Jezebel

T0244090

K.R. MEERA

Translated from the Malayalam by
Abhirami Girija Sriram *and* **K.S. Bijukumar**

PENGUIN

An imprint of Penguin Random House

HAMISH HAMILTON

USA | Canada | UK | Ireland | Australia
New Zealand | India | South Africa | China

Hamish Hamilton is part of the Penguin Random House group of companies
whose addresses can be found at global.penguinrandomhouse.com

Published by Penguin Random House India Pvt. Ltd
4th Floor, Capital Tower 1, MG Road,
Gurugram 122 002, Haryana, India

First published in Malayalam as *Sooryane Aninja Oru Sthree* by DC Books in 2018
First published in English in Hamish Hamilton by Penguin Random House India 2022

Copyright © K.R. Meera 2018
English translation copyright © Abhirami Girija Sriram and K.S. Bijukumar 2022

ISBN 9780670092468

Typeset in Adobe Caslon Pro by Manipal Technologies Limited, Manipal
Printed at Replika Press Pvt. Ltd, India

www.penguin.co.in

Translators' Dedication

For our mothers,
Vijayamma & Girijamma,
women adorned with the sun

Jezebel

1

As she stood in the family court, pelted with the blame of having paid a contract killer to murder her husband, Jezebel had this revelation: To endure extreme torture, imagine yourself as Christ on the cross.

As you stand in the courtroom in this unfinished building, consider the heaviness that weighs your chest down, as that of the wooden cross. As the short and stout defence lawyer begins his cross-examination, imagine you are climbing the Golgotha, bearing that cross. Count the barbs, both direct and indirect, in those questions, as lashings of the whip. Each time the soul is put to death, recognize that it will resurrect on the third day and there will be no pain thereafter.

The family court was a building that would forever remain unfinished. On one side of the road stood the church—where humans were united—and on the other side, the court—where humans were separated. Past the yard of the primary health centre stood the steps that led down to the court. They had no handrails. The very first time she walked down those steps, holding on to her grandmother, Valiyammachi, Jezebel turned into a prophet who foresaw someone's end. She saw in front of her, a body tumble down from above. She saw it crash into the little tea shop at one end of the court's veranda, and shatter the candy jars into smithereens.

Was that not how Jezebel, the queen of Jezreel, had been thrown down from her palace window?

What would become of the human body after such a fall? The spine would crack; the aorta, which carries blood from the heart, would sever; the neck would break; the flow of blood to the brain would cease. He or she would die, or live as good as dead.

That fall could well have been a sign. Just as Jesus Christ spoke to his followers in parables, destiny had spoken to Jezebel through signs.

Seven years ago on 16 June. She was then a medical student in her second year of MD—with classes by day and hospital duty by night. An eight-year-old with burns had been rushed into Emergency that morning. Smoke lingered in a haze along the corridor through which the gurney carrying him had been wheeled in.

As she sped home on her scooter, meaning to return to college to attend the eight-thirty class, she saw the sky—lying face down, dark and bloated, as if it had drowned in the downpour of the past few days. The lightless sun showed up like the protruding eyeball of the brain-dead.

She sensed an uncomfortable chill wrap itself around her. As she turned left at the signboard that read 'Way to the Birthplace of the Saintess', her house came into view, as did the unsightly green Indica parked in front of it. She parked her scooter next to the car and picked up the bag with her stethoscope and white coat, not pausing to straighten the dupatta slung across her shoulder. She could hear a voice from inside pleading: 'If you too forsake us, John *saar*, we will have no option but death!'

Inside, her Chachan, Kurishummoottil Poonthottathil Yohannan's son John, sat in his easy chair, spectacles in hand, lost in thought. Leaning against the door and looking on eagerly, one end of her blue-dotted brown cotton sari tucked into her waist, stood her Ammachi, Ponpally Varambel Peter's daughter, Sara. Rambling non-stop, dressed in a shiny orange Chinese-silk sari embroidered at the hem and a blouse of the same material, her sparse hair pulled into a tight topknot, was Sosa Aunty. She was a distant relative whom Valiyammachi liked to describe as the seed of a great-grandfather who taught Ouseph Kathanar, the priest, the ploy of making it seem that the north-eastern boundary of his own village fell to the west of the then marketplace, in order to fulfil a whim of building another church right next to the big church at a time when the rule allowed only one church per village.

Sosa Aunty's husband, Monichan Uncle, who wore a yellow-striped T-shirt with pants that could have been less tight and more long, sat fiddling with his teacup.

'*Dha*, here she comes!' exclaimed Ammachi when she saw Jezebel. Chachan seemed ill at ease. Ammachi muttered, loud enough for Jezebel to hear, 'Only if we start looking now will we find a suitable boy by the time her studies are over.' 'Sara is right,' chimed in Sosa Aunty. 'Sara*ye*, go ahead with it only if Jezebel and you both like the boy. Let him come and see her first, I say!' she beseeched again.

The 'boy' had been born and brought up in another city and was a doctor—an MD in Pathology. The proposal of marriage had originally been for Sosa Aunty's daughter, Tresa, and a relative of Sosa Aunty's had visited his house and fixed the date for the 'girl-seeing'. The boy's family were on their way. But, on the morning of their arrival, Tresa was nowhere to be seen!

When the boy's family arrived after travelling all that distance, there had to be a girl for them to 'see', hadn't there? Sosa Aunty implored, 'John *saar*, you have to help us. To tell you the truth, this proposal suits Jezebel better than Tresa.'

Having had his tea and biscuits, Monichan Uncle wiped his mouth and enjoined with welled-up eyes, 'I'm ready to fall at your feet, John *saar*!'

Chachan gave in. 'Don't go for your classes today, *moley*,' he told Jezebel.

Jezebel felt within herself the silence described in the Book of Revelations—the silence that spread in the earth and the sky when the seventh seal was broken. She walked past the hall—passing the dining table at one end, the television at the other, and the cane sofa set against the wall—to her room. Once inside, she set her bag down on the table and sat on her cot; she felt her body smoulder, then chill; fretted that this chill was not the cool thrill a young Catholic woman ought to have felt upon hearing about her marriage; worried about Lyla ma'am's eight-thirty class; reasoned that anyway, someday, marriage was inevitable; hoped that the one coming was a good man; imagined him to be like John Galt of Atlas Shrugged or Howard Roark of Fountainhead.

'Why the glum face, *dee*? Do you have someone else in mind?' Ammachi glared at Jezebel. 'If only,' rued Jezebel. She was yet to meet someone who made her feel that she could not live without him. A few had admired her in secret; a few others had openly expressed their feelings. Sometimes, she had set her heart on some; sometimes, in the company of some others, her heart had begun to bud. But once she headed home on her scooter, humming a tune, shared the day's news with Abel and her Chachan, then sat down to study, all thoughts of men vanished from her heart like wisps of cotton in the wind.

Then again, there had been a senior—a third-year MBBS student. His name was Ranjith. Whenever they met—in the corridors, the hospital ward, or the canteen—he would look at her with smiling eyes. Her dimples would rise to greet him. Her friends alleged that they were in love. Wasn't there some truth to that too, she had wondered. One day, in her third year of MBBS, he took leave of her saying, 'I'll see you once I'm back. There's something I need to tell you . . .' He had gone on a picnic with two of his friends—only to end up under a landslide. Never again did she meet anyone who could smile with his eyes.

Another monsoon, as Jezebel watched Jerome George Marakkaran's battered car being lifted out of the water, Ranjith showed up, eyelashes gritty with mud. He insisted he was alive under the hills and the huge rubble of rocks that had come crashing down. He shook off the particles of mud and smiled at her again with his eyes. Her dimples, and her very being, blossomed again for him, yearning for his touch.

As Jezebel stood in the witness box in the family court, she recalled the portents of 16 June. And shuddered.

Jerome George Marakkaran, his mother Lilly George Marakkaran, his father George Jerome Marakkaran, and Lilly's brother Abraham Chammanatt, arrived to 'appraise' Jezebel. Sosa Aunty and Monichan Uncle hurriedly ushered them in.

Jezebel's house, named 'Jerusalem' by her Chachan, who had never quite been able to liberate himself from the Old Testament despite dropping out of the seminary, welcomed them with open arms like Christ.

The drawing room of that house, with a grille in place of a door, was longer than it was wide. There were more doors and windows than walls. The walls were plastered with lime and the ceiling was made of teak. Christ, his heart full of shining stars instead of arteries, exuded a melancholy smile from a ledge, tucked with dried fronds from the last Palm Sunday, above the door leading to the inner hall.

Jezebel had chosen to wear a white raw-silk churidar kurta with pearl earrings and a matching necklace. 'Make haste, my beloved!' her eager heart whispered.

Back in the day, Jerome George Marakkaran was a clean-shaven thirty-year-old who wore his full-sleeved shirt tucked in. His complexion was fairer than hers. He was a hefty man—six feet tall. His thick pink moist lips were what struck her at first glance. Whenever she looked up at him, her gaze averted from those lips with a shudder. Meanwhile, his father George Jerome

Marakkaran had already shot off that problematic question, 'What is your name, *kochey*?'

Jezebel was serving cups of tea in a tray, and, with Christ and the palm fronds as witness, as soon as he heard her name, George Jerome Marakkaran put his teacup back on the tray.

'Jezebel*o*? How can any true Christian name his daughter Jezebel!'

Jezebel was taken aback at the outburst. Chachan's face reddened. He looked at the books of theology stacked on the shelf next to him, then explained, 'Jezebel was a prophet. She was the only one to challenge Prophet Elijah. I haven't seen a stronger woman in the Bible.'

'And I haven't seen a more accursed woman in the Bible either. This name has to be changed at any cost!'

It was an unexpected blow. Jezebel's limbs felt weak. Her mind caved in under a landslide.

Chachan stood up, secured his mundu tightly around his waist again, then looked at George Jerome Marakkaran.

'It is not possible to change her name, George *saar*. Not just her name, we're not changing anything in our lives according to your opinion. Jezebel is my daughter. If your son likes her, and she, too, likes him, let us consider this proposal. Please do not expect dowry. I plan to divide my assets equally between my two children. They can enjoy it after my lifetime, and my wife's. Let us proceed only if you agree to all this.'

'Agreed.'

The voice was Abraham Chammanatt's. He was gazing at Jezebel's certificates and medals displayed beside Chachan's bookshelf—the medals for first rank in Class 10 and Pre-degree; the laminated press clippings, including that of third rank in the all-India medical entrance examination; the proficiency awards for MBBS.

'Agreed,' repeated Abraham Chammanatt. 'Georgekutty, why demand a dowry for this girl? She is herself a treasure!'

At this, Ammachi's eyes welled up. Chachan sat down again. After wringing his hands awhile, George Jerome Marakkaran picked up the teacup again and set it to his lips. Lilly George Marakkaran heaved a loud sigh. Jerome George Marakkaran walked over to the bookshelf and examined the certificates and medals. After looking at all the trophies and reading all the newspaper clippings, he turned to look at her. She believed that his eyes had smiled at her then.

'Even so . . . Jezebel!' George Jerome Marakkaran muttered as he finished his tea.

That day, Jezebel realized how repugnant her name was. For the likes of George Jerome Marakkaran, it was synonymous with Satan.

For the two-and-a-half years that she lived with Jerome, George Jerome Marakkaran would mutter pointedly about her name whenever he saw her. In their bedroom, Jerome George Marakkaran would humiliate her, taking her name in vain. Years later, even the defence lawyer insulted her in the courtroom over her name.

'Jezebel. This name isn't all that common, is it? What does this name of yours mean anyway?'

'Virgin . . . pure . . .,' she had gulped, confronted by that unexpected question.

Even the dust motes in that courtroom seemed to swirl in a trance of moral indignation at the woman who had tried to murder her husband in order to shack up with another man. They clothed Jezebel with shame.

As she stood in that spacious room, inside the witness box— short-haired, clad in jeans and a shirt—she looked for all the world like some Class 12 student, a distressed teenager whose crystal heart had been split down the middle.

Smirking, the advocate opened the Bible in his hand at a page which had been flagged, and read aloud:

Nevertheless, I have this against you: You tolerate that woman Jezebel, who calls herself a prophet. By her teaching she misleads my servants into sexual immorality and the eating of food sacrificed to idols. I have given her time to repent of her immorality, but she is unwilling. So I will cast her on a bed of suffering, and I will make those who commit adultery with her suffer intensely, unless they repent of her ways. I will strike her children dead.

He looked at her, as if throwing a challenge, 'Sounds as if it is all about you, eh?'

Someone in the court laughed. Her advocate said something in a hushed tone. Soon, there was an altercation between the two lawyers. 'Come to the point,' intoned the judge.

The advocate shut the Bible, and asked, 'Did you not speak to Jerome George Marakkaran when you met him for the first time?'

And that was how Jezebel found herself recalling their first day.

It was Sosa Aunty who had insisted, 'I'm sure they have something to say to each other!'

Jezebel sat waiting in her room, ill at ease. After a while, a whiff of formalin wafted in. In its wake followed Jerome George Marakkaran. His presence seemed to fill her room—a huge man with no creases in his clothes, face or movements.

'Don't make much of Daddy's temper . . . he is affectionate at heart,' his thick pink moist lips murmured. 'My friend is getting me a job in the Gulf. We can both go once you finish your MD, *alle*?'

Intimidated by his lips, she cast her eyes down.

He glanced at the bookshelves. 'Good,' he said, 'reading is my hobby too.'

Her body trembled a little. Her heart began to pound. She was sure a fever was coming on.

'I do not have much leave—got to return by the 3 p.m. flight. If you give me your email ID, I'll keep in touch.'

That night, as Jezebel sat (having swallowed a paracetamol) in the duty room at the Medical College, typing up notes for the next day's seminar in her laptop, Jerome's email arrived: 'I'm waiting for your reply.'

She sat up. Remembered his lips. One should not loathe a man for his lips, she scolded herself. She typed a reply, 'I have many dreams about marriage . . . the marriage of my dreams is what Khalil Gibran wrote about: "And the oak tree and the cypress grow not in each other's shadow" . . . '

Jerome's reply was quick as lightning: 'In a true marriage, there is no man or woman, only two human beings, and the mutual trust and respect between them. That is my concept of marriage. "Who could refrain, that had a heart to love, and in that heart, courage to make love known?" I love you, Jezebel. I believe we're made for each other. I have already told Daddy I'm all for this marriage.'

Jezebel trembled a little. Her dimples blossomed of their own accord and smiled at the computer screen. The iron cot covered with the green bed sheet, the old wooden chair, the dark cobwebbed leaves of the fan, the case-sheets rustling on the desk— all smiled at her. Imagining an oak tree and a cypress growing side by side, with enough space for their branches to spread in their togetherness, Jezebel was filled with exhilaration.

Afterwards, there was no time to think. Neither did she feel the need for any further contemplation. The very next day, George Jerome Marakkaran and Abraham Chammanatt visited again. They prevailed upon Chachan.

'Shall we go ahead, then?' Chachan asked her.

She smiled, dimples blossoming.

Two weeks later, the wedding was fixed. The *manasammatham*, the betrothal, took place in the first week of July. It was decided that the wedding would be held at the church in the family's native village. Jerome had his premarital counselling in his city, and Jezebel in hers.

Abel, her brother, who was in England on a scholarship, flew down for the wedding. En route, he stopped over in Jerome's city to visit their family. When he arrived at 'Jerusalem' that night, Abel seemed dispirited.

'Don't go ahead with it, Jezebel,' he warned her.

The wedding had been fixed; the engagement ceremony was over; the marriage hall leased, the caterers booked, the invitations printed, and all friends, colleagues and neighbours invited. After all that, how could one decide against the marriage? Jezebel lost heart.

That had been the first death.

When she stepped out after the long trial in the court, her heart weighed heavy as a wet sack. The corridor—where there was space for only one person to walk—looked like a tunnel. When Valiyammachi, who had been seated among the audience in the courtroom, walked up to her and reached out a hand, Jezebel could only wordlessly grasp it in her own. She let Valiyammachi walk ahead. Clad in a salwar-kameez, Valiyammachi strode briskly with the support of a walking stick strapped by a belt to her hand. When they reached the veranda, Jezebel was out of breath. In the daylight, they looked at each other.

'Tired, *dee*, *kochey*?' Valiyammachi asked her gently.

Jezebel struggled to smile.

Just then, her lawyer, Philip Mathews, walked up to them with an expression that made it evident that he had taken up her case only for the sake of fees.

Smoothing his greying hair, Philip Mathews announced, 'The next hearing is on 11 October'.

'This trial, how many days will it last?' Valiyammachi wanted to know.

'They have finished their cross-examination today.'

'Is it enough if they do all the asking? Where is the time to say what we have to?'

'That will be the next time. That is when our re-examination, and my cross-examination of the other party will happen.'

Valiyammachi heaved a sigh, 'Ah! How tough it is to untie a knot! And you don't need any of this for the tie-up in the first place, *alle*?'

Valiyammachi stepped into the yard with some effort. She declared, 'All this must be done before the marriage. First, pay the fees and register. Engage lawyers. Question the ones who are to get married and capture what's on their minds. Check if they can have offspring or not, or if they even want to in the first place. See how much wealth each one already has, and decide how much, and to whom, the wealth they will make in future shall belong. Find out if there is any sickness, either of the body or the mind. Then let the judge pronounce, "Ah, let them tie the knot!" else, "Let them not!"'

People in the veranda turned to stare at them. Jezebel stepped into the yard and grasped Valiyammachi's hand.

'By the way . . .' The lawyer moved to the farther end of the veranda. 'When you come for the re-examination, please try to be dressed a little more decently.'

Jezebel went pale. She looked down at herself.

'What I meant was . . . didn't you hear them commenting on your clothes? No jeans and shirt please. And you could have cut your hair after the case was over. Anyway, make sure you wear a sari next time. Or else a salwar kameez, like your Valiyammachi. But then you must wear a dupatta too, *ketto*!'

Jezebel was astounded.

He grinned sheepishly, 'The judge's impression is of utmost importance. Right now, he doesn't think much of you. Do not make it worse!'

'Aha! Do judges pronounce verdicts after looking at clothes and accessories then?' scoffed Valiyammachi.

The lawyer was mortified, 'Not like that, Valiyammachi . . . if they feel the girl is too "modern", it could prejudice the judge. That's why . . .'

Valiyammachi laughed. 'In my grandmother's time, it was those who wore any clothes at all who were called "modern"! In my mother's time, wearing a sari and a blouse was "modern"! In our time, if a bra strap was so much as seen, you died of shame! Later, not wearing a bra became a crime! And now? Wearing a bra alone is "modern"! That's all that these words "modern" and "old-fashioned" mean! Shouldn't you lawyers be the ones explaining all this to the judges?'

The advocate grinned wretchedly again. Ignoring him, Valiyammachi walked towards the steps. Jezebel helped her climb up.

Walking past the primary health centre, with its faded fluttering banner announcing the polio vaccination campaign, they reached their car. As Jezebel settled Valiyammachi in the front seat, shut the door and got into the driver's seat, an awful fatigue seized her. Perhaps that was how the body gave in while slipping into a coma—not one cell at a time, but rather, like a light bulb exploding. She felt like weeping.

'Don't cry! Don't cry! There is no point in crying!' A dead woman scolded her.

In order to quell the tears, she tried to imagine the courtroom in another way. Thronging the dock were Jerome George Marakkaran, George Jerome Marakkaran, their lawyer, her lawyer, the judge, and all those who had laughed at her in the court. She interrogated them thus:

'Why did you not find out that Jezebel, the Queen of Jezreel, was also known as Ithabal?'

'Why did you not understand that Ithabal means "consecrated to God?"'

'Why did none of you try to find out why this name later became Isabel, meaning "woman of dung"?'

'Why did you not try to understand why women who questioned those who wished to capture power were all labelled whores?'

'No one told us. No one taught us,' they confessed, full of remorse, in her court.

And so, Jezebel began to script a New Testament about herself:

Jezebel, the daughter of Sara, the daughter of Susanna, the daughter of Eliyamma, the daughter of Saramma, born in the matrilineage of the daughter of Mariamma chosen by the ruler as the wife of Louis the mason, who was assistant to Antony the mason, who had arrived from Portugal to rebuild the old church in the sixteenth century.

Saramma was Eliyamma's mother, and Eliyamma, Susanna's; Susanna was Sara's mother, and Sara, Jezebel's. Jezebel had not become anyone's mother.

So, she became pregnant with her own self. With the moon under her feet, and a crown of twelve stars on her head, she saw her own self: a woman adorned with the sun.

Only from she who is, was, and would be, would grace and peace be hers.

2

This is how the birth of Sara, the mother of Jezebel, took place.

Before Sara's mother Susanna cohabited with Peter Thomas, son of Varambel Thomas, she was wedded to Kaattil Joseph. And so, before Sara, Susanna begot two sons. However, Joseph died of snakebite one monsoon. The very next year, Susanna married Peter Thomas and begot Sara by Peter.

Many years later, on 20 September, in the church famed as built by the king in AD 1125, Kurishummoottil Poonthottathil Yohannan's son John wed Sara. A year and a half later, Jezebel John was born. Two years later, Abel John followed. Susanna had bequeathed her dimples to both Jezebel and Abel. Not only her dimples, but also her wilfulness, rued Sara. Susanna wished that both her grandchildren would behold the world with joyous laughter. Sara desired they be immersed in the Holy Spirit.

'Why does Ammachi quarrel with you so, Valiyammachi?' Twelve-year-old Jezebel asked her one vacation, at her mother's ancestral home.

'Because I married a second time, *dee kochey*!' laughed Valiyammachi.

'Why did you marry a second time, Valiyammachi?'

'Because I needed a man!'

'Why did you need a man, Valiyammachi?'

'*Edee kochey*, I wanted a daughter! My husband had kicked the bucket. I found a man so I could give birth once more. Your Valiyappachan lost his wife in her second childbirth and was alone with his daughter. I liked him, and I married him!'

'Why would Ammachi be angry with you for marrying Valiyappachan?'

'Not because I married Valiyappachan, but because her mother married again! Ask her to get lost!'

Valiyammachi laughed again. And her dimples blossomed like two dark flowers on a honey-complexioned face. Valiyammachi's dimples.

Ever since Jezebel could remember, Valiyammachi always seemed younger than Ammachi. While Ammachi wore white voile saris, Valiyammachi got herself salwar kurtas and blouses with fashionable window-slat backs. As Ammachi wrapped herself up more and more, Valiyammachi liberated herself more and more. While Ammachi constantly complained about and blamed Jezebel, Valiyammachi always praised her and was proud of her.

'Ammachi's face is always full of anger. Yours is all joy, Valiyammachi. Why so?' Jezebel asked her once.

'That's because I lived with two men, *dee kochey*!' guffawed Valiyammachi.

'What if you had lived with three men?'

'I might have been even happier!'

'Then I shall live with ten men when I grow up! I shall marry ten times!' declared Jezebel.

'Go ahead and live with ten. Just don't marry! That's the wise thing to do, *dee kochey*.' Valiyammachi belly-laughed heartily. 'You'd better run away with some boy before Sara puts you in a nunnery. That's what's good for you!'

'Is this the kind of talk a grandmother has with her granddaughter?' Ammachi, who had overheard it all, was hopping mad. Turning to her mother, she raged, 'Don't you set foot in my house again! I will not let you lead my children astray!'

Valiyammachi laughed out loud again, 'May you lead your children astray all by yourself! I'm not in the race with you, *dee* Sara*ye*!'

Valiyammachi then reminded her of the story of Valiyammami, their grand-aunt who had eloped with Thuppayi—who had come to paint murals in the church. Muthuvaliappan, their great-grandfather, who had invited the man home in the first place, was heartbroken when his own daughter ran away with him. Ever since, they said women did not grace that family for long.

Ammachi, who went ballistic after hearing that story, tried to pull Jezebel away from Valiyammachi. Jezebel buried her face deep in her Valiyammachi's bosom. Ammachi smote herself on the head, cursing and wailing. Hugging Jezebel close, Valiyammachi laughed louder.

Valiyammachi had married a second time so she could have a daughter. And that very daughter despised Valiyammachi for having married again. In her evening prayers, Ammachi beseeched the Lord for mercy on her mother who had gone astray. 'Lead me astray again and again, my Lord,' Valiyammachi was quick to counter.

Although Valiyammachi had been at 'Jerusalem' ever since the alliance had been fixed, and had pitched camp in Jezebel's room as usual, Jezebel hadn't had the chance to talk to her properly. Jezebel was busy as both an organizer and a participant in a national seminar at the Medical College. On most days, she would rush back home in the mornings, shower, change and rush back to college. Since there was no time to go to the city, they shopped for saris for the engagement and wedding from the town nearby. She had to work even on the day before her engagement.

Jerome George Marakkaran called from time to time, but his conversations were matter-of-fact. It was while sitting next to him on the dais at their engagement ceremony that Jezebel had a good look at him, and asked herself, 'Is this my husband?'

By then, it was too late.

Everything—and everyone—was all set. The house had been painted and renovated. The pandal had been set up. Abel had arrived. The house was full of relatives. Everything had been firmed up.

From time to time, Jezebel recalled with a pang those moments when Valiyammachi, clad in a blue nightie with white frills, sat on the bed watching her as she put back the saris and necklaces she had shown Varghese uncle and Koshy uncle and their wives Reena Aunty and Lissy Aunty—who had come bearing wine, myrrh and frankincense. Abel sat next to Valiyammachi, munching on something. Closing the cupboard shut, Jezebel lay down on the bed in the space between Abel and Valiyammachi. Straightening her spectacles, and caressing Jezebel's then long, thick hair with her left hand, Valiyammachi asked Abel, 'Why does she seem so dull, *da?*'

'She knows not what she is doing,' said Abel, 'May she forgive herself'.

That was a moment of reckoning. To Jezebel it felt like someone had splashed water on her face. In the mirror, she could see all three of them. He was taller, but otherwise, her spitting image. His lips, like hers, were thin. Dimples hid in his cheeks too. Like her, he, too, had gotten down to swim in lakes of fire and brimstone. And climbed ashore, scorched and scalded.

'That house, its ambience, the people there—I didn't like it one bit, Valiyammachi. Whatever did she see in them that made her agree to this match?' And he added, 'You shouldn't have been so foolish, Jezebel.'

Jezebel's pride was wounded. Her ego was hurt. What had she seen in Jerome George Marakkaran in order to settle for him? It was a question she had forgotten to ask herself. The question terrified her.

'He is decent,' she replied stoutly. 'Over the phone and email, he is very courteous.'

It was a lesson Abel had taught her in her fifteenth year. One day, while walking to school after getting down from the bus, the boy who had given her a love letter the previous day brushed against her from behind, as if unknowingly. Jezebel mistook it for a display of love. She was about to unfurl her dimples. Abel had been waiting for her a little way ahead—his forehead creased in a frown. That evening, when she was doing her homework, he came up to her and heaved a deep sigh. 'Love only those men who respect women,' he said, addressing no one in particular. 'The one who respects you will not accost you on the road and pinch your bottom.' And then he held forth like a prophet, 'He'll spread a carpet so that your feet don't hurt. He'll carry you in his arms so that you're not pricked by thorns. He'll treat you like a princess!'

At that time, he was only a Class 8 student. Then again, when she recalled that he had always been her prophet, Jezebel fretted. The one who had stolen her right as firstborn—although two years younger, he had always exhibited the sagacity of one four or five years older. She earned more degrees, faced more hardships than him. But he had always been the more mature one.

Now, he observed her silently, stroking his chin. 'What a fool you are, Jezebel . . .,' he sighed.

She insisted that Jerome was a gentleman. That Jerome was decent. It was easy to talk to him. His phone calls were brief and proper—'How are things? How was work today? Did you have many patients to attend to? Is the duty doctor a bribe-taker? Are there enough nurses? Yesterday there was a recruitment drive for jobs in Saudi Arabia. I had applied, but didn't go. Let our wedding get over. Let your course get completed. Daddy says it's a good thing that Abel is in the UK—we can somehow soft-soap him and then get ourselves there. Then why worry?'

She insisted that he was good at heart.

'What's the problem with him?' Valiyammachi wanted to know.

'Valiyammachi . . . even looks-wise, it's not a good match. He is one hulk of a man—six feet tall!' rued Abel.

'Oh, how do height and weight matter anyway?' asked Valiyammachi, dimples of mischief spreading over her wrinkled cheeks. 'Have you seen a peacock, *da*? They used to fly by our gate back then. They're not to be seen nowadays. Men are like peacocks—well-plumed until marriage, they prance about showing off their feathers—what a sight! But after marriage, the plume falls off. And then what's left is only a crown on the head. They won't let go of that one though!'

'I don't think he is all that straightforward. He seems to be hiding something. Not only that, I don't think he is marrying her because he likes her. I don't like such people. For them, marriage is not about spending their lives with the woman they like. It is a passport they use to get to some other destination in life. What happiness will they have in life? I don't understand.' Abel was agitated.

Valiyammachi's face turned anxious.

'Jerome is better compared to many others,' said Jezebel feebly.

'Whom would you rather marry—the better among a bad lot or the best among the better ones?' asked Abel.

'How do I even find one like that, *da*?' Jezebel asked, disheartened.

'Wait a while. What's your hurry?' shot back Abel.

Just then, Ammachi, who walked in, intervened, '*Eda*, he is a good boy. His family is pious and God-fearing. Mark my words—in five years, he will build a house. And buy a car too. In ten years, he will have a rubber estate to his name! Not like you and your Chachan, running around spending all that you earn on books and useless CDs and learning to play the piano and violin.

Eda, it is far better to marry a girl off to someone like him than to someone like you. Don't you dare change her mind saying this and that now!'

Ammachi turned to Jezebel. 'Everyone has been invited, the marriage has been announced in church, your wedding sari has also been bought. If you dare say anything now . . . ! He is the man the Lord has willed for you. And what fine people they are! Was there any hoo-ha about dowry? Chachan said he wouldn't give any, and they agreed. Jezebel, you're fortunate to have found him.'

Abel burst out laughing. 'Fine people indeed! His father has asked me to make Chachan understand that their relatives are inquiring about the "pocket money",' he scoffed.

By then, Chachan had joined them at the doorway. His face fell when he heard this. Abel walked out of the room. Ammachi and Chachan followed him. Valiyammachi and a bewildered Jezebel were left alone.

Valiyammachi looked at her fondly. '*Kochey*, if you don't like it, just say so. There will be some hue and cry, but never mind. It's better than bearing a yoke all your life. If you want to say anything, do it right away. The truth that is delayed is fatal.'

Jezebel panicked. Panic made her weak. She grew uneasy, wondering if she had made a mistake. There was no need to have rushed into this decision, she rued. She should have waited, should have asked for more time. She wondered if Jerome George Marakkaran's were borrowed feathers—tucked away for the time being, not easy to spot at first glance. She worried that they would all fall off if she tried to touch them.

When she asked Jerome 'What do you think of Abel?', pat came the reply: 'He is not at all practical.'

'He is good at heart,' Jezebel countered.

'Will goodness buy you rice and wheat?'

Jezebel felt like she had been slapped.

At the engagement too, she suffered a similar blow. Only a few of George Jerome Marakkaran's relatives had come. As they stood on the stage, posing for photographs, she saw the two families stay apart, unmingling, like oil and water. She felt uneasy.

'Haven't any of your friends come?' she asked Jerome, between posing for photographs.

'I don't have many friends. Where's the time to make friends in the midst of studies? My Daddy is my best friend.'

'What about the friend who said he'd arrange everything for us to go to the Gulf?'

Jezebel thought she saw Jerome's face redden.

'Oh, that. Yes, he's there . . . but he's much more than a friend . . .'

He swiftly changed the subject before she could probe further. He said he had an interview that evening at a local hospital. It was the same when she asked him about his elder brother, who did not attend the engagement.

'He'll be there for the wedding,' Jerome replied evasively.

'How come your brother hasn't married yet?'

'Shouldn't they find a suitable match?'

'What is the age difference between you two?'

'Not much . . .'

Vague answers. Slippery answers. They bewildered her, pained her. She fretted that her notion of marriage—as the joyous coming together of two people who could read each other like open books—was drowning in formalin.

'The boy's not bad to look at. The father's a bit of a tough nut. The mother is a meek creature. Her brother seems to be the one making all the decisions. He is the one doling out the money. Then again, do you like him with all your heart or not? That's all that matters,' said Valiyammachi.

Jezebel fretted even more. 'This is not the marriage I had in mind, this is not my man,' she heard someone prophesy.

'And one more thing,' said Valiyammachi, 'if you say no to this one, don't presume that you'll get a better one, *ketto*? Things seem different only for some five or six months after marriage. After that, all men are the same—some pretence, some deceit, and a whole lot of stubbornness. At first there's love, then the squabbles begin. You will both come to blows, and it will tire you both out. And then you'll both cool off when you remember that there's only a little more of the journey to go.'

'Saying no is a huge responsibility,' sighed Valiyammachi. 'Saying yes is an even bigger responsibility. Think it through and take a decision.'

Jezebel was terrified of thinking it through. She felt it was easier to say yes than to decide against it.

'How was your relationship with Jerome George Marakkaran?' asked the defence lawyer.

'We had differences . . .'

'What sort of differences? Did he stop you from working? Or demand that you change your subject of study?'

'He asked me not to study further.'

'Over here, is it not usually the case that a good doctor needs to study only up to MD? Will the line of treatment be any different because you study further?'

'I wanted to study further.'

'You were still doing your MD, weren't you? A higher academic degree would come only after that, right? Anyway, so was this the only point of difference?'

'I like reading novels. Jerome did not like to read even a short story . . .'

'*Iyoyo*! Some difference, that! I wonder if a doctor who's studying for MD even has the time to read novels! I don't have the time after all the work in this court, you see. Even otherwise, are there any novels worth reading these days?'

She had no answer.

'Never mind. How about your physical relationship? Were there differences?'

She stood downcast.

'Didn't you hear me? Was your physical relationship satisfactory?'

She did not answer. Because the answer was meant for her alone. No one else had the right to hear it.

How would she describe to complete strangers their wedding night in her house, when Jerome entered the bedroom and went to the bathroom as she sat breathlessly on the bed, her diary echoing her beating heart from under the pillow? Her diary, which she had kept safely since her Pre-degree days, hoping to gift it to her husband on the day of their wedding. It was her life. Her world. Her heart.

He came out of the bathroom, wiped his hands and walked up to the bookshelf. He stood there for a moment, gazing at the books. Her heart surged with love. She went up to him. She opened one door of the bookshelf.

'Do you like Sethu's stories?' she asked, trying to get friendly. 'He says in one of his stories that women like to be indulged and pampered. Have you read it?'

He shut the door she had opened.

'I don't read Malayalam. We had only Hindi in school,' he said, and added in English, 'All these writers are perverts.'

Her heart sank. Still, not losing hope, she tried to find out which book in English was his favourite. 'Gibran? My favourite writer is Marquez. After reading "The Third Resignation" . . .'

Abruptly, he reached out and touched the dimple on her smiling cheek. She forgot what she had been saying. A thrill coursed through her body. He sat on the bed. Holding her hand, he stood her in front of him. She blossomed all over.

The moment has arrived. I'm going to be one with my man, her heart prophesied. My husband. My man. We will be baptized in love. We will be one in body and soul till death do us part.

He reached out and touched her on the neck.

And then without warning, he forced her head down. She fell to her knees, at his feet. He grabbed hold of her face and pressed it on to his lap. And shoved his penis into her mouth. She felt like her soul had parted from her body. Her head bobbed willy-nilly in his hands, like a broken-necked doll in the hands of a naughty child.

'I haven't read any of this rubbish, except for prescribed textbooks. Don't you bring up this 'Kibran-Kubran' with me hereafter! But your name . . . I like that one! Do you know what the name Jezebel means? Whore! Whore! Whore!' He laughed, panting.

For a moment, Jezebel blacked out. She had not been prepared for that sudden blow. One half of her brain went numb. The other half retreated to old textbooks in order to survive that moment.

The male reproductive organ has four main parts, Jezebel-the-doctor evangelized to Jezebel-the-new-bride: glans, corpus cavernosum, corpus spongiosum, urethra. Glans refers to the tip of the penis. It is pink in colour, and is covered in mucosa. Corpus cavernosum comprises the two fleshy layers of tissue on either side of the penis. Erection occurs when blood surges into these tissues. Corpus spongiosum comprises the sponge-like tissues in front of the penis that extend up to the glans. During erection, blood gushes into these tissues and opens up the urethra. The urethra is the duct that passes through the tissues of corpus spongiosum. It is through the urethra that urine and semen flow out.

'Do your name justice, *eda*, do it justice! Let me see how smart you are! *You whore! Whore! Whore!*'

He panted like a madman. Jezebel was breaking apart. He had not touched her except on the head, and yet her body hurt as if it had been torn asunder. Recall what you studied about the arousal of sexual desire in a man, Jezebel-the-doctor exhorted. The parasympathetic cells of the brain's autonomic nervous system produce acetylcholine which leads to the production of nitric oxide by the endothelial cells. This nitric oxide causes the trabecular blood vessels of the corpus cavernosum to expand, thus increasing the inflow of blood into the penis. The cells at the bottom of the penis contract, and this helps retain the blood and prevent it from draining. In this way, corpus cavernosum cells become firm . . .

A little nitric oxide, Jezebel consoled herself.

When the activity in the parasympathetic cells of his brain came to a halt, Jerome George Marakkaran got up. The production of chemicals in his body stopped. Blood drained from the cells of his body; they shrunk to their former state. He went to the bathroom, returned, flopped on to the bed without a word. His body produced melatonin. He fell asleep.

That night, Jezebel's nuptial night, the wretched rain lashed outside. Bats flew about, flapping their wet wings. The mottled wood owl screeched non-stop. Pain lurked, a serpent by the wayside, a viper on the path. Bitten on the heel, foaming at the mouth, her sleep fell dead. She got up, then lay down. She rinsed out her mouth, again and again. Felt like throwing up, again and again. In the end, someone rolled the giant boulder of darkness away from the well of the day. Like a thirsty lamb, she rushed out to drink in the sunlight. She writhed like a fish caught in a net.

She did not cry, but her eyes smarted and smouldered.

Wormwood was the star that bloomed in her sky that day. It fell from heaven blazing like a rag-torch. One third of her life was made bitter like wormwood oil. The first sky, the first earth went past. The sea, too, vanished.

'You are a woman with education and income. Your family is also educated and well respected in society. If you did not like this relationship, why did you live with this man for two-and-a-half years?' asked the defence lawyer.

In all the books I read, good wives were ready to wait until their husbands reformed their ways—she wanted to say. In all the movies I've seen, misunderstood husbands astonished their wives in the end with proof of their innocence. They taught me, at school and in church, that good things happened to those who forgave, forbore and waited patiently. They demanded that I be discreet both in speech and desire.

But she did not say anything. Even if she had, neither that lawyer nor the judge would have understood. They were balloons that flew up in the sky, held down by outdated strings. If the string broke, they would burst to pieces too. Later, she regretted not having discomfited them at least, by describing how she had gone into the bedroom when dusk fell again, resolving to speak to Jerome George Marakkaran.

The second night, when she walked in, having resolved to speak openly, she found Jerome texting someone on his mobile phone. He saw her, switched off his phone, put it away and readied himself as if for a workout. 'Jerome, I need to speak to you,' began Jezebel.

Jerome leaned forward eagerly.

'My name is Jezebel. If you disliked this name so much, you shouldn't have agreed to the wedding, Jerome,' she said, her voice faltering.

'Ha! What is this? Why do you say such things, *kochey*? Would I have come this far and married you if there had been any dislike?'

He moistened his thick pink lips with his tongue.

'Then please don't go on and on about my name.'

'I was joking, Jezebel!' Jerome pretended to be hurt.

'Jerome, I don't know if you know, Jezebel was the queen of Phoenicia. When she married Ahab, the king of Jezreel and arrived at Samaria as a bride, she was all of fifteen. The city of Tyre, which she lived in, was the world's first naval power. From a land of water and freedom, she had come to a desert ruled by tribal laws.'

'You know your history quite well!' Jerome grinned sheepishly, and then tried to placate her saying, 'Forget all that, let's go to bed.'

He sat her on the bed. And then he stood up, facing her. And she went numb all over again.

That day too, he said derisively, 'I like your name a lot, *da*!' Just the memory of it filled Jezebel's mouth with bitterness.

In the court, Jezebel-the-rabbi interrogated Jezebel-the-unbeliever thus: 'What did you go to the desert for? To see the reed blossom and sway in the breeze? Else, what other sight did you go to see? The one wearing fine clothes? If not, then what else did you go to see there? The prophet?'

'Yes, I'm telling you, someone greater than the prophet.'

'Let me state the plain truth—no woman is respected as much as she deserves to be in her own home and land. So, it is better that she walks through their midst and leaves.'

3

And this is how Jezebel's birth took place.

Shortly after her mother, Sara, and her father, John, were engaged, even before they had begun to cohabit, Sara was possessed by an overwhelming sense of sin. Her mind conceived of a perpetual unrest. Because her husband, John, was a just man and he did not wish to slight her, he put up with her behaviour silently. With great effort, John managed to have two children by Sara. In anticipation that the firstborn would be a boy, a name—Immanuel—had been chosen. 'What other name can you give one born to a mother who is still a virgin at heart?' he said. However, a daughter was born, belying all expectations. John combed through the Bible for a suitable name. He saw the name 'Jezebel' in the Book of Revelations. He was excited when he saw that the Book of Revelations had only one name from the Old Testament. The baby was duly christened Jezebel.

Despite a daughter and a son born to them, John did not come to know Sara intimately. Neither did Sara know her man. However, Sara loved and trusted her husband's mother, Mariamma, more than her own. Mariamma, who had been widowed at thirty-three, was a teacher who had devoted her entire life to raising her only son. Mariamma's house was close to the Birthplace of the Saintess of Suffering and she claimed that the saintess had been her childhood friend. Like the saintess, Mariamma firmly believed that illness was God's blessing and that there was no greater prayer than pain.

When the saintess was beatified as a blessed servant of God, Jezebel was all of four. From time to time, Mariamma made everyone lose their sleep by wailing out loud that the little saintess—clad in *chatta* and mundu and wearing the traditional *kunukku* in her ears—was sitting in the ancient church, weeping. Long after she had grown up, Jezebel often dreamt of Mariamma (whom she called Matteyammachi) and Ammachi both sitting up and praying all night with a candle in front of the Holy Mother's picture, the ends of their saris wrapped around their heads. She vividly remembered two-year-old Abel waking up startled at the sound, and crying and Ammachi picking him up, lifting her blouse, thrusting a nipple into his mouth and carrying on with her prayer.

When she was pregnant with Abel, Ammachi made Jezebel sleep separately. From then onward, she got used to sleeping—hugging a little pillow—in the next room. When Abel turned two, Ammachi made him sleep apart from her. When Abel was four, she made Chachan sleep apart as well. Ammachi was afraid of the body. She detested its pleasures.

As the second night gave way to dawn, on hearing the indistinct clatter of vessels, Jezebel rushed towards the kitchen. She wanted Ammachi's bosom. She wanted to lean her head against it and weep.

The lights were on in the kitchen. Ammachi took out of the fridge the frozen ducks killed the day before and marinated them in salt and turmeric. Their flesh bore goosebumps of lost feathers. The long necks of the headless ducks dangled out of the vessel, spattered with ice-flecks. Ammachi dropped them in a basin of water; a cloud of vapour rose. As she spooned chilli powder and turmeric powder and other masalas into a bowl, Ammachi glanced askance at her—standing around, limp and listless.

'If you're here to complain, forget it,' Ammachi said unkindly, running her finger over the blade of the knife. 'For God's sake, behave yourself.'

Ammachi went on to chop onions and check the appam batter for tartness. She diced potatoes for the mutton stew, ground the masala. The blue flame of the stove leapt to life. Pots and pans clattered as they were filled with water and emptied. Ducks that had once frolicked about in green ponds in the midst of paddy fields, now simmered in small pieces in a blood-red gravy. Jezebel lost heart all over again.

Ammachi had never pampered her. Whenever Ammachi breastfed baby Abel, little Jezebel would get restless. She was filled with longing, seeing those dark nipples on fair skin. Once, she reached out to touch Ammachi lightly on the breast through the slit in her nightie. Ammachi looked up with a start. Eyes blazing, she slapped her hard. In the days that followed, she sent Jezebel out and shut the door before feeding Abel.

Afterwards, Jezebel contented herself with feeling the little ant-like marks on her own chest. While playing with Sebin, the little boy next door, she would press her lips to his chest, and he would laugh, tickled. That was how they discovered the game of mommy and baby. In each round, she got to be the mommy five times over; then it was his turn.

When Ammachi found out about this game, she raised hell and beat up Jezebel black and blue. Jezebel's bony frame was scarred all over with red welts from an iron rod. 'Satan's child!' Ammachi wailed, 'Sins even before she's hatched out of the egg!'

Chachan stood helpless. Ammachi punished Jezebel severely for her 'sin'. She beat her over and over, scolded her again and again, took her to church, threatening her with, 'Repent for your sins to the Lord!'

She looked into little Jezebel's scared wide eyes more pitilessly than the judge at the family court later would. Whenever they faced each other, Jezebel felt that Ammachi's lips mouthed the word 'sinner'. Her guilty conscience grew faster than her little self and shattered her confidence.

Even as she smiled, talked, studied, and played, a sinner within her writhed in pain. And so, whenever she got a chance, she would weep out loud. She often sat up in bed weeping, head pressed to her knees. Chachan would come up and console her with 'Don't cry, *moley*, you're Chachan's pet, aren't you?' And his kindness would make her burst into sobs again.

Whenever Ammachi heard her crying, she would rush in with a harsh 'What is it, *dee*, have your father and mother kicked the bucket or what?' At this, Jezebel would sit bolt upright. She would hasten to brush her teeth, bathe, wear the clothes Ammachi handed her, eat the food Ammachi served her, and revise the previous day's lessons until the school bus arrived. With Sebin's family moving elsewhere, she had no more friends; there were no more games. She was left alone.

Until Abel was old enough to console her, it became a habit for her to wake up weeping. Later, Abel began to wake up earlier in anticipation. 'Please don't cry,' he would entreat as soon as she began weeping. And yet the tears brimmed, ever ready to spill at the slightest excuse. A sum gone wrong, a comma misplaced, one mark less in a test—these were reasons enough for her to sob for hours on end. It was only when she secured the top rank in Class 10 that things began to look up. She mustered the courage to crack jokes in Pre-degree. By the time she was an MBBS student, she even dared to make small talk with Ammachi.

After attending a class on 'Normal growth and development' during her MD, she finally decided to confront Ammachi. 'Exploring and touching the body is a normal phase in child development,' she said one evening over tea and dosas, throwing down the gauntlet to Ammachi who sat across the table. 'And when you see such behaviour, you should gently explain to the child about the body.'

Ammachi's face hardened.

'Remember, Ammachi, how you hit me with an iron rod?' She looked at her, expecting an apology.

'You committed a sin,' pronounced Ammachi gravely. 'It was a sin then; it is a sin now.'

'Says who?' retorted Jezebel.

'Read the Bible and find out.'

'Try reading modern medicine, Ammachi.'

'There's nothing in the world that hasn't been told in the Bible. It is God's word. Are you wiser than God?'

Ammachi was furious. Jezebel was astounded. She clearly saw Ammachi's power. It was the power of ignorance. Ammachi held her tongue when Abel was around, but always tried to tame Jezebel's. She discovered that Ammachi's God was a man, that Ammachi believed her life itself was consecrated to the service of men.

Jezebel was curious to know what Ammachi would have to say about Jerome George Marakkaran's 'sin' against her. She wanted to add that it was a sin because there was no love in it. She had not been able to understand him. She had not been able to understand his body. She had not been able to understand her own body either.

When Reena Aunty and Lissy Aunty, who had by now joined them in the kitchen, began playfully teasing Jezebel, Ammachi's annoyance grew. Ammachi did not like light-hearted banter. So she switched on Christian devotionals on the tape recorder. The lines '*Matha pithakkale marakkaruthe* (forget not your mother and father)' rang out plaintively. Ammachi poured coffee into a cup. 'The sun's up,' she declared. 'Go serve him coffee.'

That was an order. Jezebel wished she could resist. Cup of coffee in hand, she walked into their room. Jerome George Marakkaran woke up with a start, stretched, greeted her with a 'Hello, good morning'. He went to the bathroom, came back, picked up the cup. He gloated that he had slept well, inquired if it had rained at night. He spoke to her as if nothing had happened. She was at a loss for words.

Only Valiyammachi read her mind. 'Come, sit next to me,' she beckoned. She lifted her chin up and looked her in the eye. Jezebel cast her eyes down in guilt and shame.

'Sara*ye*! Is this how a bride's face should be?' An irate Valiyammachi asked Ammachi who had just walked in. Ammachi braced for battle with her mother. '*Dhey* Ammachi, don't you ruin my child's life! Now be off with you. I'm going to tell my brothers to get you packing and back home as early as possible.'

'Not even your father can get me packing, *dee*, you dimwit!' snarled Valiyammachi. And then: 'Jezebel, you are educated and intelligent. If you feel you cannot continue, you must sever it at this very moment.'

'But how, Valiyammachi? Our community, family, friends . . .,' Jezebel panicked.

'It's your life, *kochey*. If they eat, will that fill your stomach? If they drink, will your thirst be slaked? Only you know what will make you happy,' stated Valiyammachi with an air of finality.

Jezebel demurred. She was too scared to make a decision.

'Don't you dare set foot in this house if you let go of him,' threatened Ammachi. Looking at Chachan, Varghese uncle and Koshy uncle, Jezebel grew unnerved. Looking at Jerome, who behaved as if nothing at all had happened, unnerved her even more. He looked very cheerful. He discussed matters of import with Chachan and her uncles. Unmindful of her suffocation, he took her on visits to a few relatives' homes, introduced her with much pride, went along with her to the Medical College, met her friends, saw Abel off, returned, had dinner.

'So let us be honest, whatever was your quarrel with Jerome?' asked the lawyer. 'Let's set aside all this talk that he didn't read fiction, didn't recite poetry, didn't dance Bharatanatyam and so on. Pray, tell us, from the point of view of an ordinary girl in an ordinary household, what, in fact, was his failing?'

Jerome did not have the kind of failings that the lawyer would understand. He was six feet tall and weighed 90 kilos. He was a doctor with an MD. He left for work dressed in crisp, well-ironed clothes and returned home on time. He sought to work in hospitals that paid him more. He kept meticulous accounts of his income, duly deposited it in the bank, and explored ways of earning more profit. He liked to dress well and to attend weddings, baptisms, funerals. He watched television serials and movies without fail. Every night, before bedtime, he would narrate the day's happenings to his father, seek his opinion and advice, laugh while watching the 'Comedy Time' show on TV.

'Let us now hear if indeed there was any complaint,' challenged the lawyer. 'Every class you studied in, you topped with distinction. You are well-regarded in your profession. And you're no ordinary woman. In which case, if there were differences of opinion, couldn't you have talked it over?'

Looking at the lawyer's obtuse face, she was reminded of her departure for Jerome's city. It was the day a woman had taken oath as the country's President for the first time ever. George Jerome Marakkaran, Lilly George Marakkaran and her son John George Marakkaran, who had been staying at Abraham Chammanatt's for the past four days, were also with them. 'If only we had driven a harder bargain for the dowry, we could have travelled in the AC coach,' George Jerome Marakkaran kept muttering. Jezebel was silent. Even as she sat sweating in the swelter and bustle of the sleeper class, she was eager to speak to Jerome. However, he spent all his time with his Daddy, totting up the wedding expenses over and over again. When he went to the toilet, she followed him and stood outside, waiting by the door.

A cool breeze wafted in. Outside, the view was enchanting. She longed to soak it all up, standing there by the door, with him by her side. Just then, he came out and instructed her, 'Don't stand here.' In spite of herself, her courage rose.

'This was not how I'd imagined our journey,' she said. 'This is not how I'd imagined sex would be either.'

His face darkened. 'Is this the time to talk about all that?' He returned to his seat. When the breeze blew again, Jezebel felt like weeping. This is only the beginning, she consoled herself. It will change. As the journey continues, as the train reaches its destination, it will all change. He will save you from being trodden underfoot.

But nothing changed. His home in that faraway city was just as Abel had described it. It was dark even in the daytime because all the windows were always shut. In the morning, someone would reveal the greatness of God on some Christian devotional channel on television. George Jerome Marakkaran raised his voice needlessly. He regarded her with greater ire than Ammachi.

At night, in the bedroom, as usual, Jerome pushed her head down on his body. Jezebel floundered.

'Is it enough to go on like this? Don't you want a baby?' she finally mustered the nerve to ask.

Her body was aroused, then went limp.

'You're still studying, alle?'

'Aren't there other ways to manage that?'

Jerome pulled away from her. His face filled with distaste.

'It is the husband, not the wife, who decides all that,' he snapped. 'In our family, the women do not talk about sex. It does not behove women of respectable families.'

He turned away and switched off the light as if his pride had been wounded. Jezebel sat in the darkness, shaken. She found it difficult to believe all this was happening. Which century was this? Which world?

That room reeked of sulphur. Those days, she suffered great agony. She was helpless too—she desired her husband, and he regarded her desire with disdain. Her body reeled, like water sloshing about in a waterskin.

Pigeons wheezed asthmatically on the windowsill in that unfamiliar city. Jezebel cocked her ear to their cooing and tried to count them. She was petrified that she was the fledgling pigeon someone had laid at the altar, instead of a sacrificial lamb, for burnt offerings and the atonement of sins.

Jezebel had not met Sebin after his family moved out. She preferred to forget him. At one point, his memories flared up her guilt. Growing up, she often wished to see him, although she was also terrified at the thought. And yet, when she did meet Sebin out of the blue on the day of Jerome George Marakkaran's accident, her heart brimmed over with fondness.

He was one of the four young men who had rushed Jerome to the hospital. At the hospital, he recognized Chachan and Ammachi, and then, Jezebel. He deferred to Jezebel in the manner of patients.

'Sebin, I've often thought about you,' Jezebel said, trying to be friendly.

He stood abashed. He had changed so much: dark sagging jowls, a pot belly, and the stench of cigarettes, Pan Parag and alcohol. His face foretold the beginnings of a corroding liver. His ashen cheeks worried her.

'I thought you'd have become a pilot,' she said.

'Oh! I was good-for-nothing even back then!' His eyes betrayed an inferiority complex. Jezebel felt a pang.

She had cheated him. When they played the game of mommy and baby, each one was supposed to suckle five times. Even at that age, she could count up to a hundred. He was naive and always fumbled with numbers. When he counted five, she would refute it saying it was four. He'd wonder if four came after five. She bullied him into believing that five came a long way after three and four.

'But you never thought of me, *alle*, Sebin?'

He looked even more sheepish.

'I did . . . from time to time.'

'Then why didn't you come?'

'That . . . but how intelligent you were even back then, Jezebel!'

She forgot that she was a wife keeping vigil over a man battling for life in the ICU after an accident. Her cheeks dimpled.

'Hm? What of it?'

A miserable smile spread over his dark swollen cheeks.

'If we run after girls who are smarter than us, then we'll be trapped and tied up in knots for ever.'

Jezebel kept looking at him. True, she was the more intelligent one. But he was the one who had seen life. She saw that what he said was true. She felt truly sorry for Jerome who had unwittingly tied himself up in knots as well.

At the first trial, the defence lawyer had asked, 'Is it true that you paid "Shark" Sebin, the contract killer, twenty-five thousand rupees to kill your husband Jerome George Marakkaran?'

'I did not give anyone any contract.'

'Did you pay money or not?'

'I did.'

'Then what was the payment for, if not to kill?'

It had happened a few months after their first meeting. Sebin said he needed twenty-five thousand rupees. 'I won't be able to return the money, Jezebel,' he informed her regretfully. 'But I can make it up to you in another way. I can break someone's arm or leg for you. If you wish, I can even finish someone off!'

'*Iyo*! Isn't that a criminal case?'

'There are four cases in my name already. What if there is one more, or one less?'

They had both laughed then. In the court too, she felt like laughing. All traces of laughter, though, vanished at the sight of the defence lawyer.

'I did not kill anyone,' said Jezebel. That was the truth. She was incapable of killing anyone. And so, she had not killed anyone.

She had scooped out water from the river and poured it on the ground. It had turned to blood, that was all.

4

And this is how Jezebel discovered that a red star had risen above her head.

While walking to school, she was called a *charakku*, a commodity. While walking back home, she heard whispers of 'sshh' from a bicycle that swooped in from behind. As she stood inside the bus, a hand shot out of the crowd to grope her not-fully-developed breasts. As she made her way towards the exit to get off, hands reached out and brushed against her abdomen. When she finally reached home or school, having braved all the hustle and bustle, she found semen stuck to her blue skirt like snot. In the city's buses and bus stops, the organs of those who pretended to be gentlemen were flashed at her without warning. She learnt that just as Mother Mary had kept infant Jesus hidden, she had to keep her body hidden from the roving eyes of these latter-day Herods. And yet, it was marriage that presented her with a forceful revelation: *The body is an eternal cross.*

She realized that marriage was a Golgotha especially in those days that she stayed with Jerome George Marakkaran's family: a house such as she had never seen until then, people who were unlike those she had met until then, food that was unlike anything she had eaten until then, behaviour that she had not been accustomed to until then, pigeons that wheezed non-stop like asthmatics on their deathbeds, vehicles that roared past. She felt suffocated. She did not know what it was that stifled her. Her days grew arid and her nights, insufferable.

Her nights ended at 4 a.m. with the faltering voice of Lilly George Marakkaran reading out from the Bible. From within Lilly's humble being wailed a cuckoo whose throat had been slit. After this, gospels rang out from some devotional TV channel that George Jerome Marakkaran switched on, which blared on day and night.

Other than the gospels, the only other sound heard within those four walls was George Jerome Marakkaran's voice. He spoke only to Jerome; to everybody else, he barked orders. Jerome's elder brother John also lived in that house, but his voice was seldom heard. He had Lilly George Marakkaran's large, helpless eyes. Slender of frame, he always wore old, faded, ill-fitting clothes; even on the train journey, he seemed to have hidden himself away somewhere.

'Where do you work, John *achaya*?' she asked him once in an attempt to break the ice during the train journey. John had looked at Jezebel as if at a stranger.

'In a private company,' cut in George Jerome Marakkaran, and added with a touch of menace, 'He doesn't talk much, doctor*ey*. Don't trouble him with too many questions, *ketto*?'

Even at home, John often stayed invisible. He lay low like some cockroach or lizard that stayed hidden in the crevices of the walls until the world fell asleep. Early in the morning, he could be seen in the drawing room, curled up on the sofa, hugging his knees like a child who had been punished. The moment Jezebel walked in, he would make himself scarce.

The first morning at her husband's house, Jezebel woke up with a headache. In the kitchen, Lilly George Marakkaran was getting down to making breakfast. Puttu and an insipid green-gram curry. When she saw Jezebel, something like a smile flitted across Lilly's face. When Jezebel asked her, 'Can I help with anything, Mummy?' she replied in a whisper, 'It's all right, *moley*. I can manage.'

As she sipped the black coffee she had been handed, leaning against the grimy kitchen table, George Jerome Marakkaran appeared at the door, clad in a red T-shirt and a chequered lungi.

'It's almost noon! Did they teach you in your MBBS that doctors need to wake up only at this hour?'

She lacked the energy to take the scorn and disdain in his voice that morning. Lilly George Marakkaran turned pale and escaped to the balcony under the pretext of getting something from there. Jezebel froze. George Jerome Marakkaran seemed pleased that he had hit the nail on the head.

'Such are the ways at your home, *alle*? Not much piety or prayer over there, eh? Over here, that is not the case. Here, there are rules. Might be a little difficult for you to follow, but follow you must. This is a family that lives by the word of the congregation, the church and the Lord. It will be tough, but you have no option except to go through with it.'

George Jerome Marakkaran's words fell upon her like slimy frogs that multiplied in a trice and frothed all over her clothes, the floor, the coffee cup, the flour bowl. They pounced on her and stuck fast. Jezebel squirmed.

'They don't let her enter the kitchen at home, Daddy. It's her Ammachi who does all the housework. She's the studious type, remember?' Jerome, who had heard everything, threw in his lot with his Daddy.

George Jerome Marakkaran grew more animated.

'Oh, the studious one! Will something drop off if she steps into the kitchen? Daughter-in-law, you may have picked up many such habits from home. Sadly, they won't work in this house, *ketto*? Here, the Lord is the master of the church, and the husband is the lord and master of the family. Here, you see, the women abide by their men. So, daughter-in-law, get into the kitchen without further ado, and learn to make my son Jerome's favourite dishes. If you heed these words, we can get on with life.'

Jezebel thought George Jerome Marakkaran found great pleasure in finding fault with her. From the day she set foot in that house until she left, he exulted in pointing out what a worthless person she was. With a smirk in place on his clean-shaven face, he gave her lessons, his voice dripping with disrespect.

'Come, come, prophetess. Heard you're a great scholar of history? Pray enlighten us too. I'm eager to hear the story of Queen Jezebel as well. Because all this is not to be found in the Bible that we read, you see.'

Jezebel was crestfallen when she realized that he was interrogating her about something she had told Jerome in private. She saw that George Jerome Marakkaran's intent was to prove that she was inconsequential for him—a mere blade of grass.

'Did they teach you in MBBS and MD not to clean the rooms in your marital home, prophetess? Or is it written in Prophetess Jezebel's gospel?'

'Will it demean your status to take this settee's cover downstairs and wash it and dry it on the terrace, prophetess?'

'So your Chachan will send maids and servants to mop these rooms, *alle*, Princess Jezebel?'

George Jerome Marakkaran was ever alert. As soon as he saw that everyone was done with their chores, he would be quick to turn them over into the hands of God and preachers. He slipped in the CD, switched on the player, and at his call of 'Lill*ye*!', Lilly George Marakkaran would come rushing from the kitchen, wiping her wet hands on her blue nightie blackened with grime, to sit down on the floor and stare at the TV. John emerged from his room, drawstrings dangling from his pyjamas, and sat down next to his mother. Jerome ambled up and leaned back on the sofa. Just as Jezebel began to hope that she could finally retire to her room, George Jerome Marakkaran turned on her.

'Will your degree drop off if you listen to this, Prophetess Jezebel?'

'But I haven't . . .,' she whispered.

George Jerome Marakkaran's face hardened.

'Haven't listened to all these, eh? *Iyo*, don't listen, don't listen! Please don't ever listen to wise words that will improve your mind! Your head will conk off! Your glory will dim, *ketto*!'

'But Chachan says . . .'

'Your Chachan may have said all sorts of things at *your* place. But what to do, daughter-in-law, this home happens to be mine. Should you not be listening to me now?'

Jezebel stood wilting.

'Sit down. Daddy doesn't like it if we talk back,' hissed Jerome.

Consoling herself that she would be returning home in four days, Jezebel sat down on the sofa.

'Oh, when the mother-in-law sits down on the floor, the daughter-in-law ought to sit on the sofa all right. Perch high on the sofa or the wall! Don't climb down ever, *ketto*!'

Jezebel's eyes pricked with tears. She sat down on the floor next to Lilly and stared blindly at the TV. When the preacher's assistant came up on stage and began to read out a letter about the divine experience of a patient with oral cancer, she went numb.

'I've heard of mother-in-law battles, but this must be what they call a father-in-law battle!' she blurted out to Jerome that night.

'Sshh! Daddy will hear!' Jerome looked up nervously.

'Why do you always insult me like this, Jerome? What wrong have I done?'

Jezebel teared up. Her heart was swollen with pain.

Jerome's forehead creased. 'Why do you take Daddy's joke so seriously?'

'You call this a joke? Back home we call this character assassination or humiliation.'

'That's Daddy's style,' he said.

'I don't think much of that "style" then.'

Jerome's face clouded. Jezebel got up, opened her purse, popped a pill, and drank some water.

'What pill is that?'

'OCP,' muttered Jezebel.

Jerome's forehead creased once again. But he did not say anything.

'Not that this is needed here. Still . . .,' Jezebel added.

Jerome's face darkened some more. Silently, he stretched out on the bed. When she put the strip of contraceptive pills back in her purse, her eyes fell on the wad of notes in it. Of the six five-hundred rupee notes that had been there, there were only three left.

'Jerome, did you take any cash from this purse?' she asked, trying to keep her tone light.

'Ah yes, I'd taken some in the morning. Thousand five hundred.' Jerome's words were touched with dislike.

'What was it for, Jerome?'

There was no reply.

'Was it to buy something?' she asked, with no trace of rancour.

Jerome George Marakkaran looked at her sharply. 'I didn't know I had to ask for permission to take something from my wife's purse,' he said, face hardening.

She felt an inexplicable surge of fondness. Her tone softened even more.

'So where did you go this morning?'

Jerome's face reddened. His voice hardening, he said: 'Men have any number of places to go to!'

She was stunned. His words had swallowed hers whole. Jerome switched off the light and slept. Jezebel kept sitting in the dark. She was unable to understand herself. She was beginning to understand how marriage turned a woman's self-esteem upside down. Her heart blazed like a furnace. Who had grabbed fistfuls of ashes from that furnace and smeared the sky with it? How had sores festered in her heart? Sores that were not mentioned in modern medicine? She felt fear. She felt pain. Tears sprang and shamed her even when she was half-asleep.

The next morning, soon after breakfast, came George Jerome Marakkaran's call. 'If it would not otherwise inconvenience Doctor Jezebel Prophetess, could she please grant us an audience?'

Jezebel stepped out of the kitchen. He sat on the sofa and looked at her, forehead creased, eyes narrowed to slits.

'Popping pills, are we?'

Jezebel was taken aback. She felt as if someone had suddenly disrobed her.

'Just curious . . . whom did you ask before taking these pills?'

Jezebel struggled to find her voice. 'My friend Smita in Gynaecology . . .'

'Oh, like that. Of course, doctors ought to be like that. Did it occur to you to ask anyone else, though? Like this duffer here, your husband? His duffer father is here too, and his mother, and brother.'

Jezebel's blood boiled, but she steeled her heart. Rushing to her room, she fell upon the cot, sobbing. Jerome followed her in.

'What are you crying for now?'

Irate, she looked up at him.

'Wasn't it you who told Daddy I was taking pills?'

'Why? Should I not tell Daddy?'

Jezebel was flabbergasted. 'Jerome, isn't that our private affair? Even otherwise, doesn't the law say that a woman has a right to decide when she wants to have a baby?'

'Which law? In a family, what the husband says is law.'

'In that case, we don't need a constitution in this country, do we?'

'Are you crazy, Jezebel? Why do you need a constitution inside the house?'

His bewilderment was for real. Jezebel did not have an answer.

She tried a different tack to make him understand. 'If I needed sanitary pads, would you ask Daddy for permission for that too, Jerome?'

'Let me make it clear, Doctor Jezebel Prophetess. Alas, that, too, will be necessary here,' said George Jerome Marakkaran, who had just walked in. 'In this house, you will not spend a hundred and a hundred fifty every month to buy that thing you mentioned, hear? Women in our family always use pieces of old cloth, and now that you're here, daughter-in-law, you might as well do the same.'

He regarded her pitilessly.

'And keep your constitution and law points for the Parliament and the courts. In this house, what I say is law. After marriage, a woman has no money or property of her own. Before marriage, it's her father's; afterwards, her husband's. Once you get your salary, hand it over to Jerome. He'll give you whatever you need. That is the law in this house.'

He left the room. She realized that there was nothing to talk to him about from then on. His words, too, had swallowed hers whole. They scorched her, wrung the necks of the fledgling pigeons of joy and hope in her heart, ripped her wings apart. Two wings hung limp from the small body like broken blossoms.

'All right, so what would one usually find in your purse?' asked the lawyer.

'Cash, ATM card . . .'

'And?'

'Sometimes an important piece of paper . . .'

'Try and recall again?'

Jezebel could not remember.

'Don't you keep contraceptives in your purse?'

Jezebel felt disrobed all over again.

'From the very beginning, you had taken all precautions to ensure you did not get pregnant by Jerome George Marakkaran, had you not?'

Jezebel was dumbstruck.

'Or did these things have some use elsewhere too?' asked the lawyer animatedly. 'Such as when you visited your lover, Dr Sandeep Mohan?'

Jezebel wept. But the tears wouldn't flow.

'Wasn't it in order to marry Dr Sandeep Mohan that you tried to kill your husband in an accident?'

'I did not try to kill anyone.'

'But you admit you were in love with Sandeep?'

Jezebel shook her head in a helpless effort to deny it.

'Did you not borrow twenty-five thousand rupees from Sandeep to give Shark Sebin?'

'Who is this Sandeep?' asked the judge, with evident interest.

The lawyer became more animated. The court was all astir. They saw that the plot was about to thicken. The young doctor studying for her MD had borrowed money from her doctor-lover to pay a contract killer to finish off her doctor-husband. And then what happened?

Words like countless frogs, all fallen dead, all swept up in a great pile. A stench spread within her. 'Don't weep, please,' Jezebel beseeched her own eyes.

No one can enter a strong woman's house unless he ties her up first.

5

And then Jezebel was led by her soul to the desert to be further tested by Satan. She realized that marital life was a lot like a *meenkoodu*, the fishing basket that her grandfather made every monsoon to trap river fish, which lay moth-eaten in the cowshed afterwards.

This was how the *meenkoodu* was made: dried strips of coconut midrib were pared down and woven together, three at a time, with thin strands of coir. To fortify this woven basket, three sturdy wooden twigs of the same size—pared, heated and made pliable— were fastened to it. Two rings, the size of a coconut shell each, were attached to the back of the basket. A *naakkoodu*, a smaller basket with a tongue-shaped contraption, was fixed to this. And then strong sharp strips of coconut midrib were trussed up with coir on both sides of the woven basket. A wooden twig, bent to the shape of the Malayalam letter 'ra' (∩), was fixed in front and then inserted into the mouth of the bigger basket and tied up tightly.

This *meenkoodu* was placed at the mouth of a gushing canal, where fish would enter through the *naakkoodu* and get trapped, unable to swim out. When you lifted the basket the next morning, you found catfish and snakeheads thrashing about. And thus, their lives ended, once and for all.

'Had this not been the predicament of Queen Jezebel as well, when she arrived from Tyre?' she tried to console herself.

A fifteen-year-old, who had grown up in a palace that resonated with the music of the waves, was married and sent off to a desert where battles were waged for water. She woke up one morning to a scorching sea of sand instead of the familiar warmth of the ocean that would beckon to her with a thousand hands. How suffocated she would have felt! How weary her eyes would have grown! She was of the sea; he was of the land. Just like Jerome and her, thought Jezebel, her heart flailing. Those who had brought them together were sinners. They had yoked an ox and an ass together for ploughing. They had forgotten that it was forbidden. And it became her burden to keep others from finding out that one of them was an ass. The onus was on her alone.

George Jerome Marakkaran had prepared a blueprint for Jerome George Marakkaran and her. All they had to do was to live by it. On the day they were to return, George Jerome Marakkaran, whose keen eye missed nothing, saw the haste and enthusiasm with which she had gotten ready by ten o'clock to take the afternoon train. He stated, 'A rented house has been arranged for, *ketto*, Prophetess Jezebel!'

Jezebel was nonplussed.

With a triumphant smirk, George Jerome Marakkaran declared, 'In our family, the brides are always brought into their husbands' homes. Men never put up in the homes of their women.'

Upset, Jezebel asked Jerome why she had not been told about the rented house earlier. 'Shouldn't Daddy be able to come and stay with us?' he countered, annoyed.

She wanted to know what was wrong with the idea of them staying at her place.

'What? Put up at the woman's place?' It was Jerome's turn to do a double-take now.

'Woman's place, man's place! How can you think in such old-fashioned ways, Jerome?' she was irked.

'Yeah, right, I'm a little old-fashioned,' shrugged Jerome.

'But I'm not! And I had told you as much earlier. This is such a let-down, Jerome.'

'If it is a let-down, then you deserve it. Why let yourself be let down in the first place?' his voice rose.

Just then, George Jerome Marakkaran peeped in.

'Not a single paisa was given as dowry anyway. At least make sure they furnish the new place well before you move in, *ketto da*, Jerom*ey*?'

Jerome looked at her as if to say 'you heard that, didn't you'. And then he followed Daddy out of the room.

That was a dreadful moment—the moment of her undoing, but also the moment of her evolution. There was a little girl inside her who refused to grow up, even as she herself had grown up, come of age and earned her degrees. A girl who loved the world in all her innocence, and lived with hope in truth and justice. It was that little girl that Jerome and the world had now crushed. They had robbed her of the ability to trust another person. In marriage, she had hoped for a friend and a lover; instead, what she had been granted was a master, and along with him, an overlord. Their words and actions were an onslaught on her self-esteem. She turned into a rebel.

She was furious with Jerome. When they were alone in the rented house, when he tried to cosy up to her when there was nothing else to do, her fury grew twofold. At night, before he came to bed, she turned away and curled up under a blanket, feigning sleep. Under the mattress, her old diary wept. After he slept, she, too, shed tears of indignation.

She understood that matrimony was society's way of striking in the heel a woman who was otherwise well-protected at home and well-regarded among friends at school and college. She shuddered when she realized that the prince with his grand golden crown and fine-spun red tunic, whom she had been waiting to welcome with the horn, flute, zither, lyre, harp, pipe, and all kinds of music, was a mere imposter.

'Why do you pretend to be another woman?' she asked herself constantly. Thorns and thistles grew over her soul.

After everything was over, she looked back on those days with mortification. How much she had despised him without understanding what he really was!

Every morning he woke up, went to the gym, got back home, showered and set out for work—at one hospital in the forenoon, another in the afternoon, and at a private lab until eight in the evening. He meticulously collected his salary from all these places and ensured she handed over her stipend to him as well. Every month, he transferred sixty thousand rupees to George Jerome Marakkaran's bank account, went to the movies every Saturday evening, ate out every night, grew happier with every passing day. As for her, she grew more and more unhappy, and began to hate him more and more.

Later she realized that it had not been hatred but disappointment. The disappointment of her heart. The disappointment of every single cell in her body. It was a protest. A protest against injustice. A protest against the forceful drowning in formalin of her notion of marriage as the exhilaration of being able to read each other like open books.

Some nights, she dreamt that he came over and sat next to her and caressed her hair; that he spoke to her about this and that; that he burst out laughing; that he shared his sorrow with her. She imagined his lips on her forehead, on her eyelashes, on her cheeks. She sprang awake with a jolt. She looked over at him, sleeping on one side of the bed, and staunched the hatred welling up within her. Sometimes, losing all control, she made pathetic attempts to make him her own.

'Won't you come and sit next to me, Jerome?'
'What for?'
'Won't you touch me with love?'
'Don't be silly.'

She tried different tricks to teach him the ways of love. He refused to learn. She looked at her married friends with envy. When Ahana sat smiling secretly in class, she found herself wondering with a pang about how her husband might have kissed her on the lips the previous night. When Divya sighed after texting on her phone, she wondered with a touch of disappointment about all the ways in which her boyfriend might have pampered her. Seeing a man hold his pregnant wife close, she burned and smouldered with feelings of inadequacy and inexplicable rage.

On one such day, Sandeep Mohan blazed into her life like a flame on a stone pillar. She saw him first on a Monday. She was with her friends Ahana, Divya and Rani in the canteen at break time. When they saw the dark circles under her eyes and inquired, 'Honestly, Jez, what's the matter?' her tears burst their floodgates. They were taken aback. And then Ahana asked her, 'Anything wrong with your sex life?'

'Sex!' Jezebel welled up afresh. 'The women in their family are not supposed to talk about it. Don't see it, don't hear it, don't talk about it.'

'And you kept quiet?' admonished Divya. 'You didn't swear right on his face and give him one on his underside?'

'There's no point. In their family, the rule is that you live under the husband's thumb.'

'So what is one supposed to do for sex?' demanded Ahana, her forehead creasing.

'Suppress desire.'

'Couldn't you open your mouth and say something?'

'The only thing I haven't done yet is climbed on to the rooftop and announced it over a mike.'

'Is he impotent?'

At this, Jezebel broke down. Her friends rallied around, sharing in her anguish.

'*Edee*, you're a doctor, aren't you? How can someone be so stupid? Damn, it's been a while since your marriage! Are you still a virgin? Whatever did you get married for then, *moley*?'

Jezebel could not hold back her tears. That word—virgin— had pierced its way into her being. She trembled.

Her own body mocked her, despised her. She wished she could tear it asunder, hack it into pieces and throw it to the dogs.

'It's all her fault,' chided Divya. 'Five, six years of loitering about in this campus, and what does she have to show for it except a bunch of certificates and ranks? Not a single love affair! Why blame that man then?'

Rani, too, accused Jezebel of having chased away all prospective love interests. And then they began to joke about love and male psychology. They made her laugh, telling her all about how men loathed intelligent women, preferring instead the silly types that kept asking 'Is it so?', 'Really?', 'Is that true?' and so on; and how they themselves had pretended to be dumb whenever they had been in love.

That was when Sandeep arrived on the scene. A cardiologist in his mid-thirties, he had been Ahana's senior in medical college. He saw Ahana, walked up to them, said that he had come to meet a relative's child at the hospital, pulled up a chair and sat next to them.

'Sandeep! Tell us! Isn't it true that men don't like intelligent women?' demanded Ahana, straightening her white burqa over her head.

'Never! I for one prefer intelligent women. Because . . .,' Sandeep paused for effect, pushed his spectacles up his nose and smiled at them. 'They are easier to "bend".'

He was tall, dark-haired, and clear-eyed. And good-humoured, intelligent, and handsome. He spoke jovially, taking off his spectacles from time to time. 'It's difficult to charm beauties because they are well aware of their good looks. Too many fools keep chasing after them and reminding them about it too; whereas the intelligent ones are less in demand and low on confidence. So, although they have brains, they have to be told of that as well. And when you do, they'll fall at your feet.'

'What of those who are intelligent and are aware of it too?'

'Even easier to bring them round. For they're blinded by their own arrogance!'

They all laughed again. Everyone, except Jezebel.

'Look at this one here. No one to "bend" her!'

'Please don't take it amiss,' Sandeep allowed a moment's dramatic pause. 'Even your husband will be able to love you only like a daughter.'

They all burst out laughing. Jezebel laughed along as well. When she took their leave and proceeded to the ward, Sandeep Mohan came along with her.

'Can I tell you something?'

Jezebel turned around and looked at him.

'Don't forget to call me when you feel the need to laugh!'

Jezebel's dimples blossomed in spite of herself.

'But your jokes aren't making me laugh.'

'I'm ready to work harder on them!'

'And what would you gain from that?'

'Not to "bend" you or anything, *ketto*?'

'Oh, don't say that! Please "bend" me over, do!'

'The way times have changed! Would girls have dared to talk like this back in the day?'

'Oh, it runs in our family. My grandmother always prays, "Oh Lord, lead me astray over and again!"'

Sandeep laughed out loud. Jezebel laughed along with him.

Laughing, they climbed up the steps to the ward. He paused at the turn to the Paediatric ICU. 'Can I call you too, when I feel the need to laugh, Jezebel?'

In spite of herself, Jezebel's face fell. With a hasty goodbye, she rushed towards the ward so that he would not notice.

'Could you clarify the nature of your relationship with Dr Sandeep Mohan?' queried the defence lawyer.

'He's a friend.'

'Friend? Meaning? Was it love?'

'No.'

'Oh, come on. Friendship between a man and a woman? Impossible. It will inevitably lead to love and all sorts of other things. And how do you know that it wasn't love? Have you asked him if he was in love with you?'

'He hasn't told me.'

'Nice! Why should love be announced from the rooftop? Is it not for people to understand without it being stated aloud?'

'There was no love.'

'Wasn't Sandeep Mohan estranged from his wife? What was the reason?'

'I don't know.'

'Did you know why Sandeep Mohan's wife, Savitha, had filed for divorce?'

'No.'

'Then I'll tell you. The allegation was that he had a child from another relationship. Not only that, but she also alleged that he had illicit relations with many of his female colleagues, including a doctor, at the Medical College.'

Jezebel's lawyer rose to object that that was a case sub judice in another court. Not paying heed, the defence lawyer continued, 'And there's a great song and dance in the Medical College about this, saying that you are the colleague in question!'

'After marriage, I haven't listened to any songs.'

'By song, I meant the hearsay all over the place.'

'I don't know about it.'

'But you have been to Sandeep Mohan's house, haven't you?'

'Yes, I have.'

'What for?'

'Sandeep's a friend and a colleague.'

'Your husband met with an accident at 8.30 in the morning. Could you let us know where you were at that time?'

Jezebel swallowed hard.

'I say that you were at Sandeep Mohan's house at that time, in his bedroom. Can you deny that?'

Jezebel did not wish to deny it. She had, for a fact, been in Sandeep Mohan's bedroom at that time—where Ann Mary lay with high fever, her large, pretty eyes closed, raving, 'I'll kill him!'

Jezebel placed a cold compress on Ann Mary's forehead. Dipping a towel in hot water, she wiped her neck and those strong palms, darkened and calloused from holding a spanner since the age of five. When her padded bra slipped out of place, her flat chest came into view. Jezebel straightened Ann Mary's clothes. She woke up, screaming.

'It's me, *moley*, don't be scared,' Jezebel said, caressing her forehead.

'I'll kill him!' wailed Ann Mary.

Jezebel felt like weeping too. She stroked Ann Mary on the head. Ann Mary was not female. She had neither breasts nor a womb—a poor foetus that had set out to become male but ended up female. She had been brought up as a female, and therefore conditioned to fear her own nakedness and to protect her body from groping hands.

After Ann Mary slept, Jezebel came out to the living room. Sandeep Mohan, who had been lying in the chair, rubbing his forehead, looked up. Jezebel looked at him, eyes welling up.

'Sandeep, I never thought . . .'

'What do I do with her, Jezebel? I have no clue . . .' His voice, too, faltered.

Like two asses bearing the same heavy burden, they looked at each other. She went over to him and stroked his hair gently. He teared up. His lips quivered.

'I love you, Jezebel,' he whispered.

Jezebel's face reddened. Her dimples blossomed, disregarding her tear-filled eyes.

'Only like a daughter, right?'

Sandeep did not smile.

'Like Ann Mary, then?'

She smiled through her tears. He caressed her palm. She liked the touch of his warm palm. She liked his flushed, tired face. She felt like giving him a kiss. He sat with his eyes closed, thinking of something. She sat down on the sofa and held his hands tight. He pulled away.

'There's blood on my hands, Jezebel.'

His eyes welled up and spilled over. He stared hard at his own hands and closed his eyes again. Again, the tears poured, bursting their floodgates.

Jezebel sat down, exhausted. That was when her phone rang with that frantic call.

'*Main Jerome ka friend Avinash Gupta hoon.* Am I speaking to Mrs Jerome?'

'*Haan,* yes.'

'Hello Jezebel, *mujhe ek call aaya.* Someone from Kerala Police. *Jerome ka koi accident ho gaya?*'

'Jerome? In an accident? No way!' said Jezebel.

As she stood in the court, she wished she did not have to recall those moments again.

'A few days before the accident, you had brought home a girl named Ann Mary without your husband's consent, is that not so?' asked the defence lawyer.

'Jerome did not object.'

'How do you know this Ann Mary?'

'From the Medical College.'

'Aha? In that case, what was that child's illness?'

'That would affect the patient's privacy. I cannot divulge details.'

'Fine. So, who brought Ann Mary to you? Her mother?'

'Her mother is no more.'

'And her father? I mean, her mother's husband? His name is . . . ah yes, George Zacharia, the workshop owner.'

'No.'

'Then?'

'It was Sandeep.' Her voice dropped to a whisper.

'There you are!' The lawyer grew excited, the courtroom stirred, the judge sat up with new-found interest.

'Do you bring all patients home like this?'

Jezebel glared at him.

'Let that be. Dr Jerome sent Ann Mary out of the house. And his accident happened shortly after.'

'She wasn't sent out. She and I left that house together.' Jezebel's eyes welled up.

'We'll come to that later. Jerome's friend called you up and informed you about the accident. And yet you didn't call Jerome on his number or make inquiries. Why so? Normally, if a wife gets to hear that her husband has met with an accident, she would call him up, wailing and screaming. You didn't do that.'

'I did not believe the news of his accident. Also, we'd had a quarrel.'

'And what kind of quarrel was it that you did not feel like calling him even when you heard he had met with an accident? What was the reason? If you're not up to it, let me tell the court why. This Ann Mary is Sandeep Mohan's daughter from an illicit relationship. You decided to adopt your paramour's illegitimate child in order to help him. Jerome George Marakkaran opposed this. To avenge this, you plotted Jerome's murder, either all by yourself or with your paramour's help. Is that not so?'

Jezebel went quiet. The courtroom fell silent. She could hear her own heartbeat. No, no, that man sinned, her heart wailed. He ploughed, yoking an ox and an ass together; he maintained two different measures in the same house; he planted grapes and figs in the same field; he approached a daughter as he would a wife. Sin, heinous sin.

'Why did you atone for someone else's sins?' The doubting Jezebel quietly asked Jezebel-the-rabbi.

She answered soundlessly thus:

'The one who makes the fishing basket does not hear the wails of the fish trapped inside, does he? Only the other fish do.

Let those who can, hear them.'

6

In the family famed as Poonthottathil was a man named John P. John. He was the son of Yohannan, the elder son of Pathrose, the younger son of Yohannan. All four children born to Yohannan before John P. John did not live for long. And so Yohannan prayed that he would dedicate his first healthy child to the Lord. Yohannan and his wife Mariamma endeavoured to raise John P. John in accordance with the divine calling. During his Pre-degree days, John P. John was drawn to communism. He also fell in love with a Dalit girl. When he learnt about this, Yohannan died of a broken heart. John P. John joined the seminary to console his mother Mariamma who was convinced that he was the cause of the father's unexpected death. Within six months, the girl he loved took her own life. When he learnt about this, John left the seminary. 'It would have been better if I had died instead,' he wept, falling at Mariamma's feet. Mariamma was terrified that the thunderbolt of divine wrath would fall upon their family because her son had returned without completing his theological studies. And so, she took to praying for divine mercy day and night for the rest of her days.

Mother and son spent years under the same roof like strangers. Once he landed a job as a teacher, there were marriage proposals aplenty for John P. John. He was able to present to his mother a suitable enough daughter-in-law; however, he could not find for himself a suitable partner. And yet, from Sara he managed to sire two children, both of whom were bright enough to carry on the family name.

The day Jezebel returned from her marital home, though, it became clear to John P. John that, like him, his daughter too had not found a suitable partner. It broke his heart to see his daughter's face as she got off the train. 'What happened, are you not well?' he asked her at the earliest opportunity.

'Tired, Chachaa,' was all she would say in reply.

There was a certain gravitas on Jerome's face. 'We've found a house. Need to shift today itself,' he announced.

John P. John had not anticipated this. All the same, he replied, 'Why not? That's a good thing too.'

Soon after, Abraham Chammanatt arrived in his car. Thereafter, his daughter did not return to spend a single night in her parents' house. John P. John did not try to meet her or talk to her in private either. And when she came back two-and-a-half years later, like a shabby, broken-winged white dove returning to roost, there was no need to ask her anything.

Jezebel, too, lacked the nerve to talk to her Chachan. The guilt that it had all been a yoke of her own making gnawed at her. Until she realized that she had to break free of that yoke all by herself in order to walk erect, she was loath to hurt others with the truth. It took her months to understand that being herded like an obedient, overburdened wild ass by Jerome George Marakkaran and George Jerome Marakkaran wasn't going to get anyone anywhere.

When she tried to point out that this was not the right path, father and son lashed out at her. The lashes left welts on her soul, bruised it. Those wounds festered and thirsted for love's soothing balm. It was on one such day that she left in search of her Chachan—and saw how helpless he was.

That was also the day when she became the keeper of Dr Sandeep Mohan's conscience.

It was a Sunday. A day when Jezebel had no class. A day when she had gotten tired washing, cooking all that Jerome had ordered her to, doing the dishes, mopping the floor.

While Jerome sank into his afternoon nap, she had her bath and settled down on the sofa with a cup of tea and a book. It was *A History of God*, a book she had borrowed from Ahana. As she immersed herself in the joy of having found time to turn the pages of a book after many days, Jerome called out to her. She did not hear him. He came up to her. The sight of her curled up with a book irked him. 'Which exam are you always studying for?' he asked her, snatching the book to look at the title on the cover.

Muttering 'What a waste!', he flung it down with distaste. The book fell flat on its face. She went red. When he looked at her out of the corner of his eye, he had second thoughts. Trying to change the topic, he bade her, 'A tea for me too.' She did not budge. She sat staring at him.

'Didn't you hear? Make me tea!' he ordered again.

'It's there in the flask,' she retorted.

'Why can't you give it to me?' he demanded.

'Has your hand gone limp, Jerome? Serve yourself.'

His face reddened. He saw that her face had reddened as well. So he quickly softened his tone. 'Just give it to me, won't you, Jezebel? Why do you want to pick a fight with me?'

Fuming, Jezebel got up. She poured out the tea and handed it to Jerome who sat on the sofa, fiddling with the TV remote.

'Don't do this again, Jerome,' she said, struggling to keep her tone even. Jerome looked at her innocently. 'But what did I do?'

'Didn't you snatch the book I was reading and throw it down?'

'Oh, that.' He busied himself surfing through TV channels. The feeble smile of the diffident spread on his face. 'Won't you get bored if you read all this?' he tried to joke.

She walked over, picked up the book, dusted it, hugged it to her heart and looked at him. Her eyes blazed.

'If only I had known that you were the type to throw books about, I would have never married you, Jerome.'

Jerome's face betrayed displeasure, but he mustered a smile. 'Ha, it was just a joke . . . and see how you take it to heart!'

'One can make someone out from the kind of jokes he tells.'

When he saw that she was bracing for direct combat, he puckered his lips to focus on the tea and muttered, 'Yeah, Daddy was right. You live up to your name. No respect for the husband at all.'

'Maybe. But did I beg you to come and take me away?' she burst out.

Jerome was stunned. He put his cup down on the teapoy, sprang up to his feet and wagged a finger at her, gnashing his teeth. '*Chee*, stop it *dee*! Else you'll see my true colours. In our family, any woman who dares to talk back to her husband like this will have her teeth knocked out!'

'Just try hitting me if you dare! We'll see that too!' flared Jezebel.

Jerome's face drained of all colour. He raised his hand against her. She smirked.

'You don't hit your wife to prove you're a man. You prove it by sleeping with her instead!'

Jerome's face clouded with shame. 'I'm a man, *dee*! And you are not good enough for me! I'd rather sleep with a wayside bitch instead! Just the sight of your body repels me!'

Jezebel went numb. She burned and writhed as if some robot had grabbed her by the hair and thrown her on a bed of live coals.

She wanted to burst out weeping, but she was also ashamed of tears. He raised his hand again to hit her, then snatched her book and flung it down since he knew that that would hurt her more.

Jezebel lost all control. She breathed hard. She crumbled. When her tears burst their floodgates, shaming her, she picked up her bag, and rushed out with the scooter key. On her way out, she picked up the book lying in the courtyard and put it in her bag. As the scooter revved up, she could see Jerome reach the doorstep in the scooter's rear-view mirror. She sped away without turning back.

In the traffic at the crossroads, her scooter nearly collided with a couple of vehicles. People turned to stare. They scolded her. It was a wretched evening. As she sped dangerously fast on her scooter, she asked herself as to what she had gained from all those months of matrimony. Before marriage, she had had more time to study, time to rest after she got back home from hospital duty and the leisure to fall asleep reading a book. She did not have to scrub and wash bath towels and heavy jeans (that were longer than her!). She did not have to endure the heat and smoke of the kitchen in the little time she had before night duty. She did not have to feel the pain of a lacerated heart.

While caught in a traffic jam on the way home, she noticed a young couple in the car to her right. The man said something to the woman, glaring at her. The woman retorted with a vehement shake of her head. For a while, they sat facing away from each other. By the time the jam eased, they were looking at each other and beginning to smile. That's all there is to married life, thought Jezebel—quarrels in the intervals between laughter, and laughter in the intervals between quarrels. No intervals in her marriage, though. No respite.

She saw the scenes in front of her as if for the first time in her life and drove on steadily. She passed by the Vocational Higher Secondary School, row upon row of acacia trees, the archway in front of the Subramania temple, palm trees with their hair unloosed, the signboard that said 'River fish sold here', the stream in which lorries were washed, fields on both sides, a signboard that said 'Progressive Men's Welfare Association', the panchayat office, Girls' High School, toddy shop, Lower Primary School, and at last, the Birthplace of the Saint. And next to it was the Birthplace of Jezebel.

When she went in, head bent down by the yoke, she found Chachan reading. He looked up from the book. His eyes filled with fondness. Jezebel tried to smile. She wiped her face clean and sat down on the sofa like a guest. She felt as if Sosa Aunty and Monichan Uncle were still there in that room, along with George Jerome Marakkaran and Jerome George Marakkaran. And Abraham Chammanatt too, standing near the bookshelf, gazing at her medals. She wished she could rewind to that day and roar loud and clear: 'I don't want you!'

'Your Valiyammachi is not well. Sara has gone to visit her. She should be back any time now. Have you come all by yourself, *moley*? Where's Jerome?' Chachan asked her.

She looked at the thick book he was reading with a sigh.

'*The Gospel of Mary.* Heard about it? Among his disciples, Christ was fondest of Mary Magdalene. But because she was a woman, she was not respected as an apostle. Maybe that's why some people consider this gospel as a later addition and apocryphal. Do you want this book?'

All at once, Jezebel's tears sprang out. From within her, a little child cried out: 'Chachaa!'

She recalled her childhood days when Chachan would take her and Abel to the local library in the evening after school. They would both hold on tight to Chachan. Once they reached the library, Chachan left them free to browse the bookshelves. On seeing them, the books spread their plumes like peacocks; they gave their hearts a thousand eyes and gave their eyes the sight of a thousand people. Jezebel understood that eyes once opened were dangerous things. She despaired that however much you shut your eyes, sights once seen were impossible to erase.

'The Bible says you ought not to breed together two kinds of your cattle,' said Chachan, his voice trembling. Jezebel smiled, wiping her tears. She went up to Chachan, laid her head on his shoulder. He kissed her on the forehead.

It distressed Jezebel to see her Chachan crumble so. Chachan—who always had a solution for everyone's problems and who always mediated everybody's disputes. It pained her to see his pain. Her own pain was too intense for her to even remember its pathology. She stood helpless as Chachan rushed inside to stifle his sobs.

Christ with the haloed heart looked at her with bewildered blue eyes. She looked reproachfully back at Christ. By then, Chachan came back, having wept, and washed and wiped his face.

'Come back here if it's unbearable. Chachan's here for you.' There was a catch in his throat.

Just then, Ammachi walked in, holding her purse and umbrella close. 'Where's Jerome?' she demanded.

Jezebel was silent.

Ammachi stopped to look at both of them, and said sharply, 'He called and told me everything.'

Jezebel began to explain, but Ammachi didn't wait to hear her. She walked off in a huff. Jezebel and Chachan exchanged glances. From inside the house, Ammachi's voice rose: 'Wives, submit to your husbands as to the Lord. For the husband is the head of the wife as Christ is the head of the church, he is the saviour of the body. Now as the church submits to Christ, so also wives should submit to their husbands in everything.'

Jezebel looked at Chachan. Chachan was helpless. There were huge dark circles under his eyes. His voice had grown weary. His smile was full of pain. Chachan's own life was a sacrifice laid at the altar of Ammachi's inanities. 'Each one bears his own cross,' he whispered. Jezebel left without saying goodbye.

That moment, she felt orphaned. She felt weak and helpless, with nowhere to go and no one to love. Her Kinetic Honda took her to the Medical College. At the gate, her scooter grazed against an oncoming car. She fell down. It was Sandeep Mohan's car. He sprang out. 'Jezebel, *edo*, what's the hurry!' he admonished her.

He lifted up the vehicle which lay by the wayside, wheels still spinning, then helped her to her feet. He checked for bruises on her hands and feet, and insisted on accompanying her to the casualty department, where he cleaned her wounds. 'Where to?' he asked her when they came out. 'Nowhere,' she replied. 'Why don't we go for a drive then?' he suggested. 'Sure,' she agreed.

Much later, when he touched her lightly to indicate that it was time to get off, she woke up with a start and wondered where she was. They were in front of his house. She grew uneasy.

'You didn't say we were coming here,' she protested.

'You didn't ask where we were going,' he reminded her, and added, as he opened the door, 'I didn't ask you why you were crying either.'

Perplexed, she ran a hand over her face. Her cheeks were wet. Her handkerchief was wet. There were still traces of tears, which had flowed for long, in the eyes that met hers in the car's rear-view mirror. She was mortified. She wiped her face and followed him into the house.

It was a charmingly done-up room. A framed painting hung on the wall. In the painting, an orange-complexioned, green-haired female figure with blue eyes that opened up to the sky stood leaning on a blue-skinned, yellow-haired male whose red eyes drooped down to the earth. The glow of the bulb above the painting made all four eyes shine. Jezebel stood there, unable to take her eyes off those eyes.

'A woman drew that,' said Sandeep as he came out of one of the rooms. She noticed that his voice had grown tender.

'The frame makes the painting lovelier,' said Jezebel.

'I made that.'

The furniture, the colour of dried blood, looked novel and aesthetic.

'Nice decor. Where did you buy this furniture?'

'It wasn't bought. I made it myself.'

She looked at him in amazement. He took off his glasses, wiped them, wore them again and went in. She took a little tour of the house—two bedrooms, a kitchen, a study, books on cardiology stacked in the study. One of the bedrooms was done up like a luxurious five-star hotel room. The other one was shut. 'This is my bedroom, that is my wife's,' said Sandeep.

'Two separate rooms, one for each. Interesting.'

'Soon there will be two separate lives as well. She has sent me a divorce notice.'

He tried to smile. And then remembered, '*Iyo*, coffee!' and rushed to the kitchen.

He returned with two blue coffee cups and saucers laden with biscuits. Her bruises had begun to hurt. She sat uneasily on the sofa.

'So, what were we talking about? Ah yes, my wife. Her divorce notice . . .'

He handed her a cup.

'Why?' asked Jezebel.

Sandeep took his time blowing on, and cooling his coffee, then looked at her.

'Never ask anyone that. It's like asking someone, "Why did you die?" All of us die at some point in time. All relationships drift apart at some point in time. Some stay under the same roof even after they have drifted apart. Some leave immediately.'

'And some live in the same house without ever meeting each other.'

Jezebel tried to smile. Sandeep looked at her with tenderness.

'Now I know why you cried, Jezebel.'

'I didn't even know I'd cried.'

'Some people are like that. Only, they won't know that they are crying.'

'No wonder your wife left you! There's a limit to suffering such dull philosophy!' Jezebel quipped.

Sandeep laughed out loud. Jezebel got up after having her coffee. 'Time to go,' she said.

'Where to?'

'From where we started. Where else?' Her voice was filled with despair.

'I wanted to meet you, Jezebel. Just so happened that we met anyway—like the vine you went in search of coils itself around your feet. I need a favour, Jezebel.'

'Ha, how typical! Ahana always says be careful when men are nice to you. It usually means they need something from you.'

'Honestly! Women's education is the greatest tragedy to befall our society.'

'No matter how much philosophy you spout, you still need women to prop up your jokes, don't you?'

'Won't let a poor man overcome his inferiority complex, will you?'

Sandeep and Jezebel both laughed. Then his face grew serious. 'I can't tell Ahana this. I don't think she can keep a secret.'

'Ok. What can I do for you?'

Sandeep heaved a long sigh.

'There's a patient in bed number 113 of the oncology ward—a woman. Her name is Anitha. Please visit her, Jezebel, and let me know how she's doing. I'll give you some money. Please hand it over.'

'Oh, I thought it was something major!'

'It is. Please tell that woman—only her—that you're visiting her at my behest . . .'

Jezebel sat up.

'. . . . and that if anything happens to her, I'll take care of Ann Mary.'

His voice was firm. Jezebel looked at him, curious.

'Ann Mary? Who's that?'

'Her daughter.' He took off his glasses, wiped them and wore them again. 'And mine.'

Later, whenever she thought about that moment of shock, and about life that had put fire and water before her and asked her to choose between them, Jezebel grew terrified. She chose fire, thinking it was water. And that was how she was dragged into Sandeep Mohan's life.

It was the kind of story she hadn't heard until then. The story of Class 10 student Sandeep Mohan who became the lover of the thirty-year-old married woman Anitha, and their relationship which lasted many years. The story of a daughter born to her from him. The story of how Sandeep fled in fright, and how he later returned to look for her, racked by guilt. Jezebel was stunned. Sandeep's honesty shattered her. He confessed to her. 'Mea culpa, mea culpa, mea maxima culpa,' he wept. Jezebel was helpless. By receiving someone's secret, she had been crucified to that bond for life. She promised him that she would visit Anitha the very next day.

As she was about to leave, the painting on the living room wall caught Jezebel's eye again. 'Anitha drew this, didn't she?'

Sandeep flushed. 'No wonder your friends say you're intelligent.'

'Intelligence is useless. Haven't you heard that Tamil film song that goes, "Not all who are intelligent become successful in life?" And not all those who succeed are intelligent either.'

'Success is a state of mind. Wasn't it some feminist who said that if you live long enough, you'll see that all your old successes turn into failures?'

He reached for her hand. Jezebel felt shy. She thrilled all over.

'When I first saw you, Jezebel, you reminded me of my Ann Mary.'

Jezebel went limp. She felt like laughing and weeping at the same time.

'When your husband caught you red-handed after you visited Dr Sandeep Mohan at his house, didn't he advise you not to repeat it?' asked the defence lawyer.

'He didn't "catch me red-handed". I told him myself that I had gone to Dr Sandeep's place. When Jerome heard that . . .'

'Hold on, hold on. Just answer the question asked.'

'When Jerome came to know that you and Dr Sandeep drove fifty kilometres in your car to Anitha's place, he scolded you.'

'I went alone.'

'Why did you go there? To enjoy the sea breeze?'

'To bring Ann Mary.'

'The brakes in Dr Jerome's car were damaged. It was a new car. There was no way the brakes could not have worked properly.'

Jezebel swallowed hard.

'George Jerome Marakkaran had misgivings that someone may have deliberately tampered with the brakes. But you were quick to tell the police that there was no such suspicion.'

'Jerome was still getting used to driving.'

'The car that Jerome drove, who used it in the days before?'

'I did.'

'When did you learn driving?'

'We both learnt to drive after we bought the car.'

'See! How liberal of Dr Jerome!' There was admiration in the defence lawyer's voice.

Jezebel was disgusted.

It was on the day she had walked out that George Jerome Marakkaran called his son and instructed him to buy a car. A ploy to put an end to Jezebel's scooter rides. When he saw her bruises upon her return from Sandeep's house, Jerome feigned anxiety. He begged forgiveness. Do wayside bitches have any other option, she fumed in reply. And then he pulled out the trump card and declared: 'Daddy has given us permission to buy a car!'

'Do we even get to buy rice in this house without Daddy's permission?' grumbled Jezebel.

'Listening to Daddy has only ever done us good,' reasoned Jerome, and then announced that they needed a bank loan to buy the car.

Jezebel was hopping mad. Her stipend was only half of his salary, yet she insisted that she, too, wanted to learn driving. He agreed reluctantly. She called up a driving school right away and enrolled for lessons for both of them from the next morning onwards. The prospect of learning something new excited her. They were together in the morning class. Within a week, Jezebel cleared the H test. 'So quickly?' exclaimed the driving instructor. Two months after she got her driving licence, Jerome was still learning to drive. In the end, the instructor got him a licence after bribing the officer.

'Even though you both began to learn driving at the same time, you could drive long distances on your own while Jerome was still learning.'

'Jerome was a little slow to pick up new things.'

'That means you were quick on the uptake, isn't it? What if I said you were the one who meddled with the brake?'

'I learnt only to drive. Not to mess with brakes.'

'Ok, so it wasn't you. Does this mean someone else fiddled with it? Do not lie in court. Who was it?'

Jezebel stood there with a heavy heart. Even after she had thrown off Jerome's yoke, another one remained. She did not wish to sever its bonds. Because it was not easy. Because the yoke was one of compassion.

In her own court, Jezebel the pilate interrogated Jezebel-the-rabbi, 'Why could you not avert the great tragedy that befell that poor man by giving him his freedom the day he told you he was repelled by the very sight of your body?'

'Why did you not teach him that the way to prove that he was a man was not by sleeping with a woman but by respecting and loving her instead?'

Jezebel-the-rabbi replied thus, 'I was taught to feel ashamed of my own body, wasn't I? And I thought you had taught him that he, too, has to give of himself when we sleep together.'

7

This is how the gospel of Anitha Zacharia, the daughter of sorrow, begins:

'Behold, I send my messenger, and she will prepare your way.
The voice of she who cries out in the desert: prepare the way for her!'

Anitha was the wife of George Zacharia who had been sent to a juvenile home at the age of nine after stabbing his uncle who had fought with his father over a property dispute. George Zacharia left home at the age of seventeen and returned as an automobile mechanic. From time to time, he got embroiled in petty cases of fisticuffs. Later, he set up his own workshop. He looked around for a nice girl who couldn't afford dowry, and found Anitha. He married her, and sired Rosemary and Rubin, but continued to indulge in wine and women. Once, when she was pregnant with Rubin, Anitha went home meaning to stay a week but returned in two days. She was taken aback by the scene of drink and debauchery that greeted her. She stormed out. When George Zacharia came looking for her, Anitha's family coerced her into going back with him. Once home, they fought again. She stormed out again. And as this cycle continued, a Class 10 boy arrived next door. His name was Sandeep Mohan.

Jezebel went over to the oncology ward, curious to meet the woman who had, unmindful of age and stature, fallen in love with a teenager, and who bore his child when she was thirty. She lay on a green bed-sheet spread over an iron cot at the far end of the ward, curled up like the Malayalam letter 'Ꮇ'. A forty-something in an ill-fitting nightie that hung over an ashen body. She sat up when Jezebel walked up to her. Jezebel introduced herself and said she had come at Sandeep's behest. The moment she heard Sandeep's name, Anitha started. Her tired drooping eyes revived like withered leaves that perk up when spattered with raindrops. A blush spread over her cheeks, sunken and ashen with death's shadow. Jezebel examined her case sheet, trembling a little at the mention of 'CA Breast Stage-4'. That day, Jezebel was baptized in tears by Anitha. She felt the heavens open and saw the spirit of God descend like a dove and alight on her.

Outside, sunbeams bathed the earth in radiation therapy. There was a long queue at the counter for free food organized by a charity. Jezebel handed over to Anitha the money Sandeep had given, and let her know he had asked her to reach out to him in case she needed anything. Anitha replied, 'Please ask him not to worry about me.' Jezebel wondered if Anitha was all by herself. That was when she rushed in with a tiffin box full of the free food. Jezebel looked at her—a lamb, pink and unblemished. Sandeep's wide eyes looked out from her face at Jezebel. Jezebel smiled fondly at her and said, 'Ann Mary?' 'Yes,' came the reply in a gruff voice. Jezebel took her hand warmly. Her palm was surprisingly rough, strong and calloused. When Jezebel asked her if she didn't have to go to school that day, Ann Mary's large eyes filled with indifference.

'It's been two years since I stopped going to school.'

'But why?' Jezebel's forehead creased.

'Mummy's unwell,' she said, as if dropping out were no big deal.

Ever since Anitha took ill, Ann Mary stopped going to school. She was the only one available to attend to Mummy at the hospital. She knew cancer centres and medical colleges by heart. She was the one to spoon-feed her mother with juice after the chemotherapy. She blended *kanji*, rice-soup, either in a mixie or mashed it by hand, and fed it to her mother, admonishing her if she resisted. When Mummy was back home from the hospital, Ann Mary had no time to rest. She had to do all the household chores single-handedly. She had to help Papa at the workshop. Papa's workshop was in the front yard of the house. She had learnt all the nitty-gritties of automobile repair. However, her dream had been to study medicine. When Jezebel asked her why, she whispered, 'That's how it is', blushing.

Later, Jezebel realized that another sign had appeared in her life that day. It was on that day that two little girls, aged eight and four, from a family that had attempted mass suicide, had been brought to the hospital in a critical condition. Their story was the talk of the hospital. The man had mortgaged their house and taken a loan from a private financier so that his wife—a nurse—could go abroad. The job offer fell through, the interest on the unpaid loan multiplied, and the financier's goons attacked the house and raped the wife. The husband and wife decided to take their lives. The children had asked for fried rice a few days ago. The man borrowed a thousand rupees from his brother, took his wife and children to the church to pray, bought fried rice and chicken, came back home, and mixed a chutney made from poisonous seeds with the fried rice. The next morning, a neighbour alerted the police when she saw that the house remained unopened even at eight in the morning. By nine, four bodies had been brought to the Medical College Hospital. The woman was dead. The man was dying.

It was after Alexander sir's class, as she turned the corner to the ward from the corridor with dark cobwebs, that Jezebel saw the gurneys with the bodies of the children rolling towards her.

She rushed after them. The eight-year-old's name was Michelle; the four-year-old with a pink, doll-like face was Angel. Angel was calling out to her mother in a half-unconscious state. Jezebel laced her fingers with that tiny little hand reaching out for her mother. The little one gripped her fingers tight and slid back into a peaceful slumber. Jezebel stood there, despairing, soaking up the warmth of those tiny fingers. Her heart brimmed over. She thought of her own unborn children. She imagined giving birth to them, holding them close to her bosom. But when she remembered that she had to conceive them through Jerome, she felt as if a burning log had been thrust at her. Her insides burned; her mouth filled with distaste. She gently let go of Angel's grasp.

By the time she completed her rounds and returned, Michelle was declared dead. Angel was lost in a deep sleep. Before she left for the oncology ward, Jezebel examined Angel once again and smoothed her hair.

The sight of the ambulance in front of the casualty department would never be erased from Jezebel's memory of that day. When she returned after visiting Anitha, the ambulance stood ready in front of the casualty block. She remembered it all like yesterday— its doors opening like the jaws of death, two men lifting a body into it, two more bodies waiting at the entrance. Angel lay limp on the shoulder of a man in the crowd. A cannula had been inserted into her little wrist. When the man who carried her tossed her carelessly in the seat inside the ambulance, Jezebel's heart lurched.

A few months later, Jezebel saw her again. By then, seven bowls of God's wrath had been poured over her. Jezebel was clutching at straws, like one who set sail on a stormy sea and prayed to a piece of driftwood far weaker than the ship on which she stood. As she waited along with Ann Mary for the lawyer to arrive at the police station, she appeared in front of Jezebel—her hair unkempt and windblown, her skin shrivelled and sunburnt. She walked absently past her, accompanied by two policewomen. The police said that she had been staying with her father's brother after the death of her parents and sister; that a sixty-year-old neighbour had lured her with candy and sexually abused her for months on end. Her name: Angel. A tender olive branch, a piece of driftwood one could hold onto and stay afloat.

When the lawyer asked her about that day, she remembered Angel's little face. Her heart ached all over again.

'When Jerome George Marakkaran's parents arrived after hearing the news of his accident, you were not around. Must have been something really urgent that took you away. Where were you?' the lawyer asked Jezebel.

'At the court.'

'And what was the case?'

'George Zacharia had filed a complaint that Ann Mary had been kidnapped.'

'You returned late that night. And when George Jerome Marakkaran asked you where you had been all day, you raised your hand against him and caught him by the collar. Is this true?'

'It was Jerome's Daddy who hit me.'

'The question is, what did you do?'

'I did not do anything.'

'Doctor*ey*, I ask because I really don't get it. How could you drive some fifty kilometres to attend to a case pertaining to someone else's child at a time when your own husband lay critical in hospital after an accident?'

Jezebel fell silent. She was at a loss as to how she could answer that question in one word.

It was on the day of Abraham Chammanatt's angioplasty that she met Sandeep again. Abraham Chammanatt was in the cardiology ward. With him were his wife Gracy Aunty and his late brother's wife Mary Aunty. Once Sandeep had finished examining Abraham Chammanatt, Jezebel escorted him out. Sandeep asked about Anitha, and if her children had come to the hospital to assist her. Jezebel informed him that only Ann Mary was around, and remarked, 'She is your spitting image.'

Sandeep was abashed. 'I'm the father of such a grown-up girl! Wonder if she'll love me or hate me when she is older. Will she feel pride or shame?'

'I'm upset she had to discontinue her studies,' said Jezebel.

Sandeep's face fell. A flicker of pain shadowed his eyes. 'A mother's paramour does not have a father's rights, Jezebel.'

His voice shook. Perhaps fearing he would break down, he rushed to the duty room. As she stood there watching him, Jezebel felt thorns pierce her heart. She asked herself, who gains wisdom about life and the reason behind its experiences? Who understands the intimations of language or the meanings of riddles?

That day, she found herself adrift on a sea of helplessness. The home of her dreams, that promised land, had turned into a desert. Signs of disaster and miracles with intimations of evil bewildered her. Feelings of isolation and abandonment suffocated her. She knew that Jerome, too, was disturbed. It troubled him to see the woman he called his wife behave like someone else. Jezebel got closer to Ann Mary. She bought her biryani and fried rice and ice cream from the canteen. They spent time chit-chatting. Ann Mary made her laugh, filled her with tenderness, taught her to forget her own pain.

'If I kick the bucket, go stay with Doctor Aunty, *dee*. You could even help with the household chores. Doctor Aunty will take good care of you,' said Anitha, only half in jest.

'Won't your husband look after her?' asked Jezebel.

Anitha's eyes welled up. Ann Mary's face dimmed. She said that Papa hated her. She was a thorn in the side of Anitha's married daughter Rosemary and engineer son Rubin. Ann Mary had only Anitha; Anitha had only Ann Mary.

'I've told the Father in our church to put her in some orphanage if I pass away.'

'But shouldn't the others agree to it too?'

'It will be good riddance for them, *alle*? If they don't agree, she'll have to run away. Otherwise, the moment my coffin is lowered, they'll poison her to death.'

Anitha worried that there was no option but to put her in an orphanage. Only then would Sandeep be able to help her out. And adopt her. Sandeep, her Sandu, would not let her down; of this, she was certain. Sandu was a good man. Anitha wiped her tears.

Even as Jezebel wondered how Anitha could have taken up with a man young enough to be her son, Anitha exulted in the fact that it was Sandu who had made her feel like a woman. The boy who had come to stay with his uncle after his parents left for the Gulf. For Anitha, he was, at first, the boy next door, and then, her own son's playmate. Anitha's mother was bedridden at the time. Since Anitha was not allowed to see her relatives, Sandu offered to take food and medicines over to her mother without George Zacharia getting wind of it. And that was how Sandu became her confidant. One day, Sandu came over when she was all alone at home.

'I don't know how it happened, doctor. We sat next to each other. I was sharing my sorrows; he was consoling me. When I came to, it was all over.'

Jezebel swallowed hard. She tried to wrap her head around it. The bond between a man and woman. Their union, wrapped in robes fragrant with the fresh sap of desire, with love's sandal paste, youth's invigorating clove. Jezebel saw in her mind's eye a tumult of fingers, lips, a meeting of voices, gazes, touches. Her heart sank. She thought about her own self. Despaired. Raged. Grieved.

When he came to know that Anitha was pregnant with Ann Mary, Sandeep was panic-stricken. He was doing his MBBS back then. He became selfish. He became a coward. He insisted that she terminate the pregnancy.

'That was the one thing I did not obey. I did not have the heart to let the baby go.'

Jezebel was full of curiosity about whether Anitha's husband had not come to know of this sooner.

Anitha heaved a sigh. 'It was my elder daughter Rosemary who first found out about my relationship with Sandu. We haven't spoken to each other since. She informed her Papa about it that day itself. He used to quarrel with me even earlier on. With this, fights and abuse became a daily affair. He even tried to kill me. But I held on. The pregnancy gave me courage from God knows where. I told him—either we part ways now, in which case I will tell everyone that this baby isn't yours. Many more skeletons will tumble out of the closet. Or I could raise the child as yours. Only the two of us would know that this child isn't yours.'

Her large eyes brightened. Jezebel looked on in disbelief.

'That was the first time I spoke firmly to anyone. He pounced on me with an "I'll kill you, *dee*!" And I told him: "If you must, kill me completely. If there's even a wisp of life left in me, I'll crush your dignity underfoot."'

She smiled, wiping her overflowing tears.

'Later I wondered where I'd got that strength from. Honestly, doctor, it was from the realization that I had no one. I got no love from my husband. The one who had given me love and hope left me in the lurch. What other option did I have before me?'

Anitha's father had been an artist. She, too, painted. Her father's brother had a shop that sold portraits. Since her brothers were already estranged, Anitha sought her uncle's help. The uncle agreed to sell whatever she painted. She sold the only bangle she had and bought a canvas and paints. She painted. The baby in her womb grew. Her paintings grew better.

If Sandu was a coward, my husband was worse. I decided not to have anything to do with Sandu. But when Ann Mary was six years old, I was diagnosed with cancer. It was at the cancer centre that I saw him again. When he saw me, at first, he fled. But he came looking for me a couple of days later. And from that day onwards, I have been ready to die. My heart brimmed over. Even chemotherapy could not hurt me after that. If death were to come calling now, I'd go along happily. Because all that I had suffered until now was in the name of this love which cannot be spoken about. It is the reason my own children and husband hate me with all their heart. But that love was priceless. My suffering was not in vain either. Because the one I loved was a good man. He did not hate me or cheat me even after the illness, even after I lost my good looks. He loved me as much as I loved him. Even if I die, even if he dies, our love will endure.'

At this, Jezebel, too, welled up. Anitha's words, and those memories, infused the stinging burn of chillies into her veins, as if from an endless drip. They rang in Jezebel's ears. As she tossed sleeplessly in bed that night, she wept, thinking of Anitha. And felt rapture. And envy.

Ann Mary ought to have been born a man. Because of a hormonal defect, her body became that of a woman's. And yet she had no uterus. Her breasts were not fully formed. When he realized that she would never menstruate, Sandeep was distraught. 'How will Anitha endure this?'

'Plastic surgery can help set the breast right. But you do know that she won't be able to have children, don't you?'

'If Anitha gets to know, she'll die right away.'

'Don't tell her. Just let her know that the treatment is under way,' Jezebel consoled him.

Anitha died without ever getting to know about it—six months before Jerome's accident. It was cardiac arrest. As she lay tired and nauseated after a chemo session, she felt some discomfort in her chest. Ann Mary called Jezebel. Jezebel called Sandeep. They shifted Anitha to the cardiology ICU. For two days and nights, Sandeep stayed right by Anitha's side. Early one morning, at about four, Anitha vomited blood. Sandeep received those thick clots of blood in his cupped palms. He fulfilled the tenet of love that says when one dies, the other must be by their side. God received Anitha. Sandeep crashed to the ground. Ann Mary was orphaned.

'Can you tell us the details of the case filed against you by Ann Mary's father George Zacharia?' asked the lawyer.

'It was a complaint of kidnapping.'

'So when did you hatch the plot to kidnap the child?'

'I did not kidnap her. She came of her own volition. She had no food, no clothes, no safety in that house.'

'So? Did you give her food and clothes and safety?'

That was a complicated question. She had given Ann Mary food and clothes. She had given her love and compassion. But safety . . .?

'Couldn't Sandeep Mohan have gone to the court instead?'

'The case was in my name. The lawyer asked me to show up.'

'What would have happened if you hadn't turned up?'

'The lawyer said the police would take her away.'

'So let them! She's not your child, *alle*? Just a child that came to the hospital for treatment. Even if she's your colleague's child, what is the relationship between you two that you have to go and bring her, and keep her in your custody? Or could it be that you had this child before marriage and gave it away to be raised? That, too, can happen, *alle*? Like in some movies.'

The lawyer paused for effect, then raised his voice, 'Still, doctor*ey*, what is the rationale in your going in search of someone else's child just two days after your own husband met with an accident when you ought to have been by his bedside, praying for him as he lay between life and death?'

That was a big question. Jezebel did not answer. Some answers ought not to be spoken. They are the sores that blister on the soul when the bowls of God's wrath spill. Their secrets have to be kept until death. Their stench has to be covered up. One has to seek refuge in a piece of driftwood weaker than the ship on which one stands.

Some women are cursed thus.

8

In the beginning was a woman. Her name was Lilly. She came to bear witness to the light, so that through her, all might believe. She herself was not the light, but the world was illumined through her. She became flesh, and was born among us. She took birth in the ancient Chammanatt family. She was the only daughter. The Chammanatts were among those Christian families that had set up shop in the new market in the seventeenth century under the king's reign. They were adept not only at business but also at farming and healing. Lilly had four brothers. They all loved her limitlessly. She was the lamp of that home, the light of that land.

The little one grew and became strong in spirit. She had to wander in the desert until the time came for her to present herself in public. So be vigilant! Because women in some families are creatures in human form. They fly straight ahead, without looking to the left or right. Where the spirit wills them, there they go. After a while, they grow four faces and four wings. Sometimes, some recognize that the wings are meant to comfort and protect each other.

Lilly George Marakkaran and Jezebel were such four-winged creatures. They discovered that they could cover up each other's misery with their wings, hide each other's nakedness if they both held their wings together, and fly, unbeknownst to anyone.

It was unexpectedly that Lilly's faces were revealed to Jezebel. The first hint was given by Abraham Chammanatt. On the third day after Abraham's angioplasty, after class got over at five, she returned to the ward, checked the discharge summary written by the house surgeon and got ready to leave. Just then, Jerome George Marakkaran called. 'Gracy Aunty's cousin died. She'll return only tomorrow after the funeral. I have to work overtime today. Daddy asked you to stay behind with Uncle.'

'Ask Daddy to draw up my duty timetable at the Medical College as well!' snapped Jezebel.

She despised Abraham. She believed he had ruined her life. All the same, she went over to his room and attended to him as best as she could. And yet, he wondered, '*Moley*, have you come here unwillingly?' Jezebel was embarrassed.

'I still remember your face on the day we came home to fix the marriage. How radiant you were! And now it's as if someone has squeezed the very life out of that face!' Abraham sighed.

Jezebel's eyes filled. She did not say anything. Abraham's voice shook. 'Did I do you wrong, *moley*?'

'She's my sister, after all. I couldn't find her a good husband. So, I thought I would at least give her a good daughter-in-law. Who does she have in her old age? And I did think you would never forsake her. That's why I pushed for this marriage. If what I did was wrong, please forgive me *moley*.'

Jezebel sat numb. 'I'm not angry with you, Uncle,' she said. And then she asked him the question that was bothering her. 'Why did you marry your sister off to someone like George Jerome Marakkaran?'

Abraham Chammanatt's face drained of colour. 'It happened,' was all he would say before he shut his eyes and turned away.

How it 'happened' was something Jezebel found out months later—on the day Anitha died. Three days earlier, George Jerome Marakkaran, Lilly George Marakkaran and John had arrived. John's wedding was being solemnized with a girl called Christina. That, too, was an alliance arranged by Abraham Chammanatt.

From the betrothal until the wedding, all of them were staying at Jerome's and Jezebel's rented house. The day Anitha died, Sandeep's car pulled up in front of the gate at the crack of dawn. From the window, Jezebel saw him opening the gate and walking in. She grew restless. Jerome had left for the gym. George Jerome Marakkaran, who sat reading the newspaper in the veranda, announced, 'Jerome isn't here. Gone to the gym.'

'Isn't Jezebel around?' asked Sandeep.

George Jerome Marakkaran's face darkened. 'Who are you to Jezebel?' he demanded, forehead creasing. And then stood up, bracing for battle: 'Whatever it is, tell me. I'm her father-in-law.'

'Isn't Jezebel home?' repeated Sandeep.

'Whatever you have to say, say it to me,' repeated George Jerome Marakkaran.

Mustering courage, Jezebel stepped out. George Jerome Marakkaran's face hardened. 'Anitha is dead,' informed Sandeep and turned to leave.

Thunderclouds rumbled inside the house. When Jerome returned, George Jerome Marakkaran was raging at Jezebel for having insulted him. Jezebel shot back that he had humiliated her colleague. Jerome ordered her not to talk back to Daddy. There was a limit to putting up with things, retorted Jezebel. George Jerome Marakkaran slapped her hard across the face. Jezebel saw stars. Lilly George Marakkaran rushed up to her and dragged her away. 'Don't say anything, *moley*,' she pleaded. 'I can't live here any more,' Jezebel wailed. Lilly held her close, whispering, 'Don't cry, please don't cry.' Jezebel tried to wriggle free. Lilly held her tight. In the end, Jezebel gave in and leaned against her. Lilly's bosom was as soft as the down lining a bird's nest. As she buried her face in and closed her eyes, Jezebel heard the fluttering of wings. She learnt that this fluttering of wings that you heard with your heart was what they called 'mother'. She called out, 'Ammey!' Lilly's wings folded around her in an embrace.

'My mother used to say, there's no point chanting the scripture at a charging buffalo. It won't understand a word,' she whispered. Her lips grazed Jezebel's burning cheek. Jezebel's tears burst their floodgates. Lilly George Marakkaran talked without pause. 'Don't cry, don't cry. Look at me. I don't cry. I won't cry. There is no point crying. Crying won't solve anything. And no one will love you more because of your tears.'

Jezebel snuggled closer. Lilly hugged her tight and pressed her lips on her forehead.

'You can wage a war without a sound. And you can win the war without anyone knowing about it. We need to love ourselves first.'

Jezebel looked up with a start. And looked at her with wonder. She had always seen misery in those large eyes. That day, for the first time, she saw mischief in them. Mischief in the eyes of a middle-aged woman! The mischief of an eight-year-old. She had a hard time believing her own eyes.

'Only when we love ourselves will others love us too. I didn't know that. I loved everyone with all my heart. And I thought they would all give me love in return too. I waited for so long. Nobody gave me any love. I fell apart. That's when I understood that you don't give others love. Give them kindness, and save the love for yourself. We find strength when someone loves us. When you feel you'll go to pieces, muster all your strength and love yourself . . .'

Jezebel was stunned. She felt a churning within. Presently, she calmed down. Lilly helped her get ready, packed her lunch. She left for the hospital. When she returned in the evening, George Jerome Marakkaran and Jerome George Marakkaran were not at home. Lilly served her tea and steaming hot *ada*. Jezebel held her close and laid her head on her shoulder.

'Mummy, tell me honestly. Why did your family foist this man on you? Couldn't they find anyone else?' she asked.

'No.' Lilly smiled. 'He was not foisted on me; I was foisted on him.'

Her large eyes met Jezebel's. 'At the time of the wedding, I was pregnant with John.'

Jezebel was stunned.

She saw Lilly's other faces. The Lilly of the past. The one who talked non-stop and laughed out loud. The one who secured the second rank in BA Literature and was studying for her MA from the women's college in the city. Her family had fixed her marriage. The boy was handsome. He was rich. And from a prominent family. He met Lilly the day her hostel closed for the vacation. They roamed the city on his bike. He took her someplace saying it was his friend's house. There, he made love to her. And with that, his mien changed. He did not talk to her after that. 'What wrong did I do?' despaired Lilly. He dropped her at the bus stop and left. Lilly reached home, heartbroken. He did not contact her until the vacation was over and it was time to return. He did not reply to her letters. The day before college was to reopen, they received a communication that the marriage was off. Lilly was devastated. At first, she was livid, then she wept. Meanwhile, she found out that she was with child. When she sought him out, he spurned her. He offered to help terminate the pregnancy, but didn't want to marry her. 'If you were a good woman, you wouldn't have shared a bed with me before marriage. If you were a good woman, you would have told me, "*Chee!* Stay away *da!*" If you were a good woman, you would have slapped me on the cheek. I don't need a woman who spreads her legs the moment a man touches her.'

Lilly George Marakkaran held Jezebel's palm in hers and caressed it.

'I was ready to terminate the pregnancy. Where was the virtue in bearing such a man's child?'

But religion bade otherwise. Her family looked for someone who would shoulder the responsibility. Father Mathew Arackal, who had studied with Abraham Chammanatt, told him about Georgekutty. Father Arackal had been in their parish for a while.

Georgekutty's was an impoverished family. He agreed to marry Lilly in return for a hefty dowry. The wedding took place. They moved to another city. He oppressed her, crushed her underfoot. Lilly tried to love him and endured his slights.

After John was born, the abuse grew worse. Whenever the baby cried, or toddled up to George, he thrashed him brutally. John grew up starved and tortured. He developed a stammer, faltered when he walked. And then Jerome was born. After that, Lilly did not conceive. Before Jezebel could ask why, she smiled, a twinkle in her eye.

'For ten years, I stored pills in the spice box in the kitchen. And then when I stayed with Ammachi in her last days at the hospital, I secretly got rid of it there.'

'*Sho!*' exclaimed Jezebel like a schoolgirl who had been let into a secret behind the class teacher's back.

Winking, Lilly revealed that her friend Mini, a gynaecologist, stayed nearby. They both laughed. Afterwards, whenever she saw Lilly George Marakkaran, a smile blossomed in Jezebel's heart. Lilly had other wings tucked away in her heart. She hid mischief in her eyes. Jezebel, too, recognized her own wings. They were creatures with bodies of humans and wings of birds. They had haloes of crystal sparkling above their heads. They spread their wings together, one touching the other, under that halo. They had two wings each to cover their bodies.

John's wedding was a frugal affair. George Jerome Marakkaran stood ramrod stiff, hands clasped behind his back, chin tilted up at a hundred-and-twenty degrees. In his sandalwood-coloured silk jibba and gold-bordered mundu, he looked every bit the father in television serials. Unsmiling, dusky, slightly plump Christina was the bride. Jezebel felt a surge of fondness for her. John stood impassive, head downcast. Jezebel felt fond of him too.

As they returned after dropping the bride and the groom at Christina's house, Lilly George Marakkaran and Jezebel were particularly happy. George Jerome Marakkaran and Jerome George Marakkaran were not in the same car as them. Gazing out of the window, Lilly George Marakkaran grew as excited as a child. 'This is the way to my Ammamma's house. See this little shrine? It was built by my Appappan's Appan. See the road that turns left from the school? That's my classmate Susie's house. How my Appan thrashed me for spending time here after bunking class!' Lilly knew how to laugh, and how to make others laugh. Candles still glowed brightly in her heart despite thirty-two years of living with soot and smoke in George's kitchen.

Jezebel could not attend Anitha's funeral. Caught up in the bustle of John's wedding, she could not speak to Sandeep either. The day after John's wedding, she went to meet Sandeep in the interval between ward duty and the next class. He was alone in his room. Sandeep looked at her intently. Jezebel feared he would break down.

'I missed you badly, Jezebel . . .' Sandeep's voice was tender. 'I felt as if there's no one else in this wide world to hear me out.'

'Love, is it?' Eyes crinkling, dimples blossoming, Jezebel tried to make light of the turmoil within.

'I have only you to pour my heart out to . . .'

Jezebel felt fondness for him as well. Sandeep despaired that there was no news of Ann Mary. He couldn't muster the courage to go and meet her. Or even call her.

'Would you be able to go?'

The day after George Jerome Marakkaran and company left for their city, Jezebel set out after class. She reached Anitha's town at five and found out where the workshop was. Ann Mary emerged from under a stationary car, her face and clothes streaked with grease. When she saw Jezebel, her large pretty eyes welled up.

'And who are you?' boomed a loud baritone. George Zacharia's face peeped out of the door. The huge bags under his eyes spoke of his addiction to drinking. When he heard she was a doctor, his forehead creased. Putting on a shirt, he came out to the veranda and invited her in.

It was a small house with a concrete façade. A bedspread had been draped over a frayed rexine sofa. The other pieces of furniture in that room were an easy chair with a cloth seat that looked like it hadn't been washed in years and two wooden chairs. On the wall were plastic images of Jesus Christ and the Mother. 'Christ is the lord of this home' announced a sign above the door. Ann Mary peeped in timidly. George Zacharia glared at her; she turned and left, downcast.

He looked at Jezebel intently. Then began the questions: 'Did you know Anitha that well, doctor?' 'Do you treat cancer?'

'No . . . actually I'm Ann Mary's doctor. And it's Ann Mary I've come to meet.'

'But what illness does she have?'

'Anitha told my colleague that Ann Mary's periods haven't yet begun. We haven't come across too many cases like this in medical college. So, I've come looking for her.'

He looked at her even more sharply, then smiled feebly.

'It's ok to lie if absolutely necessary, doctor*ey*. But this is a useless fib. Isn't he the one who sent you here? That Sandeep Mohan?'

Jezebel turned pale. She swallowed hard. George Zacharia looked at her with scorn.

'I know he works there. I know that's why Anitha got herself admitted there too. But that did not bother me. My life was ruined long back because I let it bother me too much. You know, doctor, we men go after a thousand women. But if our wives so much as turn around to look at another man, we are finished! I've always wondered why that is the case.'

Jezebel wondered whether to tell him that it stemmed from a lack of self-confidence. But then he wouldn't understand, would he? So, she kept quiet.

'I know Ann Mary isn't my daughter. She knows it too. So do my children. From the day she was born, I have been suffocating. Whenever I see her, a fire rages in my heart. I know there is no point in getting angry with her either. Why should I be angry with her? What wrong did she do? Aren't we the ones to blame: Anitha, me, and that bastard Sandeep Mohan?'

'Why don't you hand her over to Sandeep then? Let him raise her.'

George Zacharia smirked. 'How would that work, doctor*ey*? I might as well announce to the world over a mike that my wife had a child from an affair. All this suffocation that I've experienced all these years . . . what's the point of it all then?'

Jezebel sat looking at him, numb.

'In that case, you'll receive money for all her expenses. Please allow her to study.'

'Come again? Receive money from my wife's lover and educate her ill-begotten child? Nice!'

'What else do you plan to do?'

'She helps me out in the workshop. Let her stay here. There are a few other young workers here in my workshop. It's good she hasn't had her periods. Even if those guys mess with her, she won't get big with a child. Just as well.'

Jezebel was shocked. 'How can you talk so cruelly?' she said, raising her voice.

'*Chee*!' He glared, placing a finger on his lips to shush her. 'She will stay here for now. With me. I don't have the means to educate her. We can make ends meet only if she too works. I have a debt of seven to eight lakh.'

'That's not a debt of her making,' said Jezebel.

'Some of it was borrowed for Rosemary's marriage, some of it to educate Rubin and a lot of money was spent on Anitha's treatment.'

'Please don't ruin that child's future.'

'I'm ensuring that even if I die, she will have a way of earning her own rice. Do you know, doctor*ey*, she repairs cars better than me!'

'It's against the law to make a minor work so much.'

'There are so many laws in this land, aren't there, doctorey? Do we abide by all of those? If we had, would a life such as Ann Mary's have happened upon the face of this earth? In my house, what I lay down is the law. '

Jezebel stood up. 'We are both Christians. The Bible says that we ought to forgive even those who wrong us.'

'It's not that I don't wish to, doctor*ey*. But shouldn't I be able to?'

He had tears in his eyes. Jezebel could not say anything. She came out. Just then, Ann Mary, who had been fixing a tyre onto a white Indica, leapt to her feet. The tyre slipped and rolled away, spinning on the sand in the courtyard. Unmindful, she rushed up to Jezebel. Jezebel struggled not to look her in the eye. With Sandeep's eyes, she looked intently at Jezebel. In the end, Jezebel met her gaze. Ann Mary's eyes were like a hungry pup's.

'I have no one now, Aunty,' Ann Mary's voice broke. She struggled to smile. It was a heartbreaking sight—a little girl, weeping, now trying to play it down and smile. Jezebel did not know how to console her. It wasn't merely the desolation of a child who had lost her mother. There was the feeling, too, of inferiority, of being an illegitimate child. Day and night, the sight of her pretty face fanned the embers of revenge in a fifty-five-year-old.

'Papa is not at all well,' said Ann Mary. 'He wheezes and coughs all night. I'm scared.'

Jezebel sensed a cold fire slowly spread and scald her from within.

'Will you take me with you, like Mummy said that day?' Ann Mary fought back tears.

Jezebel struggled to speak. 'Will your Papa let you go, *moley*?'

'He'll listen to our vicar, Father Michael.'

Jezebel did not know what to say in reply. She had the money Sandeep had given her. But she did not hand it over to Ann Mary, because George Zacharia stood watching them from the veranda.

'Did you not know that there would be a case against you if you took a child away without the guardian's permission?' asked the lawyer.

'I saw no other way of rescuing her.'

'So you'd break the law if you see that there is no other way out?'

'She is a minor. But she was forced to work. There was no guarantee of safety for either her life or her body.'

'And so? Would you round up all such kids and make them stay with you? Should you not have filed a complaint with the police instead?'

'I filed a complaint with the ChildLine. And George Zacharia assured us that he would not repeat it henceforth. A few days later, though, he went back on his word.'

'How did you find out that he had gone back on his word? Does that not mean that you went in search of the child again, without your husband's knowledge or permission?'

'I believe society is responsible for each and every child.'

'You may have many such beliefs. No need to dish them all out here. Wasn't it because of your prodding that she ran away from her father and came to you? Is that not the truth?'

The child ran away and came to her, true. There were only six months left for Jezebel's MD exam. She had prepared a timetable. She had stacked her textbooks and marked up the sections she had to finish studying every week. Jerome George Marakkaran was snoring away. Just then, Sandeep's car and a police jeep pulled up at the gate. Sandeep got down from his car. From the jeep alighted two policemen. Behind them, hugging her old school bag, was Ann Mary. As she saw them from the window, Jezebel was taken aback. She shook Jerome awake. The policemen had spotted Ann Mary at the bus stop. She had named both Sandeep and Jezebel. Since there were no women at Sandeep's place, the police had escorted her to Jezebel's.

'Hadn't Jerome made it clear that she couldn't stay with you?'

'Jerome had not objected—'

'In my house, if there is something I do not like or approve of, then my wife wouldn't even think of doing it, you know?'

'I believe a husband and wife have equal rights in the house.'

'Oh! Like that! In other words, if the husband drinks, you would drink too. If he breaks a pot, would you break two?'

'I have a responsibility towards a child undergoing medical treatment under my supervision. How many things I've done for Jerome in spite of not wanting to! Jerome, too, is obliged to consider my interests.'

'How would that work out, doctor*ey*? If your interest is to sleep with another man, should your husband abide by that too?' The lawyer guffawed. A smile of derision lit up the judge's face too. Except for Valiyammachi, everyone in the courtroom laughed out loud.

Jezebel could not laugh.

Once, there were two women. Each slept with one man for the sake of love, and another man for the sake of society. Whose wife would they be in the end, she wanted to ask.

She wanted to say that the creatures with the bodies of women too had four unseen wings. When they fly, you can hear the flapping of their wings. They resound like the roar of a torrent, like the almighty's grand crescendo, like an army's battle cry. Each creature with the form of a woman had two wings to hide her body and two, touching the wings of the creature next to her.

Jezebel's wings spread out for Ann Mary. The flapping of her own wings terrified her.

9

This was how Jezebel justified her stay with Jerome in spite of everything else:

Hadn't Jesus called out to Zacchaeus, who climbed a sycamore to see him, and said to him, 'Zacchaeus, come down quickly because I must stay at your house today?' Hadn't the onlookers muttered among themselves about how Jesus had gone in to be a guest at a sinner's house? Hadn't Zacchaeus given away half of his possessions to the poor and paid back fourfold the money he had made by cheating people? Hadn't Christ declared then that salvation had come to that house that day because he, too, was a son of Abraham? Shouldn't Jerome's house too attain salvation some day? Isn't it to look for and save what is lost that the daughters of man have to bear the cross?

Which is not to say that Jezebel did not show signs of defiance. They made Jerome George Marakkaran uneasy. He kept his father, George Jerome Marakkaran, informed about them too. The father advised the son that be it woman or snake, the only way to overpower both was to break their backs. But Jerome felt inferior in front of Jezebel. He saw that she was useful as a shield. She was good to live with. She was a person of truth, justice, dharma. And so, it was easy to control her. He ensured that she was never out of his sight. He accompanied her everywhere so that she did not stray too far. He pleaded for her mercy. Weeping, falling at her feet, whining and complaining—he kept her under his thumb. He did not disturb her physically. He even tempted her with the prospect that love would hatch in their marital nest as days and months flew by.

Jerome had long since stopped going to Jezebel's house and meeting her family. Jezebel, too, had stopped visiting Jerome's relatives. Chachan came to meet her at her workplace from time to time. Ammachi dropped by once in a while at their rented house. Twice or thrice, Valiyammachi, too, called on her along with her entourage from the *tharavadu*, the homestead. A couple of times, she went over to see Ammachi. Abel called occasionally. She emailed him on and off. Otherwise, she was immersed in her books and studies.

Jerome fought with Jezebel on the night of Ann Mary's arrival. He threatened to inform his Daddy. Jezebel threatened to walk out if he did. At the end of the quarrel, they turned away from each other and tried to sleep.

Jezebel woke up at the sound of the alarm at five the next morning. Her day was about to begin. Class at eight-thirty. She had to make breakfast and lunch before that. Either fish fry or beef roast was a must for lunch. Must cook chicken curry or fish curry as well. Then soak and wash his clothes from the previous day. And iron the clothes he was planning to wear that day.

Early that morning, as she walked into the kitchen, feeling resentful at the routine sight of Jerome curled up in bed, Jezebel was taken by surprise. Ann Mary was chopping up vegetables. She had taken the idli batter out of the fridge, and finished dicing vegetables for the sambar.

When she said, 'Aunty, please sleep a little more if you want. I'll take care of this. I know how to make all these,' with the air of a pup wagging its tail to please its master, Jezebel's heart melted. A little girl yearning for love. A girl who had partaken of the punishment the world meted out to her mother. A girl who had no one else. A girl who seemed to say, though not in words: 'This is my last refuge.'

Jezebel stood there with an aching heart. Ann Mary had established her suzerainty over the kitchen. Even as Jezebel looked on, she grated coconut, ground coconut-and-red-chilli chutney, added spices to the sambar bubbling on the stove. The fragrance of asafoetida filled the kitchen. Rice boiled in a pressure cooker on one burner of the stove. She picked it up effortlessly and drained the rice of starch water. She inquired about the lunch menu. She whipped up a chammanthi, scrambled eggs and fried fish for Jezebel's lunch.

Jezebel stood leaning against the door, not knowing what to do. Jerome, who had come for his morning tea, stood watching this awhile. 'Are you making her work for a wage?' he snapped. When Jezebel tried to pitch in, Ann Mary stopped her. 'Please relax, Aunty. I'll take care of everything,' she insisted. 'For how many days will you do this?' Jezebel asked worriedly. 'As long as you let me, Aunty,' smiled Ann Mary. 'And how will you become a doctor if you keep working in the kitchen like this?' admonished Jezebel. 'Oh, all those are just dreams,' laughed Ann Mary. 'There's no compromise when it comes to studies,' said Jezebel sternly. Ann Mary's face fell.

'I will get a Transfer Certificate only if Papa wants me to. But I can't bring myself to go there again . . .'

'All the same, it's sad that you had to leave without letting anyone know . . .'

'If I had stayed on, I'd have had to go to jail, Aunty. There is someone in the workshop who has a daughter my age—Johnykutty. Yesterday, he tried to grab me. That's not what upset me. When I went and told Papa this, do you know what he said, "So what if he touches you? Will you melt?"'

Jezebel's heart quailed. As she stood watching the girl, pottering about the kitchen in a black skirt and white blouse, a *thorthu* slung over her shoulder in the manner of a housewife who had spent all her life there, Jezebel felt rage and indignation welling up within. How fortunate she herself had been at this age! What had she given the world in return for that good fortune? As Ann Mary put Jezebel's and Jerome's laundry to wash, as she snatched the clothes to be pressed from her hand and ironed them neatly, Jezebel gave in, weakly. She watched Ann Mary's enthusiasm with a pounding heart. She saw that the girl was a flame struggling to stay alive, like the candle at the tomb of the Saintess. She saw the wind blowing hard. She was afraid.

Jerome liked the breakfast and lunch Ann Mary had prepared. 'Let her stay if she doesn't want a salary, right?' he said, with an air of magnanimity. And offered: 'I can tell Daddy we've sent her away.' As Jezebel changed and prepared to leave, Ann Mary walked up to her with the lunch box. She reminded Ann Mary to keep the door shut, and then they set off, Jezebel on her scooter, Jerome in the car.

The outpatient department bustled that morning. Most patients had come there with fever and coughing. In between arrived ten-year-old Sneha who had been complaining of severe stomach ache for days on end. Jezebel would always remember how she had come with her mother Jayanthi, who worked as a household help to raise her two children, and stood, eyes downcast, nervously gathering the folds of her long black skirt. She was a pale, puny little thing, in an oversized red blouse which seemed to be a hand-me-down. A vacant emptiness pooled in her eyes. Sneha's illness was six months old. They had brought test reports. Jameela ma'am and the other doctors leafed through those reports. Jezebel was asked to speak to the child.

Jezebel beckoned Sneha over, made small talk with her, asked her about her dress, about her little brother. When asked about her stomach ache, Sneha pursed her lips. When Jezebel tried to hold her close, she flinched, as if scalded. Jezebel smoothed strands of her hair, brushed a speck off her cheek. With each touch, Sneha grew more and more tense. Try as Jezebel might, she would not smile. In the end, Jezebel said, 'You know, I too had a tummy ache like this long back. When I changed schools, it went away. Shall we change your school?'

A sudden flicker of hope lit up Sneha's eyes. Jezebel sent the child to a psychologist for counselling. Two hours later, Dr Vinod from Child Guidance called her over. The hunch was right. The child had been abused by her Math teacher.

Jameela ma'am called Jayanthi in and explained this to her. Jezebel expected that she would foul-mouth the teacher, but she cursed her own daughter instead. 'Shameless one! I'll kill her today! Hasn't hatched out of the egg yet, and this is what she's up to? I don't need a daughter like her!'

Jezebel was taken aback. She saw her own Ammachi in Jayanthi. She asked her pointedly, 'She's a child! How can it be her fault if she was abused by someone?'

'Then what? There are so many other children studying there. How come none of them has a problem and only she does?'

'We don't know how he behaved with the other kids, *alle*?'

'Why did she go to him in the first place? Why did she play along when he touched her?' she screamed.

'Why did he touch her in the first place? Is that not what we should be asking? Should this little kid be punished for that?'

'Doctor*ey*, please stop preaching. We are poor people; our honour is all we have. Who will marry her now?' And she broke down.

Jezebel was flabbergasted. 'Which century are you living in, *chechi*?' she asked.

'Never mind which century, if a girl goes astray, all goes astray.' Jayanthi burst into heart-wrenching sobs.

'It's the child's mother who needs counselling,' Jezebel told Dr Vinod.

'I can make the child understand, but the mother . . .' Dr Vinod shrugged, while preparing to inform the police.

'For heaven's sake, please do not destroy this child,' Jezebel pleaded with Jayanthi. 'That teacher only bruised her body. Now please don't scar her mind as well. Instead of offering love and support, don't push her to her death!'

Jayanthi's eyes blazed. 'Why should she live any more? Might as well die!'

Jezebel grew limp. 'You're saying this about a ten-year-old? Would you have said the same thing if a dog had bitten her?'

'There is some dignity even in that, doctor*ey*. A man has touched her. Will that stain disappear even if you scrub and wash it away?'

Jezebel followed her to the door as she stormed out, weeping inconsolably, dragging the child by her hand. The child turned to look at Jezebel. 'What wrong did I do?' her eyes seemed to be asking Jezebel. With a sinking heart, Jezebel realized that this was the gaze that met her own eyes when she looked at the mirror every morning.

Livid, Jezebel shared this news with Ahana, Divya and Rani. They were astounded. On the one hand was the progress of modern medicine; on the other, the hardening of superstitions and social stigmas like never before. What a wretched state of affairs, they bemoaned. When the body is abused, it reacts in the same way, thought Jezebel. She remembered her own nights, and felt her stomach ache too. It ached again when, just before the afternoon class, she opened the lunchbox Ann Mary had packed. Her eyes welled up as she had her first mouthful. She shuddered as she thought about the little ones. What was the need for so many children in such a cruel world, her heart quailed.

The doctors called for a strike as the afternoon class was in progress. Someone had barged into the ward and roughed up a doctor. Which department? Cardiology. Who was the doctor? Dr Sandeep Mohan.

Ahana, Divya, Rani and Jezebel rushed to the cardiology department. Dr Sandeep Mohan had been kept under observation. Jezebel made her way past the postgraduate students crowding around his bed. When he saw her, he sat up in bed, smiling, taking care to push the saline drip to one side. His blood-red shirt had been torn apart, buttonholes and all.

'It was out of the blue,' he said, wearing his spectacles, the stems of which had been bent out of shape.

'Was George Zacharia all by himself?' Jezebel dropped her voice to a whisper.

Sandeep Mohan looked at her in disbelief. 'Jezebel, you are smart!'

'They would have gone to my place as well,' she predicted.

It turned out to be true. They had reached her house as well. But since the gate was locked from outside, they stood around, uncertain. Jerome George Marakkaran was on his way back after the morning shift. The moment he saw people standing outside his gate, Jerome's brain swung into action. He drove the car past the open gates of his neighbour's compound. From the kitchen yard behind the house, he jumped over the wicket gate to his own compound. He went over to the kitchen door, called and escorted Ann Mary out, left her at the neighbour's house and then drove over to his house as if nothing had happened. George Zacharia and his men were also contemplating jumping over the wall. Jerome went up to them and made inquiries. When they told him they had come in search of Ann Mary, he replied: 'Oh, but the police took that kid away this morning!' Without missing a beat, he opened the gate and the front door, invited George Zacharia in, and told him he was free to take the child if she was around. When George Zacharia coughed a little, Jerome even opened a drawer and presented him with a cough syrup sample that Jezebel had brought home. George Zacharia took a liking to Jerome. He left after making an apology. By the time Jezebel rushed home on her scooter, Jerome was getting ready to leave for work at another lab after drinking the tea Ann Mary had prepared for him.

'Jerome did not want to raise a child born of someone's affair with some woman. Was that not the reason for your difference of opinion with him?' asked the lawyer.

'I had only let her stay with me for the time being. There was no thought of the future.'

'Then why did you and Dr Jerome George Marakkaran quarrel on that day?'

Jezebel wondered what to say in reply. After George Zacharia had come looking for her, Jezebel began to take Ann Mary along with her every morning. The first day, they took an auto from home, and returned by Sandeep's car. The second day, in order to avoid travelling in Sandeep's car, Jerome let her use their car. Jezebel left Ann Mary in the care of a charitable home named Punarjani while she worked at the hospital, and picked her up on the way back home. At home, ignoring Jezebel's protestations, Ann Mary finished up the kitchen chores quickly and efficiently— prepared tasty food, swept and mopped the house. Jezebel got more time to study. Jerome got tasty food. Life went by without a hitch. All until the last quarrel, two days before the accident.

Two incidents occurred on that day. After class at three-thirty, as Jezebel stepped out, having signed the discharge summary of a child with jaundice in the ward, George Zacharia stood blocking her way.

'Where is she?' he demanded.

'Who?' countered Jezebel.

'My daughter,' he raged.

'How would I know?' she shot back.

'I'll show you, *dee*!' he threatened, and then broke into a fit of coughing.

Jezebel wished she could pin him down to a hospital bed and treat him. He was clearly unwell. And slowly crumbling.

He followed her to the parking lot, repeating, 'If you don't return my daughter to me, I don't care how great a doctor you are, I'll kill you!'

Paying him no heed, Jezebel revved up the car and drove over to Ahana's apartment. She spent some time there chatting with her. Afterwards, she picked up Ann Mary. When they reached home, Ann Mary was running a slight temperature. Jezebel gave her medicine, fed her some kanji, put her to bed, and sat down to study. That's when Kurien sir called up, asking her to report to work urgently because the mother of the doctor on night duty had passed away at eight o'clock. She informed Jerome, who was watching TV, and rushed to the hospital.

The second incident was at two in the morning. There was a call from Jerome's phone. Jezebel was in the duty room, reading. She reached out and picked up the phone. 'Aunty, please come soon, Aunty!' It was Ann Mary, screaming like a wounded rabbit.

Jezebel froze with dread. She dialled Sandeep's number. The phone rang but he didn't pick it up. Telling the nurse on duty that she would be back soon, Jezebel sped home. More than once, her hands slipped off the steering wheel. The car lost control several times. Somehow, she reached home. When she unlocked the gate, the keys rattled. Opening the door, Ann Mary ran up to her. She saw Ann Mary's body as something else. All bodies are not the same. Someone may ask: how are the dead resurrected? How do their bodies appear?

When the lawyer persisted about the reason for her quarrel with Jerome George Marakkaran, it was Sneha that Jezebel remembered—a child ruined by the touch of a man. What had become of her life?

'Jerome did something unpardonable,' was all Jezebel would say. She did not wish to drag Ann Mary into the case.

'And what is that thing that a wife cannot pardon her husband for?' The lawyer's face was full of disbelief. 'Fine, so your husband did something unpardonable. Was that your motive to kill him?'

'This is a family court, not a magistrate court,' interjected the judge.

Her lawyer gently reminded the court that the defence lawyer was being needlessly dramatic. Unmoved, the defence lawyer kept staring at her.

Those moments when she held Ann Mary close came to mind. At that time, her vision blurred. Her ears slammed shut. Her body was aflame. Fire spewed out of each cell. 'Why are you afraid?' Jezebel asked herself. Ann Mary, too, was burning hot. On her cheek, a bruise from hitting the leg of the bed had turned blue.

'Don't be afraid, don't be afraid,' Jezebel told Ann Mary what she had to tell herself. Fear is a figment of our imagination. You will learn that when you become a doctor. There is a part of the brain called amygdala. That is where fear is born. The amygdala wakes up the hypothalamus. The hypothalamus simultaneously awakens the sympathetic nervous system and the pituitary gland. Don't you know about the nervous system? It's the job of our nerves to make the body feel tense. Don't be afraid. When you feel fear, remember that the pituitary gland stimulates the adrenal cortical system and pumps adrenaline into your bloodstream. That stimulates the muscles. Then the poor heart has to pump more blood. It beats louder. Don't be afraid, don't be afraid. You know nothing about our body. It's just a bunch of chemicals. Love, kindness, fear, none of this is our doing. It's just the level of chemicals in us.

'I'm not afraid,' screamed Ann Mary, wriggling free of Jezebel's grasp. 'I want to kill him, I want to kill him!'

Jezebel wished the hormone that calmed the body would flow into Ann Mary's bloodstream post-haste. Must calm down. The mind must calm down. She hugged Ann Mary tighter. 'I'm there for you. Whatever happens, I'm there for you.'

'But Aunty, your husband!' she wailed.

He's not my husband, rued Jezebel. A man who harms a child is no husband of mine. He has sinned. The man who assaulted my daughter's body is my enemy. I have only hatred for him.

She realized that the production of adrenalin had reduced in her body. Her mind was calming down. It was hardening. She walked into the house. Ann Mary opened the door of her room which had been bolted from outside. Jerome George Marakkaran emerged from the room. He had heard the car and figured that Jezebel had reached.

'Jez! She tried to steal jewellery from our almirah!' he shouted, a quaver in his voice. As Ann Mary sprang forward, furious, Jezebel held her back.

'But the almirah is in our room, Jerome. How did you get to her room?'

Let the mind calm down more and more, Jezebel prayed. Let the voice become even gentler. Let the body grow stiller.

'She saw me, got frightened and ran over to this room,' Jerome was still shouting. His face grew sallow, then reddened, then darkened. Jezebel laughed out loud. Again and again. 'Great, Jerome. Thank you very much. For all the new wisdom you've given me these short two-and-a-half years.'

Jerome grew more nonplussed. 'Jez, listen to what I have to say. Don't jump to conclusions. Trust your husband, not someone you met just the other day. She is a thief! She's here to ruin us. I haven't told Daddy about her. If I had, he'd have taken the next train here!' he blathered on.

Jezebel laughed out loud. She asked Ann Mary to go and change, then packed Ann Mary's clothes in a bag. She picked up her certificates and a few clothes.

'Jez, where are you off to?' Jerome trailed her anxiously.

'I will not live with a criminal.' For the first time, Jezebel's voice filled with sadness.

'Criminal? Mind your words!'

'What else should I call someone who tries to rape a minor? An angel?'

Jerome looked like he had been slapped. He gnashed his teeth. 'So? What are you going to do?'

'You'll see, soon.'

Jerome burst into sudden tears. Much later too, Jezebel saw that tears were the last ace up men's sleeves. She felt nauseated seeing Jerome weep. Later too, she would feel nauseated at the sight of men's tears.

'How proud I was that I had found myself a smart and intelligent wife! I deserve this. How much I've sacrificed for your sake! I left Mumbai and came here for you. Leaving behind my Daddy and Mummy, leaving behind the place I was born and brought up, to a place where I don't even know the language properly. I don't have a single friend here. How much my family is struggling over there without me! Daddy and Avinash insisted I stay on there. I even fought with my Daddy so I could come stay here with you. And am I leading a cushy life? From eight in the morning to ten in the night, it's work upon work. For whom, for what am I slogging like this? For you, for our family. How you forget all that, Jezebel!' and he added, 'I'm really sad.'

'So? Is it all right to rape a minor girl who comes seeking refuge?' Jezebel asked him calmly, as she zipped up the bag.

'Don't talk nonsense!'

'No, I'll just file a police complaint.'

Jerome George Marakkaran was shocked. It looked like he was making some other mental calculation. When Jezebel picked up the car keys, he blocked her. 'The car is mine,' he said, lunging for the keys. Throwing the car keys at him, she rushed out with the scooter key instead. It was cold. Ann Mary rode pillion, hugging her from behind. Jezebel could feel her thin body burn and shiver with fever, could feel her sob now and then. She drove on, numb.

She stopped at a lamp post near the road leading to Sandeep's house. The road was empty.

'Shall I drop you at your father's place?' Jezebel spoke with some difficulty. She saw Ann Mary looking up from behind her shoulder in the rear-view mirror. Ann Mary buried her face back into Jezebel's shoulder. Jezebel waited for her reply. As she sat there, she felt the throbbing of a fledgling, burning hot on her shoulder—a fledgling with its wings broken and hanging limp. Her heart grew tender. A small child, bruised both in mind and body. A turtle dove sacrificed at the altar of her mother's love.

'There . . . won't someone else be there?' Ann Mary asked, choking.

Jezebel looked intently at her in the mirror. Ann Mary whispered without looking up, 'Achan has never called me "*moley*". Has never accepted me as his daughter. How will I go to him? Not only that, but Achan also has a wife, no? She quarrelled with him over Mummy, no? If I go there, won't it ruin Achan's life? Achan is still young, isn't he, Aunty? And he is a big doctor, no? Won't his name be spoilt? Won't everyone get to know everything?'

It was almost four in the morning. The blowing of a conch could be heard from a temple somewhere. Jezebel shuddered. A fifteen-year-old was leaning on to her, agonizing about her father's future. It was cold. Jezebel turned around and kissed Ann Mary on the forehead. 'It's your father who should be worrying about your future,' she consoled her. She drove on towards Sandeep's house.

Even before George Zacharia had attacked him, Sandeep was in the habit of taking sleeping pills. And now, having had painkillers as well, he had fallen into a deep sleep. So it was quite a task to wake him up. Jezebel left Ann Mary in Sandeep's care and drove back to the Medical College. When she finally sat down in the chair in the Duty room, she thought she would collapse. Her head felt foggy. The cells in her brain drooped as if sedated.

After her shift, she went to the apartment where Ahana and Remitha stayed. She told them that she'd had a tiff with Jerome. They didn't ask her anything more. She went to Sandeep Mohan's place in the afternoon to discuss about filing a police complaint. Ann Mary had a high fever. Sandeep was by her side, attending to her. Jezebel examined her and gave her medicine.

Sandeep walked back with her till the gate. 'Ann Mary has had a huge shock. I'm scared.'

'We'll arrange for counselling. Let her fever reduce first,' said Jezebel feebly.

'She isn't saying a word to me, Jezebel,' said Sandeep, his voice faltering.

'Your daughter is worried that your future will be ruined because of her.'

Sandeep's eyes filled with tears. 'What a sinner I am, Jezebel,' he sighed.

Jezebel could not stay there for long. She rushed back to class. She managed to pay attention in class despite her fatigue. She did not allow her mind to slip out of control. When she stepped out after class, Jerome George Marakkaran called.

'When will you be home?'

'We will not stay together in the same house any more.'

'What does that mean? Divorce?'

'Yes, divorce.'

Jerome laughed aloud. 'Nice idea. But our church will not allow it.'

'But the marriage can be annulled, can it not?' Jezebel laughed too. 'If one of the partners is mentally ill, a marriage can be declared null and void. Assaulting minor girls is a kind of mental illness, is it not?'

Swearing at her in Hindi and English, Jerome disconnected the call.

Shortly after, George Jerome Marakkaran called. 'Doctor Jezebel, what are you gunning for? Out to ruin my son's life, are you?'

Jezebel did not reply. She knew it was pointless to say anything. Her silence enraged George Jerome Marakkaran even more. There was a menace in his tone, 'Better get home by evening. All this MBBS and MD is only in the hospital. At home, you are just a wife. Submit to your husband. That's the rule in our household.'

'I'm afraid I won't be able to follow that rule then.' Jezebel disconnected the call. She felt a sense of daring that she had never felt before. She drove to Ahana's apartment, bathed, changed and went back to Sandeep's place. Ann Mary was asleep, all worn out.

'I'm worried for you, Jezebel,' said Sandeep. Jezebel struggled to smile. Her vision was blurred. It was as if she was seeing everything through the veil she had worn on her wedding day. 'What will you do?' Sandeep asked anxiously. Jezebel had no answer.

Soon after she got back to the Medical College from Sandeep's place, Jerome George Marakkaran arrived. There were scratch marks on his face. He wore a mask of anger in order to confront her. Jezebel's blood boiled. But she asked him formally, as if addressing a stranger, 'Yes, what can I do for you?'

To his 'Jezebel, you must come home,' she responded with a 'Sorry, I don't have a home.'

Jerome grew agitated at first, then pleaded with her, then got worked up again. Jezebel heard him out impassively.

'You had better get home by eight tomorrow morning,' he delivered an ultimatum.

'And if I don't?'

Jerome's face reddened. 'I know how to get you home,' he dared her. 'Don't force me to come here again.' With that, he stormed out. Jezebel stood watching him, hands folded across her chest. She watched him unblinkingly as he reversed the car with great effort and drove away. As the car neared the gate, it skidded. A cloud of dust rose. Just then, a voice prophesied from within Jezebel: 'We will never see each other again. He is not the one for me.'

10

After Jerome George Marakkaran left, Jezebel quoth unto herself: 'If you wish to be my follower, you must give up your own way, take your cross, and follow me. Those who try to save their own happiness will lose it. She who gives up small joys will find great happiness. What is the use of gaining the whole world if she has lost her own soul?'

Jezebel later recalled with a pang that even as she left from Ahana's apartment and visited Ann Mary at Sandeep's house, she was always thinking about how to confront Jerome. What she told the lawyer was true. She was at Sandeep's place when Avinash had called her, but she had not believed the news of Jerome's accident. She thought it was a ploy he had devised to carry out his threat of 'I know how to get you home.' So, without missing a beat, she called Chachan and asked him to enquire whether Jerome's car had met with an accident. Only when the police called did she realize that something serious had happened. The sky was overcast, so, she borrowed Sandeep's car and rushed to the site of the accident.

At that time, her mind was totally blank. Fear, anxiety, tension—she felt none of these. Her eyes, ears and brain felt dull, as if half asleep. As she drove, she could see in her mind's eye only scenes of those brought into the casualty department after an accident. Red lights. Beeps. Ambulances. The blazing headlights and flickering indicators of the ambulances that came roaring in.

Doors thrown wide open. Rolling gurneys. Bodies bathed in blood.
The images kept flashing across her mind, as if from a movie. As
she neared the accident site, the vehicles in the opposite direction
seemed to slow down. She could see people craning their necks out
of bus windows, unmindful of the drizzle. Drivers of two-wheelers
were moving very slowly. Pedestrians had surrounded the area,
eager to watch the goings-on.

Jezebel parked the car near a pile of timber meant for the mill,
took a look at the crowd and moved towards the bridge in a daze.
The river was turbulent. A police jeep was parked on the bridge.
The sub-inspector stood resting his elbows against the jeep. In
front of him, twisted steel bars protruded from railings that had
been rammed open. Just then, like a fish caught on a hook, the
car emerged from the river, hanging on to a crane. The front of
the car had been smashed out of shape. The door that was forced
open to pull Jerome out flapped in the air like a broken wing. At
first, water poured out, then dripped, as if squeezed out of a wet
cloth. Jezebel thought she saw Jerome behind the steering wheel.
That was when, after many years, Ranjith, on whom she had had
a crush in her MBBS years, rose from oblivion.

They had rescued Jerome earlier. The sub-inspector said that
when they saw the car crash into the railings and fall, fuming,
into the river below, a few youths who had been bathing on the
other shore swam across, opened the car door and pulled Jerome
out. A few others who were passing by in an autorickshaw helped
get him to a private hospital nearby. Meanwhile, one of them had
taken Jerome's phone from his pocket and handed it over to the
police. Luckily it had not been damaged. The sub-inspector said
that when they called the number listed in his phone as 'Wife', a
Hindi-speaking male responded; that there was no response when
they called the number 'Dad' listed below that one; and that only
after that, they saw the name 'Jez' right below. Jezebel heard him
out with no particular emotion.

They had admitted Jerome to a small hospital near the next bridge. She was seeing that hospital for the first time. It was built by a well-known doctor couple after their retirement from the Medical College. Since there was an ongoing case over the property among their children after their deaths, the maintenance work was pending. The roof above the ICU in front of the veranda was leaking. Water plopped at regular intervals into a bucket. Jezebel introduced herself to a nurse who was passing by and asked her to inform one of the doctors. Shortly, she was called inside. There, on a cot with a green bed-sheet spread on it, bandaged in white all over and with an oxygen mask on his face, Jerome lay like a space traveller. Two young doctors stood by his side. One of them told her animatedly, 'We have resuscitated him, don't worry!' The other one added, 'Heartbeat is normal now.'

Jezebel looked at Jerome again. She felt she was in a deep sleep and dreaming. As if she was floating up and plummeting down. She saw the hospital room and its paraphernalia in a blur. She was not conscious of where she was, and with whom. But she remembered that she was a doctor. And the lessons she had learned.

'Conscious?' Jezebel asked, half-conscious herself.

'No, not conscious,' said the first doctor.

In that half-conscious state, Jezebel went up to Jerome and lifted open his eyelid. One of the doctors shone a pen-torch at his eye. His grey irises came into view. They were still. They stared vacantly. She couldn't take her eyes off them. Was all this for real or was she imagining it all, she asked herself. She was in the midst of huge mountains, small hills. The mountains were battering rams, the hills were frolicking lambs. The room slipped away from her. After a moment, for the first time after hearing the news, Jezebel's body and brain woke up with a start. She must have been frightened. Her body must have pumped more hormones into her blood. With no warning, her heart drummed loudly. Fear. Such fear. Fear is not a condition; it is a preparation. The preparation of the body and mind to face what is to come.

Later, Jerome's grey staring eyes would recur in her nightmares. She would be frightened at the sight of two eyelids opening and two dilated grey protruding eyes staring at her from the endless dark. When she realized that this was her husband lying there, bandaged from top to toe, his body going into spasms from time to time, she felt her head would split.

When she came out of the ICU, Chachan and Ammachi rushed up to her. Chachan looked weary and distressed. Ammachi stared at her. The moment she saw Ammachi standing there, the end of her white cotton sari pulled over her head, her umbrella and purse clasped to her chest, her eyes silently accusing her with a 'What did you do to him?' Jezebel's urge to cry evaporated.

Two days later, when Abel arrived, she still wanted to cry. As he rushed in, backpack on shoulder, she went up to him. But she could only smile miserably, dimples spreading on her cheeks. Abel broke down. Later too, he wept for her, many times.

The emotion that lingered in her mind afterwards, like the haze of smoke that lingers after an explosion, was disbelief. Disbelief about her life. This cannot be happening, she kept telling herself. This was a nightmare from a long sleep. Or else, this was a story she was reading. In the story, the smart heroine, who studied well and lived happily, marries a stranger. They live together for two-and-a-half years, not making love even once. A girl like Ann Mary stays with them. He assaults the girl. The next day, he meets with an accident. She stays by his side as he lies unconscious, unable to love him or hate him . . . did all this actually happen? This man, was he her husband? Had there ever been a young man called Ranjith in her college? Was he still there under the rubble? Was Dr Sandeep Mohan for real? Was Anitha, the woman he loved, for real? Jezebel felt she was going insane.

Just then, she could hear Ammachi chanting proverbs from the Bible. 'Who can find a virtuous wife? For her worth is far above rubies. The heart of her husband trusts in her, and he will have no lack of gain. She will do him good and not evil all the days of her life.'

It was a twenty-four-hour-long wait. And then there was George Jerome Marakkaran's phone call. 'What happened to my *kochan*?' was the first question. 'Was it an accident or did you and your secret lover finish him off?' was the second. Jezebel felt like she had been hit on the head. Like a steel lunch-box banged against the corner of the school desk and forced open, she felt her brains toss and turn and scatter inside her skull. Perhaps, that was what had happened to Jerome George Marakkaran too.

She could see that accident in front of her eyes. While driving, he would have either swerved right instead of left trying to make way for the lorry coming head on. Or else, he must have turned the steering wheel hard to the right in order to regain balance when the car swerved left. The car would have lost control, hit the bridge on the right, crashed into the railings and nosedived into the river. His head would have hit the steering wheel or the windshield, and been thrown back, and forward to hit the wheel again. His brain would have rammed against the walls of the skull, damaging the rubbery dura mater, the moist candyfloss-like arachnoid mater and the pia mater that wrap the brain, shattering the frontal and temporal lobes. That would have caused diffuse axonal injury. She remembered the diagram of the nerve fibre, the neuron like a child's drawing of a sunflower, the axon like its stalk. She saw it in a flash: the axon snapping, the nerve fibre breaking, all communication to and from the brain ceasing, the axon swelling, pressure increasing inside the skull, the brain pressing against the sockets of the eyes, the eyeball protruding, losing vision—TBI, traumatic brain injury.

Darkness clouded her eyes. Her thoughts scattered. She felt as if her body were emitting waves of heat and cold. She worried about how Jerome's accident would affect her, then felt ashamed. When Sandeep Mohan called, she spoke disconnectedly.

'Yesterday I hated Jerome so much, Sandeep. But I don't understand what's on my mind now. The first man in my life. The one I lived with for two-and-a-half years. I cooked for him and served him, washed his clothes. I wanted to move away from him. But I never wanted him gone, not even in my dreams. Is it because of me that this has happened to Jerome?'

'Jezebel, this is not the time to analyse your relationship with him. Think about the treatment. Isn't it better to shift him to the Medical College as soon as possible?'

'Until yesterday, I was a doctor. Now, I'm the wife of a patient. I don't know what needs to be done. My mind is going blank.'

She found that it was better to be a doctor than a wife in a situation such as this. When you are a wife, the worry is about how his accident would affect your future. When you are a doctor, you worry only about what would happen to the patient. Choking, she disconnected the call. She was too exhausted to cry. In the meantime, two policemen arrived. She saw them talk to her parents and walk up to her, as if in a fog. They introduced themselves and asked her if she had any complaint to record about the accident.

'*Illa*, no.' Jezebel said to no one in particular.

'Are you sure it's an accident?' asked one of the policemen.

'Yes,' she said, as if half-asleep.

'Why do you think so?'

'Jerome often lost control while driving.'

It happened even when we met last—she wanted to say, but the words wouldn't come. When we quarrelled, when he drove away after threatening me, the car skidded. Dust rose. Everything was a haze. I knew even back then . . .

'Did you meet the patient? Did you talk to him?' asked the policeman. Jezebel did not understand. What did she have to talk to Jerome about? What would he have to tell her? Perhaps, he would smirk at her. And call out, 'Whore! Whore!' What if he did that in front of the doctors and nurses, what if he blathered, 'Do your name justice, *edee*'? She shuddered and perspired in shame.

'He's not conscious yet,' Chachan said. And then, in a fog, Jezebel saw him walking away, talking to the policeman. Meanwhile, Ahana, Rani and Remitha came rushing in a panic. When Ahana asked her what happened, Jezebel sank weakly against her shoulder. Remitha held her close. Rani went up to the ICU, spoke to one of the doctors there. Ahana and Remitha kept asking Jezebel this and that. She could barely comprehend. 'Why are you asking me all this?' she smiled. 'Don't you know you lose memory after a TBI? Sometimes short-term memory loss, sometimes long-term . . .'

And then Jezebel recalled an incident. 'Do you remember that excursion in our final year? That ten-day trip. The second night, when I was sleeping all by myself in the seat, some guy came up and kissed me on the cheek. He vanished before I could open my eyes. I told you about it. But you all made fun of me, told me I'd been dreaming. You did not believe me. If only you had, we could have found out who that guy was. Do you remember, it was someone with a moustache, without a beard? There were six guys with moustaches in our class. What's the point of having friends like you? Did any of you help me find out who it was? Did any of you help me find a boy? If you had, would I be like this today? If only there was a man like that, I would have married him. He would have loved me. He would have kissed me a lot. Do you know, Jerome never kissed me? Hasn't said a decent word to me? He didn't like me. He didn't like my face. He was disgusted with my body, you know? Am I that bad? Am I such a good-for-nothing that no man can love me?' She punched Remitha on the shoulder in a fit of pique. 'What are you saying, *moley*?' sighed Remitha. Ahana turned away, blinking back tears. With a long face, Jezebel went and sat on a chair some distance away. They sat by her side for a long time, trying to console her. 'Go away, you two!' she snapped. Finally, they left her alone, saying they would wait for her to feel better. The moment they left, she called Ahana with a 'How could you leave me like that as soon as I asked you to?'

The next several hours of waiting in that hospital corridor would always return to her in her dreams. She did not feel any pang of hunger or thirst. Ammachi continued to chant from the Bible. The proverbs she had made Jezebel and Abel memorize as children, from 'The purpose of the proverbs' to 'A good wife', she would recite them all.

That was when Sebin and Chachan walked in. When she recognized Sebin, Jezebel tried hard to smile. He stayed by her side. From time to time, Jezebel went over to the ICU. The doctors greeted her brightly, reassuring her that there was improvement, that he was responding to calls, that he had started breathing on his own, that the seizures were under control. They said that he could be shifted to the Medical College hospital if necessary.

Just then, a senior doctor breezed in, saying, 'What's up? Will he kick the bucket or what?' The junior doctors hurriedly introduced Jezebel to him. He greeted her, trying to hide his embarrassment. 'Nothing to fear. He had a cardiac arrest at the time of the accident. That happens . . .' he tried to reassure her.

Jezebel was irritated. 'Tell me how he is now, Doctor.'

'When he was brought here, his ECG was a flat line. How much these two doctors struggled to get his heart pumping again! Hats off, they have done a wonderful job!' he said, avoiding her eye.

'Doctor, please, how is he now? What exactly is his condition? That is what I need to know.'

'You know what happens when hypoxia occurs, don't you, Doctor? Hypoxic brain injury. The heart stopped beating all of a sudden. The flow of oxygen to the brain stopped too. And so, the brain cells . . .' The senior doctor paused and looked at her.

'The CT scan, ECG and bedside echocardiogram are all normal,' the junior doctor hastened to add.

'Yes, nothing to fear.'

'Nothing?' Jezebel's voice faltered.

'No. We have had patients who were worse off. And all of them walked out of the hospital fully recovered. You can trust us. If you permit us, we could try hypothermia. It has been seen to be successful in treating cases of hypoxia the world over.'

Jezebel stood there, caught in a dilemma. The senior doctor explained that there were two methods of inducing hypothermia. One was by injecting cold fluids to bring down body temperature. But this was risky, because the heart could suddenly stop beating. The other option was to place ice on the head. The damage to the brain could be mitigated by bringing down the temperature of the brain. The first method was more effective, but the risk was greater too.

'No, the second will do.'

'That's not it, Dr Jezebel. Whichever of the two we try, one cannot expect him to be his old active self even if he recovers. I would therefore recommend the first option.'

Either he would recover. Or he would die. That was the 'ease' of the first option. Jezebel's blood boiled. Something buzzed and stirred in her brain. It was not possible for her to make a guinea pig of Jerome. There was still a dreamer left within her. 'That's my husband,' cried out that dreamer. 'He took me as his life partner. We lived happily. Like the oak and the cypress, one offered shade to the other. The boughs of one brushed against the other's. Both loved each other. Did not hide anything. Never hurt the other. We were happy. We were in love.' Jezebel-the-dreamer wished she could believe it all. She wanted to cry, but the tear glands refused to come out of their coma.

Jerome was shifted to the Medical College that day itself. Thanks to the principal's intervention, they got a room in the pay ward. As soon as they reached the room, Ammachi's Bible chanting began. Jezebel hadn't eaten since morning. Ahana, Divya, Remitha and Rani dropped in. They gave her a sleeping pill. She slept. When she woke up with a start sometime in the night, she could still hear Ammachi, 'Who has gone up to heaven and come down? Who has wrapped up the waters in a cloak? Who has established all the ends of the earth?'

Struggling to keep her bleary eyes open, Jezebel went over to the ICU. She flipped through the case sheets kept at the head of Jerome's bed. She became a doctor once again. She carefully examined the body lying on that bed.

'When Dr Jerome George Marakkaran was admitted to the hospital, he was conscious, was he not?' asked the defence lawyer.

'The doctors said he wasn't.'

'You're a doctor, aren't you? When you saw him, what did you feel?'

'He wasn't conscious.'

'No, I mean what was his condition like?'

'His pupils had dilated. There were seizures.'

'And whatever does that mean, doctor*ey*?'

'The enlargement of the pupil of the eye indicates brain damage. It is also common for convulsions, like epileptic fits, to occur at such a time.'

'So, you knew on that day itself that your husband was a goner?'

'No, the doctors in the first hospital said that he responded to calls. I believed them.'

'That's why I asked. Doctors said he responded to calls. There's no reason to doubt them, is there? So he did respond to calls. Then why did you pack him off to the Medical College Hospital?'

'Everyone said it was better to take him there since there were better doctors in the Medical College.'

'Or did you think "Why waste money, let him kick the bucket if he must"?'

'No.'

'Why else would you dump him there and then go on a trip some fifty-odd kilometres away the very next day? Right from the start, you didn't believe he would make it, did you?'

Jezebel did not reply. The lawyer raised his voice.

'Even otherwise, did you shed a single tear after your husband met with such a major accident? Did anyone see you crying?'

Jezebel fell silent. She recalled how the police had arrived with a court order based on George Zacharia's complaint that the child had been forcefully detained. Jezebel had to appear in court. She deposed to the magistrate, who issued an interim order that the child be sent to a short-stay home. When she got back, George Jerome Marakkaran and Lilly George Marakkaran were getting down from the car. It was dark by then. In full public view, George Jerome Marakkaran caught her by the throat and roared, 'What did you do to my son, *edee*?' Humiliated, Jezebel ran to the room. He followed her, cursing loudly. In the room, Jezebel's teachers Dr Sukumaran and Dr John Joseph were talking to Chachan and Ammachi. George Jerome Marakkaran raised his hand to slap her again in front of them. Jezebel rushed to the ICU. She pulled up a chair next to Jerome's bed and sat down, panting. She did not cry even then. But her mind said, 'This man will never wake up again.'

And that turned out to be true too. A week later, when they took an MRI scan, white patches showed up on his brain. The brain had begun to shrink. Abraham Chammanatt and Lilly George Marakkaran met her in the corridor outside the ICU and inquired about Jerome's condition. 'He's in a coma,' she said.

'When will he wake up?' demanded George Jerome Marakkaran.

'I don't know,' Jezebel said stoically.

Lilly George Marakkaran stood stunned. George Jerome Marakkaran's eyes popped out. Abraham Chammanatt's face too changed colour.

'I have no hope after seeing the MRI scan,' she said. Jezebel's voice was calm. 'Such patients should wake up after twenty four hours. If not, it may take up to seventy-two hours for any sign of recovery. Or else, a week. If there is still no change, four weeks. That's the prognosis for coma.'

'What does that mean? That my son will lie endlessly like this?' burst out George Jerome Marakkaran.

'Not just your son, it's the same for any patient in this condition.'

'How can you talk so heartlessly about your own husband?'

'Can I rewrite medical science just because he happens to be my husband?'

'Didn't you go and inject him? Isn't that why he's like this?' He made a lunge for Jezebel's throat again.

'If I inject your son, will his brain shrink?' Jezebel retorted. She was losing control over herself. A clean-shaven, neatly dressed Jerome George Marakkaran now stood in front of her, the odour of formalin about him. He sat on the bed. He placed a hand on her shoulder. She trembled. Bitterness filled her mouth. She felt nauseated. She was furious with everyone. 'You were unjust to me,' her own body raged at her. Her heart demanded an account of all the love and honesty it had been denied. She did not feel kindly towards anyone. Because nobody had been kind to her. She had lived with a man for two-and-a-half years. Did he love her? Did he pamper her? Did he make her happy? Did he speak to her about things she liked? Did he travel with her? Did he assault a minor girl? Nobody had asked her. How many clothes did he get her? How much jewellery? How much did he earn? This is all they wanted to know. She despised them all. None of you deserves to be happy—a grievously wounded woman growled from within her—having wiped all the happiness out of my life, not one of you deserves to be happy.

George Jerome Marakkaran tried to hit her again. Just then, Sebin sprang on him out of the blue, grabbed hold of him, swung him around, pinned him to the wall and raised a fist at his nose. Abel and Chachan tried to restrain him. George Jerome Marakkaran shouted, '*Eda*, she is the one who tried to kill my son! Like Naboth was killed for his vineyard. Kill her! I'll give you how much ever money you want.' Sebin unclenched his fingers as if to strangle George. His muscles flexed; his nerves grew taut. 'If you lay a finger on her again, I'll finish off both father and son!' he growled.

As Abraham Chammanatt, Lilly and Chachan escorted George Jerome Marakkaran inside, the onlookers dispersed. Jezebel stood leaning against the wall, unsure of what to do. Only Sebin stood in front of her. They looked at each other. She felt a rush of fondness for him. He looked worn out. His liver had started corroding. It seemed that he was ready for the final journey at that young age.

'It's time for you to get a complete medical check-up done,' Jezebel whispered. 'If you drink any more, you will die, Sebin . . .'

Sebin kept looking at her in disbelief. He tried to smile. His jaundiced eyes welled up. 'Oh, what life do I have left? But your case is not like that, Jezebel . . .' And then his forehead creased as if he just remembered something. 'Tell me, who is this Naboth? Why did you try to kill him? Couldn't you have told me if you wanted to finish him off?'

In spite of herself, Jezebel's dimples blossomed. When he learned that it was a story from the Bible, he grew sheepish. Trying to cover up his embarrassment, he said, 'If I ever get to know that that geezer tried to mess with you again . . .!'

Wiping his eyes, he walked off. Jezebel stood there, miserable. By then, having heard everything, Ahana, Divya, Remitha and Rani came rushing up. They took her away to their apartment. They forced her to freshen up. Then they forced her to have some tea and buns. They made her lie down on the bed, tucked her in and sat by her side. Jezebel recalled Sebin and his words. She burst out laughing. When she laughed, her eyes filled with tears.

She laughed and wept at the same time. In the end, the laughter vanished. She wept inconsolably. Ahana, Divya, Remitha and Rani held her close and wept along with her. The sobs subsided. All the cells in her brain burnt out, she slept. She heard Ammachi's voice in her sleep. Ammachi was reciting the Proverbs: 'Four things are intolerable: a slave who becomes a king, a fool who is filled with food, a maid who displaces her mistress, and an unloved wife.'

Three of the four were intolerable to men. Only the fourth was intolerable to women. Jezebel recited it again and again, 'An unloved wife . . . unloved wife . . . unloved wife.'

11

From then on, Jezebel began to tell herself that she had to go to Jerusalem, that she would have to endure much at the hands of the noblemen, high priests and scholars of law, that she would be killed but also that she would be resurrected someday. She consoled herself, 'May the Lord bless you, Jezebel, may this never happen to you.' She admonished herself, 'Go away from me, Satan! You are a stumbling block for me. You do not have in mind the concerns of God, but merely human concerns.'

Every time they met near the ICU, Jezebel could hear George Jerome Marakkaran cursing her. She saw in his face the kind of frenzy one saw in the mentally ill. The first day, she was furious. And then she thought, you could win some battles in this way too. She was tired. Her heart was immersed in doubt—about what was right, what was wrong; about what was good, what was evil. She loved and desired her man. But she had no love lost for Jerome George Marakkaran because he had never wanted to be her man. And yet, she felt for him. She was pained that he was dying and in pain. At the same time, the very prospect of his recovery frightened her.

It was on the day she went to pick up the neurologist's report that she realized she had lost control of her mind. She had not met the neurologist Dr Kiran Varghese before. Looking at her and the reports, he asked her, 'How long have you been married?'

'Two-and-a-half years,' she replied.

'Children?' he asked.

'No,' she said in a low voice.

He smiled with something like relief. 'You're lucky. You'd have been trapped if you'd had kids. This man will not get up again. And even if he does . . .'

Later, Jezebel would recall with embarrassment how she had sprung up from her chair. She would regret screaming 'Shame on you!', and feel guilty about snatching the sheets from Kiran Varghese and trying to hit him. Kiran Varghese rang a bell, a few people came rushing in, then they brought Abel. Abel dragged her out. She was screaming, 'A doctor ought not to say this! That man is no doctor! Even butchers have more mercy!' Abel clapped a hand over her mouth and took her away. He somehow managed to get her out of the hospital and into an auto. He took her to the nearest cafe.

It was around eleven in the morning. The tables were empty. In a corner, a pair of teenage lovers sat, ill at ease. He ordered juice. She was still fuming. And then slowly, she calmed down. Clutching her forehead, she stared at the cartoons in the paper table-mat on the glass table in front of her. Abel reached out for her hand. She was reluctant to look at him. She feared that he would despise her. She was accursed like the prophet Jezebel in the Bible. Her body was destined to be devoured by dogs. Her head felt numb.

'I don't understand you, Jezebel. You have changed so much. This is not the Jezebel I know. What happened to you?' asked Abel. He looked intently at her. She recognized the distance of two-and-a-half years. He rarely emailed. When he called Chachan and Ammachi every week, he inquired after her then. They told him she was fine. He preferred to believe that. And she, too, preferred it that way.

'If it were a shock about the accident, I can understand. But this is not that. I've been observing you since the time I arrived.

Your whole personality has changed. There's some sort of darkness on your face. You even look different, Jezebel!'

Jezebel's eyes filled with misery. She looked at that young man, but turned a deaf ear to him. 'I don't want to hear anything,' she fumed. 'You don't have to love me. Why should you be the only one to love me?'

'Is there any truth to what George Jerome Marakkaran said?'

'That I seized Naboth's vineyard and stoned him to death?' She tried to smile, miserably.

'He says this was not an accident. He says it was a plot hatched by you and another doctor. That you have an affair with that doctor. And that his daughter stayed with you. Jerome caught her red-handed when she tried to steal money. You fought with him over this and walked out. And that you moved in with the doctor.'

Jezebel looked Abel in the eye.

'I don't believe all of it, of course. You wouldn't hurt a fly, I know that. But the bit about the affair, is that true?'

'What if it is?' Jezebel retorted.

Abel looked at her intently. And smiled in sympathy.

'Jezebel, only your looks have changed. But your behaviour is just the same.'

Tears threatened to burst their floodgates, but she put up a brave front. Abel asked her about her life with Jerome. Jezebel told him everything, seething. Abel was taken aback. He raged. Scolded her. Abused Jerome. 'Why did you not speak up? Why didn't you take him to a psychiatrist?' he demanded.

Jezebel felt like laughing. 'For by your standard of measuring, it will be measured to you in return.'

By then, the waiter brought them their glasses of juice. She finished hers in one gulp. But Abel sat with his glass, stirring it with a straw. His tears dropped into the glass. 'The juice will get salty,' Jezebel teased. He tried to laugh, wiping his tears. 'What should I do, Jezebel?' he asked.

'You must go back,' she said.

'How can I leave you like this?'

'However much we try, sometimes we are all alone, Abel. Some crosses are to be borne all by ourselves. That is our fate.'

'Even the Lord carried his cross only for as long as it took to climb a hill. How long will you bear yours?' he despaired. 'What if Jerome never wakes up again? And if he does, how will it be? Will he walk? Talk? And even if he does, will you be able to live with him? Why did you quarrel with that doctor? Isn't what he said true? We're lucky it turned out like this.'

'Oh yes, I'm truly lucky—a husband lying in a coma, an MD that's unlikely to be completed, a father-in-law who's such a fount of love. What luck! Such luck!' she sneered.

Abel consoled her. He insisted that she must take charge of her future. Upon his insistence, Jezebel agreed to go home. 'I'm taking Jezebel home. Jerome's parents can stay with him at the hospital tonight,' announced Abel.

'How is that possible? Without her around?' George Jerome Marakkaran demanded.

'What if she too ended up on a bed like him?' Abel asked calmly. George Jerome Marakkaran didn't say a word after that. One look at Abel, and Ammachi could not say anything either.

They took a taxi to 'Jerusalem'. No one said anything. Ammachi was counting the beads of the rosary. Abel sat next to her in the backseat, holding Jezebel close. When they reached home, Jezebel went to her room. It smelled of dust and damp, having been shut for a long time. It felt unfamiliar to her. It was difficult to believe that she had slept in that room all her life. Her cot, mattress, the cupboards in which her books were stacked up neatly, her study table, the green steel almirah in a corner in which her wedding saris and jewellery were stored—everything looked the same. She sat on the cot, not bothering to switch on the light or to open the windows.

She was a warrior who had returned from battle, wounded and defeated. The battle had been with her own self. She was the one who had attacked, she was the one who had been hacked. She remembered the first time Jerome had come into that room. She saw the sheen of his thick moist lips. Every day they spent together sped past her. It seemed like he was still sitting, spread-eagled, on that bed. Abel came in, switched on the light and sat next to her. Behind him came Chachan, who pulled up a chair and sat down. Ammachi stood leaning against the door. Jezebel's heart surged with emotion. She felt she was not alone. Everyone was around: Chachan, Ammachi, her brother. Her heart melted.

Jezebel would recall much later how important that day had been in her life. Ammachi's first question was, 'Where were you yesterday?' 'Don't you know, Ammachi?' she had countered. 'With whose permission did you leave?' asked Ammachi, spoiling for a fight. Jezebel got angry. 'You all stood there, watching, when that man hit me and cursed me. You didn't say a word then, did you, Ammachi? And Chachan didn't even try to stop him.' Her voice broke. Tears sprang up.

Ammachi walked up to her. 'Jezebel, if your plan is to get people to gossip, that won't happen here. You ought to have stayed on at the hospital yesterday. It wasn't proper, your going off to someone's place without even informing anyone. You forgot that it was your husband lying there. Are you really my daughter? What will people say?'

Abel stopped Ammachi. 'Ammachi, don't think in this old-fashioned way. What else was she supposed to do? Did she have a moment's peace there? Did you not see the standards of the 'family' you all found for her? Didn't they point fingers at her and blame her rather than console her after an accident like this?'

'That is all her doing. What do you know? She never liked that boy anyway. She hated him from day one. Why did she have to make some girl stay at her place? Which man wouldn't take advantage of a girl if he had the chance? Don't you know what the Bible says? "There are four things I don't understand: the way of a serpent on a rock; the way of a ship on the ocean; the way of an eagle in the sky; and the way of a man with a virgin!" Who is that girl to her? Who is that girl's father to her? What is his relationship with her? Can you blame people for asking? When her husband lies struggling between life and death in the hospital, she goes off to some court far away—to defend some ill-begotten girl. I should have thrashed her to death that day itself.'

Abel intervened again. 'I cannot agree with you Ammachi. Do all men grab a minor girl simply because she's there in the house? No decent man would do it. And I would never justify one who does it either. My sister need not stay with a man like that.'

Ignoring him, Ammachi scolded her again. In the end, Chachan looked up. 'Sara, enough!' he said firmly. And then Ammachi stopped. Chachan turned to Abel. 'What is your decision?'

Abel heaved a long sigh. 'I'm going back tomorrow. And then I'll make arrangements to bring Jezebel over. I don't want anyone to say anything against this later.'

'You aren't taking her anywhere until her husband gets up,' raged Ammachi.

Jezebel leapt to her feet. She picked up her bag.

'Where are you going? Sit down,' said Abel.

She did not reply. The room filled with silence.

'Please, don't go,' pleaded Abel, going after her. Jezebel did not pay him heed. It was past eight in the night. But she found an autorickshaw when she stepped out of the gate. She went to Sandeep Mohan's house. It was locked. She called him on the phone. His phone was switched off. Jezebel took the same auto to Ahana's apartment. It was locked too. She went back to the hospital. And sat down, tired, on one of the chairs outside the ICU.

From that day onwards, for twenty-one long days, she stayed on stubbornly at the hospital. She realized that she had nowhere else to go—not for want of a place but because there was no opportunity. She remembered Gibran's words, 'The wounded deer lives in a cave until it is healed or dead,' and waited.

Every morning, Chachan and Ammachi arrived at six-thirty. The moment he saw them, George Jerome Marakkaran would leave for home. That was when Jezebel would go into the room, shower and change. Either Ahana, Remitha or Rani would turn up with breakfast and take her old clothes back with them. Once George Jerome Marakkaran was back, she'd step out of the room. But he would still find some reason to complain—Jerome wasn't being given his medicines, the nurses were standing around giggling, and so on. If the doctor doing the rounds was even a little late, he'd growl at her, 'Go and bring him, right now!' She complied wordlessly. There were no questions, no answers. On the twenty-first day, Jerome was taken off the ventilator. The Head of Department, Kurien P. George, came over to meet her. Jezebel rose hurriedly from her seat.

'How many days has it been since you've been sitting around like this?' His voice rang in the corridor. Patients and their attendants, standing around, turned to look. George Jerome Marakkaran, Chachan and Ammachi came up. He raised his voice, 'And for how many more days will you sit like this?'

Jezebel's eyes were downcast. A sea of tears surged within.

'You're a doctor, aren't you? If you sit here like this, do you think the man lying inside will get up and come out? You know his condition, don't you?'

Silence again. And then Dr Kurien's voice rose again.

'You're a gold medallist in MBBS. And you sit here with no thought about either your own future or your social responsibility.

Get up. You shouldn't be seen around here henceforth! And if you don't turn up for class tomorrow, I'll teach you a lesson!'

He glared at George Jerome Marakkaran. 'Aren't you supposed to ensure she attends class? Aren't you ashamed to behave like this, with no sense of responsibility?'

'When her husband is lying there . . .' began George Jerome Marakkaran.

Dr Kurien wouldn't let him finish. 'Let him lie there. There are other doctors and nurses to take care of him. Her sitting around here like this won't bring about any change in his condition. Would you do this if she were your own daughter? Would you ruin her future?'

George Jerome Marakkaran was at a loss for words. Kurien sir stormed out. Jezebel looked at Chachan, Ammachi and George Jerome Marakkaran. George Jerome Marakkaran stomped back into the room, and came out after a while. 'Enough of your sitting around here. Go home.'

Jezebel didn't quite get him. 'I meant your rented house. Jerome's mother is there. Go and sit there. I'll call you when you're needed here. Never mind this man, even if the Lord himself comes and tells me, there's no way you're attending any class unless my son wakes up.'

His voice was pure evil. Jezebel recoiled as if a burning log had been thrust at her.

'I will go. Even if the Lord himself stops me, I will attend class.' Her voice was firm.

George Jerome Marakkaran flinched. Jezebel shut the book in her hand. She went into the room and picked up her bag. And went over to Chachan and Ammachi.

'I'm going to class from tomorrow onwards. I need to write my exam.'

'And who will be here then?' George Jerome Marakkaran rushed in. 'I'm not well. I'm over sixty-five. And I have sugar and high blood pressure.'

'We'll be here,' Chachan hastened to assure him. 'Let Jezebel write her exam.'

George Jerome Marakkaran would not budge. He kicked up a ruckus again. Jezebel did not stop to talk to him and left for Ahana's apartment.

She was back in class from the next day onwards. And pored over her lessons with a vengeance. She was at the ICU every day in the morning and evening. She checked the case sheets every day. He lay motionless on the bed. The bandages on his face had been removed. His forehead and cheeks bore the scars of wounds that had healed. Sometimes, Jezebel would look closely at him. She saw in front of her the sight of him getting ready for work, wearing cooling glasses, clad in the shirt and pants that she had ironed for him and the shoes she had polished to a shine for him, his hair slicked back with gel, perfume in his armpits and chest. She saw him counting out money, writing accounts, approaching her at night with a lecherous leer. Every day, her heart asked of him: why did you enter my life, only to blow it to pieces? Whenever she looked at him, she was seized with dread about the rest of her life. She could see that his muscles and his skin and cells were beginning to give up. It was apparent that his looks were changing. His body had begun to shrink. Clearly, he would be reduced to a fistful of skin and bones in no time.

'When your husband was moved back to his home in a critical condition, you did not accompany him. Why?' the lawyer asked.

'I had exams.'

'Are exams more important for a wife? Or the husband's life?'

'There was no danger to his life.'

'Right! When a man who's hit on the head and strung between life and death is taken home, wouldn't any other wife go along with him, weeping?'

Jezebel could not help thinking: Dear Lord, the onus of explaining why the wife didn't cry is a yoke around my neck alone.

She did not wish to recall how Jerome had been taken back to his city just the day before her exam. When she went to see Jerome that morning, she found Lilly George Marakkaran packing the bags. Chachan and Ammachi were standing around, bewildered. When he saw her, George Jerome Marakkaran announced, 'An ambulance has been arranged for 3.30 p.m. We are going back to our place. The rest of the treatment will be over there.'

Jezebel was nonplussed. 'Tomorrow's the exam,' she whispered.

Ammachi cleared her throat. 'Exams can be written next year too.'

Jezebel looked at Chachan. Chachan looked away.

'It's good to have a doctor around to explain things when you take him to a new hospital, that's why we're begging you. The vehicle will arrive at the casualty department at 3.30 p.m. Go, get your bag.' George Jerome Marakkaran ordered again. Jezebel stood benumbed for a moment. She looked around for help. Those around pretended they had not noticed. She walked out on leaden feet. She thought about death. She cast about in her mind for the names of medicines that would help her with a quick death. That was when Lilly George Marakkaran called out to her from behind. '*Moley*, a minute.'

She turned around. Lilly rushed up to her. 'He asked you to pack your certificates as well,' she said, panting. Then, turning back to make sure there was no one at the door, she took Jezebel's hand. 'You don't have to bring your bag. You don't have to come at all. I know my son is dead. *Moley*, go and write your exam. Become a great doctor. Your life is meant to rescue many others from death. It is not to be wasted on one who's already dead.' Saying this, she slipped away like the wind. Jezebel grew numb.

That afternoon, the ambulance stood ready outside the casualty department at 3.30. Ammachi stood there, counting the rosary. Chachan and a couple of others had lifted Jerome into the ambulance. Seeing Jezebel, George Jerome Marakkaran's face lit up with an air of triumph. Jezebel got into the ambulance. She looked at Jerome. He had turned into someone else. His once chubby cheeks were now sunken. The skin was pallid and dry. She took Jerome's hand, cold and numb and waxy. When she got down from the ambulance, George Jerome Marakkaran's forehead creased. She stood in front of him and looked him in the eye. 'I need to write the exam.'

She saw blood rush to George Jerome Marakkaran's face. Lilly George Marakkaran stood holding a heavy bag, pretending not to see or hear any of this. Jezebel clasped Lilly's hand tight for a moment. Lilly let go of her hand as if she had not seen her, and got into the ambulance. Jezebel walked towards the Medical College. She could hear George Jerome Marakkaran ranting. She did not pay heed.

She walked towards the casualty department. She rushed up the steps blindly. After she had climbed a few flights of stairs, she looked down from the first window. The ambulance had started moving. It made its slow way down the road canopied by rain trees on either side. As she looked on, she felt something leave her body, roaring. A great emptiness filled within her. Her body twisted as if it had been stabbed from behind. 'My man has gone,' her body screamed. 'He left without ever letting me experience the secret of intimacy between man and woman,' it cursed.

When she heard that Prophet Jehu had arrived in Jezreel, Ahab's wife Jezebel lined her eyes, arranged her hair and sat looking out of the window. 'Jehu, please take me,' she had called out. But Jehu did not accept her. 'Throw her down,' he had ordered. Jezebel stood there, feeling for the Jezebel of the Bible. Her body trembled; her legs grew weak. If only some man had thrown her down from above, with love. If only dogs had devoured her fallen, blood-spattered body. Alas, no one had taken her.

12

Life prophesied to Jezebel thus: 'On that night two people will be in one bed. One will be taken, and the other left. Two women will be grinding grain together. One will be taken and the other left.' Where, O life? asked Jezebel. Life answered, 'Wherever there is a carcass, there the vultures will gather. So, make sure you keep yourself alive each day.'

Many were the furnaces of experience that helped Jezebel gain notoriety as the young doctor who had discarded her comatose husband like a tattered old doormat and escaped to safety seeking her own comfort—furnaces where the fires had died down. She wanted to sketch a few pictures with the charcoal she had gathered from those furnaces. Some of those pictures were of men who could not forgive women. A few others were distorted sketches of her own self.

As advised by Dr Prashant Narayanan, the psychiatrist she met after Jerome had disappeared from her life, Jezebel sorted her experiences and emotions post Jerome's accident into five stages—DABDA, as Elisabeth Kubler Ross named it. The first stage, denial. Then anger. Then bargaining. Followed by depression. And in the end, acceptance. As far as she was concerned, there was no stage of denial, or 'This will never ever happen to me.' Even if there had been, it must have been earlier. For her, denial was flight. She had not denied; instead, she had run away saying,

'I don't want to hear this.' As she ran, she grew terrified. And the more she ran, the more ferocious and obstinate George Jerome Marakkaran grew. He chased her relentlessly. She ran farther and farther.

The chase began on the day of her first exam, Basic Sciences. Barely an hour before the exam, he called: 'Satan's offspring, you're going to write an exam and get all smart after killing my son, are you *dee*? The Lord will punish you, *dee*. My son and I will be around to see your ruin. Go, write your exam!'

Jezebel was shocked. Sitting in the moving ambulance, he poured all the evil in his heart into his words. Words she hadn't heard until then. That too from a man who ought not to have spoken to her like that. Her nerves, which had been tense in anticipation of the exam, hurt as if they had been severed. A numbness spread from her toes up to her brain. Her body shivered. Her limbs froze. She kept shivering. Ahana, who noticed this, took the phone from her hand and put it to her own ear. Hearing the words from the other end, she turned red. She switched off the phone, put it in her bag and told Jezebel, 'No one needs to speak to you until the exam is over.' Jezebel tried to muster courage. When a child who has lost one leg struggles to get up, the world throws her down again by striking her on the other leg.

The exams were on alternate days. Although she had not switched on her mobile after that, on the day of the second exam, as she was walking towards the exam hall, a clerk from the college office called her and handed her the receiver of the landline. '*Edee* whore, you thought I wouldn't get through to you if you switched off your phone?' growled George Jerome Marakkaran at the other end. Although the next couple of exams went by on the strength of her friends' insistence that she did not pick up any calls, she lived in constant dread that George Jerome Marakkaran could call any time. If any mobile phone or landline rang, she shuddered in reflex. Even the thought of his voice was enough to drain her of courage. The hatred in that voice rained stones on her.

Even after Ahana returned her mobile the day the theory papers got over, she was reluctant to switch it on. She got herself a new number so that he could not call her again. She tried to take comfort in the fact that the exams were over. But the relief was momentary. Each step that she took forward seemed to sink her in a swamp of disquiet. She wandered aimlessly around on her scooter. Each trip brought alive some bitter memory. Tired and heartbroken, she returned to her friends' apartment.

Now that the examinations were over, Satan's tests resumed. It began with Ahana and Divya going back home and Remitha's husband Shaan Mohammed arriving at their apartment. They were newly-weds. Theirs had been a tempestuous love marriage— while Remitha's father was a daily wage labourer, Shaan's Vaappa was an NRI billionaire. When Remitha and Shaan went out for a movie, Jezebel found herself all alone in the apartment. She showered, made noodles for herself and dozed off, reading. Around midnight, when she woke up startled by some sound and opened the door, she found Shaan and Remitha on the sofa, fighting for the TV remote. As Remitha tried to wriggle away with the remote, Shaan grabbed her and pulled her on to his lap. He bit her on her ear and neck.

Jezebel retreated, her eyes scorched. When she tried to sleep again, she could hear the pitiful beating of her own heart. That house, where Remitha and Shaan rejoiced, rained live coals on her. Her heart pounded as if she had committed some great sin. She felt a sense of inferiority for no reason. Her body kept trembling. Her heart rattled within her body as if it had crashed in some major accident. She began to weep.

Weeping, she slept. She dreamt about the watchman at the mortuary. He was over forty-five. She watched frozen as he walked into the apartment, untying the shabby red towel with green threads from his head, flinging it over his shoulder, smoothing his grey hair, undoing the buttons on his khaki shirt. He came up to her cooing, 'Aren't you my sweet little lovebird?' She felt a surge of love for him. And then his face changed into that of George Jerome Marakkaran. She sprang up in shock. George Jerome Marakkaran grabbed her throat, screaming, 'Whore!' She saw a large knife in his hand.

She was jolted awake by the sound of knocks on the door. She was drenched in sweat. When she switched on the light and opened the door, Remitha and Shaan came inside, asking her what had happened. Jezebel tried to smile through her tears. Smoothing Jezebel's hair, Remitha asked her if she was afraid to sleep alone. 'And if I were, would you come and sleep here, leaving your husband alone?' asked Jezebel angrily. Remitha smiled fondly at her.

'He became my husband only two months ago. But I have known you for five or six years at least. You've given me money to pay my fees, sat up with me when I had a fever, helped me with lessons. So, if you are scared to sleep alone, I will sleep right here with you.'

Tears streamed down Jezebel's cheeks. Remitha's affection deepened the wound within. She buried her face in the pillow. 'I was just joking. Go, sleep,' she said without looking up. Remitha tucked her in, caressed her forehead, kissed her on the cheek and left. Jezebel tossed and turned sleeplessly for the rest of the night. Images blurred and fused in front of her eyes. She tried to dissect her life as if it were a dead body. Which ones were the diseased cells? Was it Ranjith's death? Was it her marriage to Jerome? Was it Ammachi's temperament? Was it the encounter with Ann Mary? She worried about Ann Mary. And despised Sandeep for having disappeared with Ann Mary without letting her know. She had nowhere to go. She felt as if someone had buried her in a casket of darkness. She panicked that the trial in her life had only just begun.

Since the MD course was over, there was no duty in the Medical College hospital any more. With nothing to do, nowhere to go, nobody to talk to or be comforted by, she wallowed in uncertainty. She was terrified of the void waiting for her with its jaws wide open once her practical exams too got over, two weeks later. She was reluctant to visit Valiyammachi because she was afraid of facing her uncles and their wives.

One day, when Remitha and Shaan had gone out, she tried to watch TV for a while. When that failed, she got up, got dressed and went over to the children's hospital. She entered the hospital feeling like a child that had been cast out of the house, now walking stealthily around in search of at least one open window. Dr Babu Mathews was setting out on his rounds. He did not ask her anything. Instead, he asked her to accompany him on his rounds. As he examined patients and wrote out medicines, he turned to her for her opinion. After the rounds, he called her over to his room. When she first met him, Babu sir had been a still-young forty-nine-year-old. Ever-smiling, Babu sir, with his salt-and-pepper hair and moustache, was well-loved by students and patients alike.

'Tragedies happen in everyone's life. For some, on a large scale; for others, on a small scale. Great people, and those with the potential for greatness, will suffer greater tragedies. That's the math.' Babu sir began without preface.

Jezebel tried to smile. She had been in her second year of MBBS when Babu sir's wife, son, daughter, son-in-law, and his daughter's second child all died in a car crash. He was taking class when the news of the accident reached him. 'Something has come up, I'll be back,' he told them before leaving. And he did get right back, after taking a look from afar at the mangled dead bodies lying in the casualty department. And resumed his lecture, panting. When people came and tried to escort him out, he told them gently, 'Please, let me finish this. I need some time . . . please.'

He went on to lecture non-stop for the next fifteen minutes. All along, he was sweating profusely as if he were standing next to a great furnace. And then, he began a sentence and fell silent midway, unable to complete it. Finally, he said, 'I'm all right,' and walked out of the class, wiping his forehead and neck. When she saw him the next day at the funeral service in the church, Jezebel could not recognize him—his hair had turned completely white overnight. She remembered discussing with her classmates the medical reasons for a person greying rapidly in the space of a day.

'Some tragedies present us with great opportunities. To change our own selves . . .'

Jezebel's tears burst their floodgates when she heard these words. 'Why did this happen to me? What opportunity has it ever given me?' she quailed.

'There is no need to get to the bottom of why something happened, my child . . . pray with all your heart. You may not get an answer. But, you will find the strength to move ahead. That's what matters for people like us . . .'

Babu sir looked at her kindly.

'We're starting a child development clinic in this hospital. Will you be able to spend the day there? The Director wants someone to help out. If it's you, he'll be happy.'

Jezebel was terrified that she would break down.

'It's only when a tragedy struck that I understood who my greatest enemy was. It was time. Time is like a demon with many hands. One needs to make sure there's work for each one of those hands. Otherwise, it will grab your throat with its free hands and scratch and bruise you. When your heart aches, remember: your time has sprouted an extra hand and it's time to give that hand something to do. Never sit idle. You must be busy doing something or the other, always. When your worries increase, make sure you take up more responsibilities—study more, or take up an extra job.'

Jezebel sat listening.

'From here on, your life isn't going to be easy. Always keep that in mind. Often, you might feel you're losing it. No. At such times, attend to one more patient. That is the best cure.'

Babu sir continued. 'You are no ordinary girl. I see the promise of a great doctor in you. A brain that medical science can be proud of. Don't ruin it. Go, study, work, live your life.'

Jezebel's eyes welled up. Later, she recalled with gratitude that his compassion was the last straw she had clutched onto in those days.

'You did not go along when they took your husband home. Did you visit him at least once?' asked the lawyer.

'Once,' she said.

'How many days did you stay then?'

Jezebel did not want to remember it. It was while she was leaving Babu sir's room that Remitha called her. Chachan and Ammachi had come to the apartment, and were waiting for her. She went to the apartment. When she saw her, Ammachi's face hardened. Remitha, who was dressed in shorts and a sleeveless top, served them coffee. Shaan, dressed in a T-shirt and bermudas, brought biscuits. Their bodies, not fully covered by their clothes, made Ammachi uncomfortable. Ammachi always despised bodies. 'No time for coffee. Pick up your bag, we need to go,' snarled Ammachi.

'What's the matter?' asked Jezebel, surprised.

'Your classes and exams are over, *alleyo*? And your practicals are only after a few days. Let us go visit the ancestral home. Ammachi isn't too well. She asked to see you.'

Jezebel gave in. She too was eager to meet Valiyammachi. She wanted to laugh; she wanted to cry; she wanted to bask in Valiyammachi's love.

But the next morning, when the taxi sped towards the airport and she realized they were headed for Jerome's city, Jezebel froze in terror. 'No! No! I have exams!' she raised a din. 'Your exams are only after two weeks, *alle*?' scolded Ammachi. Chachan placed a hand on her shoulder and pleaded, 'Whatever it is, let's visit them this once.'

'No need to fall at her feet and beg her like this. It is her duty to go. Let her stay there till her next exam. Don't we need to have something to say when people ask?' Ammachi snapped.

'I'm not going,' she protested.

'You have to come,' Ammachi glowered.

It was their first ever flight, hers, Chachan's and Ammachi's. But she could neither remember how she boarded that flight nor the experience of her first time on an aeroplane. When the flight landed, she felt drained. When they got into a taxi, she threw up. Ammachi pinched her hard on her upper arm and sneered, 'Don't act too smart!' She grew feverish as well. 'That man will trap me and make me stay there!' she wailed like a child. 'If he makes you stay, then stay you must,' said Ammachi. 'He's not going to kill you or eat you up, is he?'

'My practical exam!' Jezebel whimpered.

'I'll come and take you back the day before your exam,' Chachan reassured her.

When the grill gate of the old-fashioned lift in George Jerome Marakkaran's apartment opened noisily, a wolf howled in her memory. The pigeons pecking about in the courtyard scattered and rose in flight.

It was Lilly George Marakkaran who opened the door. Her face lit up when she saw Jezebel. Jezebel wanted to fall into her arms. Lilly's hands seemed to twitch too. But she quickly assumed an expression of seriousness and turned to go in. Jezebel dragged her feet behind Chachan and Ammachi. Her fever was aggravating. Jerome lay in the room where Jezebel and Jerome had stayed earlier. Ammachi and Chachan went inside. Jezebel stayed at the doorway. Dropping her voice, Lilly asked her, 'Why did you come?' Jezebel was distressed. As she looked in, she could make out the figure on the adjustable bed, next to the oxygen cylinder, in what now looked like a hospital room. She felt dizzy. She could scarcely believe her eyes. Jerome George Marakkaran, who had towered as tall as the loft in her room the first time they met, had shrivelled to a small body of some thirty-five kilos or so. Her eyes burned; Jezebel stepped back.

'Come here. Sit next to him,' called out Ammachi, annoyed. She had wanted her daughter to run weeping to her husband. Ammachi's attempt was to prove to the world that her daughter was a virtuous woman. Jezebel stood there, frozen and dying. Fever raged in her brain. She sweated profusely; her ash-grey kurta turned a shade darker. Rivulets of sweat trickled down her forehead, drenching her curls as if in a downpour. That was when George Jerome Marakkaran walked in with a bag of groceries.

'Aha! Guests, I see! And who gave you permission to enter my house?' he demanded.

'Why do you say so, George *saarey*? Isn't it our duty to visit?' Ammachi said ingratiatingly.

George Jerome Marakkaran grew more furious. 'If you were so duty-bound, would a wife have had the heart to send her husband off like that?' he growled. Jezebel took a step back.

'Please forgive my daughter. And her ignorance. She stayed back only because she had to write her exam and not let three years of study go to waste. She will stay here from now on.' said Ammachi. Jezebel's body smouldered. Her ears clamped shut. George Jerome Marakkaran looked at her with menace.

'I know you are a woman from a good family, so I'm not saying anything to your face, Saramme. But one thing, if she stays here, she has to stay right here. My son's wife must live here and attend to him. She may be a doctor, a collector, whatever. But in this house, she is my son's wife, that's all. She needs to be around here till he wakes up. She can't do as she pleases, saying "I need to go work, I need my salary" and so on. Woman is more bitter than death.'

Ammachi and Chachan looked at each other. 'Of course, she'll stay here,' Ammachi hastened to assure him. Jezebel wished she could run away before Ammachi completed her sentence. She picked up her bag and stepped out. 'Stop right there, *dee!*' George Jerome roared. 'Get back in here!'

With all the ferocity of a wolf pouncing on its fleeing prey, he grabbed her by the hand. Jezebel wanted to scream and attract attention, but fear overpowered her. She saw that the first thing fear stole from a woman was her voice. He dragged her back to the room. She dreaded that she would have to spend the rest of her life within its walls. That was when Lilly George Marakkaran raised her voice, 'No!'

Jezebel saw George Jerome Marakkaran shudder. Since he had never heard his wife raise her voice, it must have taken him a while to realize that it was indeed her. Lilly George Marakkaran picked up Jezebel's bag from the floor and pushed her towards the door. 'This wretched one need not stay here!' she cried out. 'I'm here to take care of my son. Let her go. His ruin began the moment she set foot here. If we make her stay here, she might inject him with something and kill him. This form lying there, that's all I have of him. I'm not ready to lose that as well.'

George Jerome Marakkaran began to say something. Lilly turned to face him. 'Till date, I haven't gone against your word. Like a dog, I have only obeyed you. But if you are planning to make her stay here, it's all over between you and me.'

George Jerome Marakkaran stood aghast. Lilly swung around to Jezebel. 'Leave! Leave my sight!' she raged again. She was weeping. Jezebel understood that those tears were because she hadn't escaped to safety despite having had the opportunity. Chanting to herself, 'I have found what my soul seeks, and searched for long,' she slowly walked down the steps. She feared that it would take her hours to get to the courtyard where the pigeons sat pecking. Chachan and Ammachi had already taken the lift and reached the ground floor. As she walked out following them, she turned to look up at that apartment one last time. She saw Lilly George Marakkaran standing on the balcony, wiping her tears, bidding her farewell. Ammachi wept in the taxi. Chachan called his travel agent, worried about how to arrange for one more ticket at short notice. As the taxi inched forward in a road full of vehicles, Jezebel, seated at the back, wanted to tell Lilly George Marakkaran: 'One man among a thousand have I found, but a woman among all those I have not found. Oh woman, how do you know whether you can save your husband?'

13

When Jezebel returned from the field after ploughing and shepherding, no one told her, 'Come at once, sit down for a meal'. Instead, they only told her, 'Gird yourself and serve me till I have eaten and drunk.' Because she was counted as a slave, no one thanked her, although she had done their bidding. The fruit that her soul longed for had gone away from her. All riches and splendour were lost to her. She feared that she would never get to see them again. Later, whenever she looked back on those days, she saw everyone and everything as signs. Everything that had appeared had been to reveal what was to happen in her imminent future, she panicked.

Those days, she had pangs of ravenous hunger. There are two kinds of hunger: that of the flesh, and that of the soul. Jezebel experienced both these hungers as one. Satan tempted her: 'Tell these stones of yours to become appams.' She conceded defeat that man lived for this alone.

On their way back from Jerome's city, she kicked up a fuss, wanting to stop at a restaurant. Ammachi tried to dissuade her. Jezebel insisted, Chachan gave in and asked the driver to stop. Jezebel rushed in and ordered everything she saw on the menu. When the food arrived, Ammachi and Chachan were taken aback—appams, prawn stir-fry, mullet fry, porotta, beef roast. When she saw Jezebel tucking away without paying attention to anyone else, Ammachi made a face and scolded her: 'What behaviour is this, *dee*!' 'Is it unsightly to eat food, Ammachi?' shot back Jezebel. 'I came here for the first time with Jerome, Ammachi,' she went on, her mouth full of food. 'That day, I ordered a prawn roast. Jerome got angry. He said it would be too expensive, and cancelled the order. Instead, he ordered three appams and chicken curry. And just a tea for himself. Finally, when the food came, he said I would waste it and had one appam first, then another, and then finished all the chicken pieces. You know, Ammachi, after marriage, I haven't been able to buy anything to eat for myself. There was no money in my purse. Jerome would not let me order what I wanted. Man lives not by bread alone, Ammachi, but by love too.'

As tears streamed down her face, Chachan and Ammachi looked at each other. The driver got up and left with his cup of tea. 'Speak softly, *dee*,' hissed Ammachi. 'Women from good families do not whine about food like this.' Jezebel laughed out loud, choking on her food. Later too, whenever she remembered Jerome, her body craved food. Now that he was not in her life any more, she ate with a vengeance. She rued that he had mercilessly killed even small pleasures like these.

She experienced not only hunger but also extreme rage. As if her blood pressure had increased, she grew restless and quarrelled with Ammachi and Chachan over trivial matters. She laughed aloud like never before. Cried aloud. Raved and ranted for hours. Sometimes she would throw things. When Ammachi tried to confront her, Jezebel turned on her like she had never done before. When Ammachi muttered, 'If women don't get a grip, men will do all sorts of things. One must behave accordingly. That's what makes women smart!' Jezebel shot back, 'So why didn't you teach me this smartness before?'

'Whose fault was it, *dee*? Wasn't this wedding fixed after asking you if you liked him?'

'Didn't Abel say no? Wasn't it you who didn't agree then, Ammachi?'

'Can one break up a wedding after it has been solemnized?'

'And so, what happened? Your only daughter's life went to rack and ruin. Did you go and see the house your daughter was going to be married into? Did you inquire about those living there? Someone packed them off here, seeing that the proposal wouldn't suit their daughter. Those here made a grab for it.'

'You must make peace with the ways of the house you're married into. If you behave like some high-up doctor, then this is how things will turn out.'

'Was it my fault that that man drove his car headlong into the river?'

'"That man?!" *Dee*, God will curse a woman who does not respect her husband. No wonder all this happened to you.'

'What should I respect that man for? For grabbing a minor girl? He has had no respect for me from the day we got married. He hasn't respected my likes or desires, not once. I have neither respect nor love for that man.'

'Shut up! However worthless the husband is, a good woman will not ever speak a word against him.'

'I'm not a good woman, Ammachi. I don't want to be one either.'

Each time, after such a war of words, she felt her blood boil, her bones melt. Night after night, she tossed and turned, unable to sleep. She felt a deep enmity towards Ammachi and fondness for Lilly George Marakkaran. She felt sad that for Ammachi, it was society's endorsement, not her own daughter's happiness, that mattered. Society had taught Ammachi how her daughter ought to be happy. Whether or not her husband loved her, she was obliged to love him, respect him, serve him. She was obliged to keep his misdemeanours away from the eyes of the world, and protect his fake honour. Until he returned to consciousness, she was fated to wait by his bedside, praying, without food or sleep. She did not have the right to sit in judgement on him as a good or bad person, since he had already been judged by God; she was only meant to bear her cross as best as she could.

Society was unmoved by her nerves being racked at night. Society was not inconvenienced by her inflicting wounds on herself so that the pain of the heart would dissolve in the pain of the body or by her calling up friends late in the night and breaking down over the phone—sometimes cursing life, sometimes talking of unconnected things. Society was not troubled by her friends sleepily consoling her or her bursting into tears, burying her face in the pillow, when they disconnected the call saying they would call her back in the morning, scared that their husbands would say something.

That's why whenever Ammachi prayed, she got hopping mad. Once, when Ammachi was praying, and Chachan was writing something, Jezebel threw a vessel down to the ground and raised a din. When Ammachi came rushing, Jezebel said loudly, 'I need to talk.' Ammachi raised her hand to hit her. She gripped Ammachi's hand. To Jezebel's 'If you or Chachan have a problem with my staying here, you must let me know. I will find another place,' Ammachi replied, 'We married you off. Once the knot is tied, married women do not stay in their parents' homes.' 'That knot has come undone,' said Jezebel, to which Ammachi retorted, 'For Christians, marriage is not a knot that can be untied.'

'Who is Christian?' countered Jezebel. 'That man who has no mercy for the poor, is he a Christian? The man who assaulted a little girl who sought refuge, is he a Christian?'

'Then go and stay with that Hindu,' said Ammachi.

'Either I'll stay here or I'll stay with whoever I please,' replied Jezebel, just as stubbornly.

Tired, Ammachi said in a conciliatory tone, '*Ente kochey*, my child, you have a husband. If the others hear what you're saying when he is lying bedridden, won't they make up all kinds of stories?' That only made Jezebel angrier.

'All these years, I lived the way you wanted me to—prayed before every mealtime, went to church every Sunday, confessed, partook of the holy communion, fasted during Lent, and did not do a thing you forbade—Ammachi. I agreed to the marriage proposal you found me. The very first night, I found out that he was not the one for me. But you kept me trapped in it, Ammachi. For two-and-a-half years, I suffered his, and his father's, cussing and swearing. And what did I get in return? I'm a doctor. If I diagnose an illness, I treat it with medicine. If one medicine doesn't work, I give another. If nothing works, I surgically remove the infected part. All these days, I had the medicine you prescribed. And what did I gain? I ended up with an illness I hadn't had in the first place. All my happiness has gone. I can't take it any more.'

Chachan got up, went over to her and placed his hand on her shoulder. He stroked her on the head. 'You needn't go. As long as I'm alive, you needn't go elsewhere,' he said, choking. Jezebel gave in. She leaned her head against Chachan's shoulder. 'You are my firstborn. The first one to call me "Chachan". It was in your smiles that I forgot my sorrows. You were the one who inspired me to live. This home is yours. There is no need for my daughter to wander around with nowhere to go. You must stay here. Let anyone say anything. I know my child.'

Later she would smile, remembering how she had wept loudly, hugging Chachan who, too, broke down, and how she had gone to her room, challenging Ammachi. Like a scene in a play, she would see her old musty cobwebbed room with its old bed again, as if for the first time. That day, she opened the windows, cleared the cobwebs, dusted and stacked her books, arranged her cupboard and spread a new bed sheet. She stared in disbelief at her reflection in the cupboard mirror—an apparition with sunken eyes and cheeks, protruding collarbones and a blank face. She picked out a book from the shelf. It was *The Prophet*. She heard Jerome's voice: 'Don't you bring up this Kibran-Kubran with me hereafter!' Her heart pounded in fear. That day, poor her, the road she was fleeing had neared its end. Only deep chasms lay ahead. It was impossible to turn around and retrace the vast distances she had travelled, and the very thought terrified her.

Later on, she realized that it was not only hunger and anger but also anxiety that had burnt her heart down. Her heart smouldered, red-hot, like a brick on a kiln. Its cracks and crevices hardened. In those days, she turned utterly superstitious, hoping against hope that she could fix the broken pieces of her life like before with the glue of faith.

Later, she would feel mortified about joining a prayer group. The prayer was in a small auditorium teeming with people. Pain was writ large on all the faces. Everyone was praying with all their heart. An acquaintance called her on to the stage and shared the sad story of her life with the audience. He declaimed loudly, 'This child, though a Christian, did not believe! And so, the Lord punished her!' She became an object of display. She bent her head. This was repeated for several days. Every day, she would be summoned to the stage. In the end, indignant with herself, she left the place.

That was when an old classmate of hers whom she happened to meet asked her, 'Have you heard of Ranjini deivam?' Ranjini deivam, Goddess Ranjini, was a young woman with thick eyebrows who wore *jimikki*s on her ears. She prescribed a 'twenty-one' puja for a thousand rupees, assuring her that she would hear good news on the twenty-second day. Jezebel paid a thousand rupees and got a puja performed. Goddess Ranjini tied a red thread around Jezebel's wrist and smeared her forehead with sanctified *sindooram*. She instructed that Jezebel apply the *sindooram* to the parting of her hair for twenty-one days. Ignoring Ammachi's ire, she wore the *sindooram* for twenty-one days. Thrice a day, she chanted *mantras* from the 'Saundarya Lahari'. On the twenty-second day, nothing happened. Nothing happened on the twenty-third and twenty-fourth days either. Nor on the thirtieth and fortieth days. Jezebel wiped off the *sindooram*. She snapped off the thread from her wrist and threw it into the kitchen hearth. Hadn't she been under the impression that her happiness could be gifted by someone else? Hadn't she been living in a fool's paradise thinking that there was a special happiness destined for her and that it was now in someone else's custody? Hadn't she failed to realize that her happiness was her own responsibility?

Later on, she recalled that it was not only hunger and anger and anxiety but also all sorts of fears that had tied her down at that time. One of those was the government order that pressed those who had cleared MD into government service, in order to tackle the strike by government doctors. Although she had passed the MD exam with a good score, she worried about having to leave the Medical College. New places and new people frightened her. As he struggled to console a weeping Jezebel, Dr Babu Mathews advised her to write to the health minister. He even prepared a letter for her: 'I request you to kindly post me in this Medical College itself considering the treatment requirements of my husband who is in a coma after meeting with an accident.' Later on, she would feel ashamed of how she had called Rani and cried all night, worried about being posted elsewhere.

She agonized over what she would do in case she got a job elsewhere. She stayed awake, terrified, imagining going to another place to work, the people there ridiculing her, George Jerome Marakkaran landing there to drag her away, her being forced to leave with him because there was no one to help her. The next morning, sleep-deprived, she left for the capital city.

It was not only hunger and anger and anxiety and fear, but a peculiar habit of baring her heart to anyone who would listen, that possessed her in those days. Later, she would feel ashamed recalling how she had behaved—like one carrying a load, stopping to put the burden down at every resting place on the wayside. Tears threatened to break as she waited at the health minister's office. As people moved in and out of that big room, she felt like she had shrunken into a worm—a worm curled up in terror that crawled from one place to another, taking care not to get trampled underfoot by bigger creatures, or get caught in brambles. She struggled to let the world know she was not a worm.

Sitting next to her was a balding, thickset, middle-aged man who had come seeking the transfer of his wife, a nurse. The moment he asked her something, she unpacked the story of her entire life before him. It did not occur to her that she needn't have told him all that—a man she was seeing for the first time in her life. As he heard her out intently, his wife and another woman she had been talking to, turned around and cocked their ears. Jezebel narrated the sad story of her life to them, all tears.

She was the last one to meet the minister. When the nurse and her husband were called in, two others came and sat down next to her. She repeated her story to them as well. After listening to everything, when they asked, 'Still, no matter what kind of a person he was, was it right to leave your husband like this?' she started as if someone had hit her on the head. She struggled to fight tears.

The minister was a retired teacher. As she peered at Jezebel over her glasses, that childlike face and those bright eyes must have stirred some fondness within her. When Jezebel pleaded with her with folded hands, 'Please don't transfer me elsewhere madam,' the minister immediately called her secretary and instructed her to resolve Jezebel's request. She consoled Jezebel. When Jezebel came out of her room, she was still sobbing.

Poor Jezebel did not realize until much later that what she had spoken that day had not been with others but with her own self, and that it had all been to deflect attention from the stench and the burden of the waste bin on her head. She had not understood that she did not have to try hard to make the world understand that she was not obliged to love Jerome. Because the world was constantly accusing her, 'He was your husband; it was your duty to conquer him with love.' And so, she allowed people like Nandagopan, who claimed he was not accusing but accepting her, to take her for a ride.

After meeting the minister, Jezebel stayed over at Rani's sister Rini's apartment. It was Rini who put an end to Jezebel's tendency to narrate her sob story to everyone she came across. When she met them at their apartment, Rini's husband Varun inquired after Jezebel's family. As Jezebel prepared to repeat her story one more time, Rini called her in with a 'Just a moment' under the pretext of showing her the room she would be staying in. And then she whispered, '*Moley*, you do not have to let Varun know that your husband is in a coma and that you haven't had a physical relationship with him.' As Jezebel looked at her, surprised, Rini's voice dropped even lower, 'Most men do not make good friends. They cannot keep a secret that isn't theirs.'

'Where's the secret in this? Doesn't everyone know that my husband is in a coma?' Jezebel asked, a little tired.

'Yes, but you don't have to be the one to go around telling everyone that.' Rini caressed her warmly. 'Jez, what you have seen so far is not the real world. You are yet to see it. I don't tell my husband things even about my own sister. Because I'm not sure if he would turn it into a ruse to use her. The men I've seen are all unreliable ones. I hate them.' Rini's fair face flushed. Her eyes filled with hatred.

'Not all men are like that, *chechi*,' Jezebel tried to argue.

Rini laughed out loud. She told her about how she had worshipped Varun in the early days of their marriage and shared all her secrets with him. Once, a friend confided in Rini about her husband's sexual problems. As was her wont, Rini told Varun about it. Varun sympathized and gave advice. But within weeks, that friend came back to Rini with 'What I had told you was what a woman would tell her most trusted friend. Do let your husband know that he will be the first person I'll call in case I get really desperate for sex.' That had been such a blow. 'With that, I lost that friend. And so, I have only one piece of advice to give you: never share either your secrets or your guilt with the man you love. Our society has not brought up men with the magnanimity to grasp it all.'

Jezebel did not want to believe it. She even tried to argue about it. But the next day was an eye-opener. When Varun gave her a ride to town in his car, he brushed against her not once but twice on the pretext of adjusting the side mirror and the door lock. When he played the film song '*Nin maniyaraiyile nirmala shayyayile, neela neeraalamayi njan maariyenkil* (If only I were a blue brocade over the spotless bed in your nuptial chamber)' on the car stereo, and beat time to it, and said with a sort of leer, 'I simply don't understand how your husband could ever think of leaving a tender little thing like you . . .,' it was as if a great mountain had crashed down on her.

'If I were to say that you dumped your husband on his family and then lived it up here with your lover, would you be able to deny it?' asked the lawyer. 'There is proof to show that barely three months after Dr Jerome George Marakkaran was moved back to his city, you stayed with Dr Sandeep Mohan at Holiday Hotel, some hundred kilometres away from your place.'

Jezebel struggled not to go pale and to keep her voice steady. 'I have not stayed with Sandeep.'

'But these hotel records say that Dr Sandeep Mohan did stay with you! Look here, you checked in on Monday afternoon at 1.45. You checked out the next morning at 6.'

She did not feel angry with the lawyer. Jezebel remembered what Rini (who had by then moved out after the divorce and was living by herself) told her when she called her after reading Varun's feminist posts on Facebook: 'Yeah right, some feminist indeed! But you know what, Jez, I'm not sore at him. Once you meet, get to know and then break up with some four or five men, you don't feel sore at anyone any more. All *paavams*, poor things. Hapless souls.'

By this time, Jezebel too had, in her own way, arrived at similar conclusions. So, it was possible for her to smile again. But until it became possible, like an archer who took aim at everyone who came into view, she respected the fools and even dispatched messages through them.

Man, what's between you and her?

Isn't her time still to come?

14

After what little she had was taken away from her, Jezebel lit a lamp but did not cover it with a jar or hide it under the bed. Instead, she set it on a pedestal, so that those who entered could see the light. For she hoped that there was nothing hidden that would not be disclosed, and nothing concealed that would not be made known and brought to light. And so, telling herself the old had gone and the new had come, Jezebel dreamt of new 'rights' to correct all the old wrongs of her life. But she had learnt from her life that from the moment one challenged the sole God of matrimony and family, every woman would become the Jezebel of Samaria.

George Jerome Marakkaran's vengeance against Jezebel did not die down despite the distance of two thousand kilometres. Jezebel wished she could have told the court that George Jerome Marakkaran was like Prophet Elijah who had pronounced a drought on Jezreel, enraged by the building of a temple for Baal as desired by Queen Jezebel.

In truth, Elijah's ire had not been against Ahab or the gods he installed. It had been against the self-confidence of Jezebel who worshipped those gods, she later realized. Those four years when Jehovah's people suffered without water, Prophet Elijah went and stayed in Queen Jezebel's well-watered land. Unable to comprehend neither a god who got angry and punished his subjects nor his taskmaster the prophet, the Queen was aggrieved. When it was about to rain again, Elijah returned to Jezreel and challenged the prophets of Baal to make it rain. But the prophets of Baal could not make it rain. And so, Elijah massacred them all. Queen Jezebel could not forgive a prophet who was ready to kill men to prove that his god was more powerful. Pointing a finger at Prophet Elijah, she swore, 'May the gods deal with me, be it ever so severely, if by this time tomorrow I do not make your life like that of one of them. If you are Elijah, so I am Jezebel!' Elijah fled in fear and sought refuge in the caves on the mountaintop. But his vengeance did not die down.

Just like those who gathered to help Prophet Elijah who wished to see Queen Jezebel being torn apart by dogs, there were people who arrived to assist George Jerome Marakkaran as well. They strewed thorns and glass and landmines along Jezebel's path. As for her, fool that she was, she rushed recklessly along the path in front of her in search of her promised land.

She had booked her return ticket from the capital city by the evening train. Taking leave of Varun, she went to meet her classmate Jayapal who worked in a private deluxe hospital. As she waited for Jayapal to return from his rounds, in sauntered Nandagopan, down the corridor with doctors' rooms on either side. He was a head-turner, and he knew it too. He paused in front of her with a 'Dr Jezebel, *alle?*' Jezebel was astonished. When he invited her into his room with an 'If you don't mind, you can come sit in my room until Jayapal returns', she clutched at it like a last straw. A smile played on his lips. There was a particular fragrance about him. The way he walked, the way he tilted his head to look at her, all of it exuded confidence. Her first impression was: here's a man who is so sure about everything. She was quick to take him at his word.

Nandagopan showed her that very first day that pleasing words were like honey that sweetened the soul and nourished the

body. As they went into his consultation room, he searched for
something on his laptop and then turned his screen around so
she could see it too. An old photo, enlarged—a photo from her
MBBS days in which she was seen walking with Rani and Saju
who had moved to the United States after MBBS. 'When was this
taken?' asked Jezebel, surprised. She looked happy in the photo.
That made her happy.

'I had been waiting to see you, Jezebel. I was determined to see
you and click your picture . . .' Nandagopan's eyes shone.

'And what made you so determined?' She asked, a tad
nervous.

'How could I not be? In the men's hostel, when a student tried
to teach the others something, one of them told him: "Go away,
man! You should hear Jez teach this! Let's ask her tomorrow."
That made me greatly curious. I wanted to know who this Jez was.
When I heard the name Jezebel John, it suddenly struck me. The
one who topped Class 10, Pre-degree, and the entrance exam! I
still remember the photo that appeared in the newspapers. You
had dimples back then.'

Hearing that, her dimples blossomed in spite of herself. He
looked at her closely. 'Oh, you still have them, *alle*?'

She reddened. 'How much I've changed,' she thought. She
thirsted for admiration. There was a hunger in her heart . . . to
be acknowledged, pampered, praised. As she sat there in front of
him, wondering if all women felt this way, and as he gazed into
her eyes, stroking his thick moustache, a butterfly emerged from
a chrysalis from within her. Watching its own wings unfurl in the
sunshine, the butterfly, too, marvelled, 'Is this really me? Were
there so many hues in these wings all along?'

'There has been a great upheaval in my life,' said Jezebel.

'Well, one can make that out from the dark circles under your
eyes,' he said.

He hooked his eyes onto hers. She trembled.

'Don't you know, doctors are experts at gossiping? There are many stories and allegations about you doing the rounds here. But I told them, if a girl like Jezebel has to have an extramarital affair, no one can be blamed. If such a thing happened, it only means the marriage was a failure. Failed relationships, even if they are mere friendships, cause us so much stress and tension. The energy that we spend in taking them forward, in proving to the world that we are happy, how much else could be done with it! It's also important how we define happiness. A girl as smart and studious as you would never be able to cross her limits. We don't know each other, but I'm sure you'll never do anything wrong.'

Jezebel teared up. She wiped her eyes and nose, and struggled to find her voice. 'Thanks. But I didn't have an affair with Sandeep,' she said. Nandagopan brightened like a child who had baited a fish. 'Even if you had, what of it? It's only human to have relationships. What's wrong with it? When your stomach is hungry, you seek food. When your heart is hungry, you seek love. I haven't given it more importance than that. Take my own case. When my relationship with my wife soured, I told her, "There is no need for any pretence between us. Honesty is the cornerstone of all relationships. You have all the freedom to find yourself another man. If you want to break the marital bond, so be it. I'm ready. Or else, if you are okay with carrying on like this, that's fine by me too . . ."'

Jezebel looked at him in disbelief. 'What about the children?'

'We have two. I have ensured that they will always have their mother's and father's affection. Even if we are estranged, they won't cease to be our children, *alle*?' His face grew serious.

'Did you really break up?' She wondered.

He smiled, avoiding her eyes. 'I don't admit that to anyone. Breaking up is such an abstraction, isn't it, Jezebel? If people can live peacefully, whether or not they have broken up, then why should the break-up itself be an issue? If ever there is another relationship, I will be very careful. I need a person who understands the nature of my job. See, Jezebel, most people do not understand the problems of our profession. If ever I marry again, it will be a doctor. And someone who understands the problems of a mismatched relationship. Anyway, why talk of all that and ruin this moment? I'm really happy, Jezebel. I got to see you after all these years.' He leaned back in his chair and looked intently into her eyes.

'I'm amazed you recognized me,' she said, trying to repay his kindness.

'I was looking for you all these years, Jezebel. And hoping we'd get to meet some day. That's all.'

His voice grew tender. A butterfly fluttered within Jezebel. Suddenly he seemed more handsome and desirable. When Jayapal returned, the three of them went out to lunch together. There, Jezebel narrated her life story once again. Jezebel did not fail to notice that Jayapal remained silent throughout. Nandagopan, on the other hand, grew terribly emotional. He consoled her, bad-mouthed George Jerome Marakkaran (and Jerome), and even offered to speak to him. Whenever she looked at Nandagopan, Jezebel felt the butterfly flutter. This is the man you had been seeking, it thrilled. All these years, no one else had set her heart astir. She was mortified that as soon as she had met a man her mind was filled with the possibility of romance with him. What a handsome man! What a smart conversationalist! What a kindred spirit! In the course of the lunch, he asked for her phone number and George Jerome Marakkaran's. Once he left, she felt lonely. While going to the railway station in Jayapal's car, Jezebel tried to find out more about Nandagopan.

'There was no need to tell him your personal matters in such detail,' remarked Jayapal.

'What's wrong in telling him?' She wanted to know.

'Nandagopan is a peculiar type. Be careful,' was all Jayapal would say.

'What's there to be careful about in my life any more?' she sighed. 'See what came of living so carefully?'

Jayapal was not making an effort to understand her, she thought. She grew piqued with him too.

Nandagopan called her at night and spoke for a long while. Free of all inhibitions, she, too, chatted for hours on end. He consoled her, encouraged her, made her laugh. Told her stories of wicked men and warned her to beware of them. Told her Rini was right and that she must keep a distance from her husband. Gladdened her heart with news that doctors who had passed MD were filing cases in court against their transfer orders from the Medical College. He had read Gibran and Neruda. He was able to tell her all that she wanted to hear. He landed up at the Children's Hospital several times just in order to meet her. With each day, their friendship grew stronger. Her life was filling again with music and light. She imagined it was love. She believed it would be.

And then Sajni arrived—a thirty-six-year-old who had been deserted by her husband, and worked as a salesgirl in order to bring up her thirteen-year-old son. One day, she was shocked when she saw a photo of herself undressing on her son's mobile phone. She was shattered to discover that her son had made several peepholes in the bathroom walls. When she wept, 'Doctor*ey*, I want to die!', Jezebel, who was preparing her case history, wept along with her. That night, when Nandagopan called, she told him about Sajni's problem. Nandagopan reacted even more emotionally than Jezebel. 'That child needs behavioural modification,' he advised. 'Don't you know Dr Arun Gopal? Head of the department of psychiatry at Hitech Medicity. He's a friend. I'll book an appointment. Bring that child over, Jezebel.'

As she prepared for the trip, marvelling at Nandagopan's broad-mindedness, Jezebel couldn't help wondering that if it had been Jerome, he would never have reacted the same way. When the day before, Nandagopan announced that he, too, would be coming there, Jezebel was thrilled. When he asked her, 'If you won't take it amiss, shall I tell you something?' her heart beat faster. 'I will be staying in a hotel there. If you trust me, will you also stay with me? I want to tell you something important. It's something I want to tell you in person. I will be able to make a decision on this only after hearing yours.' When he said this, Jezebel was breathless. A thousand butterflies fluttered in her cells. She was almost sure that Nandagopan had applied for a divorce from his wife and was about to propose to her. She believed that a man was calling her with love for the first time in her life. She debated with herself whether she should go or not. From time to time, her brain wondered, 'What if he wasn't trustworthy?' But her greedy heart shut her brain up.

She woke up early, and packed two sets of clothes and a nightie in a small bag. She left home with a pounding heart. The train reached on time. Jezebel got into the train with Sajni. Nandagopan had taken the same train from the capital city. He came and sat next to her. He was around when they met the doctor and booked an appointment for Sajni's son. After they had seen Sajni off in an auto to the bus stand, Jezebel went along with Nandagopan to the hotel he had booked a room in. When the receptionist asked them to fill out a form, Nandagopan regretted that he had no identity card on him. Jezebel handed over her driving licence. But it was Nandagopan who filled out the form. They walked to their room. Her legs were trembling. Her body felt cold. She knew what was going to happen. After all, knowledge was the only thing she had earned, by dint of staying up and studying sleeplessly, in her short life. She wasn't sure if Nandagopan was as knowledgeable. But her fears were unfounded. As it is written, he that had gathered much had nothing left over, and he that had gathered little had no lack.

The moment they were in the room, Nandagopan changed colour. The man who had been a friend until then now turned lord and master. He came up to her and looked into her eyes. When he placed a hand on her shoulder and lifted her chin, she thrilled in anticipation. She dreamt that he would kiss her gently. But, tearing that dream asunder like a butterfly's wing, he grunted, 'I knew you wanted this.'

Jezebel's taut body shattered. Her eagerness to be kissed retreated into its shell. The memory of Jerome George Marakkaran and their first night flashed across her mind. With a start, she realized that there was no love, only triumph, in Nandagopan's eyes. As he grabbed her and pressed his body against hers, she felt each cell in her body slip into a coma. She averted her face from his lips. 'Hm, what happened?' he asked, irritated. She tried to smile. When he approached her again, she tried to evade him with a 'Let me go take a bath.' The leer on his face and his 'Let's bathe together' only froze her even more. She saw her reflection in his eyes. She saw how pitiable her situation was. His smell repelled her. When he laughed, the mould she could see on the inside of his teeth revolted her. She took a step back. His fingers reached out for her again. Bile rose in her throat. Just then, his phone rang. She stood watching as his face drained of colour. He moved away with a 'Just a moment', and went into the bathroom, as if to take a leak. The moment the bathroom door closed, she picked up her bag without thinking too much about it. She got out and ran towards the lift. Rushing past the receptionist, she got out of the hotel, got into the first auto she saw and reached the bus stand.

As she leapt into a crowded Superfast bus that had just started moving and stood holding onto its bars, her heart gasped, 'Oh God, oh God!' Nandagopan was calling her phone non-stop. Messages from him, like 'What happened? Did I do something wrong?' and so on, came thick and fast. It was dark by the time she reached home. She did not respond to Ammachi. She washed up, changed and flopped on her bed, not bothering to eat. She wanted to cry, but the tears wouldn't come. A great weight pressed down on her chest. She wanted to die. She smouldered, fumed.

To understand a man, you must fight with him. When she fought with Nandagopan, she truly understood him. '*Chee* you fatherless bastard! Daughter of a prostitute! Who did you think I was? Inviting a man over and then humiliating him! Did you think I didn't have the stamina to satisfy you? Sleep with me once and then you'll know!' He abused her non-stop for ten minutes. Jezebel disconnected the call, too weak to continue.

Later, when he tried to call her, she did not pick up the phone. Instead, she texted him, 'Do not call me henceforth. I'm not interested in a relationship with you.' He tried to make up to her. He complained that she had hurt him. She did not reply, but she lost sleep. She paced about the room. It was dark all over. She was angry with the God who had made two lights: the greater light to rule the day, and the lesser light to rule the night. She screamed in maddened agony, and hit her head against the wall.

When Nandagopan's harassment increased over the next few days, she turned to Jayapal for help. 'Did I not warn you to be careful with him?' scolded Jayapal. Then he sighed and assured her, 'Ok, I'll handle him.' And so Nandagopan's calls came to an end. But a spurned man is also one who thirsts for revenge. Like Prophet Elijah who avenged Queen Jezebel when she declared 'I do not believe in a god that punishes and exacts revenge', Nandagopan added Sandeep Mohan's name to the hotel bill and mailed it to George Jerome Marakkaran.

'You used to take narcotic drugs, *alleyo*?' asked the lawyer.

'No.'

'Would you deny that drugs were found in your bag?'

'I do.'

'There is proof that you regularly bought drugs. What do you have to say about that?'

She closed her eyes and tried to muster strength. When they fight, some men turn into devils. They come to acquire the faces of some creatures—a lion for some, a bull for others, still others, a vulture.

The ones to be feared the most were the ones who wore the faces of humans. They could destroy another's soul more effectively.

15

When she recalled those days, Jezebel grew troubled in spirit and rued, 'Very truly I tell you, one of you betrayed me'. One whom she had loved had already done what she herself had wanted to do. It was necessary for the daughter of God to be glorified. And yet, she feared three things: the infamy that had spread in the city, the trial in public, the false witnesses . . .

At that point in time, when she was angry with her situation, she sought several possible answers to why she had rushed foolishly—like a lamb that had sighted blades of green grass—wearing the blindfold of marriage. Had she hoped for a time when love would sprout under the sun? Had she feared Ammachi? Had she sympathized with Chachan? Had she thought it was better not to have eyes till her legs became stronger? Had she found comfort in pretending to be someone else? After a long time, it was Father Ilanjikkal who told her how the environment played a role in completing every being's life cycle. It was after the manger and the exodus and the temptation by Satan that Christ had evolved. It was after that, that the crowds came to listen to him; that he satiated the hunger of five thousand with five loaves; that he spoke through parables; that the lawyers and high priests began to consider him their enemy. These are situations that all human beings undergo in their own ways. Everyone's own Golgotha awaits them. Everyone's crucifixion awaits them. Their resurrection and second coming await them. There was no end to the temptations of Satan in Jezebel's life. It was to fulfil the Lord's words that 'wisdom is justified by those who receive it.'

When Ahana and Remitha went abroad, and Rani moved to another medical college, Jezebel was more pained than she had been by Jerome's accident. Unable to bear the burden of loneliness from the time she woke up every morning, her brain collapsed like a broken-legged donkey. She woke up weeping, terrified about how to push each day through. But hadn't the universe earmarked mercy for each grain of sand, for every day and for all time, like a letter with its address pasted on it? Doesn't someone always arrive as a postman and hand the letter over to the addressee even though he doesn't know what's inside?

It was Dr Haritha Sadanand who arrived with that day's ration of mercy. The devil had possessed Jezebel that morning in the form of a burning headache. Sajni had come to inform her that her son's counselling sessions had begun. Jezebel felt pinpricks of grief seeing the dark circles under her eyes. When she asked, 'My son will get better, won't he, doctor*ey*?', Jezebel's heart ached. She opened her bag, counted out five hundred rupees and gave it to Sajni. When Sajni pleaded, 'No, doctor*ey*,' Jezebel's grief turned to rage. She scolded Sajni non-stop. Taken aback by the change in her expression, Sajni accepted the money. But Jezebel's rage did not die down. She shouted that it was Sajni's fault that her son had turned out this way. Passers-by turned to stare at them. Some of them wanted to know what the matter was. In the end, Sajni burst into tears. Even after she had rushed out, weeping, Jezebel was hopping mad.

That was when, tapping her on the shoulder from behind with a 'Relax, Dr Jezebel, come let's have a cup of coffee', Dr Haritha Sadanand walked into her life. She was a senior resident in the department of gynaecology. At her appeal, 'Don't get so hot under the collar, it's scary to watch!', Jezebel cooled down. She sensed affection in Haritha's touch. They had coffee together. They discussed this and that. Then they exchanged personal grievances. Haritha said, 'Everyone has problems. Take my case. My husband and I are both doctors. My parents are doctors. Everyone in my husband's family is a doctor. We have everything. But would you be able to understand if I told you about the suffocation I experience in my family? My mother-in-law is the one who decides everything. I was not too fond of gynaecology. But who can I tell that to? My mother-in-law told me to specialize in gynaecology because they have a hospital, and they need someone to work there. I have no wish to work there. Even my salary will be written-off by them. With that, I'll lose all my freedom. Sadanand is a *paavam*, a harmless guy. It's his mother and elder brother who decide everything.'

Jezebel told Haritha that her mother-in-law was a *paavam* and a very loving person, and that it was her father-in-law who was the villain. She said that she lived in dread of him, that she feared that any moment he could pounce on her from anywhere and drag her away. She disclosed that she had even changed her mobile number for fear of him. 'Really!' exclaimed Haritha.

That evening, Haritha persuaded her to go along for some window-shopping. Having someone to talk to and somewhere to go gave Jezebel solace. When Ahana and Remitha called that night, Jezebel told them about Haritha. At first, she laughed, then whimpered, then burst into tears. Ahana and Remitha wept along with her. Jezebel tried to joke. They laughed between their tears. After a while, Ahana called again. 'Jezebel, you must see a psychiatrist,' she said and added, 'I think you need help.' Jezebel, too, had begun to think she did. She discussed it with Haritha, who agreed it was a good idea. From a number of psychiatrists, they chose Dr Prashant Narayanan.

Dr Prashant spoke as if he had been waiting to hear from Jezebel. He welcomed her with: 'Aren't you the one who scored more than me in the exam and broke my heart? Come, come, let me have my revenge!' He was a boyish thirty-five-year-old, with mischief in his eyes and a bright smile on his lips, always waiting for a chance to crack a joke. He knew everything about her, including the marks she had scored in each paper. They spoke about common friends, doctors they both knew and shared jokes about the Medical College. She laughed out loud after a long time. Then, after a moment of silence, when he spun the paperweight around on his table, Prashant got down to business.

'Now, tell me, Jezebel. I'm ready to listen.'

She recited the same old story she had repeated several times—a husband who had met with an accident, coma, husband's family, work, studies . . .

Prashant sighed. 'Jezebel, this story is good enough to tell others but not a psychiatrist. This story is only a "dressing". I want to examine the real wound.'

Jezebel's face drained of colour. 'Jerome's accident . . .' she began again. Prashant grew serious. 'What if I tell you, it was you who met with an accident? If you're not staying with your husband now, does it not mean that there had been an emotional distance between the two of you even earlier? That is what we need to address.'

Jezebel's throat constricted.

'The relationship was that much of a failure, *alle*?'

Jezebel looked down guiltily. Prashant looked at her with empathy.

'Jezebel, I know your husband since before. His friend Avinash is an acquaintance. They had been staying together for a while in my cousin's apartment. Rest assured that you escaped.'

Jezebel was at a loss. 'I don't know what to do, doctor . . .'

'Call me Prashant.'

'Sometimes I feel like dying, Prashant. Sometimes, I want to fight back. No one seems to understand me. No one believes me. I feel I'm all alone in the midst of a great crowd. It has been so long. No one is bothered about me.'

'You have acute depression, Jezebel. If you can manage without medication, that would be great. But if that's not possible, you must have medicines. You must sleep well. As far as possible, try not to be alone.'

He wrote out medicines, boosted her morale and saw her off. She found it interesting that he had prescribed medicines to increase serotonin.

As she stepped out after meeting Prashant, Haritha called. She told her, 'Haritha*echi*, it was such a relief when I spoke to him. I set down the burden from my heart. I've understood one thing. Every human being needs happiness. And it's your own body which produces that happiness. And when the body cannot produce it, there's no need to fear. There are chemicals to help your body artificially produce that happiness. Honestly, I'm so proud of modern medicine!'

'Yes!' agreed Haritha.

The next two days were those of good sleep. Jezebel tried to laugh. She tried to reclaim her life. But on the third day, as she was slipping into sleep after having had her medicines, the phone rang. The moment she picked it up mechanically, everything shattered to pieces.

'*Dee*, did you think I wouldn't find out if you changed your phone number? You ruined my son and now you're living it up, *alle*? Your mind isn't well, *alle*? You met a psychiatrist, *alle*? No matter where you go, there's no escape for you, *dee*. Wherever you go, I'll hunt you down. The true God watches over my son. He will be back on his feet. He will stand in front of you and make you account for everything. Will you be able to answer him then, *dee*?'

Jezebel sat up, jolted. Her hair stood on end. She sensed that she was falling into a deep abyss. The darkness terrified her. The swinging of the clock's pendulum in the silence of the night startled her. She shivered when the leaves of the mango tree rustled outside the window. She feared that either George Jerome or Jerome George was standing behind the green almirah. Fear left her breathless. Panic-stricken, she called Ahana. She called Remitha. Ahana was on duty. She consoled Jezebel—told her to switch off the phone. Jezebel got up and knocked on Ammachi's door. Ammachi scolded her. Hearing the noise, Chachan came up. She fell into Chachan's arms, weeping. Chachan held her silently.

The next day, Dr Haritha was waiting for her at the parking lot of the Children's Hospital, with a parcel of snacks. 'Yesterday was my daughter's third birthday—made all these at home,' she said warmly. When she saw Haritha, Jezebel broke down. Wailing, she told Haritha about George Jerome Marakkaran's call. Haritha held her close. She consoled Jezebel saying he must be reeling from the shock of seeing his son bedridden. She insisted Jezebel come along for a matinee show. As she sat in the air-conditioned cinema hall, Jezebel felt sleepy. Leaning on Haritha's shoulder, she slept deeply. But that night too, George Jerome Marakkaran called. 'You went for a movie, *alle dee*? You left my son to die and are enjoying a movie, *alle*? I'll show you. Let my son get up.'

A baffled Jezebel called Haritha and wept, saying, 'Haritha*echi*, I'm going to change my number.' Haritha reminded her that even if she did, it wouldn't take much for him to find that out as well. And then she wondered how he was able to trace every move of Jezebel's. 'He's stalking you, Jezebel,' she said, bewildered. That night too, Jezebel lost sleep. She called Prashant, who tried to give her courage.

Although George Jerome Marakkaran did not call for the next several days, Jezebel came to expect it all the time. One day, Haritha insisted on taking her to a beauty parlour where Jezebel got herself waxed and was given a massage. When Jezebel got emotional, saying 'What would I have done without you, Haritha*echi*?', Haritha soothed her with an 'I'm there with you.' That night,

George Jerome Marakkaran called. 'What are you plucking hair off your armpits and thighs for, *dee*? To show whom?' That night too, Jezebel lost sleep.

The next day, the police arrived at the Medical College. They seized drugs from her scooter box.

'How many cases are there against you, doctor*ey*?' asked the lawyer, raising his voice to ensure that everyone in the court heard him. 'Illicit relations, kidnapping, attempt to murder husband, substance abuse. Is that all or have I missed out something?'

A few laughed out loud. Jezebel stood silent.

'So could you explain to the court how you managed to wriggle out of the drugs case?'

Jezebel wanted to say: 'On some days, we seek death but will not find it; we wish to die but death flees from us.' The day the headline 'Narcotic Drugs Seized from Lady Doctor's Scooter' flashed all over the news, she had truly wanted to die.

At that time, she was in the labour room, in order to assist Dr Irshad Mohammad at Dr Kurien P. George's behest. Nurse Sumitha came up to her and told her that Dr Haritha had called her. Jezebel opened the glass door of the labour room and peeped out. Dr Haritha had come to borrow Jezebel's scooter. Jezebel went back to the room and took out her key. 'Where are you off to, Jezebel?' asked a surprised Dr Irshad. She assured him she wasn't going anywhere.

It was a complicated case before them. The patient was a twenty-two-year-old who was bleeding after she had been kicked by her husband. Even in that unconscious state, her face was full of shock. The surgery took a long time. The body that the surgeon lifted out was that of a baby girl. She had died in her mother's womb. Her hands drooped listlessly on either side. Her legs were stretched out. Her little mouth was half open, as if in mid cry. Jezebel checked the infant's heartbeat. She tried to resuscitate the infant with bag-valve-mask ventilation. The little body lay like a wet cloth-puppet between Jezebel's gloved fingers.

The nurses were whispering to each other that the young woman had been assaulted for two sovereigns of gold remaining to be given as dowry. Jezebel cleaned up the little body and looked at her face. Her eyes, full of dark eyelashes, were scrunched shut as if frightened. Jezebel tried not to look at her. As she was telling Irshad how to write a report, the attender rushed in saying the police had come and that she was wanted in Kurien sir's room.

Later, when she thought about it, Jezebel could not recall how she had managed to reach Kurien sir's room. Had it been in an autorickshaw? Or had she walked? Under the framed picture of the Hippocratic Oath sat Kurien sir, his face filled with anxiety. In front of him sat a trim, clean-shaven, dark-complexioned sub-inspector. Next to him stood a pot-bellied policeman betraying signs of cholesterol, hands clasped behind his back. She could not recall what happened afterwards. Kurien sir must have asked her where her scooter was. She could not even remember what she asked Dr Haritha. But her reply, and the fake annoyance in her voice when she replied, rang in her ears from time to time. 'Are you mad, *kochey*? Why would I need your scooter? I come in my car, *alle*? Even otherwise I don't know how to ride a scooter.'

The sub-inspector announced that they had seized one-and-a-half kilos of cannabis from her scooter. 'Ganja! From my scooter!' exclaimed Jezebel. Darkness swayed about her eyes. 'Where do you keep the key?' asked the sub-inspector. Jezebel handed over her purse. There was no key in there. 'Do you have any other bag?' asked the sub-inspector. She went to the duty room. The sub-inspector and Kurien sir went along with her. Her bag was on the table. And it had the key too. But Kurien sir affirmed that Jezebel had not been there since morning. The sub-inspector grew pensive.

'The doctor you say you gave your key to says she did not take it. Is there anyone who was around when the key was given?'

Jezebel remembered that Sister Sumitha had been around. Kurien sir called for Sumitha. Sumitha confirmed that Haritha madam had asked for Jezebel madam. But she hadn't seen any key being handed over. The sub-inspector went on to grill her, 'Is there any witness to the key being handed? Did you lie that you keep your key in the purse? Don't you ever keep it in your bag? The doctor you mentioned, why would she ask for your key? Have you given her your key before? Does she come by car or scooter to the hospital? When a doctor who has a car asked you for the scooter key, didn't you ask her why? If someone asked you for a key, would you give it to them even without asking them why?' The sub-inspector's voice grew gruffer. Jezebel felt more and more depleted.

'You may ask my colleagues to find out what kind of person I am,' she said, with a catch in her throat.

The sub-inspector scoffed. 'We've done all that. We know you're a clever doctor too. But you also abandoned your husband who's in a coma, *alle*? Does that not mean that you are a woman who has the strength of mind to do anything? Sorry, doctor, if you don't have evidence to support what you're saying, we may have to arrest you. There's one-and-a-half kilograms of ganja in there. It's a non-bailable offence.'

Jezebel could feel the darkness storm into her eyes. The flow of blood to the brain was being broken. She panicked. Reflex syncope. The body's little trick to face any terrifying situation. She felt such self-loathing. Could the earth not break open and swallow her up so that she did not have to descend the steps of the Medical College, handcuffed, then ascend the steps of the police station and stand holding on to the bars of the lockup?

Kurien sir seemed even more shaken than she was. He summoned everyone who had been in the labour room, one after another. No one had seen anything. Finally, it was Dr Irshad Mohammad's turn. Irshad said he had seen Dr Haritha taking the scooter key. The sub-inspector subjected him to a sharp, thorough interrogation. As all eyes turned to him, Irshad turned red with unease. But he stood his ground: 'I saw it. I saw Sister Sumitha coming, I saw Jezebel sticking her head out of the baby room, and I saw Haritha madam standing there. Jezebel came in and took her key. When I asked her where she was off to, she said she wasn't going anywhere. Jezebel did not go anywhere. She was trying to save that baby.' Irshad's voice was firm.

The sub-inspector turned to Jezebel. 'So, this isn't a simple case. Looks like you have bitter enemies, doctor,' he said. She did not have the energy to respond to him at that moment. The sub-inspector left saying he would come back again if necessary. She stood ashamed in front of Kurien sir and her colleagues.

The news of drugs being seized from the scooter of a doctor in the Medical College (without her name being revealed) was splashed across television channel debates and the next morning's newspaper. But who that doctor was, became the talk of the town, at least in the Medical College. That day, Jezebel was scared to step out. She switched off her phone, shut the door and sat in the darkness. Daylight peeped in through the cracks of the door. She despised light. Despised every crack through which the light entered. She shut her eyes tight and fortified the darkness around her. Memories swirled in front of her eyes. She saw her childhood and youth in them. She saw the paths she had walked. Heard her own peals of laughter. Heard Dr Haritha's berating. She recalled with a pang the movies they had seen, the meals they had shared, the paths they had taken together. 'Why did my soul sister, the one I had trusted, the one I broke bread with, raise her heel against me?' she grieved. 'Why did George Jerome Marakkaran cast a net and dig a pit to trap me in for no reason? Even otherwise, how do we know why people strike each other on the heel? Perhaps their souls are gratified when they see another person bemoaning his sudden ruin. Perhaps the prophets, self-aggrandizing by subjecting their own people to severe hardships, fulfil their mission through them.'

But it was not easy to cross that stage of trial. She trembled, imagining that Chachan sprung upon her and stabbed her when she opened the door in the morning; that Ammachi served her black coffee laced with poison. She saw the police take out an infant's dead body and a woman's head from the scooter box. She saw Abel call out to her fondly and then push her off the third floor. She broke into a sweat seeing Ahana share nude pictures of her on YouTube. Her body burnt like tar, emitting an acrid black smoke. Afterwards, she heard a voice from heaven: 'Write this down. Blessed are those who die in the Lord.'

She decided to overdose on one of the medicines Prashant had prescribed, and thus, solve her problems once and for all. She bought medicines from three different medical shops. As she stood at the fourth medical store, Kurien sir happened to pass by. Asking her 'What are you doing here?', he took the prescription from her hand and took a look. 'Is this what you have been having?' He admonished her. 'Come to my room right now,' he ordered. As she entered his room, Jezebel felt that she had already died. She sat in front of him, unemotional, like a wilted sapling. As he looked at her, Kurien sir's face filled with anger and then sadness. 'I have prepared a timetable for you. This will be your new schedule today onwards.'

Wiping the tears that streamed down her face, Jezebel tried to read the sheet of paper he had handed her. She had to reach at eight in the morning. Then discuss the day's topics with PG students. After that, accompany them on their rounds. And then the main rounds with the Head of department. As she read the next item in the timetable, she looked up at Kurien sir, baffled. Kurien sir took off his glasses, wiped them, wore them again and leaned back in his chair. 'I'm entrusting you with the undergraduate class I teach.' He looked at her fondly. '*Moley*, you have a long way to go. People will tread on your toes, stab you from behind, but you take care that you don't fall.' Jezebel found herself whimpering.

She somehow managed to reach home where she shut herself in her room, and sobbed her heart out. With the sounds of her own sobs ringing in her years, she drifted off to sleep. The next day, as she sat in the duty room going through the notes for her first class, she could still hear the sobbing. But when she realized that it was a child crying, she got up and went out. It was a one-and-a-half-year-old boy of a young couple. The boy lay on his churidar-clad mother's shoulder, squirming and wriggling and tugging at his forehead. Jezebel could make out from the sound of his crying that something was stuck in his nose. The mother told her that he had been crying all night. She examined the child. When she said it was likely that something was stuck in the child's nostrils, the parents argued that that was not possible. She called her classmate Lal Mohan who was an ENT. She went along with them—she had to convince herself that her diagnosis was correct. Lal Mohan examined the child. She held the child's head along with the mother so that he kept still. As he squirmed and wriggled and as they tried to pin him down, the child came into her arms. Lal Mohan removed a small stone smeared with blood and pus from the child's nostril. The child stopped crying at once, looked at the stone and then touched his own nose. Then with eyes full of tears, nose full of pus, he smiled shyly. Seeing this, his father smiled in relief and the mother, through her tears. Jezebel realized that she too was smiling. She wiped the child's face, slung her stethoscope around his neck, and made him laugh.

She was still smiling after she had seen them off and proceeded to her class. When she stood in front of the students, she was still smiling. Kurien sir sat in the last row at the back of the class. 'There is a major difference between a paediatrician and other doctors. Other doctors aim at sitting birds. But we paediatricians aim at flying birds. Children are like flying birds. Depending on the age, the criteria for diagnoses change. For a paediatrician, more than money, a child's smile is the greater reward. A paediatrician's job is complete only when you see the child off with a smile.' When she started her lecture thus, she had in her mind the face of the child she saw that morning. She remembered the soft petal-like touch of his body and his baby smell. She remembered every little face she had seen. She felt an urge to call them all back and shower them with love and affection.

The class was a grand success. After the class the students mobbed her. As she spent time with them clearing their doubts, sharing experiences, she could feel the great burden in her heart begin to thaw. Back at the department, she asked Kurien sir how the class had been. 'Oh, it was a colossal bore!' he replied with mock anger. 'So I've decided to assign you two more classes.' She laughed once again, her sorrows forgotten. Later, standing in the courtroom, when she recalled how little it took to make her laugh, she felt like laughing again.

'You are laughing when I ask you about the ganja seized from your bag! Aren't you something, doctor*ey*!' The lawyer's face hardened. The judge's face hardened even more.

Jezebel did not wish to tell them that on the day of great slaughter, when the towers fall, streams of water would flow on every high mountain and every lofty hill. Even if she had, they would not have understood. In every story, some characters are never revealed. The moment they are revealed there begins another story, does it not?

As she stepped out after taking leave of Kurien sir, she saw Sebin waiting for her. His face looked even more ashen; he had bloated even more. 'So much has happened, Jezebel! Could you not have called me?' he complained. 'Oh, why bother you as well with all this,' she sighed.

'When problems like these crop up, it's people like me who know how to tackle them.' He was upset that the news splashing all over the newspapers could have been avoided if he had been informed as soon as the police arrived. He asked her not to worry about the case. He also said that the person who had committed the crime would own up to it in court. He said that it was drug trafficker Ganja Suresh who had done it and that someone from outside had made him do it. That person had sent across the ganja and paid ten-thousand rupees to place it in Jezebel's scooter box and inform the police. When Sebin said 'It could be your father-in-law,' Jezebel saw stars. She knew that George Jerome Marakkaran was capable of talking harshly, but she had not expected him to act in cold blood. 'Just say the word, I'll take care of it,' Sebin consoled her. 'You went to such trouble on my account,' she said, getting emotional. Sebin looked at her with adoration. 'At least I could do this much, Jezebel*ey*,' he whispered. And Jezebel found herself weeping once again.

Sebin kept his word. Ganja Suresh admitted to his crime. The next day's newspapers announced: 'Police Nab Culprit Who Hid Ganja in Doctor's Scooter.' Jezebel came clean in the drugs case. And yet, she would find out why Haritha had betrayed her only much later.

When junior resident Geethu came rushing up to her, saying, 'Please come fast, *chechi*. The gynaecology senior resident's child is not stirring,' Jezebel put down the book she was reading and rushed over. The moment she saw the three-year-old—her body blue and stiff, her eyeballs protruding—Jezebel knew that it was a case of poisoning. She could even tell what the poison was. It was when she asked where the child's mother was that she noticed the woman, her face puffed up with weeping. They were meeting for the first time after the drugs case. Dr Haritha Sadanand's face went pale. 'Call Kurien sir,' she screamed at Geethu. 'This woman needn't look at my child. I don't trust her.' Jezebel paid her no heed. 'Did the child consume poison?' she asked. 'This is a cardiac problem. Call Kurien sir!' Haritha shrieked. But Jezebel ignored her. The nurses and junior residents stood around, taken aback. Weeping, Haritha ran towards Dr Kurien's room. Jezebel removed the child's clothes. Washed her body. Administered an Atropine injection. The child opened her eyes in a couple of minutes. By the time Haritha arrived with Dr Kurien in tow, the child was sitting up on the bed. Haritha was taken aback. Hearing Dr Kurien chide her, 'Didn't I tell you that if Jezebel is there, there is no need for me to come?', Jezebel's dimples unfurled despite herself. As Haritha gathered the child in her arms, Jezebel returned to her room and picked up her book again.

The next day, after the rounds, as Jezebel stood talking to a young nineteen-year-old mother who was worried about the symptoms of jaundice in her child, Haritha came looking for her. Her face was wan from crying non-stop. As Jezebel took leave of the nineteen-year-old, Haritha came up to her and clasped her hand. Her eyes streamed. An old wound opened afresh in Jezebel's heart. It throbbed with growing intensity.

'What I did was a grave mistake. But trust me, it was done with the best of intentions . . .' Haritha's voice faltered.

Haritha told her that Jerome and her husband Sadanand were gym mates, that she had inquired after Jerome at Sadanand's behest and got acquainted with George Jerome Marakkaran. George Jerome Marakkaran's tears moved Haritha greatly. What a father! Haritha took to calling him frequently. One day when she called, George Jerome Marakkaran was sitting in the ambulance. 'I am going home with my son, *moley*. You know, my daughter-in-law isn't coming along with us. In this old age my wife and I are taking home this living corpse that my son has become. As long as we can, we will take care of him. When we can't, the three of us will take some poison and . . .' When he broke down, Haritha felt close to tears herself. From that day onwards she nursed a growing hatred towards Jezebel. No matter how vile the husband may be, was it right for a wife to abandon him? Was an MD degree more important than a husband? She called George Jerome Marakkaran from time to time to inquire about Jerome's health. When George

Jerome Marakkaran told her that his son was getting better, her hatred for Jezebel grew twofold. Once when she called, he told her that Jezebel was preparing to remarry, that he had enough proof that she had a secret lover, and requested Haritha to befriend her in order to follow her movements. Haritha, too, wanted to teach that woman—who had deserted her husband after his accident and gone in search of her own happiness—a lesson. From that day onwards, she befriended Jezebel and kept George Jerome Marakkaran informed about her. She did not demur even when George Jerome Marakkaran called her one day and told her, 'A chap will come to see you. Get Jezebel's scooter key and give it to him. You won't get into any trouble, doctor. But I do want to teach her a lesson.' But she hadn't known that it was in order to plant drugs. It was only when the police came inquiring that she understood the gravity of the situation. Haritha's husband called up George Jerome Marakkaran and threatened him with dire consequences in case anything happened to his wife. She hadn't called George Jerome Marakkaran or taken his calls ever since. 'But I received my just deserts. And today it had to be you who saved my child, Jezebel!'

Later, Jezebel tried not to remember how shaken she had been hearing that story. That day, her heart dried up. That Dr Haritha despised Jezebel, not for anything she had done to her but for what she thought Jezebel had done to her husband, shattered her. Society had clearly determined how a wife ought to serve her husband. And it would not allow even an inch of compromise. But who cared for the suffocation a wife underwent in her marriage?

'I betrayed your trust, Jezebel. But all I wanted was to ensure that you would go back to Jerome at the earliest. When I spoke to Jerome's daddy, I felt miserable. Isn't he growing old? Isn't it your duty to take care of your husband, Jezebel?'

'That's the question I've been asking myself all these months. Do I have a duty to take care of that man? Was he a good husband to me? Did he give me all that I wanted? Was his criminal act pardonable? What place do duty and obligation have in a relationship that is already broken? Is a relationship in the mind? Or is it on paper?'

Jezebel's voice was soft but sharp. Haritha was somewhat startled—she could not bring herself to think so deeply. She was the kind of person for whom thinking was hard work. Thinking exhausted her; so, she was careful not to question herself too much. Instead, she had learnt to answer others' questions just the way they wanted. She was convinced that those were the right answers as well.

'All said and done, there is something called society, *alle* Jezebel? Is it even possible to live without respecting it?'

Jezebel did not feel angry. She did not feel sad. Instead, she felt light. 'Thank you for everything,' she said. 'I came along with you for coffee and shopping and movies because I really thought you were fond of me. I can't bear to think that you took me around despite not liking me. I can't forgive myself either, for loving you like a sister.' She looked her squarely in the eye. 'Please, go! It was not because she was your child that I treated her. It is my job to treat patients. All patients are the same to me. So, there is no need to thank me.'

Later she tried to read the Jezebel of that day as if from a book. She tried to measure the exhaustion and the injustice she experienced that day. There are those who do not get to know or to take the path of light, but oppose it instead. The murderer wakes up before it is light to kill the poor and the defenceless. Who knows what is good for a woman in this brief life that flits by like a shadow? Who would be able to tell her what would happen under the sun after her?

Later, Jezebel-the-rabbi asked Jezebel her disciple, 'To what shall I compare society?'

The rabbi herself answered: 'It is like leaven that a woman took and hid in three measures of flour, until it was all leavened.'

16

Afterwards, Jezebel-the-rabbi went to the tax collector 'Shark' Sebin's house for a feast. There was a great company of tax collectors and others that sat down with them. The lawmakers and Pharisees asked, 'Why do you eat and drink with tax collectors and sinners?' And Jezebel said unto them, 'It is not those that are whole but they who are sick who need a physician.'

But that day she was terrified. At that stage, it was by terrifying her that Satan tested her. All sorts of fears surrounded her like a pack of wolves. She tried to imagine all the possible ways in which George Jerome Marakkaran could attack her next. If the phone rang suddenly, if someone from among the patients stepped forward abruptly, if a car or lorry trailed her while she rode the scooter—she dreaded it was him. She realized that when faced with fear—the fear of what could happen—there was no body, no desire, no appetite, no taste, no sleep even.

'The police were amazed at how the contract goondas came forward to own up to the crime on your behalf, *ketto*!' The lawyer scoffed. Jezebel felt her temper rise.

'It was Jerome's Daddy who arranged for those goondas . . .' she said.

The lawyer laughed as if he had heard a joke. 'Ha, that's a new story! Listen, answer to the point, *ketto*.'

'The police were convinced that this was a deliberate ploy to frame me.' Jezebel stood her ground.

The lawyer grew angry. 'There was no evidence against you. Say that!'

'There was no evidence because I hadn't done it.'

'Doctor*ey*, instead of MBBS, you could have joined LLB. How convenient it would have been. You would have had cases every day. Your own cases are so many. Hats off to you! Such thick skin at such a young age. Anyone else would have gone to pieces long ago.'

She wanted to say that there were riches stashed away in the homes of lawmakers. But she realized that there was no point in saying it.

'I say that you had close connections with the ganja mafia. You had financial transactions with many of them. You moved closely with the notorious goonda Shark Sebin. You used his services for several hit jobs. You, along with Sandeep Mohan, paid Shark Sebin to cause Jerome's accident. I'll tell you exactly how much. Twenty-five thousand rupees! There is evidence, and there are witnesses, to show that the amount was withdrawn from Sandeep's account and handed over to Shark Sebin. Want to see?'

The lawyer finished his little speech in one breath and looked at Jezebel challengingly. She did not know whether to laugh or to cry.

She wanted to describe how Dr Sandeep Mohan landed up in front of her one day as she was leaving the classroom. He had lost a lot of weight; there were dark circles under his eyes. As he stood in front of her in an ill-fitting shirt and the doctor's coat sagging from his shoulder, she found it hard to believe that it was indeed him.

'This is a summer of mist and rain, is it not? Oh! How hot it is, how hot!'

She ignored his sheepish remark and looked at him intently.

He went on talking non-stop as if he did not expect her to reply. 'This must be what they call climate change. See, is this anything like the old monsoon, summer or winter? The rain pelts down as if a pot has been emptied. Jez, were the rains of our childhood like this? How cool it was when it rained back then, no? Such peace in the earth and the air. And now, neither the rain nor the water has any moisture. Like the throat isn't slaked even after you have gulped so much water, *alle?*'

Irritated, Jezebel walked on, saying, 'I'm busy,' to which he replied, 'I'm not busy. Finished the morning's O.P quickly. Not many issues in the ward either. It's such a lovely day. Shall we go have something in the Coffee House?' He walked along, not waiting for a reply. And then he told her, 'Jez. I've got a job in a super-speciality hospital in Dubai. Decent salary. I think it will be good to get out of here.'

When she heard this, something tugged at Jezebel's heart. 'That's nice,' she said, forcing a smile. 'Earn a lot of money; become a rich man. I'm happy for you!' She felt close to tears. Her heart told her that he was a wicked man and that he came looking for her from time to time just to remind her that she was all alone in life.

'Jez, forgive me. I wasn't able to be with you or help at a time of crisis in your life.' When Sandeep said this, she prayed that her eyes would not well up.

'I kept away against my own will, Jez . . . There were so many problems . . . I did not want to upset you too with them.'

'It's all right. I am not upset with you. Because now I know well that you are nobody to me.' She held her head high and walked on fast without noticing where she was headed. 'I have no love for anybody now,' she said. 'Not even for myself. I will not trust anyone hereafter. No one deserves it either.' Sandeep Mohan was struggling to catch up with her. It was after sometime that she realized that she was headed in the same direction as him. She

stopped in her tracks. 'Please carry on. I have work to do,' she said
firmly. That was when Sebin came rushing up to her.

'Jezebel*ey*, I was looking for you everywhere. There was no
balance in my phone so I couldn't even call you . . .'

When she saw Sebin, all her anger vanished. Perhaps because
he had walked fast, he was bathed in sweat. There was a big dark
circle of perspiration on his red shirt.

'I need some twenty-five thousand rupees, Jezebel*ey*. A loan
will do. I'll return it later.'

Fumbling because she did not have that much money, Jezebel
began to remove the single gold bangle on her wrist. Sandeep
Mohan intervened, 'Is it okay if I give the money?' The rivulets
of sweat on Sebin's forehead announced loud and clear that he
was in urgent need of the money. 'I have the money, Jez,' Sandeep
Mohan insisted. Sebin was looking at her with great hope. She
did not have the heart to disappoint him. She agreed to accept
the money from Sandeep. As Sandeep left to withdraw it from
the nearest ATM, Sebin told her that his sister's marriage had
been fixed and there was a shortfall of twenty-five thousand rupees
in the money they had promised the groom before the betrothal.
'Dowry was banned some twenty-five years before we were even
born, *eda* Sebin*ey*,' Jezebel told him. '*Iyo*, but no one around here
has come to know about it yet, *ketto*' he joked in return. They
looked at each other and laughed like they had as children. As she
stood in court, Jezebel regretted that she lacked the gift of the gab
to describe to the lawyer the warmth in Sebin's laughter that day
as he stood wiping his sweating forehead.

That was the day he had told her, 'I may not be able to return
the money, Jezebel, but I can make it up to you in another way.'

'Do something: just marry me. Then you may keep this as my
dowry,' she quipped, and laughed when he blushed.

Just then, the hospital attendant Murali happened to pass by.
He greeted her deferentially. and asked Sebin, 'What's up, *da*?'

Sebin moved a little away with him and got chatting. Murali was an acquaintance of Abraham Chammanatt's. By then, Sandeep Mohan arrived with the money. Later Jezebel realized it was through Murali that Abraham and George Jerome Marakkaran got to know that Sandeep had handed the cash to Jezebel who handed it over to Sebin. 'I will return it as soon as I can,' Jezebel repeatedly told Sandeep. 'No rush,' Sandeep reassured her. Both of them walked silently up to the rain tree in the courtyard. Without bidding him farewell, Jezebel got on to her scooter and went home.

'You had given Shark Sebin the money on 16 November. And you sent Jerome George Marakkaran a divorce notice on 19 November. Come to think of it, wasn't there a connection between these two incidents?' The lawyer inquired as if waiting to hear a great secret. When she thought about the connection between those two days, she felt like laughing. But she lacked the gift of the gab to explain the reason behind that laughter to the lawyer and the others in the court. In any case, the good Lord had not blessed them with the ability to understand the developments of that evening, when she went home after meeting Sebin and Sandeep.

When she saw the gate wide open, it was clear that they had guests at home. In the courtyard, Koshy Uncle's black Qualis glinted in the twilight that hesitantly peeped in after the rain. Then she realized that the white Ford parked next to it was Abraham Chammanatt's. As she parked the scooter, she could hear loud male voices inside the house. Her feet itched to turn and run away. As she entered, she could hear Abraham Chammanatt's faltering voice, 'We need to take a decision on this.'

Seeing her, an uneasy silence welled up in that room. '*Kochey*, come, sit. We need to talk,' said Abraham Chammanatt, taking off his glasses and holding them in his hand. Next to him sat his wife Gracy Aunty with an expression of seriousness, the end of her sari pulled over her head as if she were about to partake of the holy communion. Koshy Uncle sat staring on the floor; Chachan sat at his writing desk, propping his head on his hands. Ammachi stood in the doorway, one arm akimbo.

Although her first impulse was to run away, Jezebel remembered that if she ran now, then she would have to keep running all her life. So, she went in, sat down next to Koshy Uncle and asked him, 'When did you come, Uncle?'

'Before noon,' he replied somewhat coldly.

'*Kochey*, Jezebel*ey*, what shall we do about this?' began Abraham. Jezebel's heart beat faster.

'Georgekutty has been giving me a hard time for the past few days. We Catholics have some beliefs and norms we need to follow, don't we? How can we live in society if we don't follow them? *Kochey*, you are a doctor, aren't you? You don't need to be told all this, do you? I would never force anybody to do anything. But we do need to take some decisions. Georgekutty wants the car to be handed over to them . . .'

Jezebel felt ashamed at the way her heart beat thrice as fast the moment she heard that name.

'Don't they have another car over there?' she asked calmly.

'But wasn't this car bought by Jerome?'

'Jerome may have bought it, but the loan is in my name. And I'm the one repaying it.'

The room fell silent. A minute later, Gracy Aunty cleared her throat. 'So, keep the car. But then you must go there and take care of Jerome.'

'I'll take care of Jerome if he is brought back here. I'll bear the expenses of bringing him over too. But that man must not come here. I don't want to see his face.' Her voice quivered.

'Jerome is Georgekutty's life and soul. He won't be able to live without him,' said Abraham Chammanatt.

'My parents won't be able to live without me either,' said Jezebel.

Gracy Aunty got angry. 'What kind of talk is this, *kochey*? Girls are meant for others. The husband's place is where they ought to stay.'

She lacked the gift of the gab to describe to the lawyer the utter orphanhood she experienced that evening when she looked at Chachan, Ammachi and Koshy Uncle for help, and not one of them said that girls were not meant for others.

'So then arrange to send the car to Georgekutty,' Gracy Aunty insisted. Jezebel, too, grew obstinate: 'If the loan too can be transferred to Jerome's daddy, then I will send the car over.' Silence filled the room. 'As long as you are legally his wife, isn't it your obligation to pay off his loan, *kochey*?' Gracy aunty raised her voice.

Neither Chachan nor Ammachi nor Koshy Uncle said a word. They kept quiet as if it was Jezebel's battle to fight. In fact, it was Jezebel's battle alone. And continuing to wage it was her job. That was when the tap-tap of a walking stick could be heard from inside, and Jezebel leapt to her feet crying, 'Valiyammachi!'

Dressed in a white nightie with blue embroidery and wielding a walking stick with brass hoops, Valiyammachi made her way into the room, past Ammachi who moved to one side, sulking. Abraham Chammanatt and Gracy Aunty rose to greet her. Jezebel went up to Valiyammachi who held her hand and sat down in the chair next to Koshy Uncle with difficulty. Even after she sat down, Valiyammachi kept holding Jezebel's hand. 'Oh, you were here, were you, Ammachi?' said Gracy Aunty by way of exchanging pleasantries.

'I came along with him. I was lying down. Felt tired,' said Valiyammachi. 'What's the big argument here?' She said, getting to the point. Abraham Chammanatt explained that it was about the car.

'Jezebel is still Jerome's wife. So, isn't it her duty to pay off the loan in his name?' Gracy Aunty began confidently.

'That's right.' Valiyammachi, without leaving Jezebel's hand, twirled her walking stick, and turned to look at Jezebel. 'In that case, just call off this relationship, *moley*. Why do you need a husband just so you can pay off his loan?'

For a moment, it was as if there had been a great explosion of silence, Jezebel would recall later. Everything shattered to pieces. Chachan sat up straight. Abraham Chammanatt shifted uneasily in his seat. Gracy Aunty's face turned pale; Ammachi's wilted.

'Abraham*ey*, if she pays off the bank loan, do you think the bank manager will come and take care of her needs? She needs a husband for that, not a bank manager, doesn't she? Your boy met with an accident. If you can't take care of him, bring him over here. We will all take care of him. Otherwise, you take care of him. That's your choice. But if you insist that our child take care of him, and that she throw away her education and throw away her job to go elsewhere and suffer someone's curses and abuse, I say you try that elsewhere.'

At that moment, Jezebel knew that her eyes were overflowing with tears. But she did not have the strength to lift her hand and wipe them. Valiyammachi was still holding her hand tight.

'Our faith . . .' began Abraham, but Valiyammachi cut in before he could complete. 'Our faith is in the Lord, not in men. The Lord will never give anyone the power to ruin a girl's life. That too, a girl as smart as this one.' Valiyammachi turned to look at Koshy Uncle. 'You've been sitting there all this while with your mouth open . . . she is your sister's child. Why don't you use that tongue of yours and say that you will not allow her life to be ruined?' Then Valiyammachi turned to face Chachan. 'John *saarey*, won't you learn to speak up when you need to speak up at least now? Sara has no brains. She is stark raving mad. Instead of trying to change her, don't you encourage her.'

Valiyammachi had finished saying all that she had wanted to. So she got up and told Jezebel, 'You had better come inside

and eat something, *kochey*,' and led her in. Until they went in
and sat on her cot, Valiyammachi did not look at her face. She
sat down on the cot with some difficulty and made Jezebel sit
down next to her—then wiped her tears. 'What are you crying
about, *kochey*,' she said softly. 'Why these tears for someone who
couldn't make you love him while he was in good health? Don't
you have anything better to do? Will your tears bring him back?
And even if he does, will you be able to take him back with
love?' Jezebel lacked the gift of the gab to describe in court how
she lay sobbing on Valiyammachi's shoulder that day, feeling
her kind heart beat like a great rippling lake inside her pale
shrunken body.

That night, she cuddled up to Valiyammachi like she had as
a child. 'I have lived with two men,' sighed Valiyammachi. 'After
a while, I felt there was only one point of difference between the
two. The second one had a little less brain. So when he lied, it
was easier for me to make it out.' Jezebel wanted to laugh. But she
realized that it was not meant to be laughed at.

'You haven't slept with him even once, *alleyo*?' A wave of great
grief lashed Valiyammachi's voice. Jezebel lay numb. She wanted
to ask, 'How do you know, Valiyammachi?' But she could not find
her voice. 'Don't I know from the look in the eyes of a woman who
has known a man intimately, *kochey*? It's been some seventy years
since your Valiyammachi was born, *alleyo*?' Valiyammachi scoffed.
Then she darted questions at no one in particular: 'Has he ever
shared a joke with you? Touched you? Kissed you? Has he ever
seen you without your clothes at least once?'

Jezebel did not reply; she lay sobbing. Jerome George
Marakkaran seemed to be there in that room still, sitting on that
very cot. It seemed that the room was filling with the odour of
formalin. The rustle of his starched, pressed polyester shirt pierced
her ears. Valiyammachi gave her a sharp nudge. 'Shame on you!
She throws away two-and-a-half years of her life and lies here

whining! Are you even my blood, *dee*? Oh, this blood must be that
faint-hearted John *saar*'s. Your father may have many virtues, but
lacks one important quality—the spine to speak his own mind!'
And then Valiyammachi pulled her close to her again.

'Don't cry, *kochey*. People will say all sorts of things. If you
don't have a husband, they will ask you to chant the name of God,
rein in your tongue and rein in your desires till the end of your
days. It's easiest for people to sit in judgement on others' affairs.
And then they'll go their own way. Not their problem. If you try
to abide by all that, what you'll lose is your life and your happiness.
You don't have to let all these bother you. We'll cross the bridge
when we come to it. There is only one life *kochey*. Do whatever
needs to be done now, and quickly.'

When Jezebel began 'But Ammachi . . .', Valiyammachi
turned furious. 'Tell Sara to mind her own business. If she dares to
say even a word against you, I'll show her.'

It was the following day that, on Valiyammachi's insistence, and
with the help of a friend, Chachan booked an appointment with
Advocate Philip Mathews. She signed the legal notice. Chachan
explained the situation to the lawyer. The lawyer's face, which had
been waiting to hear her story with a soft and tender expression,
changed colour and hardened the moment he heard that Jerome
George Marakkaran was in his house. As he asked 'Who is there to
take care of Jerome? What's George Marakkaran's financial situation
like?' the lawyer's voice filled with anxiety. When the lawyer asked
'Aren't things difficult there without you?' Valiyammachi cut in,
'What kind of question is this? It's better if she is not there. Is
that not why they don't want to send him over here?' The lawyer
sheepishly explained, 'No, I asked because the court should not feel
that she came away deserting a bedridden husband.'

'What he needs now is not a wife but a home nurse,' retorted
Valiyammachi. 'And that's why we came to you now—to make the
court understand that.'

'No, Ammachi . . . since the wife is herself a doctor . . .' Jezebel closely observed the way the lawyer smiled sheepishly, making his lack of conviction apparent.

'It's because she's a doctor that you need to make the court understand that he needs a home nurse. She became a doctor funded by tax paid by ordinary people like us. Her job is to treat lakhs of patients. Not to sit by the bedside of one person twenty-four hours a day, changing the tube in his nose simply because she happens to be married to him. If you can't make the court understand that, then why do you strut about calling yourself a lawyer?'

Not wishing to argue with her, the lawyer dodged the question, joking, 'Luckily for the judges, you didn't become a lawyer, Valiyammachi!'

After that he did not ask any questions about Jerome. He asked Jezebel a few questions, pondered deeply and said hesitantly, 'One lie is enough to settle this case once and for all.'

'The case will be closed if you say that the marriage was not consummated. But then you're a doctor, aren't you? The court will never believe that a woman as educated as you are, stayed with a man for two years without any physical relationship with him.'

Jezebel started as if she had been slapped. She looked desperately at Valiyammachi who turned crimson and raised her voice, 'So many people who've tied the knot live that way, *alleyo*? I know so many people! They live together under the same roof as man and wife. But they do not so much as lift the finger to touch the other person. She will cook for him and serve him, wash his clothes, they'll even go to church and weddings together like a pair of lovebirds!'

Jezebel sat with her eyes downcast, pretending not to notice Valiyammachi looking at Chachan mockingly and Chachan's face draining of colour. She felt a pang of guilt. She regretted that she had done everything that an educated young woman ought not to have done. She anticipated that this would be the next sign in her life. Once again, she realized that half an hour of pain would completely erase all the pleasures of the past. Love never harmed anyone; so, she wished to prove to the court that the fulfilment of the law is an act of love. She regretted that she lacked the gift of the gab to do so.

'Still, doctor*ey*, you wanted a divorce barely six months after your husband fell into a coma! Are you really a woman?!' The lawyer had humiliated her that day. She did not respond.

She ought to have asked him what the word "really" meant. That was the kind of woman she wanted to see. They were all a delusion; their graven images were as empty as the wind.

Which woman, who when she has ten coins and loses one, would not light a lamp, sweep the house and search carefully until she finds it?

17

This was the prophecy her husband granted Jezebel through experience:

The husband said thus: 'I loved you. But you ask me, in what way did you love me? If I am the husband, where is the respect that is due to me? If I am the master, where is your fear of me? The husband who is the lord of Jezebel's wealth, wisdom and happiness said thus: I despise divorce. I despise the one who covers her garment with violence. Therefore, move carefully. Do not betray trust.'

Jezebel said angrily: 'It is futile to serve you. What is there to be gained by abiding by your orders and going about like mourners before the husband? From now on, I will consider the arrogant to be fortunate.'

Back then, the fact that everyone—not just her husband and his father—opposed the idea of divorce bewildered her; later, it would amuse her. They believed that it was a great sin for the fish trapped in the *meenkoodu* of marriage to break free. When they returned home after meeting the lawyer, Ammachi crossed swords with Valiyammachi. She declared that divorce was a great sin and that a thunderbolt would strike Valiyammachi. Valiyammachi retorted, 'If there is anything of that thunderbolt left after falling on your head, you who do not have a single loving word to utter to your husband, then let it fall on mine, *dee*!' When George Jerome Marakkaran called again and abused Jezebel, Valiyammachi took the phone from her and roared, 'Talking inappropriately to a girl who is young enough to be your daughter? I'll knock your teeth off!' After that Jezebel felt courage rise within her. She discovered that courage was a blanket and that it would keep out the cold at least for the time being. She believed that Valiyammachi was the blanket of her soul. 'Valiyammachi, please don't leave me,' she begged. Valiyammachi laughed 'Don't talk nonsense, *kunjey*, Valiyammachi is ready to leave any time. But even the Lord may not call me before your matter is settled.'

It was on the day her divorce notice was readied that her lawyer brought another man into her life. In 2004, in a similar case, the court had granted divorce to a Malayali journalist who worked in a city outside Kerala on the grounds of 'a mentally unsound partner.' His name was Balagopal. The lawyer gave her the name of the newspaper he was working for. She called him. He was reluctant to speak. When he asked, 'What is it that you want to speak to me about?', she stammered. 'Is your husband in a coma?' His voice had the intensity of a raw bleeding wound. 'Yes,' she replied. He inquired about Jerome's present condition. She wound up the conversation quickly, regretting having called him. An acute pain, like that of a woman in labour, besieged her. She despaired that she was a prisoner being punished for a crime she had not committed, that she had been imprisoned without the truth being found out, and that no one had bothered to find out who the real culprit was.

But two days later, Balagopal called her and asked, 'Are you free on Sunday? I'll be in town. Will it be possible to meet?' She waited for Sunday with a pounding heart. She realized shamefacedly that just the sight of a piece of paper with the word 'man' written on it was enough to set her heart pounding. She berated herself for it too. She asked herself, 'Who are you seeking each time? Who do you find?' She told herself indignantly that she had nothing to lose. She rued that her life had been trampled underfoot, defiled and made useless by all sorts of people, and that she had nothing with her now that she once held dear. And yet, as she waited for him, wandering the empty corridors of the Medical College on Sunday morning, she bemoaned that she hadn't been able to find even one man worthy of loving in this wide world.

As she sat alone in the duty room, leafing through a journal, he entered, knocking softly on the door. The first thing she noticed was his head full of straight greying hair. She liked its sheen. Then she saw his eyes. His was a fair face with great dark circles under his eyes. The face announced loud and clear that he was a loner. In spite of herself, her dimples unfurled as she smiled at him. He looked at her for a moment. Then a smile blossomed on his face as well. When he smiled, his face grew sadder. 'I need to go to the town. You can come along if you don't mind. We can talk in the car,' he invited her.

A six-year-old boy lay asleep in the back seat of his car. He got into the back seat and laid the child's head on his lap and asked her to sit in the front next to the driver's seat. During the ride, he asked her about her work and she asked him about his. After these questions and answers sprouted a great silence, which grew, swaying its boughs and spreading its shade over them, as the car sped—past the family court, then turning left, crossing fields and streams until it stopped in front of an old house near the old seminary.

It was a cool, pleasant day. Hearing the car, an elderly man in a lungi came out and took the sleeping child from Balagopal's lap. Like Jezebel's house, it had a tiled roof and a concrete facade. There was an old sofa-cum-bed and a couple of cane chairs in the front room. Jezebel's gaze fell on the old Onida TV with a shroud over its head in a corner of the room and the faded orange curtains draped over the window with horizontal wooden bars. A lean old woman came from inside and tried to wake the child. Slinging a thorthu over his shoulder, the old man sat down on the cane chair. When Balagopal introduced Jezebel to him as a doctor from the

Medical College, he inquired politely 'To examine Sandhya?' and proceeded to ask her where she lived, about her family and so on. When the question 'Are you married?' came up, Balagopal got up, saying, 'Come, let's go and see Sandhya', thus rescuing Jezebel. For no reason, anxiety and fear gripped Jezebel. It was apparent that Sandhya was his wife. He led her into a room with a wooden loft and low shut windows. With a pounding heart Jezebel looked at the form lying on the bed under the dim white light of the CFL bulb. Another body. All skin and bones, with eyes shut. A long tube attached to her nose. Hanging below, from between her legs, an empty catheter bag. 'This is Sandhya, my ex-wife,' Balagopal was saying. Just then, they could hear the child waking up, whimpering. Balagopal brought him in and pointed at the bed saying '*Kunju*, look, Amma!' However, the child kept staring at her. Balagopal took the child closer to the bed, coaxing him, 'Give Amma a kiss.' Unable to watch that sight, Jezebel looked away and made her way back to the front room.

Sandhya's mother brought tea and a plate of snacks. Sandhya's father came and sat on the old cane chair, handed Jezebel her cup of tea, and repeated his earlier question, 'Are you married?' She nodded. As she sat sipping her tea, the child came running and hugged Sandhya's mother. She went inside, petting him. Balagopal counted out some rupee notes and handed them over to Sandhya's father, who placed them under a stack of papers on the teapoy.

'Someone I know told me about a girl who teaches in the NSS School. Her husband is no more. He was in the army. Why don't you go and see her, Bala?' asked Sandhya's father.

'Have you told them about our conditions?' asked Balagopal matter-of-factly, picking up his teacup.

'Will anything work out if we tell them all that beforehand?' wondered Sandhya's father.

'I'm not for misleading anyone,' said Balagopal firmly. Finishing his tea quickly, he turned to Jezebel and said, 'Shall we

leave then?' Sandhya's mother came out with the child, having
made him drink his tea and wiped his face. Jezebel looked on
as Balagopal rinsed his mouth and washed his face at the rusted
washbasin in a corner of the room, pulled out a handkerchief from
his pocket and wiped his face, took the child in his arms, wiped
his face and smoothed his hair. As she sat in the car, she wondered
why she had come to that house. Balagopal who sat in the front
seat with the child turned to look at her.

'I inquired about Dr Jerome George Marakkaran through a
few friends.'

It was as if a blanket had slipped away from around her heart.
Jezebel shivered. Jerome George Marakkaran's clean-shaven face,
narrow eyes and thick moist lips appeared before her eyes. Dressed
in a gaudy blue-polyester shirt tucked into his pants, he stood
towering at the threshold of a room without walls. She dreaded
the odour of formalin that pierced its way into her nose.

'Sandhya and I were classmates. We were in a relationship for
ten years. Then we got married. The accident happened just after
the child was born. They were taking him for his vaccination. A
car hit the autorickshaw they were travelling in. The autorickshaw
turned turtle. Onlookers said that they saw Sandhya fall out of the
auto and hit the road head first. The baby was saved because he
was caught in my mother's sari and fell on top of her. My mother
died on the spot. It's been six years now.'

There was no change of expression or emotion on his face
as he said this. Jezebel swallowed hard, unable to take in more.
Balagopal turned to look at her.

'I need a woman to raise him. House help is too expensive. A
marriage would help save that expense. Sandhya's treatment alone
costs ten thousand rupees a month. Then rent, petrol, bills . . . no
matter how much you earn, there's nothing left in your hand . . .'

Sweat streamed down Jezebel's forehead. For a while,
Balagopal sat silently, caressing the child in his lap.

'They say all the cells in Sandhya's brain are dead. She can't see us, hear us or remember us. She is as good as dead. But that body lies there before us, *alle*? Sometimes I get furious. Can't she just die, I think. After that the heart is always overwhelmed with guilt. What if it had been me in her place? There is no sense in thinking like this. I am not in her place. Neither is she in mine. We can never predict how each person would respond in a particular situation. She is still here. She may not be Sandhya, even to herself. But to us she is still Sandhya. Even if she dies and even after her death, she will continue to be our Sandhya.'

Jezebel felt choked by all sorts of emotions. She asked him why he got a divorce then.

'Sandhya's family compelled me.' Balagopal looked pained. 'It's their need that I get married. If something happens to them, then I am the only one left to take care of Sandhya. I wouldn't be able to both look after the child and take care of Sandhya on my own. So, another person's help is required.' As Jezebel sat there frozen, the child got up and looked at her over Balagopal's shoulder. There was a pale mark on his cheek. When she reached out to touch that spot on his cheek, he sank shyly into his father's chest. The car had neared the Medical College. When Jezebel got down, Balagopal sat the child in the front seat, picked out an envelope from a bag kept under the front seat and got down. 'Was I of any use to you, doctor?' he asked with an air of detachment. 'It was good to meet you,' said Jezebel. Balagopal gave her the cover saying that they were copies of his divorce petition and the court ruling. Jezebel took them from him. 'Sandhya's father testified that his daughter was mentally unsound. If your husband's family too testifies similarly, it will be easy to get a divorce,' said Balagopal. That is when Jezebel noticed his eyes. She thought his eyes had no doubts about life. His was a gaze that looked at the world with clear eyes. Perhaps he was not seeing anything new now; only the past flashing again before his eyes.

'Most people would look at you, doctor, as a woman who is trying to abandon a bedridden man and saving herself. I would never think so. Because what you have gone through these past six months is what I have been experiencing for the past six years. At this age, someone like you needs companionship for physical and emotional reasons. So, you must file for a divorce as soon as you can. Get married again as soon as possible. If you wish, I can go and meet your husband's family and talk to them.'

Jezebel felt mortified when she realized that it was not her face but her heart that he was able to see so clearly. He was also abashed at having to struggle not to weep in front of a stranger. As he bid her farewell and began to get into the car, she mustered strength, cleared her throat and called out to him. He turned around and looked at her inquiringly.

'Make sure your son eats enough leafy green vegetables,' she managed to say.

He looked at the child with anxiety and despaired, 'He does not eat vegetables! It's so difficult to make him eat anything at all.' Even later she would remember how she stood there numb, watching him get into the car and the car speeding away.

When she told Valiyammachi about him she said indignantly, 'See the difference between a man and a woman. When his wife was down and out, her own family insisted that he remarry. And here, your own family is asking you to drop everything and sit by his bedside. What's the point in saying that the times have changed?'

'How can you claim that Jerome George Marakkaran is mentally unsound, doctor*ey*? How do we know if a person in a coma can hear our voice or understand what we say?' asked the defence lawyer.

'You can find out by doing a brain test.'

'But the tests have shown that he does hear voices.'

'But it's not clear whether he recognized the voices. Not even ten percent of Jerome's brain cells were functional. And that means he is not able to see or hear—or even wish to speak.' And Jezebel added, 'That means the brain is almost dead.'

'Ho! What enthusiasm, Doctor, to let us know that the husband is as good as dead. Alas, not to treat him and save him!'

'Alas, I'm a doctor,' she replied.

The court fell silent. Either because she had countered him or because he did not have a good enough counter argument, the lawyer's face hardened and his eyes narrowed menacingly.

'Learn to be a good woman, wife and householder first, then you can think of becoming a good doctor,' he roared.

She wanted to roar right back at them, 'Was it after becoming a good man, husband and householder that you became lawyers and judges? Learn to be a good citizen and a good human being first.' But she did not say anything.

Iyo, but you are not supposed to say that. Even in the twenty-first century, powerful men are authorized to order rape and disgrace upon those who do not plead: 'We will eat our own appam and provide our own clothes; only let us be called by your name. Take away our disgrace!'

And hence, Prophet Jezebel said thus, so that those with ears could hear and those with eyes could see, 'When you cannot see the scales in your own eyes, how can you bring yourself to say, 'Sister, shall I remove the grit from your eyes'? Oh hypocrite, first remove the scales from your own eyes.'

18

Afterwards, seeing Jezebel's tiredness, Valiyammachi asked, 'Are you the one who was to come, or should I expect someone else?' Then Jezebel healed her own self from her many fears, mental tortures and unclean spirits, and gave her own eyes more sight. She said to Valiyammachi, 'The blind one receives sight, the deaf one hears, the lame one walks ahead, the sick one is healed, and the poor is blessed in spirit. Blessed is she who does not stumble.' 'Do not write your sorrows with an iron stylus on lead, or chisel them in stone forever,' reminded Valiyammachi. 'Do not let your hope be uprooted like a tree either.' Later Jezebel would remember with embarrassment how miserable she felt the day the divorce notice came back unaccepted. 'Do not fear seeing all this,' said Valiyammachi then. 'The winds of justice will blow. The sea will cover them. They will sink like lead in the mighty waters.'

Valiyammachi was not one to falter. And so, even as Jezebel struggled sleeplessly Valiyammachi slipped into a deep sleep, talking and laughing. Jezebel lay watching with a tender heart as Valiyammachi lay at ease in a cotton nightie—either a white-dotted blue or a blue-dotted white—propping up her forehead with her left palm, a couple of strands of silky hair glittering like silver threads falling across her forehead, dimples unfurling on her wrinkled cheeks in her sleep. Jezebel dreamt of a grandchild who would stay by her side in her old age and sigh fondly, 'How beautiful my grandmother is!' But when she wondered if that child would also have to suffer like her, she panicked and erased that desire off her heart. Although Valiyammachi seemed to sleep oblivious to her sobs or her staying awake, each time Jezebel woke up, she found herself covered by a blanket and wondered when Valiyammachi had tucked her in. She found herself folded in Valiyammachi's embrace. Each time her heart beat quicker with love and the desperation that she had only this love.

Valiyammachi reined in the storms in her life and calmed her earth and her sky— and Jezebel's days gained a semblance of order. She now had a home to return to. There was now someone at home to greet her with a smile and a hug. Valiyammachi woke up each morning along with her and as she got ready, took to insisting 'Wear something a little more colourful, *kochey*', 'Wear a *pottu* on your forehead, *kochey*', and so on. She reminded her to powder her face and tie her hair up neatly. The breakfast that Ammachi would serve with a long face, Valiyammachi served with love, all the while insisting 'Have a little more, *dee kochey*.' Even as Ammachi muttered, 'Hm, keep eating and getting fat, let everyone say that you have gobbled up your husband in the end!', Valiyammachi retorted, 'So be it. If you are hungry, you can eat anything you want as long as it's not poisonous—even a husband! If you can gobble up your own offspring, she too can happily eat up her husband, *dee*!'

If Ammachi grumbled any further, Valiyammachi would raise her voice, 'Hm? What right do you have to blame her, you who have been torturing that poor man for some twenty-five years now? Some care you lavish on your husband! That man has been reduced to such a state that even if you tickle him, he cannot laugh. If you are thrown out of here, I will have to bear your burden as well. Otherwise, Sara*ye*, I would have gladly sent you a divorce notice on John *saar*'s behalf long back!'

The divorce notice returned undelivered a second time too, with a message: 'Not accepted by addressee.' Dreading that

George Jerome Marakkaran would take her away by force if the divorce was not granted, Jezebel stayed up all night with a heavy heart. 'Are you crying, *dee kochey*?' Valiyammachi asked her twice. She wasn't. And yet her heart was heavy with pain—pain mixed with humiliation and disappointment. Memories blurred. Images blurred. Being felicitated by teachers at the school auditorium, receiving the best outgoing student award in college, smiles on the teachers' faces when the mark lists were published; Jerome George Marakkaran getting ready to go to work, emerging sheepishly from the room when Ann Mary unlatched the door, lying in a coma with his eyes closed . . . Why, why, why did you give me this cross? She kept wailing within. Why had that man cheated her so cruelly? Why had that man hurt her so grievously? Throwing away the last particles of love, why had he brought all the winds of my life to a standstill?

The next morning, Valiyammachi said, 'I am coming along with you to the Medical College, *dee kochey*. I need a complete check-up.' Jezebel brightened. She called Irshad, who arrived in his car. Dressed in an off-white sari embroidered with white flowers and a long-sleeved hakoba blouse, and brandishing her brass-hooped walking stick, Valiyammachi strode briskly along with her. She met all the doctors and the nurses at the children's hospital, and laughed and joked with them. She went along with Irshad and Geethu and got her ECG test done. When Jezebel left for her classes and went on her rounds, Valiyammachi sat in Kurien sir's room, chatting with him. After the junior residents' class got over, they went along with Irshad and Geethu to the town in Irshad's car. Throughout the ride, Valiyammachi made them laugh with her wisecracks. As they stopped in front of a restaurant, she hailed the long-haired boy with earrings who was taking out his bike: '*Da mone*, let me take a good look at you. What's your name?' When he responded with a stylish 'I am Varghese,' she said, 'Whatever your name is, you are a stunner, *ketto*! If only I were younger . . .' Turning red, the boy sped away on his bike. Irshad and Geethu, who had become Valiyammachi's fans by then, struggled to control their laughter. 'Oh, Valiyammachi! if you carry on like this, then we will have to get back to the Medical College right away,' ribbed Jezebel. Valiyammachi countered, 'I have found a few people there also, *dee moley*!'

After lunch, they went shopping. Valiyammachi encouraged Geethu and her to try out new clothes. Valiyammachi tried out a few nighties and kurtas herself. 'Do you wear all these, Valiyammachi?' asked a surprised Geethu. 'At this age is there anything that I cannot do?' Valiyammachi laughed heartily and said with a twinkle in her eyes, 'What if we can't buy all of these, at least we can try them out and feel happy.' Jezebel's eyes popped out as she took a look at the trendy kurtas, kurtis and shirts that Valiyammachi had picked out for her. 'Valiyammachi, are these for me? I have never worn such fashionable stuff,' she grew diffident. 'So start wearing them now,' ordered Valiyammachi. 'If you don't do the things you like right now, then when else are you going to do them, *dee*? When you have one foot in the grave? If you want to wear a sleeveless top like people your age do, then you must wear it right away. Or else, will someone place a sleeveless dress in your coffin when you are about to be buried? And even if they do, what use will it be to you then?'

Valiyammachi bought clothes for all three of them. At the billing counter when the cashier asked, 'Paying by cash, Valiyammachi?' she took out her debit card and said 'Plastic cash, my son.' The three of them watched awestruck as Valiyammachi keyed in her pin number. 'You kids, you keep gawking around like this. If only I were young now, how I would have lived it up!' Valiyammachi sighed. From the textile shop, they went straight to a beauty parlour. She told the beautician to trim Jezebel's hair. Clutching her long hair curled up at the ends, Jezebel quailed 'Valiyammachi . . .'

'It will grow back, *dee kochey*,' quipped Valiyammachi. Turning to the beautician, she ordered, 'You cut it, *dee kochey*, Diana style.' Geethu looked at Valiyammachi in amazement. Valiyammachi declared, 'We don't need this Jezebel any more, Geethu *moley*. Let there be a new Jezebel. A super smart girl who, if someone so much as dares to say *"Ennaa dee?"* to, will give it right back to them with an *"Ennaa da*, who are you to question me?"'

As she sat covered in an apron on a high chair in front of the large mirror at the beautician's, it was Valiyammachi's face that Jezebel's gaze fixed itself on. She soaked up the sight of Valiyammachi seated expansively on the chair at the back, holding on to her walking stick with one hand, watching intently as her grandchild's hair was being trimmed. Valiyammachi seemed to exude the majesty of a queen who ruled over a great kingdom of happiness. Jezebel's heart grew tender at the natural splendour of old age. Her confidence grew as she realized that she would always have a special place in Valiyammachi's heart, that Valiyammachi took in her dimples with pride and joy, and that as she smiled, Valiyammachi's dimples, too, blossomed. She looked at herself in the mirror only when the beautician said 'It's done.' The one who had, until then, been weighed down by life had now transformed into a pretty young woman. 'Wow!' Geethu exclaimed admiringly. Jezebel felt that she had become a new person. If only the new person would not remember the wounds of the old one. If only she could be a child again, unscarred by life's wounds, smiling at the world, unfurling her dimples.

Outside, Valiyammachi looked at Irshad who was waiting for them leaning against the car. She said, 'Look *da*, a new Jezebel! I am entrusting you both with the job of ensuring that she never becomes the old Jezebel again.'

Back home, it became the reason for a huge earthquake. 'This old woman will not rest until she has ruined my life,' ranted Ammachi. 'She goes and gets the girl's hair chopped off and her eyebrows shaved when her husband is lying unconscious after an accident! How will I ever look at people in the face?' she wailed, slapping herself on the forehead.

'It's all right, *dee*,' consoled Valiyammachi. 'We'll give them all the hair that was chopped off. And if you can't look them in the face, look elsewhere, will you?'

'She's stark raving mad. But what happened to you? You're a doctor, where's your decency and decorum, *dee*?' Ammachi sprang upon Jezebel.

'My Sara*ye*, go and take a look at the Medical College. How stylish all her teachers are! Don't you know, patients won't spare a second look for doctors who are not stylish?'

Enjoying their argument, Jezebel went to her room and stood in front of the mirror. She liked her reflection very much. Dimples blossomed on her cheeks time and again. Her heart swelled with love time and again.

'Doctor*ey*, so many people struggle to grow their hair, buying oils and unguents and whatnot. There are so many companies in the business of helping one grow one's hair! In your wedding photos, you have nice long hair. What happened then? Why did you suddenly change your hairstyle? Who advised you to cut it this way?' asked the lawyer.

'My Valiyammachi.'

'Ha, what a grandmother! She told you to cut your hair, and you went right ahead?'

'It was Valiyammachi who took me to the parlour and got my hair cut.'

The lawyer fell silent for a moment.

'And then? Did your hair not grow back? Or did Valiyammachi get it cut again?'

'I went on my own.'

'Ah, that's what I asked. And who told you to? Surely, someone would have told you: "Doctor*ey*, this suits you better" and so on, *alleyo*?'

'I thought so myself.'

'Were you like this at the time of your wedding, doctor? In matters of dress? What did you wear back then?'

'Churidar, salwar.'

'Ah, and did you wear jeans?'

'No.'

'Sleeveless tops?'

'No.'

'But now you wear only jeans and sleeveless tops, even in the court. Why?'

'I feel it is more convenient.'

'When you say convenient, in what ways are jeans more convenient?'

'To move around in the ward and while driving.'

'Oho, so those women who wear saris and salwar kurtas must be struggling to walk or drive around, *alleyo*?'

'. . .'

'Still, if a woman feels like cutting her hair and wearing low-waist jeans and sleeveless tops like some teenager even as her husband lies paralysed, what could be the motivation?'

The motivation behind that question was clear enough. Jezebel did not reply.

'All right, was it before you filed for divorce or after that you cut your hair?' The lawyer grew more animated.

'Before.'

'So, first cut your hair, wore sleeveless tops and then filed for divorce?'

'I had decided to file a case earlier.'

'So, you first decided to file the case, then wore sleeveless tops and figure-hugging jeans, and then filed the case?'

'. . .'

'Ah, well, your husband Jerome George Marakkaran, the thirty-two-year-old young man who spent two-and-a-half years with you—he was a smart, healthy, hardworking doctor who worked simultaneously in two or three hospitals back then. His father George Jerome Marakkaran suspected foul play behind the accident which caused him brain damage and made him bed-ridden and filed a complaint with the police . . . did the police not come to your place to investigate this complaint?'

'They did.'

'Did you file for divorce before that or after?'

'It was after I sent the divorce notice that Jerome's Daddy filed the complaint. But that case . . .'

'We will get to the details of that case later. You don't have to answer questions that have not been put to you. No need to stretch your leg before you sit down.'

Jezebel was speechless.

'During the investigation it was discovered that the car's brakes had been tampered with. And that was found to be the cause of the accident. Do you know if the police interrogated anyone in connection with this accident?'

'George Zacharia.'

'That is, that girl Ann Mary's father. Sorry, Ann Mary's mother Anitha's husband, to put it in clearer terms—the husband of the woman who was earlier in a relationship with Dr Sandeep Mohan with whom you are in an illicit relationship?'

'I am not in any such relationship.'

'Yes, yes, everyone knows that. Let that be. So, when did you file for divorce? Let's hear that precisely.'

Jezebel swallowed her shame.

'I sent the divorce notice thrice. Twice, they returned it unaccepted. After that, Jerome's Daddy filed a case against me. The police investigated it and found that there was no case against me. It was after that that I filed for divorce.'

'We will come to whether there is a case against you or not later. Tell us where George Zacharia is now.'

'He is dead.'

'How?'

Jezebel refused to answer. In the court room, the hot breeze of noon blew. Dust swirled in from outside. Dust in the room also swirled upwards along with it. She saw that that was the way of all dirt. She learnt that dirt always seeks out, finds, and intermingles with more dirt and then soils all that is not dirty as well.

George Zacharia's death had been horrific. There is one— she—who is, has been, and is pure. In her own judgements, she was the fairest of them all.

19

'Jezebel, you are testifying about yourself; your testimony is not valid,' accused the doubting Jezebel of herself. To this Jezebel-the-rabbi replied: 'Even if I do bear witness to myself, my testimony is true, for I know where I came from and where I am going. However, you do not know where I come from or where I am going. There is no justice in your judgement. And I judge no one.'

Jezebel realized that even if she judged no one, she would always be judged by others. Right after George Jerome Marakkaran accepted the divorce notice, the Deputy Superintendent of Police (DySP) Saif Mohammed called her about coming over to inquire about the complaint that the accident had been premeditated. That day, during the rounds, she felt her mind slip out of control several times. Jezebel sat beside an eight-year-old named Jwaala, who lay limp in the ward after her inebriated stepfather had inflicted cigarette and beedi burns on her skin. She felt it was her own self there, lying spent, in place of the eight-year-old. She could feel the scalding pain of the burns on that tender young skin as if it were her own. Jwaala looked sympathetically at the doctor who was weeping even as she was attending to her. Jezebel was amazed that even a body that was writhing in pain could look at another human being with such sympathy.

That was when she felt a rush of sympathy for Jerome George Marakkaran as well. If only he had had the honesty to admit, 'I don't understand all this,' when she had quoted Gibran's lines to him in their first email exchange . . . In that case, she would not have married him. He would not have had to come to Kerala. She would not have had to cook and clean and wash clothes in the time she could have spent studying. He would not have assaulted Ann Mary. There would not have been any reason for her to feel the kind of hatred she did for him. It was terrifying to take stock of how many lives one man's dishonesty had destroyed.

Disturbed by the sight of her teary eyes, Irshad and Geethu escorted her home at noon. Her voice faltered as she told Valiyammachi and Chachan that the police would come home that evening. 'So what, *kochey*? Let them come and ask what they have to and go,' said Valiyammachi. 'Ah, who knows what more we have to endure,' lamented Ammachi.

The DySP was a young, well-mannered man. He brought with him a file opened by the previous DySP who had since been transferred. The forensic report said that the brakes of the car were not in order. Who had been at home the day before that? Where were you at the time of the accident? What was the reason for you to go to Dr Sandeep Mohan's place that morning? What is the relationship between you and Dr Sandeep Mohan? Do you suspect anyone in connection with the accident? Do you suspect George Zacharia? Is it not reasonable to suspect that he may have tampered with the car's brakes in order to endanger your life?

Jezebel answered each question patiently. After drinking the tea that Ammachi had brought, Saif Mohammad said to her, 'Doctor, you have answered every question put to you. But there are things I haven't asked and that you haven't answered.' 'There are,' agreed Jezebel. 'Sir, if your question is going to be one that has the potential to push a fifteen-year-old's life into misery for ever, how will I answer it? What kind of answer am I to give?' The DySP looked intently into Jezebel's eyes. At that moment, she felt neither fear nor anxiety. The relief of stating the truth as plain truth energized her nerves. The DySP grew thoughtful for a while. When he sighed and said 'I have a fifteen-year-old daughter too . . .', Jezebel felt a wave of relief wash over her.

'That child has SDD, sexual development disorder. She has the appearance of a female, but no uterus or breasts. She cannot conceive a child. What awaits her in life is a long nightmare. Will anyone love her? Will the world, which measures the worth of a woman's life based on her marital status and her capacity to produce offspring, ever spare her when the precious few people that love and understand her are no longer around? All that we can give her is an education, self-confidence and the means to earn her livelihood. Even that will be denied if there is a legal case, with all its tangled baggage, against her. As long as she's not the accused, should we not try to save her as much as possible from the horrors of the law?'

The DySP sat thinking for a little while longer. Then he got up to leave. As he prepared to leave, he asked only this, 'You are such a compassionate person, doctor. Then how could you abandon your husband? That too, when he was bedridden like that?'

'Weren't you one of the accused in the police case?' asked the lawyer.

'I was a witness.'

'But Dr Sandeep Mohan was one of the accused?'

'No. He was a witness.'

'The police found that it was the enmity in connection with the abduction of the girl named Ann Mary that resulted in the attempt to murder Jerome George Marakkaran. But the attempt was targeted at you.'

'I don't know about that.'

'If seen in that light, it was because of you that poor Jerome George Marakkaran met with an accident. If only you had minded your own home and family and not gotten into tangles with other men, *paavam* Jerome would have continued to be perfectly healthy now.'

'If only Jerome had not married me in the first place.'

'Right. So the fact that he gave you a life was his undoing! Ah, let that be. It was George Zacharia's need that you and Dr Sandeep Mohan, the person everyone calls your paramour, be eliminated, *alleyo*?'

'I have no paramours.'

'*Iyo*! How unfortunate.'

Sounds of laughter rose in the court. Jezebel closed her eyes and heaved a deep sigh.

'Let that be. Whether there were paramours or not, we'll come to know in due course. But George Zacharia's death took place in the hospital where you work, *alleyo*?'

'Yes.'

'Was it a natural death? Or was it premeditated, like Dr Jerome George Marakkaran's accident? And was it for this that you paid Shark Sebin blood money?'

Jezebel smiled kindly at the lawyer. She did not wish to describe how George Zacharia had been granted bail when his health deteriorated in the sub jail and had to be admitted to the hospital where she was working. His liver had broken down. It was DySP Saif Mohammad who informed her that he was alone and that his children had abandoned him once they had learnt about the police case. When she heard this, Valiyammachi said, 'Send someone across to inquire about his health, *kochey*. If he needs money or medicine, make sure to get it across to him. What could be a greater triumph in this world than to help one's enemies without their knowledge?'

Accordingly, Jezebel sent Irshad across. George Zacharia was critically ill. Except for a helper, Shobi, there was no one with him. Irshad got back to her with a list of the medicines the doctors had prescribed. Jezebel bought him the medicines. When Irshad handed them over, George Zacharia turned the packet of medicines around this way and that and asked, 'So he's still around here, *alleyo*?'

'Who?' exclaimed a surprised Irshad.

'It was he who sent you here, *alle*, doctor? Sandeep Mohan!' George Zacharia was angry now. But when he heard the reply 'That doctor has been on leave for several months now,' he grew pensive.

That afternoon, as she walked out of the third-year MBBS class, George Zacharia was waiting for her, leaning against the wall, panting and coughing and looking like he would keel over any moment. Jezebel did not see him as George Zacharia then; she saw him only as a patient. A patient whose liver was malfunctioning and whose ashen face had turned red from disruptions in the pumping of his heart. She went up to him and told him firmly, 'Please go and lie down in the ward, won't you? If you walk about like this, you'll die.' At first, he did not recognize her. And when he did, his face reddened even more. 'How does it matter to you if I die?' he raged. He seemed to have lost a lot of weight since the last time she had seen him. The waxy sheen on his dark bloated cheeks made him look worse. 'Why did you send me those medicines?' he demanded.

'Why did you tinker with the brakes in Jerome's car?' she asked him in return. His thick eyebrows shot up in surprise. Doubt clouded his eyes. 'If I did, it hadn't been in order to kill him,' he muttered. Jezebel did not feel any fear just then. He was just a patient. The doctor in her did not feel any fear or anger towards her patients, only curiosity and compassion for the inner chambers of their bodies. 'Was I not your target?' she asked him. He looked at her sharply. She seemed to have transformed into another person altogether after cutting her hair. Earlier, her face had borne the burden of all the hair tied up at the back. Now her face had the lightness and ease of a young girl's. 'I'm not afraid of getting killed. How can you kill someone who has died several deaths already?' she asked him. He stared at her open-mouthed.

'I have no feelings of enmity or bitterness against you. I wanted to save a young girl you tried to ruin, that's all,' she explained.

'You knew that without her at the workshop, no work would get done,' he said, gnashing his teeth.

'I did not bring her away in order to disrupt your work but because I felt she has a better future awaiting her,' she explained.

'What's wrong with work at the workshop?' he demanded.

'Nothing wrong. But she wanted to study further,' argued Jezebel.

'There are so many children in the world who wish to study but do not have the means to. Why don't you rescue them all?' he got angry again.

'There are so many heart patients in this world too,' she countered. 'Will I be able to help them all? And is there any sense in not helping you simply because of that reason? Please go and lie down on your bed. If any of the senior doctors sees you standing here, I will get pulled up too.'

George Zacharia's face fell. 'I don't need your help,' he grumbled.

'You will,' she declared, like a dare. And then said kindly, 'Everyone needs someone or the other. It's better to go peacefully rather than hold stubbornly on to a grudge in your last days.'

He walked away, as if defeated. She stood watching him as he walked down the corridor. In the bright glare of the corridor lights, his white polyester shirt appeared yellow. He looked pathetic. She could see that he was just a body—a body with a heart that had given up its ghost. It was bracing wearily for battle with death. She saw his shadow trailing him like an upper garment as he climbed down the stairs, holding on to the railings. Chanting to herself 'Death walks along with one like a shadow,' she turned around to look behind herself. She could not see her own shadow. But she knew for sure that it was around somewhere nearby. The very thought vexed and consoled her at the same time.

That evening, she emailed Sandeep Mohan a two-liner: 'George Zacharia has been admitted to the Medical College hospital in a rather critical condition. There's only a worker from the workshop by his side.' She did not hear back from him.

The next day, however, as she stood talking to the junior residents after her rounds, she heard someone call, 'Doctor aunty!' From among the throng of patients and their helpers—some sitting, some lying down, some standing around and chatting—Ann Mary came running up to her with a great big smile. She seemed a little leaner. But her face looked brighter. She had grown taller. She had grown up a little more. When she first saw her with Anitha, she had seen her as a cancer patient's daughter. When she saw her at the workshop, it had been as a worker. Months later, Jezebel saw that she had transformed into the daughter of a rich man. Holding tightly onto Jezebel's hands, she exclaimed, with tears in her eyes, 'How much you've changed, doctor aunty! I didn't recognize you at first!' Jezebel looked eagerly around for Sandeep Mohan. She said, 'No, Achan hasn't come. Sister Daisy and Sister Goretha from the convent have come with me.' 'And where are they?' asked Jezebel. They were by George Zacharia's bedside, praying for him.

Later, every time she recalled the moments when she walked along with Ann Mary to George Zacharia's bed, Jezebel would feel like weeping. All along the way, she was chattering brightly, giving her all the news. She was now studying in a convent school in a faraway town. Her Achan called her every evening from abroad. When he called the day before, he told her that Papa had been hospitalized. She told him she wanted to meet Papa. At first, Achan had not agreed. And then after some time, he called her again and told her she could go if she wished. Achan was worried Papa may do something to her. That's why he insisted the nuns accompany her.

In the ward, Sister Daisy and Sister Goretha were speaking to George Zacharia. Ann Mary introduced Jezebel to the nuns. Sister

Goretha was an ever-smiling thirty-five-year-old. Sister Daisy was a fair, slender, melancholy forty-year-old. 'We've heard so much about you. But we didn't expect to see someone so young,' said Sister Goretha. The moment he saw Jezebel, George Zacharia closed his eyes. Jezebel was worried that a dying person would not be able to endure so much heartburn.

The nuns got up to leave. Sister Daisy hugged Ann Mary. When she advised her, 'Be good. Remember, it's a hospital. Take care of yourself,' Jezebel realized with a start that Ann Mary was planning to stay on at the hospital. 'Dr Sandeep was not for it. We, too, are not keen. But Ann Mary was insistent. We've asked the sisters in the Palliative Care Centre nearby to take care of her,' they said. 'Commando protection? For me?' laughed Ann Mary. 'From the time I was six, I've stayed with Mummy so many times in so many medical colleges. Back then, there was no one else with me. I felt safer staying in a hospital than at home, Sister*ey*!'

The nuns took their leave. George Zacharia lay feigning sleep, his arm over his eyes. Jezebel took Ann Mary outside. 'Are you not scared to stay here, *moley*?' she asked her.

Ann Mary smiled confidently. 'I'm not scared of anything any more, Aunty. I have my Achan. I have you, Doctor Aunty. There are people who love me. But Papa has no one. Not even his own children. He let me stay in his place for so long, *alle*? He taught me car repair work, *alle*?'

Jezebel tried to study her. She tried to understand the reason for the determination in Ann Mary's eyes. She told Jezebel that she hadn't called her all this while because her Achan told her not to disturb Aunty. There were many new developments. She told Jezebel about how Sandeep had filed a case to prove his paternity and how Father Michael of their parish had helped him in this. And that's how she got back her Achan. It was on Father Michael's suggestion that Sandeep admitted her to the convent school run by the nuns. In the meantime, George Jerome

Marakkaran had spread rumours about Sandeep and even filed a complaint stating that he was the one behind Jerome's accident. Ann Mary told her that Sandeep had not kept in touch in order to avoid any further taint on Jezebel's reputation. Jezebel grew angry hearing this.

The next day, when Jezebel went to meet George Zacharia after her classes, she found Ann Mary massaging his feet. Jezebel saw her wipe his face and help him wash his mouth when he coughed up sputum and blood. He followed her instructions like an obedient child. Jezebel remembered the first day she had gone to his house. She remembered Ann Mary—her clothes soiled with grease, her face pleading for mercy. And could only imagine the suffocation she would have undergone in the interiors of that shabby house. She watched in disbelief the child who compassionately received the sputum and vomit of the man who had humiliated and wounded her from birth as an illegitimate child. In the days that followed, Jezebel went to meet Ann Mary every day with food and other things she needed. However, Jezebel did not bother to meet George Zacharia.

Before a week was over, Ann Mary came to meet Jezebel in the duty room. 'Papa says he wants to meet you, Aunty.'

Jezebel went to his ward on her way home. George Zacharia looked a little better. He was wearing only a vest and a lungi. He sat up when he saw her—wrapped a towel around his shoulder by way of showing respect—and looked at her with his round yellow eyes.

'It's only now that I'm seeing her properly, doctor*ey*. She knows I'm not her Appan. Anyone who looks at her would say she's a girl from a well-to-do family, *alleyo*. She's not a workshop mechanic's daughter any more. She's a doctor's daughter now, *alleyo*?'

Jezebel stood there, heart pounding, unsure of what he was trying to tell her.

'A child who's now the daughter of a doctor. That too, a child who's only fifteen years old—she's come to the general hospital to care for a workshop mechanic. And her doctor Appan has agreed to it too!'

He tried to smile at Jezebel, but his lips drooped as he ended up whimpering.

'I was thinking . . . she was born in my house fifteen years ago. I remember the births of my Rosemary and Rubin—seeing them in their cradles for the first time, the first time they crawled and took their first steps—I remember it all as if it were yesterday. But I don't remember anything about this one here. Because I haven't looked at her at all. If I heard her crying, I would smash everything in sight. So Anitha would clap a hand over her mouth to stop her from crying. If I saw Anitha feeding her, I would kick her. So she would feed her and put her to sleep before I returned from the workshop.'

Jezebel stood there, her heart aching. He heaved a deep breath.

'Poor thing, *alleyo*? A little infant. What would she know? She looked at me as an Appan. How much she would have longed for her Appan to pick her up once? To get her a dress? Or just to touch her? Or at least to smile at her? Why ever did I not feel like doing any of those?'

He coughed once again. Ann Mary came rushing up, received his phlegm in the plastic mug lined with sand kept at the foot of the bed. She wiped his face with the towel kept at the foot of the bed and offered him hot water from a flask. His eyes welling up—either from coughing or out of helplessness—he told Ann Mary, '*Moley*, go out for a bit. I need to tell this doctor one more thing.'

When she had left, he looked at Jezebel. 'I'm not asking for forgiveness. There is no point asking for forgiveness, is there? So, I shall pray for her. May good things happen to my child, only good things . . .'

He wiped his eyes. It was difficult to watch tears and agony on that face which had always been hardened with malice. He wiped his face hard with his towel.

'We men have this problem, doctor*ey*. All our lives, we keep fighting to conquer. In the end, when we can't fight, we crumble. We can't hold on for long when we feel there's no one for us. Now I think this was probably why I forced Anitha to stay with me, threatening her, torturing her—because of this fear. The fear that if she wasn't there, then I would have no one else.'

It was clear to Jezebel that he knew he wouldn't live for much longer.

'But I apologize to you, doctor*ey*. May the Lord bless you.'

George Zacharia was on the ventilator for two days. Before his daughter and son could arrive, he passed away. The day he died, it rained incessantly—flooding the road to his native place. As vehicles moved forward, waves of floodwater surged into the huts by the roadside. Behind the ambulance, Jezebel sat in Irshad's car, holding Ann Mary close. A rain that had lost its brakes crashed down on the tarpaulin sheet tied like a pandal outside that small house and on the roofs of the vehicles waiting for repair in the workshop next to it. But the sound of Ann Mary's wailing rose above it all.

The righteous woman will receive her recompense for sure.

20

Thus promised Lilly George Marakkaran the holy spirit, offering peace on earth to Jezebel who was restless at heart, 'Peace I leave with you; I do not give you peace as the world gives. Do not let your heart be troubled; do not be afraid. You heard me say, "I am going away, and I am coming back to you." And now I have told you before it happens, so that when it does happen, you will believe. I will not speak with you much longer, for the prince of this world is coming. But he has no claim on me.'

One Thursday morning, news arrived of Valiyappachan's eldest daughter Alice's hospitalization for hysterectomy, and then Koshy uncle arrived to take Valiyammachi away. And so Valiyammachi returned to the *tharavadu*. Jezebel felt she was left all alone. She tossed and turned sleeplessly in that room where Valiyammachi's scent lingered. In the days that followed, she was tossed about all over again in wave after wave of depression. She struggled to conceal a torn, tumultuous sky within her heart. When she taught her classes, she fervently hoped that they would never end. When she went on her rounds, she was loath to leave her patients. When work got over, she was terrified. Reluctant to leave, she wandered around the hospital's corridors aimlessly. Sometimes she would go to the nurses' room to chat with them. Sometimes she would go to the casualty and stand around joking with the junior residents. And sometimes, she would stand watching food being distributed by the NGO Navajeevan. She turned into a little schoolgirl who was reluctant to go back home—a little girl who dragged her feet but preferred to watch the sights of the wayside even though she had left home early in the morning. Sometimes she rode her scooter all the way to town and back. Sometimes she went window-shopping. If sometimes Geethu or Irshad went along with her, she watched movies at the theatre too.

When she found herself routinely waking up with a start from a dream in which a great mountain came crashing down on her, only to spend all night trying to dust the invisible particles of mud off her eyes, nose and lungs, she decided it was time to book an appointment with Dr Prashant.

It was dusk by the time she reached the super-speciality hospital where he worked. While the throng at the outpatient department had begun to disperse, the pharmacy was still crowded. She was called in soon after she handed over a slip with her name written on it to a nurse at the door.

Even though the sight of Dr Prashant greeting her brightly with a 'Hello, who's this? I didn't recognize you at first. You look so stylish! Very good!' restored her confidence, her anger broke its banks the moment she sat down. She looked at Prashant as if at an enemy. 'No, no need for any compliments! I understand everyone perfectly now. You're Haritha's friend, *alle*? I know what's going on in your mind. Even otherwise, there's only one thing on the minds of everyone who interacts with me. Outwardly they speak nicely, and are all kindness. But deep down, they're gnashing their teeth: "Aren't you the one that dumped your husband, *dee*?" You too are one of them. I know, I know.'

Dr Prashant was taken aback for a moment. Then he asked her with a sigh, 'Are you done?' That infuriated her even more.

'There's such joy on your face, Prashant. How would someone like you ever understand what I'm going through? You lack nothing in your life. You'll never understand the pain of the have-nots. When Valiyammachi was around, I had peace of mind. There was the feeling that I had someone for me. The moment I saw Haritha, it became clear to me that this world will never look at things from my point of view. Do you know what she asked me? She asked me if it wasn't my duty to look after Jerome. As far as I'm concerned, Jerome George Marakkaran died long before his accident, Prashant. I cannot think of a single reason to love him, but the world wants me to. How do I bring myself to feel a love that isn't there? My life was a blank sheet of paper. Why did he scratch all over it, crumple it, tear it up and stain it with mud? What wrong did I do that man? I told him clearly what kind of man I had wanted. Why did he lie to me saying, 'Jezebel, we are made for each other'? Neither could I love him, nor could he love me. For him, marriage was a transaction, a business deal. Is there a sin worse than that? And yet the world blames me. I do not feel any love for him, Prashant. Do you have any medicine that will make me love him? Can you change my mind and make it to everyone's liking by talking to me or injecting me with something or performing an operation on me? Can you make me unlike myself? Can you please kill my capacity to think, at the very least?'

She struggled to hold back her tears. But tears burst forth with a vengeance. A dense silence filled the room. Prashant sat watching her without uttering a word. After ten to fifteen minutes, the tears stopped on their own. She wiped her face. Prashant sat expressionless. Jezebel was embarrassed. She looked at him and tried to smile again. Weary, she got up to leave. Prashant smiled sympathetically.

'Leaving already? Sit. I have a lot of woes to share too, *edo*. Aren't we psychiatrists humans too? Don't we too get angry and upset and disappointed?'

She sat holding on to a corner of the chair like a guilty child. Resting his elbows on the table, his palms propping up his cheeks, he smiled at her.

'Napoleon once said, give me a seven-year-old and I will make of him whatever we want him to be. But I say, give me a person of any age, and in two years I can make them mentally sick. But don't ask me to make them normal again. I may not be able to do that . . .'

Jezebel looked at him bewildered.

'Do you know the easiest way to make someone mentally ill? Put him on a leash. Try to control him. Scoff at even his little pleasures. Follow him around everywhere. You don't have to say anything. Just keep looking at him with contempt. At first, he may pretend not to notice. But do not give up. After a while, he will try to turn his face away. Keep persisting. In time, he will try to run away. At that time, throw some little pleasures at him like bones at a dog—a word of praise or a gift. Then tighten the leash a little more. All men have a breaking point, Jezebel. The moment we realize that we are not as great as we are made out to be—we just have to lead a person to that moment. After that, he will be forever at our feet. Afterwards, he will begin to genuinely believe that the leash around his neck is his greatest safety net. He will never try to escape after that. But there is a problem. He will insist that everyone around him wears a leash as well. All those in the leash will get together and form a great chain. We all hold a little bit of that leash in our hands, Jezebel. Any moment, either our limbs or our necks may get caught in it. There is only one way to escape—the determination that we will not get trapped in it.'

Jezebel sat listening to him, baffled.

Prashant leaned back in his chair and looked at her.

'What I don't understand is how a person like you who has studied the science of the mind and the body is prepared to stay trapped in someone else's leash?'

Prashant had hurt her ego.

It was as if Jezebel was shaken out of a stupor. She was ashamed of herself.

'But this society . . .' Jezebel's voice faltered.

'Society itself is like one big mentally-ill patient, Jezebel. It always keeps so many leashes ready because it does not want anyone else to be happy. Some people break free of the leash. Some give in to it of their own volition. Still others make the world think that they are at the ends of their leashes even as they are breaking free in their own ways.'

'I'm not sure what I want,' Jezebel demurred.

'This is the problem,' said Prashant. 'We are never sure what we really want. When I saw you walk in in jeans and short hair, I was really happy. The way we dress is our style statement. It's the most apt way to announce to the world that one doesn't wish to toe society's line. That is how we say "I do not need the endorsement of the likes of you, *da*". Society always wants to keep everyone on a leash. That's why everyone has an opinion about what a woman should wear. But this is not applicable to women alone, *ketto*. Like women wear shorts in public, what if men wore long skirts and blouses? Or else, what would happen if I were to turn up tomorrow in a *pavada* and blouse to meet my patients?'

Jezebel heard him, rapt. Prashant continued.

'What I mean is, what society wants is not people who live their lives on their own terms. It only wants those who obey. It wants people who live according to the opinions of others who decide what you wear, which god you pray to, how you conduct yourself. Our society says a beautiful woman is one with long, well-oiled hair. When a woman chops off her hair, and hurls it at society's face with a "here, take it, *da*!" it disturbs society greatly. When we were kids, we have seen short-haired girls being ridiculed as *mottachi*s, baldies. But when they grew in numbers, we had to concede defeat. But that doesn't mean that if you cut your hair, you have broken free of the leash within. What you needed to cut first was the leash—the leash of guilt.'

She felt a sense of calm. She looked at him gratefully and said, 'You are a good counsellor, Prashant.'

Prashant laughed out loud. 'But I haven't even counselled you! This wasn't counselling. This was just a friendly conversation I had with you.' And then he talked for a long time. They laughed and shared jokes from their MBBS days. When she realized with a start '*Iyo*, it's very late,' Prashant leaned forward in his chair with an expression of seriousness, 'Now what I'm going to tell you is a counsellor's suggestion. Please listen. Jezebel, life is full of unexpected blows. That's life. How soon a person recovers from its shock and returns to status quo ante is an indicator of their mental health. When a relationship breaks it takes six months to two years to recover. To recover from a crisis like what you've been through, you will need a minimum of two years. Why don't you start a blog?'

Jezebel looked at him in disbelief, 'A blog!'

'Just give it a try. You know when the path ahead clears up for those who are clueless about what to do?' he smiled mischievously. 'When they advise others.'

She could not bring herself to smile just then. Once it has begun to count the number of links in its chains, no dog will smile until it has broken completely free of the leash.

The defence lawyer would remind her in the court, again and again, of her efforts to smile then. 'Usually, in your community, when problems of this nature occur, the parish priest and the church intervene, *illeyo*?' he asked.

'Yes, they do.'

'Had anyone come to discuss a compromise in your case?'

'I believe they spoke to Chachan and Ammachi. No one spoke to me.'

'How come?'

'I don't go to church.'

'Why? Have you converted?'

'My God is in my heart.'

The judge's expression hardened. For a moment, everyone fell silent.

'Don't you need to have a heart first, and a conscience, to have a God within?' The lawyer scoffed. 'Let that be, Doctor. It seems that although you don't go to church, you have considerable clout over the church and the priests. Do you know that a priest visited Jerome George Marakkaran's house to intercede on your behalf?'

'I do. Father Martin Ilanjikkal.'

'How do you know him? Was he the vicar of your parish or something?'

'No, he got in touch with me after he read my blog.'

'Ho! You used to blog? Dear Lord! When the husband lies on his deathbed, a wife cuts her hair, takes to wearing jeans, blogging . . . Ho! I've got to give it to you, *ketto*!'

'Thank you.'

'Tell me, is this priest still with the church? Or has he quit? Does he read only blogs written by women? Tell me, how old is this Father?'

'Ninety,' said Jezebel.

The room fell silent. Ninety years. Whoever has ears, let them hear. Such is the endurance and faith of the saints. She did not wish to explain, how on the day she returned after meeting Prashant, she explored the possibilities of the internet in the life of a lone woman and set up an email account and a blog at bellasthoughts. blogspot.com.

She had no idea what to write. As she sat staring at the blank screen for a long time, she decided she had to write something and began to write about a girl she had met that day.

Today I met a girl. She was ten years old. One fine morning, she woke up and found that she could only limp and not walk like before. Nothing showed up in the diagnosis. The family

said that she used to dance at school. That gave me an idea. I
compelled her to dance. She wept. When I probed further, she
told me the truth—that a relative, a religious scholar, who came
to know that she had danced at school, had warned her. He had
said that God did not like dance and that she would not be able
to walk if she danced. The fear that it created in her young mind
crippled her.

Her story took me back to my own childhood. How all
religions inject each of their follower's heart with so many don'ts
and difficulties! Why so many rules and commandments to get
to know God? I was one who lived according to the rules laid
down by my religion. But that religion does not give my life the
value of even a twig. What has religion ever done for me? Why
does religion never consider my health and peace? Why does
it not insist that the love and justice I was denied be restored
to me? I have seen kids who when they spot a worm, crush it
underfoot for no reason at all. I understand religion as that child
that crushes underfoot the desires and joy of poor people who
mean no harm to others. The child I saw today, found happiness
in dancing. The idea that that happiness was sin was dinned into
her. Perhaps it will never be possible for her to dance with joy
again. The fear that has been dinned into her will afflict her in
the form of some illness. She will never be happy. She will not
be able to feel any joy at others' happiness either. Is this what
religion wants—the perennial unhappiness of people?

Two days later, she saw a comment under that blog post in the
name of one Martin Ilanjikkal.

'I happened to come across this blog by accident. There is a
major error in what you have written, Bella. Religions were formed
not to snatch away people's happiness but to increase it twofold.
But those who interpret the ideals of religion always forget it.
People with small minds turn religions against people.'

She replied right away, 'What you say is absolutely right. Throughout history, people with small minds have controlled and ruined the lives of ordinary people like me. Why do we subject ourselves to it even in this day and age? My life slips by like this. When I lie down to sleep, I ask myself, "Why am I not happy?" In a world with so many religions, how come people like me end up praying, "May I be able to sleep somehow or the other?"'

Replies and responses went back and forth. Then he asked her for her email address. She gave it to him. Deep down she hoped that he would be a young man. But in the email, this is what she read:

> '*Moley*, I am a ninety-year-old priest, now leading a retired life. All these years I tried to study God and religion. And now I have reached a stage where I find no great difference between me and God. When God is within me, what is the difference between me and him? The pain in your writing moves me. What is your problem? Here is my address and phone number . . .'

Jezebel noted with surprise that he lived in Jerome's city. She called Father Ilanjikkal. She heard a deep voice that made each word resonate with meaning.

'I really like the name Jezebel. What a beautiful name! It means one who is dear to God.'

It was comforting to hear that voice that sounded like it came straight from the heart.

'My husband's Appan wanted that name changed. According to him the name meant prostitute,' said Jezebel.

Father Ilanjikkal's laughter rang out at the other end.

'*Ente moley*, my girl, you are educated, *alle*? What's the easiest way to ruin a woman? Ruin her dignity. And what's the best way to do that? Call her a prostitute. Then again, prostitution in the Bible has little to do with sex. It has to do with faith. It is a word used to label the acts of deviating from monotheism and, indeed, any act of disobedience.'

She found it difficult to believe that it was a ninety-year-old priest on the other end. To her it seemed that it was God himself talking to her over the phone. It was clear that Father Ilanjikkal loved to talk.

'Religion is a big institution. The most important thing for any institution is the bonds that hold it together. Faith is what binds religion. Without people to unquestioningly obey, there is no religion; there is no bond of faith. Man is safe only as long as he stands as part of a group. And religion is the cement that helps any kind of society to stand together. Because it is not only the sense of safety that men give men but it is the sense of safety that comes from the belief that one can, through constant worship, manipulate even the one who is beyond the firmament, above the clouds, who has the power to create the sun and the moon and light and darkness. Without faith, there is no God. Without God, there is no religion. Without religion, people would become like elephants without trunks—their power, strength, and tusks will all be pointless.'

In the months that followed, though they called up and spoke to each other often, he never asked Jezebel even once, 'What is the wound in your heart, *moley*?' If at all he were to ask her, if she told him upfront about Jerome's accident and all that transpired afterwards, she could guess the kind of questions a ninety-year-old would ask: 'He is your husband, *alle*? Were you not united by God? If you had met with that accident instead and he deserted you, how would you feel? Isn't there such a thing as humaneness? How can you bring yourself to abandon someone you lived with?'

And then one Sunday afternoon, escorted by Chachan and Ammachi, arrived an ochre-khadi-kurta-and-white-pyjama-clad gent whose abundant hair and beard shone like silver. As he stepped out of Father Sebastian Elakkatt's white Qualis unsupported by a walking stick, he asked her 'Do you recognize me?', she quipped '*Ilanjippoo manam*', alluding to the famous film song about the fragrance of the ilanji blossom. Father Ilanjikkal laughed out loud. He was a man who exuded peace. After lunch, he took her for a walk in the garden, chatting about the fertilizer used to improve the yield of black pepper, the tangy curry prepared from the stem of yam, twenty kinds of jackfruit dishes, the red worm that carries oil for the Messiah, the differences in the idea of a prophet in the Bible and in Islam and so on. He told her about the study conducted in Jerusalem to ascertain the stone used to seal the tomb of Jesus, and how they found that it was cork-shaped. After tea, he got up to take leave, saying, 'Got to go to the Bishop's house. A priest who was with me at the seminary is bedridden. Need to go and see him as well.' And then he addressed everyone, 'I know all about the situation here. There is no need for Jezebel to nurse a young man who is as good as dead. There are so many institutions run by our sisters. If he is admitted in one of those, they will take care of him.'

Father Sebastian, Chachan and Ammachi looked at one another. But no one said anything.

'But Jezebel, you need a companion. You need children. There is an age for all this. So I shall go and meet them. Only if you, especially Jezebel, permit me.'

Jezebel welled up. Afterwards there was no news for about a week. But the next Sunday night, came a call. Jezebel heard him out eagerly.

'I can read Hebrew. Once I got back here, I picked up my Hebrew Bible and read the Old Testament. When you read it you understand one thing. The marriage between Jezebel and Ahab was an agreement between two communities that worshipped two different gods. Jehovah's prophets did not approve of this. If there are many gods in a society the control of the prophets is considerably reduced.' Father Ilanjikkal heaved a sigh. 'It's all power play, *moley*. Everyone wants to exercise control over everyone else. They want to lord it over the others. The adamance that others should live and die for them.'

Trembling, Jezebel asked him, 'You did go there, *alle*, Father?'

After a moment's silence, Father replied, 'His is a closed mind, *moley*. You can knock all you want, but it won't open. It's as if he is living to prove Christ's words wrong.'

His voice faltered as he continued, 'That man's mind has lost its balance. He imagines that you are responsible for what happened to his son. I fear for you, *kochey*. Be careful. He has such hatred for you. When I went there, I was wondering why the Lord has led me there. There must be some reason. There may be some opportunity some day when I may be of use.'

'Is it true that Jerome George Marakkaran's mother Lilly George Marakkaran came to your house to meet you and asked you to stay with her and help look after her son?' asked the defence lawyer.

'She came to meet me.'

'What for?'

Darkness rushed into Jezebel's heart. As she recalled that day, her body shuddered all over again.

One evening when she returned home, she saw Abraham Chammanatt's car parked outside. Inside were Abraham Chammanatt and Lilly George Marakkaran. She rushed to her calling out 'Mummy!' Lilly held out her arms towards her and Jezebel fell into them and held her tightly. She had lost a lot of weight. She looked like an apparition. She affectionately patted Jezebel's trembling back as if lulling her to sleep. Her Ammachi stood there frowning as if she had not noticed. Chachan wiped the corners of his eyes as if they were itching. Jezebel took her to her room. 'You have pulled down so much, Mummy,' she rued.

'Who wouldn't pull down if they have to keep vigil over a live corpse, *moley*?' Her voice faltered.

Jezebel winced as if nails had been driven into her body.

'I thank the Lord every day that you escaped. I feel relieved that I could do justice to you. I will not ask you whether you are well. I know that you are not. You look weak. As if all the flesh has evaporated from your face. Dark circles under your eyes. How are you getting along, *kochey*?'

Jezebel's eyes welled up and her vision blurred. She stared at her blindly.

'Georgekutty curses you all the time. But have I ever been able to make him understand? I did try to, back when I was newly married. And stopped trying right after. Georgekutty is an empty, upturned vessel. He will never fill up, nor will he ever stop clattering. I believe that sending you away from there was the only good thing that I have ever done in my life.'

'Did Jerome's Daddy scold you that day, Mummy?' asked Jezebel, distressed.

'Scold?' she smiled. And touched the left part of her forehead. There was a dark scar there. Jezebel examined the scar anxiously.

'He grabbed me by my hair and hit me against the wall.' She smiled. 'I thought my hair had been torn off my scalp. Georgekutty's hands were full of my hair. Later, when I swept the room, there were curls of hair lying all over. For many days afterwards, I could not bend my neck. If I moved, my head would hurt as if it had been prised apart.'

Jezebel did not wish to hear any more. She wished she would black out. She fantasized that she was lying with eyes closed, brain-dead, like Jerome. But words rammed against her chest. The sternal rib, where the bones of the ribcage meet, is what hurts the most when hit. Someone was hitting her hard there. 'Don't tell me more Mummy. It hurts,' Jezebel whimpered.

'It doesn't hurt for me any more.' Lilly George Marakkaran smiled.

'Are you not upset that I did not take care of Jerome?' asked Jezebel.

'I was the one who asked you not to come. We are there to look after him, *alle*?'

'Well, well! Wouldn't any mother feel some spite for a daughter-in-law who abandoned her own son? Otherwise, are you a mother at all?' Ammachi, who had entered the room, raged.

'There has not been a day in my life where I have not rued my fate that she had to be born my daughter and cursed my womb that bore her. In that case, how much more should you curse her! A son who is the pillar of support for the family, a son whom you raised with such difficulty to be a doctor—how can you bring yourself to pamper a girl who got up and left when he was felled down?' Ammachi was hopping mad.

Lilly George Marakkaran's expression changed. 'Stop it, Sara!' she raised her voice. 'The day we left after seeing Jezebel for the first time, I fervently prayed that this wedding should not take place. But God has never heard my prayers at the right time. I was not for this wedding. I did not want her as my son's wife.' She paused for breath, and wiped her face.

Ammachi and Jezebel stood stunned. She turned towards Ammachi with growing anger.

'Do you know why? I knew that my son did not need a woman to sleep with. For that, Avinash Gupta was enough.'

Frissons of lightning criss-crossed Jezebel's body. Lilly George Marakkaran stood there, lifeless. In a dead voice she said, 'He married in order to keep up appearances. He needed someone to deck up and take out, to slog in the kitchen, to keep the house tidy, to wash his clothes, to work and earn money so that he could buy a big house and car. It was only for all these.'

'What are you saying, Lilly?' shuddered Ammachi.

'We knew it earlier.' Lilly smiled sadly. 'His Appan feigned ignorance. He was his Daddy's boy all the way. When I tried to talk to him, he shooed me away. Georgekutty brought him up to disrespect the womb that bore him. Perhaps that's why he couldn't bring himself to love bodies with wombs. Jezebel, I've always agonized about you. I hoped that marriage would change him. I understood that it was not so the morning you came to stay with us after your marriage. When he came back after going out that morning, I could smell that boy, Avinash, on him. A smell that always filled Jerome's room. He would often come home under the pretext of combined study. I have seen them in bed together. The first time I wished my eyes would go blind. I thought it was a great sin. Then I thought this must be his way. This is how God has created him. When Georgekutty began to look for a bride for him, I thought he would protest. I was wrong. Then I thought he would have changed. I was wrong again.'

Lilly George Marakkaran stopped, weary. Ammachi stood rooted to the spot.

'Sara, have we all not ruined her life enough? At least now, can't we leave this poor thing alone?' Lilly George Marakkaran asked, pained.

Silence filled the room.

'Lilly, shall we leave?' When Abraham Chammanatt's voice came from the other room Lilly George Marakkaran got up, wiping her nose and eyes. Jezebel fell into her arms, held her tight and tried to weep. The tears would not come. They swirled around in her heart like a sandstorm. Lilly George Marakkaran held her close. 'I came to tell you one more thing' she whispered. Jezebel waited for the next blow.

'Ever since the divorce notice came, Georgekutty's madness has grown twofold. After Father Ilanjikkal's visit it has grown even worse. He is determined never to let you live in peace. How long will you carry on like this? Don't you need a good life? Don't you want to find someone who loves you? Even if you win the case in court, will the church ever allow a divorce? Your best years will be well past you by the time all this gets resolved. Otherwise, Jerome should go. I pray daily that he should die. But it seems unlikely that he will go any time soon.'

Jezebel felt like weeping again. She kept looking intently at Lilly.

'I fear for you, *moley*. For Georgekutty this is not just a case of bullheadedness against you. It is his attitude against all women.' She sighed again. 'I feel it is best for you to go stay with your brother. There, you will not have to be scared of Georgekutty. If the court grants a divorce, you can even get married to someone else there.'

'It's not like you fear, Mummy . . .'

'As long as I am around, I will make sure that you come to no harm. But I don't know how much longer I will live. Georgekutty will not hesitate to even kill me in order to bring you there. After Father Ilanjikkal's visit, Georgekutty threw John and Christina out of the house. They are now in Christina's house. She has given birth. It was a pre-term delivery. I came to see the baby. Even that was possible only because my brother put in a word.'

Jezebel stood there as if she had been hit hard on the head. After they left Ammachi went into her room and shut the door. Jezebel could hear murmurs of lines from the Bible rising from the room. At night, when it was past dinner time Chachan came up to Ammachi's door but went back, reluctant to disturb her. Jezebel got up and called out to Ammachi. 'I am praying, can you serve the food?' came the teary response.

Jezebel served Chachan dinner. She did not eat. Ammachi did not come out of her room either. She knocked repeatedly on the door. In the end, Ammachi opened the door. Her face was puffed up with weeping. She looked at Jezebel as if for the first time.

'Don't you want dinner, Ammachi?' asked Jezebel.

'You go ahead. I am not hungry,' whispered Ammachi.

'If you are not hungry, I am not hungry either,' sulked Jezebel.

They looked at each other. Ammachi held the Bible in her right hand close to her heart. With her left hand, she reached out to touch Jezebel's short hair. Jezebel held on to Ammachi's hand tightly. For the first time in her life, Ammachi hugged her tight. For the first time in her life, Jezebel leaned her head on Ammachi's shoulder. For the first time in her life, she realized that Ammachi smelt of fresh milk. She realized that Ammachi's skin was as soft as that of babies in the neonatal ward. She hugged Ammachi tight.

'Please forgive me,' said Ammachi. Jezebel hugged her. 'Never. I will never forgive you. I will kill you with love.'

Ammachi burst out weeping.

For Jezebel it was a day of tears but also a day of love.

'When Lilly George Marakkaran came to meet you, was it not to beg and plead you to go back with her?' The lawyer asked, somewhat irked.

'No . . .'

'Then what did she come to your house for?'

The lawyer grew more impatient.

Jezebel heaved a sigh. She was feeling drained.

'She didn't say anything?'

'She told me to go to the UK and save myself as soon as possible.'

The lawyer burst out laughing. There was a smile on the judge's face as well.

'Will any mother-in-law say something like this to the wife of her son who is lying in a coma?' The lawyer could not control his laughter.

Jezebel stood silent. Stifling his laughter somehow, the lawyer continued, 'And then? Was that all she said?'

'She asked me to drive that car . . .' Jezebel's voice broke.

The lawyer recoiled as if a burning log had been shoved at him.

'Which car? The one in which Dr Jerome met with an accident?'

The courtroom fell silent.

'And? Did you drive it?'

'Hm.'

Unable to contain himself, the lawyer looked at the judge in shocked surprise, then turned to her lawyer, then turned to everybody else in that room.

'The car in which your husband met with an accident . . . the very car . . . You say that even now? Did you come to argue this divorce case driving that car even today?'

'Yes,' said Jezebel.

To conceal his discomfiture, the judge tapped his pen on the sheet of paper in front of him, in a sort of rhythm.

'I wanted to buy an Innova. But then what if I went and crashed it somewhere and slipped into a coma and then my wife drove that same car to the family court to file a case and ended up marrying some Sandeep Mohan . . . So, I decided not to get one after all, *ketto*?'

The lawyer tried his own feeble brand of humour. Nobody laughed. And hence, in an attempt to reclaim his confidence, he asked, 'Okay, all agreed doctor*ey*. But I have a small doubt. Why did this mother-in-law, who was so fond of you, commit suicide, saying you did not go back with her?'

The courtroom fell silent.

'Oh! She committed suicide?' The judge looked shocked. The lawyer's face filled with sorrow.

'Yes sir. That poor woman committed suicide, consuming poison. She left a note saying her husband and she were unable to care for their bedridden son in their old age and that she hoped that her daughter-in-law would take over the responsibility. That poor mother fell at this one's feet, begging her to stay with her and help her take care of her son. But she didn't go. In truth, she is responsible for abetting Lilly George Marakkaran's suicide, sir . . .'

Jezebel felt a rush of sympathy for the lawyer then. But she realized in that courtroom, that car had been a metaphor in her life—life had tried to speak to her through that metaphor.

But there is a moment in everyone's life—a moment that speaks without the help of similes. A moment when others say, 'It is now that you are speaking plainly.'

21

Jezebel regretted that everyone in her life who had ever thrown a feast served the fine wine first and then the cheap wine after she was drunk. And so, she saved the fine wine until the end of the feast. It was the blood of her heart.

Much later, when she tried to read her life like someone else's story, Jezebel was intrigued. That is when she realized that each person who had entered her life was making way for the next one and that together, they were all contributing to making her life complete. When Lilly George Marakkaran took leave of her, she made sure to remind her, 'Do not cry. When you cry, nobody will come to cry along with you.' As she stepped out, she glanced at the garage on the right. The car that Jerome George Marakkaran had driven last stood there covered in tarpaulin. 'Do you drive this car now?' she had asked. 'If you don't, then you will lose touch with driving, and the car will also fall into disuse,' she added. 'But this is the car that Jerome drove, Mummy,' Jezebel had replied. 'You mean the car he drove and ruined,' said Lilly George Marakkaran, 'like he did your life. Unlike me, do not let what is broken stay broken. Reclaim it. Reclaim what is lost as much as you can.'

After the car carrying Abraham Chammanatt and Lilly George Marakkaran faded into the distance, she fetched the car key. She pulled off the car's cover, opened the door. The car started at once. It glided out, carrying Jezebel. She did not once feel that she was driving after months. She thought of Jerome. Whenever she thought of Jerome, she thought of Avinash as well. The car took her through the busy road right up to a signboard that said 'Aishwarya Workshop.'

Jezebel knew the owner of the workshop, Madhavankutty. When he had rushed his daughter Aishwarya to the hospital one night, following a bout of acute asthma, it was Jezebel who had resuscitated her. She had stayed by the child's side all night through nebulization. On the day the child was discharged, Madhavankutty came home with an envelope. She told him off, accusing him of trying to bribe her. He apologized. Afterwards, whenever Aishwarya had an attack of asthma, he came in search of Jezebel. Jezebel prescribed medicines and offered advice: sweep and mop the child's room every day, change the bedsheets at least once in two days, avoid fast food, canned juice and cold food items, wash and wipe the hair if the head sweats too much, do breathing exercises . . .

The gaps between Aishwarya's and Madhavankutty's visits to the hospital grew considerably. Then they were not to be seen at all. Just as Jezebel began to think that they might have started consulting a private hospital, one day, Madhavankutty came to meet her with a whole bunch of plantains, 'This is from our back yard. I would like to offer it to you.' She accepted it happily. He made her happier when he told her that Aishwarya had not had an episode of asthma for the past one year and that he was indebted to Jezebel. Madhavankutty was among those who had come inquiring after getting to know about Jerome's accident.

In two weeks, the car was made as good as new. The first trip Jezebel made was to Christina's house. Ammachi came along. They bought baby clothes and towels from a shop in town. Although she was going there after a very long time, Jezebel reached Christina's house without losing her way.

As they stopped the car near the gate, they could hear the wail of a baby from inside the house. Jezebel cocked her ear to the sound of that squirming cry and diagnosed it as 'gas'. John rushed to greet them at the gate. Just like Lilly George Marakkaran, John too had changed drastically. John, who had seemed short-statured because of his drooping shoulders and bent head back in those days when he would stay hidden inside the house like some rat or cockroach in its hole, now appeared as tall as Jerome when she saw him after a year and a half. He did not look either Jezebel or Ammachi in the eye. And, yet, his movements reflected traces of confidence. Though when Jezebel asked him 'John *achaya*, have you forgotten me?', he slunk away as if he had not heard her.

Christina's house was a two-storey building that looked at least twenty-five years old. Her Appachan, a cancer patient, sat in the sit-out on an old, faded easy chair, wearing an ill-fitting shirt and a hastily clad lungi. Although Appachan had made a lot of money working in the merchant navy, when he returned sick, the family lost its rhythm. As hospital visits and treatments became routine, Christina's education suffered a setback. Years passed. there was no one to think of a marriage proposal for her or to conduct her wedding. That was when Abraham Chammanatt arrived to sell off a plot of his land next to their house. The old acquaintance was renewed. Abraham took a liking to Christina and thought he would consider her for John. Having heard of the fame of the Chammanatt family, Christina's Appachan agreed. And that is how that wedding took place.

Christina's mother was a thin, withered woman. Years of caring for an ever-ailing husband had robbed her eyes of any hope. Her smile seemed to suggest that it was pointless to weep or despair. She received Jezebel and Ammachi as though she had been waiting for them for ever.

Christina's mother took them to the room from where the baby's cry could be heard. As Jezebel and Ammachi stood at the door, Christina, who was struggling to soothe the crying baby, looked up and forced a smile on her face. She was disturbed by the baby's wailing. But she was just as disturbed by Jezebel's presence. Jezebel went up to her and held out her hand. Christina seemed reluctant to hand the crying baby over to her. Jezebel took the child anyway, sat on the cot, held the baby down, and pressing its tummy to her knees she patted it on the back. 'I did that already,' said Christina. Jezebel didn't pay heed. After a minute, the child burped all of a sudden. The crying stopped as if a switch had been pressed.

'It was gas,' said Jezebel. Christina looked sheepish. She laid the child down on the plastic sheet spread on the cot. Just then, John peeped in. 'The crying stopped!', he exclaimed. 'It was gas,' repeated Jezebel. 'I had burped her after feeding,' Christina said feebly. 'From now on, I'll burp her. You don't have to,' said John sternly. Jezebel was hearing his voice for the first time. It was exactly like Jerome's. Perhaps because it was the voice of authority. John's movements, too, bore the same stamp of authority as he walked in. He took the baby and went out. Jezebel watched his firm footsteps with surprise. Perhaps when there is a woman to obey his command, a man grows taller and his tread grows firmer, she thought. When he takes his own child in his arms, perhaps his chest swells with pride. The greatness of a man is evident in the submission of those around him.

Probably remembering the convenience of having a doctor at hand, Christina began to ask Jezebel this and that about childcare. After a while Ammachi got up and went to the kitchen. Silence spread around the room as Jezebel and Christina found themselves alone. 'You are angry with me, *alle*, Christina?' Jezebel asked.

'Why?' Christina looked away.

'Do you feel I dumped Jerome on you both?'

Christina was silent. Her face hardened. Jezebel felt sad. For the world, Jerome was her cross to bear. He was her husband. The world demanded that he was entitled to be loved by her simply because he happened to be her husband.

Christina began to fold the washed baby-clothes heaped on a chair next to the cot. Jezebel asked her once again about how things were over there. Christina looked up. Her eyes filled with tears of indignation.

'What do you mean, "things over there"? I can speak for myself. They got me married not to their son but to that man's enemy. John*chayan* is not that man's son. So as far as he is concerned, John*chayan* is not even a human being, and the woman John*chayan* is married to is not a human being either. Haven't you heard of slaves in olden days? Just like that. At first, I didn't know what to do. I called my Ammachi and told her I was coming back home. Ammachi said, "Don't come right away. People around may say something. After a while, I'll call you over saying that Appachan is unwell. And then you can come." And so, I made up my mind that as long as I stayed there, I would not give in. And then whenever that man tried to hit John*chayan*, I began to step in. One day, I called the police and complained that he was assaulting me. That man bribed them and sent them away. After that whenever he raised his voice, I raised mine as well. With that, his ruckus stopped. The wife who wouldn't talk back and the son who wouldn't cry were his strength. He finally piped down when he saw that I would tell the world the truth about John*chayan* . . .'

Christina had finished folding the clothes. Jezebel listened speechless.

'And then Jerome*chayan*'s accident happened. They brought Jerome*chayan* over. From day one, that man was hopping mad. From then on, Jezebel became his enemy. That man did not sleep at night. He would pace up and down, cursing. He wouldn't let anyone sleep. He would sit next to his bedridden son and keep telling him, 'I'll teach her a lesson, *eda*! Get well and get up soon. We'll show her!' Sometimes he would laugh. Sometimes he would rage. But that man would never cry. But then, Mummy never wept either. Sometimes he would hit Mummy. I would intervene. One day, I got hit too. At that time, I was six months pregnant. I thought I had lost the baby. But when I fell down, John*chayan* came running. That was the first time I realized that my husband could stand up straight. John*chayan* not only stood with his spine erect, but he also grabbed hold of that man's hands and pinned him down. And screamed, "If you ever lay a finger on my wife or my mother again, I will kill you!" And then he pinned him to the wall. And stood like that for a long time. The fear on that man's face then! He said he didn't want to see him around in that house ever again. I was terrified. Not for myself or for John*chayan*, but for the child in my womb. The next morning, we left. We hadn't booked train tickets. We travelled by the general compartment. I didn't get back any of my gold jewellery. We didn't have any money either.'

Her head stayed bent. Jezebel heard her out silently. Tears dropped from Christina's eyes. Jezebel could see everything in her mind's eye—that world where a thousand pigeons wheezed asthmatically, those four shabby walls. And inside, George Jerome Marakkaran hitting Lilly George Marakkaran like a madman. A pregnant Christina falling down after being kicked. John George Marakkaran, who had, until then, not even looked George Jerome Marakkaran in the eye, standing upright and screaming. An electric current blazed through Jezebel's body. In what myriad ways the doings of some men transform other men!

'Until then, I had no love for John*chayan*. I thought he had ruined my life. But that day, all that changed. He does love me. I do have some value in his heart.'

Jezebel was not ashamed that her eyes had welled up. She was relieved for Christina. And envious too, that she could feel that sort of certainty about someone else. What a stroke of luck that was!

With a sigh, Jezebel inquired about Jerome. Christina's face filled with pity.

'Oh, what's there to say? Still the same. All laid up. His clothes need to be changed every day. He has to be turned to one side and then the other from time to time, and powdered all over, and fanned. Mummy does all that. Appan sits by his side all the time.'

'Does anyone come to meet Jerome?' Jezebel struggled to speak.

'A friend comes. He brings flowers. Gets medicines. Sits next to him.'

'Avinash?' Jezebel asked with bated breath.

'Yes,' replied Christina.

Jezebel felt suffocated and pained. She wondered why she was feeling so much pain. She had wanted to love Jerome. And tried to, too. But he had never allowed it. Even while living with her, the one he had loved and longed for was Avinash Gupta.

She came out of the room and stood in the dining hall, where the walls were still fresh from the coat of paint they had received just before Christina's wedding. A large picture of Christ hung above the door leading to the kitchen. Dried palm fronds from the last Palm Sunday lay curled up between the nails that propped up the picture. Just then, John came in from outside holding the baby. He and the baby were both smiling. The baby had John's long eyes and Lilly George Marakkaran's lovely lips. When she grows up, she will be a beauty, Jezebel prophesied to herself. When he saw her, John paused and began to take a step back.

'Make sure she is vaccinated at the right time, *ketto*,' said Jezebel.

John turned around quickly. He surprised her with his accurate recalling of the vaccination dates.

'They have asked us to come after three months for the next dose—on the 25th. Should we give her any other medicine before that?' asked John.

'No need,' Jezebel reassured him. He came a little closer.

'Anything else . . .? There's no other problem, no?' he asked diffidently.

'What other problem?' asked Jezebel, perplexed.

'No . . . her brain . . . I'm scared she'll turn out like me . . .'

His voice then became unlike Jerome's. It seemed like two babies were looking intently at her. She was moved.

'What's lacking in your brain John *achaya*?' she asked, her voice faltering. 'You are intelligent. It's just that you hadn't been using it, *alle*. And now you have begun to, *alle*?' she joked.

'No, I never had as much brain as Jerome even in childhood,' John said gravely.

'Jerome never had as much brain as you think, John *achaya*,' sighed Jezebel. 'You can make out how intelligent a person is by his capacity to love. Those who can love more are more intelligent. In that way, John *achaya*, you are more intelligent than Jerome. Jerome has never been able to love like you do, John *achaya*.'

John brightened. 'Ah yes. I do like everybody.' His innocent voice firmed up and filled with confidence.

Jezebel's heart was at ease even after she left that house. She tried to understand why. She smiled when she saw that it was because of the realization that Jerome George Marakkaran, too, had suffered just like her. How vile people are! Nobody is at ease until and unless they realize that the other person is suffering just as much. The moment you realize that no one else is any better off is when your self-confidence is restored. The moment you find someone to pin the blame on, is when you reclaim your inner strength.

The more she saw how pathetic it was that a man incapable of loving a woman's body had to marry a woman in order to convince the world, the sorrier she felt for Jerome. If only he had told her openly about it at least once. She would have been able to understand Jerome. She would have been able to forgive him as well. But would she have been able to role-play a contented wife for the sake the world as he wanted? It was a vicious cycle. Society had bound Jerome's hands and feet with its shackles of ignorance. He had hooked her too at one end of that shackle. As for her, she spent the best days of her youth choking and stifling and chafing within those shackles.

Jezebel thought of Avinash Gupta. She recalled his anxious voice, '*Jerome ko koi accident hua.*' She had not met Avinash. He had not made an effort to meet her. Was it because seeing Jerome's wife in person would have broken his heart? Perhaps Avinash felt the same intense heartache that a woman would feel when her lover married another woman. Perhaps Jerome married her with the same sense of helplessness felt by a man who leaves the woman he loves to invite a stranger into his life.

That night Jezebel kept thinking about those two men. She remembered that Jerome had a photograph of him with Avinash in his purse. She remembered that the screen saver on Jerome's laptop too was a picture of them together. She remembered that there were good morning and good night messages from him daily on Jerome's mobile phone. She felt ashamed that she had not been able to discern their relationship. She was ashamed that despite all the evidence in front of her, she had not been perceptive enough to suspect anything. She tried to imagine Avinash walking in with flowers and waiting next to Jerome's inert body. She wanted to thank Jerome for his having loved at least someone well enough for that person to keep vigil by his bedside. Startled by the sight of the damp pillow and moist strands of her hair when she woke up the next morning, she wondered when she had wept so much. She pledged to herself that she would never weep again.

A few days later, Christina's phone call came when she was in the midst of her rounds. 'John*chayan*'s Mummy . . .' she said and paused. Jezebel did not understand.

'What is it? What is it?' Jezebel asked anxiously.

'Mummy . . .' Christina paused again.

'Mummy?' prodded Jezebel.

'Mummy committed suicide!' screamed Christina.

Jezebel stood in disbelief.

Then she ran to Kurien sir's room. She told him something incoherently, breathlessly. With shivering hands, she searched for Abraham Chammanatt's number. She had Kurien sir call Abraham Chammanatt. The news of the death was confirmed. She had been found dead by poisoning in the morning. Abraham Chammanatt and his wife had already reached Jerome's city by then.

Jezebel stood rooted to the spot. She was worried for Jerome. Who would change the tubes on his body hereafter? Who would sponge his body? Who would turn him over so he wouldn't get bedsores?

Jezebel took the day off and drove to Christina's. The car sped as fast as it could through heavy traffic. As she neared Christina's gate, she could hear sounds of screaming from inside the house. A few neighbours stood around in the courtyard and the sit-out. In the courtyard, John was sprawled on the ground, wailing. Inside, the baby was bawling in fright. Jezebel went to Christina's room. A couple of women stood in the corridor, whispering among themselves. Christina was struggling to calm the screaming baby. Tears overflowed from her eyes. 'There is no one to go with John*chayan*,' whimpered Christina. 'How can I go in this condition?'

Jezebel was taken aback. It pained her to think of Lilly George Marakkaran setting out on her final journey without John seeing her.

'Shall I go with him?' she asked.

Christina was jolted.

'I will go with him.' Jezebel's voice filled with courage. 'You have his identification cards, *alle*? I will book flight tickets.'

She booked tickets for herself and John. The flight was at five in the evening. Christina called Abraham Chammanatt and asked them to wait till John's arrival for the last rites. When he realized that he would be able to go, John's wailing stopped as if it had been switched off. He quickly packed a bag. Wiping his tears on the sleeve of his shirt, he followed Jezebel like a lamb. They got into the car. Jezebel drove home. She informed Chachan and Ammachi about her decision to go to Jerome's city. They were shocked. She asked Chachan for some money. Chachan went along with them to the airport.

From the time they reached the airport John held on to her hand nervously like a little child. When they had to stand in separate lines at the security check, he kept turning back anxiously to look at her. When she came out of the screening, he ran up to her and clasped her hand tight again. Jezebel consoled him. She bought him food. But he would not let go of her hand. Even after they boarded the flight, his grip on her hand would not slacken. When the aeroplane rose into the air, he leaned his head on her shoulder. She thought he must have gone off to sleep. She felt fond of him. When her shoulder felt damp, she was taken aback. He was weeping, leaning on her shoulder. She tried to comfort him. But he did not wipe his tears.

'Mummy's gone!' he said in disbelief. It was a voice from a heart torn asunder.

Jezebel was unnerved.

'Mummy won't go away like that. She would never go away like that,' he said.

Jezebel felt like weeping. She tried to smile. She tried to distract him with what the airhostess brought them. After drinking some juice, John laid his head on her shoulder again.

'That man killed her. I know it.'

Jezebel was stunned. The chill of fear gripped her heart.

'I knew that that man would kill Mummy,' he said. 'I came away because I was scared that he would kill Christina and Kunjumol.'

'All that is just your fear, John *achaya*,' Jezebel tried to console him in a trembling voice.

John suddenly sat upright. 'Mummy's family has willed her share of the property in my name. That's why he has not killed me.'

Jezebel shut her eyes tight. John kept talking. 'Whenever I sat down to eat, he would fling away my plate of food. Even if my clothes were torn, he wouldn't get me new ones. I grew up wearing Jerome's old clothes. It was after he started going to school, and Mummy pleaded with Uncle, that I too was sent to school. Whenever Jerome hit me, Daddy would clap his hands and laugh out loud. If I ever hit back, Daddy would kick me to the ground. One day, Jerome ground my face into the floor. My lip began to bleed. The skin on my cheek peeled off. I cried. I began to run. That was when Mummy hit me for the first and last time. "Run if you want. But when you feel you can't run any more, you must stop. You must turn around. And you must ask him why he is hitting you. He must answer you. You must make him answer. Only when you stop and turn around will you grow."' John heaved a sigh. 'That day, when he kicked Christina, I turned around.'

John did not say that afterwards, he grew and became a "man".

Jezebel leaned back in her seat, eyes shut tight. She was scared to open her eyes. The world was a burning lake of fire. The world was a sea of piercing spearheads. The world was a valley of wolves sinking their fangs into flesh. Two-and-a-half hours sped by quickly. The journey came to an end. She dropped him outside the apartment. She told him to tell everyone that he had come alone. Then she went to Father Ilanjikkal's place. He arranged for her to stay in a convent nearby. The next day, accompanied by nuns sent by Father Ilanjikkal, she arrived at the church for Lilly Marakkaran's last rites. The nuns escorted her discreetly up to the coffin, before the lid was closed. George Jerome Marakkaran did not see her. She did not see him either. She kissed Lilly on the forehead, withdrew and came out. But when she emerged into the glare of sunlight from the shade of the huge gulmohar trees in the church compound, she sobbed her heart out. The being called man, how weak he is! The being called man, how helpless he is! The being called man, how insecure he is!

The face she had seen in the coffin was ashen. She tried to figure out what poison she may have consumed. Would she have felt a burning pain in her gut while dying? Would she have felt the tumult of everything inside her shattering to pieces? Would she have writhed on the ground, eyes popping out, tongue thirsting for water, throat smouldering? Jezebel wept a great deal that day. Death is that moment when life declares independence from the body. Lilly George Marakkaran's life had escaped her body. Jerome's life was still trapped in his.

'Doctor*ey*, answer the question put to you. Let's assume that all you have said is indeed true. Why did such an affectionate mother-in-law take her own life? Why?'

Jezebel looked at the lawyer with pity. What a meaningless question 'why' is! She wanted to tell him that wisdom is proved right through those who receive it. But she did not say it. She doubted if there was any point in saying it.

The doubting Jezebel asked Jezebel-the-rabbi thus: 'Why did Jerome George Marakkaran, who loved Avinash Gupta, marry Jezebel? Why did he assault Ann Mary? Why did Ammachi keep Chachan away from her? Why did George Jerome Marakkaran despise women so? Why does society shut tight even the graves of those who cannot be resurrected, with cork-shaped stones?'

Jezebel-the-rabbi replied thus: '"What is this?", "Why is this?" It will not be possible for anyone to answer these questions. All will be revealed in good time. It will not be possible to say that one is worse than the other. Each will be revealed as goodness in good time.'

22

Then Jezebel asked her own self, 'Who do you say I am?' She said, 'you are a woman full of life.' Happy to hear that, Jezebel told herself, 'I tell you, Jezebel you are the rock. And with this rock I will build your heart. The gates of hell will not prevail against it. I will give you the keys of the kingdom of heaven. I promise you, God in heaven will allow whatever you allow on earth, but he will not allow anything you don't allow. Those who wish to protect their own happiness will never destroy or forsake their freedom'.

Jezebel had imagined in many ways the day she would meet George Jerome Marakkaran again. Each thought of George Jerome Marakkaran getting aggressive again terrified her. She thought long and hard about how she would confront him. Sebin's face came to mind. If Sebin were by her side, she would not have to fear George Jerome Marakkaran. 'Don't be scared Jezebel, I am here, *alle?*' he reassured her. And yet the day she faced George Jerome Marakkaran in court, Sebin could not come to her aid.

Two months ago, Jezebel had attended Sebin's sister's wedding. The ceremony took place in an Orthodox Church since the groom belonged to that faction. As she sat down to partake of the feast after the wedding, Sebin came rushing up, all smiles.

'You've given me a loan all right, but don't eat too much, there are people waiting to eat in the next batch too.'

'Shouldn't I get value for my money, *da*?' Jezebel quipped.

'Money? What money?' he teased. And then he asked her eagerly, 'Wasn't it grand, the wedding?'

Jezebel looked at the stage decorated with a pair of plaster-of-Paris turtle doves, and at the bride posing for photos with family, her face bright with joy and pride, and agreed, 'Yes, it was grand.'

And then she teased him, 'Now that your sister is married off, isn't it your turn next?'

A mock shyness spread over Sebin's face. 'Oh, who would want to marry me?'

Dropping her voice to a whisper, Jezebel said, 'Do one thing. Marry me. When you are asleep, I will harvest your kidney and liver and make good the money I lent you.'

'You wicked one!' he exclaimed in mock horror.

Both of them laughed aloud as they had in their childhood.

When the laughter subsided, his face grew serious. 'Jezebel*ey*, I wanted to ask you a few things. Am I fit for married life? How to find out if there is anything left of my liver and kidney?'

'Aha, another wedding feast in the offing then!' teased Jezebel.

Shyness spread across his swollen face. 'Enough of the joking now. Tell me, if I marry, will there be any problem with the babies? That's what my friends keep saying.'

'We can do some tests and find out,' she reassured him. 'Who's the girl?' she asked.

Shyly he turned to a table a couple of rows away. Jezebel followed his gaze. A young woman, who had been feeding a child sitting next to her, looked up at him at the same time. Perhaps because she met his gaze, a spark lit up her eyes. Smiling at no one in particular, she nervously pulled the end of her blue silk sari around herself. She wiped bits of food from the child's mouth. Jezebel was startled—a married woman, and the mother of a child. Her eyes fell on the child. 'Intellectual disability', she whispered to herself.

'Jezebel*ey*, how do you like Princy?' asked Sebin. Jezebel tried to smile. She looked intently at Sebin. A new Sebin—one with sagging jowls. The damage in his liver reflected in his bloated cheeks, sweat beaded on his receding hairline, bags under his sunken yellow eyes—but his eyes shone bright.

'Your lover?' she asked him.

His eyes flickered. Lips quivered. Not hiding the pride men feel when they are loved, he turned to look once again at that young woman. 'Friend's wife,' said Sebin. 'He is dead. She had eloped with him. Her family will not take her back if she goes back. When that kid was born, the father was in jail. I was the one to first take him in my arms. She is bold. She will bring him up somehow. But how can I leave him to bear the brunt of someone's cussing and swearing?'

Jezebel looked at that child once again. A chubby face. An expression on him as if he was visiting the earth having left his mind behind on another planet. A face untroubled by the burden of having to think. He chewed his food absentmindedly. Food spilled from his mouth from time to time.

Jezebel's heart brimmed over. 'And yet you continue to drink and ruin your liver so,' she scolded him.

Sebin's face filled with guilt. 'I've stopped, I've stopped. But that's not what I'm worried about. If Princy has another child, will it also turn out like Rupesh?'

'Don't worry, Sebin. We will do a test and find out,' Jezebel reassured him. 'But first things first. First marry her. And then think about children.' She put the last bit of cutlet into her mouth and smiled at him. 'Nice cutlet. Get the same caterers for your wedding too, *ketto*?'

He looked away, unsure whether to tell her or not. 'Ammachi is kicking up a ruckus.' And then he looked at Jezebel with an air of come-what-may. 'No matter who agrees or not, this can't be put off any longer. I need to get the tests done as early as possible. Should I come see you? Or is it better to go to another hospital?'

When she realized that he was hinting that Princy was pregnant, she laughed. She teased him. She asked him to come and meet her at the hospital after the wedding bustle was over. He said he would come to the hospital on Friday with Princy.

As she drove home, Jezebel felt a great disquiet. Lives, she mused, such strange lives. She remembered the Sebin of her childhood—his innocence, his stupidity, his trust in her. May good things happen to him, she wished with all her heart.

Jezebel would never forget that Friday. After her class with the junior residents at the Medical College that morning, as she rushed towards the Neonatal Intensive Care Unit to attend to an emergency case, the phone in her kurta pocket vibrated. She disconnected the call without checking who it was and rushed into the NICU. The patient was a baby born the previous day—a scrawny little thing that wasn't crying or feeding. The phone rang again as she prepared a needle to do a lumbar puncture to extract cerebrospinal fluid from the baby's back. She ignored the call again. She laid the baby in the shape of a 'C'. The nurse held the baby's hands and feet. She put a needle and took out the fluid from between the L2, L3 discs in the baby's spine. The phone kept vibrating even then. The fluid she took out was all pus. She worried at the severity of the infection. She examined it under a microscope in the NICU. She prescribed a high dose of antibiotics. As the phone began to buzz again, without looking at who had called, she switched it off. The baby's mother was a young woman, not yet twenty. Wearing a towel over her nightie she slowly waddled over to Jezebel. 'Who asked you to walk around?' scolded Jezebel. 'My baby . . .' she wept.

As she came out after having consoled the mother, a young woman whose face had been washed clean by tears came up to her with her son. As she whispered, 'Sebin told me to come,' Jezebel suddenly recognized Princy—a slender woman, about five feet eight inches tall. Her abdomen protruded slightly from under her striped black kurta. The little boy dressed in a red T-shirt and three-fourths stood holding her finger tight, shaking his head, his gaze not focused anywhere. 'Where is Sebin? Why didn't you call before coming?' said Jezebel.

Princy smiled politely. 'I called you many times, doctor*ey*. Sebin is in the hospital—a case of stabbing.'

Jezebel was shocked.

But Princy continued in a low voice as if nothing unusual had happened. 'I came to know about it only this morning. He had gone to work in a lorry last night. He was particular that we come and get the tests done. That's why I'm here. Will it be possible to do the tests today itself, doctor*ey*? I am scared especially because this one is like this. If both children turn out like this it would be hard on them and on us. And if we delay it further, it may be too late to decide against having the baby.'

Jezebel was scared to look at her. Swallowing hard, she struggled to find her voice. 'Case of stabbing? Is it serious?'

'The friend who called me said it was a little serious. The lorry had come with goods from Mumbai. There was some quarrel about parking. Sebin had gone to mediate . . .'

'Which hospital? Is there a number to call?' There was none. But Princy assured her that someone would keep her informed. She stood in front of Jezebel betraying no sign of fatigue or sorrow that would be expected of a woman who had come for a test even as the father of her unborn baby lay with injuries in a hospital. Jezebel told her about the need for a genetic test. She called Dr Khadeeja who had been her teacher. She gave her Dr Khadeeja's number and the address of the private hospital she worked at. Princy looked at it. '*Iyo*, that far!' she gasped. Jezebel felt her breath constrict. She opened her purse and counted out the money in it—about five thousand rupees. She gave it to Princy. She looked at her, then at the rupee notes. Then she took them and put them in her own bag.

'Don't worry, Princy. Please don't hesitate to call me if there is anything. I will give you my number.'

'No, I have your number, doctor.'

'I think you are a brave woman, Princy. So I need not give you any other advice,' Jezebel said, trying to cover up her own nervousness.

'This is not courage, doctor,' Princy smiled. 'Courage is something that comes with thinking. This strength doesn't come from thoughts. Whatever happens, one has no option but to face it, *alle*? I know the work Sebin does. Earlier too he has been hit. Hit others. Killed. Gone to jail. We know that we will get as good as we give, *alle* doctor? What's the use of refusing to accept what we get? That's all that life is about for them. And when we live with them, that's what life is about for us too.'

Jezebel liked Princy's attitude. She felt grateful to Sebin for having found her and loved her. Jezebel patted Rupesh on the head. 'You must let me know if you need money. If you tell me two days in advance, I will keep it ready' she said.

'Doesn't Sebichan owe you money already, doctor?' Princy asked politely.

Jezebel went to meet Sebin. The sight of him laid up in a hospital reduced her to tears. He wept too. And then scolded her. And then made her laugh. And begged her not to come there again.

'Let me recover from all this. I'll finish off those two for you,' said Sebin. 'Your father-in-law and husband. I will go to your husband's place disguised as some plumber or electrician. I'll remove his oxygen tube. Two minutes. I will smother your father-in-law with a pillow. Five minutes. Five plus two: seven. In seven minutes, all your problems will be solved.' Sebin laughed out loud.

As she stood in the court, Jezebel recalled how she had felt a surge of fondness for him then.

'Can you explain the present condition of your husband who spent two-and-a-half years with you, loving you and caring for you?' asked the lawyer.

'He is in a coma.'

'Have you ever thought about the moment he recovers from all this?'

'He will not recover.' Jezebel's tone was calm. But the faces of those present in the court filled with distaste, as if she had stripped in front of them. The judge's face filled first with shock and then disgust.

'Who are you, doctor*ey*, to say that he will not recover? Are you God?'

'All the medical experts who examined Jerome said that . . .'

'*Sho*! So many people written off by doctors continue to live happily to this day. Do you know, a big doctor told a cancer patient near my house that he wouldn't live for more than four months? And I went along with him to that very doctor's burial. Ten years ago . . .' The lawyer's voice was full of rage and scorn. 'Okay, let's say he will not get up. How long will he remain in this condition?'

'The doctors said five years.'

'Then what is the need for this case, doctor*ey*? This case has been going on for two years. After the verdict on this case is returned, then the appeal in a higher court, and then the decision of the church . . .'

'I want a legal separation.'

'What for? That's the question.'

As Jezebel prepared to answer, the lawyer cut in again. 'Because you know that your husband will recover eventually, and when he does, he will ask you a whole lot of questions. You will not be able to answer any of those questions. And that's why you have filed this case—in order to escape before he confronts you.'

If only Jerome George Marakkaran could get up and come, thought Jezebel. But Jerome did not come. Instead came that man—George Jerome Marakkaran.

That day, she left for the court alone since Valiyammachi was down with a fever. She was scared of being on her own, yet she decided to go alone. A wedding ceremony was just getting over in the church opposite the court. The bride and the groom stood on the steps and smiled sweetly for the cameras. She looked at them with sympathy. As she stopped the car and got out, she stood for a moment outside the health centre, gazing at the banner that read 'Should you stop your wife's pregnancy? Don't!' and billowed in the air like a pregnant woman's belly. And then, trembling, she descended the steps to the court.

As she walked into the box-like court, near the steps leading to the counselling centre, she saw her lawyer talking to the defence lawyer. George Jerome Marakkaran stood next to them, his hands clasped tightly behind his back. His long face had grown thinner and longer. His jaw and nose seemed to have grown sharper and jutted out into the air. Hatred glittered in his sharp eyes. Jezebel's eyes clouded over. Her feet begged her to turn and run away. She lacked the strength to run. 'When you feel you can't run any more, you must stop.' She heard Lilly George Marakkaran's voice. 'You must turn around. Arriving at a decision either way rather than running endlessly is better for everyone.'

Jezebel went straight up to him. She greeted him with folded palms. And then she turned to her lawyer Advocate Philip Mathews. He told her, 'We feel that a compromise would be better, doctor. That's what we were discussing.'

'What compromise?' Jezebel's voice grew louder. 'Compromise with whom?'

'Not like that. Even though the cases in the court are decided based on documents, the credibility of the complainant is of utmost importance. In your case, they have placed several complicated details about you before the court. We will not be able prove that those things did not happen either because of the nature of those allegations. So, rather than the court quashing the case, will it not be better to reach a compromise and reach some sort of cash settlement?' asked the lawyer.

Jezebel's blood boiled. 'No. There will be no compromise. I need to win this case at any cost,' she said. 'I can't keep running in fear all my life.'

That was when she realized, she had grown. Not as a man or as a woman, but as a citizen.

It was time for harvest. The crop was ripe on earth.

23

Later, Jezebel who arrived at the Gethsemane of sufferance asked Jezebel-the-disciple, 'Are you still sleeping and resting? Look, the hour is near. Arise! The ones who will betray me are approaching.'

She knew that it was the day of the crucifixion. She foresaw that they would give her bitter wine, nail her to the cross and divide up her garments by casting lots. They would mark her forehead with 'Here is Jezebel, queen of the wayward.' They would line her up along with thieves and murderers. The passers-by would berate her. Her memories of the court that day were from the perspective of the topmost step leading from the health centre. From up there, she could see in the courtyard a rich young man wearing thick gold jewellery on his neck and hands, along with a group of other young men. They reminded one of soldiers ready for war or revolutionaries preparing for an attack. She guessed that they must be witnesses in a divorce case. She recalled Valiyammachi's words 'How easy it is to tie the knot. If the man and woman agree, then the job is done. But to untie it, you need the approval of the whole community.' But later she came to know that it was not just a divorce case. They were there to trap and punish the autorickshaw driver who had eloped with the wife of the rich young man.

Jezebel's re-examination began immediately. Philip Mathews asked her, 'What is the status of the cases in your name?' She told him about each case.

'So, which are the cases in your name right now?'

'There are no cases against me.'

'What happened to the investigation in the case that the brakes of your husband's car were found to be tampered with?'

'The accused is no more.'

'Are you among the accused?'

'No.'

'The police had given you a clean chit in the drugs case.'

'Yes.'

'Since when have there been cases against you?'

'After my husband's family took him back home.'

'What was that for?'

'To put pressure on me.'

'What was your opinion about taking Dr Jerome George Marakkaran to their place?'

'Nobody asked me for my opinion.'

'When were you informed about the decision to take Jerome away?'

'The day before my MD exams began.'

'Why did you refuse to go with your husband?'

'If I had gone, three years of my studies would have gone to waste.'

'Why is an MD degree so important to you?'

'It's difficult to get a good job without an MD.'

'Why did you not ask your husband's relatives to wait until after the examinations?'

'I was not given time for that. Everything was decided beforehand.'

'Had you not given your word that you would take care of him here?'

'They didn't listen to me.'

'Why did they not agree?'

'I don't know.'

'Who has the jewellery and the cash that you received at the time of the wedding?'

'Jerome's Daddy.'

'Why did you stay in a rented house although this is your home town?'

'Because Jerome's Daddy insisted.'

'What was your opinion?'

'They did not ask me for my opinion at any point in time.'

'You received a stipend, didn't you? Who used to spend it?'

'Jerome. The car loan was paid from my stipend.'

'Who earned more? You or your husband?'

'Jerome.'

'Then why did he make you pay the loan?'

'Because Jerome's Daddy said so.'

'In other words, who controlled your lives after your marriage?'

'Jerome's Daddy.'

'You are an educated and intelligent woman, *alle*? Could you not have tried to take responsibility for your life?'

'Neither Jerome nor his Daddy ever valued my words.'

'What about your family?'

'They told me to live by my husband's word.'

'What is the relationship between you and Dr Sandeep Mohan whose name was mentioned earlier?'

'Friendship.'

'Where is Sandeep Mohan at present?'

'In Dubai.'

'When did you last meet Sandeep Mohan?'

'When he came to tell me that he was going to Dubai. That's when he gave Sebin the money.'

'What is the relationship between you and Sebin?'

'We were neighbours. We grew up playing together, and then they moved elsewhere.'

'At what age were you playmates?'

'Until the age of five.'

'Okay. After that what was your relationship with Sebin?'

'I had met Sebin's mother and sister sometime but saw Sebin only years later, at the hospital where Jerome had been admitted. Sebin and his three friends had rushed Jerome to the hospital although they did not know who he was.'

'So did you recognize him at the hospital?'

'Sebin recognized my father. Chachan used to meet them even after they moved house.'

'Right. Why did you give Sebin twenty-five thousand rupees?'

'It was Sebin's sister's wedding. He said he was short of twenty-five thousand rupees for the fixing of the wedding.'

'Did you go to that wedding?'

'Yes.'

'Did he return the money?'

'Sebin is bedridden after an accident.'

'Why do you want a divorce at this point in time?'

Jezebel was silent.

'Go on. Tell us. There are no women who do not wish to become mothers, *alle*? You, too, might want a family life and children of your own, *alle*, Dr Jezebel?'

'No,' said Jezebel.

The lawyer was taken aback. The defence lawyer laughed out loud. The judge laughed too. Philip Mathews, too, laughed to cover up his embarrassment.

'So, you don't plan to marry again?' asked the judge.

'No.'

'Don't want children?'

'No.'

The courtroom fell silent again.

'Then why do you need a divorce?'

'I want freedom.'

All at once Jezebel felt the shackles of fear slip off her soul. She declared with all her heart, 'I want to live without fearing anyone.'

The courtroom was silent. Then a wave of whispers rose, and someone could be heard talking and laughing at the same time. The judge called for order. The defence lawyer announced, 'She is not interested in toeing the line, she wants to run wild.' And people laughed again.

Advocate Philip Mathews stopped his re-examination, as if defeated. 'That was a bit much,' he admonished her in a low voice as she got down from the witness box. 'I told you specifically to mention that you want to become a wife and a mother, hadn't I?'

'But I am not interested in that,' said Jezebel.

'You may not be interested. But had I not told you that this is how you put it in court?'

'One should not lie in court, *alle*?'

Philip Mathews' face reddened. 'Ah! Well, then face the consequences. Don't blame me if you lose the case.' He swung around and walked away to the front. George Jerome Marakkaran was getting on to the witness box for cross-examination.

With a new-found confidence Jezebel went to the back of the room and stood behind the benches. When he saw her, George Jerome Marakkaran's eyes narrowed further. His face hardened even more. George Jerome Marakkaran took the oath placing his hand on the book. Her lawyer began the cross-examination lackadaisically. Jezebel looked intently at George Jerome Marakkaran. She looked at him without fear for the first time. His eyebrows had greyed. There were creases on his forehead. Great dark circles had appeared under his eyes. His cheekbones jutted out. His eyes blazed. To Jezebel, he looked like he was smouldering. A man with a furnace burning in his heart. He would always smoulder—and suffocate others.

'Your son Dr Jerome George Marakkaran is bedridden after an accident. What is his present condition?' asked her lawyer.

'By god's grace, he is much better. I believe he will get up and walk about very soon.' George Jerome Marakkaran said with an air of solemn calm, raising his eyes heavenwards. Jezebel was stunned.

'What do you mean by "much better"? Dr Jerome's medical report says he is in a coma.'

'I had complained long back that that report was incorrect.' George Jerome Marakkaran paused to look bitterly at Jezebel.

'I came to know later that some people had tried to tamper with that report. Some people were very keen to prove that my son would never get up and walk again. But there is nothing that God the all-powerful cannot do. Today my son's condition is far better. Even yesterday, Dr Paul, who is treating my son, said that he would recover fully and return to work as a doctor very soon.'

'Who is this Dr Paul?'

'He has treated several such patients and made them walk again. He practises a branch of medicine called electro homeopathy.'

'Is it possible for a patient to recover completely and walk again after being in a coma for so long?'

'If the court would permit, I am ready to bring my son and present him here in court exactly a year from today. All I plead is that the court grant me time until then.'

'And what if you don't keep your word? My client will have to wait for a whole year more, *alle*? And even if your son recovers, what's the guarantee that he will be as healthy as before? Your son's wife is twenty-seven years old already. Medical science says that, ideally, the first pregnancy should occur before the age of twenty-eight for the child to be born without disabilities. In such a situation, it is already late for Dr Jezebel. So is it not better to grant her a divorce now?'

'First, Dr Jezebel has made it clear here that she is not interested in either marrying again or becoming a mother.'

'That could be due to her ignorance at this point in time. She is, after all, a woman. If, tomorrow, her family and relatives compel her, is it not likely that she may change her mind?'

'I am more concerned than anyone else here about Dr Jezebel. For me she was not a daughter-in-law. She was a daughter. She was my son's very life. And we loved her as much as he did. And we still do. Like her father, I, too, wish that she has a good life. But, *saarey*, nobody can love her like my son. She will not get that kind of love and care from anyone else.'

'But had you not humiliated and tortured Dr Jezebel during the time she spent at your place?'

'Who? Me? Did Jezebel say so?' George Jerome Marakkaran stood open-mouthed. Jezebel was bewildered to see his ability to act so bewildered.

'I have always thanked God for giving me a daughter-in-law as smart and intelligent as Dr Jezebel. Of course, she is a bit impulsive, but that's about the only problem I've seen in her so far. My wife, who passed away recently, and me, we both loved Jezebel dearly.'

'In that case, are you not obliged to ensure that your daughter-in-law gets a good life? Isn't it better to allow this divorce to happen rather than to object to it?'

George Jerome Marakkaran smiled a pained smile. 'The honourable court should understand one thing. If something happens to my son, I am ready to take the lead in arranging another marriage for my daughter-in-law. But Dr Jezebel is not the kind of woman you think she is. She is not interested in getting pregnant or having children. Ever since she got married, she has been on contraceptive pills. This was something that upset my son greatly. He has told me about it too.' George Jerome Marakkaran paused for a moment. 'If what I said is untrue, then why did Dr Jezebel not have children in the two years that she spent with my son? If she hasn't had pills, then is it because Dr Jezebel cannot become a mother anyway? That needs to be confirmed by a test.'

The lawyer was momentarily caught off guard.

George Jerome Marakkaran continued, 'And now about another wedding. Even if she is granted a divorce from here, only if she is granted a divorce by the church will she be able to marry again in the church. We Catholics do not have the right to put asunder what God brought together. The church will never allow a wife to abandon a bedridden husband—a husband who carried her around in his palm like a prized possession for two-and-a-half years. A woman who runs around trying to get married again the moment he falls sick—who will marry her?'

George Jerome Marakkaran gasped for breath.

'And let me make it clear that I have never wished to ruin the happiness of my daughter-in-law, because my son loved his wife so deeply. He has never refused any of her wishes. He has never laid a finger on her. But if you ask me if she returned that love, I have no answer. He has confided in me about all that he had to endure each day of his life with her. Each time I would tell him, "Son, she is your wife. Even if there are failings on her part, you must forgive her." If my daughter-in-law wants a divorce, so be it. I will agree to it. But not now. After a year. Because I promise this court in the name of the Lord that my son will get up and walk again. Let him come and take a decision. Anyway, we have come this far. One year, I request the court to give me just one more year's time.'

George Jerome Marakkaran paused for a moment—he heaved a sigh. The courtroom was silent. Under the cement stairs, a baby mouse scurried about in the dust. Jezebel sat watching it impassively. The lawyer cleared his throat.

'What do you mean by "give me time"?'

'My son's condition is improving day by day. He will walk one day. We have shown him to so many eminent doctors. All of them say that Jerome will be back on his feet soon, but it will take time. I have great hope. My wife observed fast after fast for his well-being and eventually lost her mental balance and died. Jerome's health has improved. His weight has increased. When we call out to him, he responds by tilting his head and moving his eyeballs. If you have any doubts, come home with me. I will pay for the flight tickets. If you need to find out how much improvement he has made, please come and see him at least once.' He stopped again.

'My daughter-in-law Dr Jezebel was not a daughter-in-law for me. She was my daughter. I will only be too happy if she gets a good life, but she is stubborn by nature. She left us after a small misunderstanding, and my wife died broken-hearted because of that. But I have no ill will towards her. I have only one request to make to Jezebel. One year, until my son recovers, bear with us for just one year. Let her have a word with him and then go with whoever she pleases.'

The court was silent. George Jerome Marakkaran heaved a sigh.

'Dr Jezebel is young. She is not old enough to understand the pain of a father. I had given a healthy young man in marriage to her, but what she returned to me was a living corpse. I have taken good care of him so far. His health has improved considerably. He will become his old self very soon. Until then, I need time. Just a little more time is what I am asking for. I only ask this honourable court to have mercy on this father, this old man.'

A loud wail rose. The sound of George Jerome Marakkaran's sobs reverberated in that hall. The women lawyers and women sitting next to Jezebel wiped their eyes. Jezebel sat with the disbelief of seeing a villain in a movie suddenly metamorphose into a virtuous character. George Jerome Marakkaran shed all the tears he had not shed earlier in his life. The judge wiped his face.

As he got down from the witness box, George Jerome Marakkaran's feet gave way. His lawyer rushed to support him.

The judge announced that the next hearing would be four months later. The court had to be informed of any progress in Jerome George Marakkaran's health after four months. A doctor's certificate would have to be produced. Jezebel fumed. Four months was a short time, but for her, it felt like an eternity. She came out and stood on the veranda. Her lawyer who came up from behind said, his face hardening, 'We lost the case.'

'But the verdict is not out,' said Jezebel, surprised.

'What verdict? That man has walked away with the case,' said the irate lawyer. 'Even otherwise you failed to impress the court. Your looks and the way you dress had a negative influence on the court. I told you many times not to come to the court in jeans. How will the court respect a woman who does not show any sign of sorrow even though her husband has been caught in such a tragedy?'

Seeing the lawyer's irritation, Jezebel felt mischievous. 'What if we tell the court that the marriage was not consummated?' she asked.

'Who would believe that a doctor like you would live like that with someone for two years?' The lawyer grew more irritated.

'If necessary, we can do a virginity test. Then the court may believe me.' She smiled.

The lawyer flinched as if he had been hit. He struggled to understand if she was joking or not.

'It's too late,' he said timidly. 'Whatever you have to say, you have to say at the outset. That's how it is in the court.'

Jezebel smiled, her dimples unfurling. 'And if I had, would the accusation that I don't look sad enough change?' she asked.

The lawyer turned away uneasily, but the irritation and aversion on his face had mellowed. A little softness and empathy were evident. Jezebel wondered why. Would that be the kindness of a man towards a virgin? Who knows the way of a man with a virgin?

Jezebel stood at the foot of the stairs. She felt tired. Just then a woman dressed in a churidar called out to her from the top of the stairs, 'Doctor*ey*!' She carried a baby who looked about one-and-a-half years old. As Jezebel climbed up the steps, the woman called out, 'Do you remember me doctor?' When she reached the top, the woman held Jezebel's hand and began to introduce herself, 'Doctor*ey*, when my son had burns, in the Medical College . . .'

After a moment, Jezebel recognized her. The mother of the eight-year-old who was admitted with burns on the day Sosa Aunty arrived with Jerome George Marakkaran's marriage proposal! She remembered how, crazed with grief, the woman had tried to jump off the second floor when she heard the news of her son's death. But now, there were no traces of grief on her face. 'My daughter, doctor*ey*,' she said. Jezebel held the little one's hand—a healthy baby. The twinkle in her eyes and her abundant hair told of her good health.

'She has been vaccinated, *alle*? You have started giving her everything you cook at home, *alle*?' Jezebel asked her.

'A mild fever, so we came to the health centre to pick up medicines,' said the mother.

'No need to give medicines for a mild fever,' advised Jezebel. The smiles on the faces of the mother and child made her smile too.

Just then, Jezebel's eyes fell on the courtyard below. George Jerome Marakkaran had reached the foot of the steps along with his lawyer. He, too, was smiling. The tears of the courtroom had evaporated, and instead, a smile beamed across his face. When he saw her, his face hardened. Another kind of smile gleamed in his eyes. Jezebel did not feel anger or spite. She looked intently at him; he looked intently at her. His eyes seemed to emit sparks of fire. Jezebel's head felt heavy. She felt the pain of the wounds left by the nails he had driven into her body. On his face you could see the dark shadow of the miseries he had undergone for the past several months. The veins on his forehead bulged. His stoop was more pronounced now. She thought he might kill her if he came any closer. That was when the gang of young men who had come to witness the divorce case swarmed out. A young man rushed up the steps, trying to flee them. As he fled for his life, he pushed George Jerome Marakkaran, who lost his footing on the steps and fell down to the ground below.

The uproar of the chasers and the chased faded. Only George Jerome Marakkaran's cries could be heard. Jezebel rushed down the steps. People were helping him to his feet. The left elbow had been twisted out of shape. 'Is it a fracture?' someone could be heard asking. '*Iyo*, my back!' he cried out. Jezebel made her way through the crowd and reached his side. The crowd parted for her. She examined his hand and leg. 'We have to rush him to the hospital,' she said. It was not clear whether George Jerome Marakkaran had recognized her voice. Pain shrouded the usual sneer on his face. She could see the pain wrenching his bones and flesh like a naughty child would pull out a plant by its roots. His face turned blue, then black and was drenched in sweat.

In pain, people dissolve like a lump of salt in the sea. They become unlike themselves. They become the water of the sea— mere water that rises and crashes with the tide and plunges into the depths with the ebb. Because all men are like blades of grass— their greatness is like the flowers on those blades of grass. The blades of grass wither. The flowers wilt.

Even after four months the case would drag on. George Jerome Marakkaran would ask for time until his broken bones healed. He would ask for more and more time. Her head reeled. She could feel the last nail piercing its way into her body.

'*Eloi, eloi lama sabachthani?* My god, my god, why have you forsaken me?' Jezebel wanted to cry out. But what if those who heard her thought she was calling out to Elijah?

Prophet Elijah left for Jordan. There, he met his end. Before he left, Elijah cursed Jezebel: Within the limits of Jezreel, Jezebel would be devoured by dogs.

But before that, I will line my eyes, arrange my hair, brace for battle and look down from the window—Jezebel grew headstrong.

And so, I say with all my heart, I live like a queen. I'm not a widow. I will never need to weep and wail.

It was all over. Jezebel's head slumped, and she dedicated her soul to the heavens.

24

Later, when Jezebel took stock of what she had gained from pursuing the divorce case, this was the revelation she had: The punishment for the daughter of man does not end with crucifixion alone. Her legs will be fully broken. To make sure she is dead, they will insert spears into her sides. They will rejoice when blood and water spurt out. They will stand watching and laughing at the one they have wounded. If someone accepts her body and wraps it in a clean cloth and buries it in a tomb hewn out of rock, they will close its mouth with a boulder.

As she drove behind the ambulance carrying George Jerome Marakkaran, Jezebel found it difficult to breathe. Jezebel-the-doctor reminded Jezebel-the-crucified that it was not easy for someone to breathe while nailed to the cross. Like when you get married, when you are nailed to the cross, too, you feel weighed down by the body. When you hang, the weight of the body is borne by the legs at first. That is why they bend your knees at forty-five degrees before nailing you to the cross. As long as the legs can bear the weight, death will be delayed. They break your knees to quicken death. Once the knees are broken, then the weight of the body is borne by the two outstretched hands. The wrists are bound so that the flesh is not prised apart from the nails. When they hang for long, the shoulder bones detach from their sockets. And so, the hands grow longer. The ribcage begins to sag. The body struggles to exhale. It suffocates. The body sweats profusely and blood keeps oozing from the wounds. A cardiovascular collapse owing to hypovolemic shock—with that, it's all over.

Since the lawyer had informed them about George Jerome Marakkaran's accident, Abraham Chammanatt and Gracy aunty had already reached the casualty department at the Medical College. Jezebel stood watching the sight of the doctors examining George Jerome Marakkaran, speaking to Abraham Chammanatt and then wheeling George Jerome Marakkaran away in a gurney, as if in a movie. Some of the nurses were familiar with Jezebel. Attenders greeted her politely. As she stood alone in that bustling crowd, Jezebel thought about death by crucifixion. If you were nailed to the cross, how long would it take for you to die? One hour? Three hours? How would the body endure such excruciating pain? Would brain death occur at the peak of pain? And when that occurred, what would happen to all the memories and fears stored until then in the brain?

After sometime, her feet led her outside. Her hands opened the door of the car. The car took her home. Her feet took her inside, into her room, flung her on to the bed. It was when Valiyammachi shook her with an '*Ennadee kochey*, what happened?' that she was jolted awake.

'Did they rip you apart in the court today, too?' asked Valiyammachi anxiously. As Valiyammachi ran her hands, still warm with fever, on her hair and shoulders, Jezebel's soul quivered. It rushed back to the body it had left behind. The brain which had died throbbed back to life as if it had received an electric shock. She sat up. She reminded herself that she had to resurrect herself from the dead.

When she heard what had happened to George Jerome Marakkaran, Valiyammachi's eyes widened in disbelief. 'How on earth did that happen?' wondered Chachan. 'The Lord gives man the fruits of his deeds,' said Ammachi, drawing a cross. As she left for the Medical College along with Chachan, Jezebel thought about all the wounds the man called George Jerome Marakkaran had inflicted upon her. How he had upturned her life in so many ways! How he had trampled her soul, like kicking a rabbit and sending it hurtling! And what did he gain? Why did he have to meet with that accident in the family court itself, in front of her eyes? She saw that the ways of justice were full of danger. Her heart filled with terror. It struggled to muster courage and beat weakly.

George Jerome Marakkaran had suffered two major fractures. He required immediate surgery. Jezebel sat waiting in the duty room of the children's hospital until the surgery got over at two in the morning. Irshad went to the operation theatre to make inquiries whenever he got time during his night duty. When she heard that it would take at least six months for the bones to get fused again, Jezebel felt like laughing and crying. Who knows how long one has left? Man decides his path, but someone else controls his footsteps.

The next morning, as she left for the post-operation ward, Jezebel's mind was blank. She consoled herself that this was the void the crucified one felt at the height of pain. Having been informed by Abraham Chammanatt, George Jerome Marakkaran's only sister Rosamma Varghese arrived at the hospital, dressed in a shiny sari and heavy ornaments of imitation gold. She was about the same age as George Jerome Marakkaran. Although she had heard many stories about her earlier, perhaps because Jezebel was a doctor, she was not hostile towards her. Jezebel bought her lunch. She got her medicine for her joint pain from the orthopaedist Dr Shaheed.

The next day Jezebel came face to face with Abraham Chammanatt at the parking lot. She saw that when he looked at her, his eyes filled with fear. She rejoiced at the thought that he was afraid of her. She wanted to add to that fear.

'Who is there to take care of Jerome?' she asked with an air of authority.

'A friend of his, who is also a doctor,' replied Abraham Chammanatt meekly.

'Is Avinash Gupta just a friend?' Jezebel was breathing hard despite her best effort to stay calm.

Abraham Chammanatt fumbled and floundered and stood embarrassed in front of Jezebel.

Jezebel was livid. 'So you knew everything, *alle*, Uncle? Knowing fully well about the relationship between Avinash and Jerome, you ruined my life, *alle*?'

Abraham looked miserable. 'I thought he would stop all that after marriage.'

Jezebel felt that her body was set on fire. She stood there, burning. She felt like smashing everything in sight. They were standing in the hot sun. Around them people were coming and going—countless people, patients and others, passers-by and vendors. They all looked like conspirators to her. Everyone had known everything beforehand. Jerome's Daddy knew that his son could not love women. Jerome's Mummy knew that her boy was sexually attracted to other men. Abraham Chammanatt knew that his sister's son had a physical relationship with a male friend. Perhaps his wife and all his relatives knew all of this, too. Like in a clichéd script, all of them had sacrificed her at the altar in order to see a man play his role in society.

'Lilly was our only sister, *moley*. She was our very life. The man we chose for her ruined her life. And then we had to marry her off to the one who was available. Those were different days. What other way was there to save face in front of the community? The better option was to kill her off. Not that we didn't know that. We Christians are forbidden to kill, *alle*? But we can crucify. And we can stand watching as the blood drains and life ebbs on the cross.' Abraham Chammanatt tried to smile.

Jezebel could not. How could a body nailed to the cross, a body whose blood was draining away little by little, smile?

'To save face, you first sacrificed Mummy's life and then, mine. How come it's always women you sacrifice in order to save face, Uncle?' Jezebel fumed.

'What's the point of talking about something that's past, *moley*?' Abraham Chammanatt was helpless.

'It's past for you,' hissed Jezebel. 'For me nothing is past. And it won't get over. How will it get over? As long as the man lying inside with broken limbs lives on, it is not over for me. It's not over for me until the heartbeat of a man lying unconscious two thousand kilometres away stops. Try living my life for just one day. Any one day—from the day you set foot in my house with the marriage proposal till today—do you dare? Do you dare?'

Abraham Chammanatt looked around nervously, hoping no one had heard her. His constant need to keep saving face enraged her even more. What was so great about all their faces that they needed saving? What does the world gain by seeing these faces like this? As she was crucified, the saints were being canonized. Lilly George Marakkaran rose from her grave and narrated the story of her ruined life. She confessed: I am a woman who has never known love, who had no self-respect, who was hurt and humiliated every day, and who died somehow. The thought that like Lilly, she too was walking down a path of no return, terrified her.

'It says in the Bible that man is in the hands of the Lord like clay in the hands of the potter. He acts according to his will.' Abraham Chammanatt tried to reason.

Jezebel's anger blazed again. 'Is the Bible meant only for you to quote from according to your needs? I have also read in the holy book: "Don't say that the Lord is the reason for my downfall, for he will not do anything that I despise. Do not say the Lord led me astray for He does not need a sinner."'

Abraham Chammanatt looked at her, defeated. 'I have nothing to argue with you about, *kochey*. What is to be done now? Tell me. I'll do what you say.'

'Please give me back my life. That's all. My happiness . . . my ability to laugh.' Jezebel's lips quivered. Her left cheek throbbed. 'That's all I want, Uncle. I want to be able to forget everything and laugh. I don't want to feel resentful when I see other people laughing.' She gasped for breath. 'I have promised myself that I won't cry. I don't like to break promises.' With a look of contempt, she walked past Abraham Chammanatt who stood there defeated and helpless. That night, unable to bear the burden of her own body, she wept all night long. Valiyammachi tried to console her. 'You promised not to cry?' she protested feebly.

'These are not tears, Valiyammachi. This is the pericardial fluid that spurts out when a spear pierces the ribs,' she said soundlessly.

Irshad's call came just as she had begun to sleep. 'Jez, Arifa has gone into labour. Most probably she might deliver today. Umma cannot manage it all by herself. Geethu is the only one around here. If you come over and relieve me I could go home . . .'

Jezebel got up, washed her face, pulled on a pair of jeans and shirt and rushed to the Medical College. As she entered through the back gate and turned towards the Children's Hospital, a police jeep and an ambulance, its siren wailing, pulled up in front of the casualty department of the Medical College. In a flash she saw a young man, his clothes drenched in blood, rushing towards the casualty with a baby in his arms.

Jezebel's eyes saw only the child at first, and guessed—three years old. When she entered, the young man had laid the child on a stretcher and was screaming, 'Sister, please call someone! Take the child to the ICU!' And then as if he could not bear to wait for anyone, he began to wheel the gurney himself, shouting, 'Where is the ICU? Tell me! Tell me!' Jezebel ran up and checked the child's pulse. She could not feel the pulse. She gave the child CPR. She called out 'Oxygen! Oxygen!' She rushed to the ICU with the child. When she saw that it was her senior Dr Sivaprasad who was on duty, she felt reassured. They could not resuscitate the child despite both of them trying for a long time. When she came out, exhausted, the young man was standing at the doorway, his eyes half-closed.

'Sorry,' whispered Jezebel.

'Is she really dead?' he asked. As the truth sank in, a kind of calm descended in his eyes, and he quietly sat down on the floor, eyes closed. The sight of that man stretched out on the bare floor in the midst of that bustling crowd, as peacefully as if he were on his own bed at home, astounded her. His pulse was normal. It was clear that he was weak from exhaustion. She requested Dr Sivaprasad to put him on a glucose drip.

The ward was teeming with patients. The walls rang with grunts, moans, cries, scoldings and complaints of the relatives. People were talking about the accident. A hospital attendant said that a woman and a ten-year-old child had died earlier. She felt a rush of empathy with the man who had tried to save the second child. Whoever he was, whether an officer or a businessman, rich or poor, an intellectual or an artist, he was just a living being impelled to action like a man possessed, when he felt that the last link in a bloodline was about to be broken. What if he did not have anyone else left in this world?

As she sat reading under a noisy fan in the duty room at the children's hospital, Jezebel felt the unbearable heaviness of her body. She was distressed that it was because her body had been nailed to the cross. She could see Jerome George Marakkaran, who had nailed her body on to that cross, lying in an apartment in another city, having lost the weight of his body for all time. She could also see Avinash Gupta who waiting by his bedside with flowers.

Jezebel-the-doctor reassured Jezebel-the-wife that Avinash Gupta, a general physician, would take better care of Jerome than she ever could. Avinash, who had been Jerome's soulmate for years, would happily nurse Jerome, unlike Jezebel who had never been loved. She marvelled at the ways in which nature brought together two people in love. George Jerome Marakkaran had tried to separate Jerome and Avinash by placing her in between. But the accident helped Jerome to return to Avinash. True, they could not see each other. True, they could not rejoice in each other. And yet, they were together. The love of their bodies endured. Perhaps, she consoled herself, it was for their sake that she had to die on the cross.

Jezebel wanted to see that nameless man. How would he receive her if she removed his blood-soaked clothes and wiped clean the wounds on his body? How would he react if in the midst of that milling crowd, she leaned over him to apply medicine on the wound on his forehead and her breast brushed softly against his?

Her body thrilled with pleasure, shaming her. She was mortified once again by her shameless body. Jezebel-the-doctor consoled her, 'This is just the body's reminder that the ova are ready, just a human being responding obsessively to nature's prodding to ensure that the bloodline is not broken.'

The next morning, she went back home, showered, had breakfast, came back to the children's hospital, finished her morning class, and then went to the casualty ward in search of him. En route, she had picked up a T-shirt, a pair of pyjamas and a towel from a wayside shop. He was there on the same bed. He had washed his face and combed his hair. She greeted him and handed over the bag of clothes. He looked into the bag, looked up at her, and smiled gratefully. Jezebel could not help wondering how a father who had fallen unconscious in shock after hearing about his child's death could smile so charmingly at her. 'How are you now?' she inquired.

'I'm perfect,' he said. 'I was jet-lagged and hadn't slept in four days. Sleep sorted that out. And then a bottle of glucose has gone in, no? I'm ready to leave after a bath and a change of clothes.'

He looked at the bag in his hands once again. 'You are so thoughtful. I was worried that my suitcase and passport were not at hand.' He smiled at her once again. 'I was looking for you, doctor, to thank you.' Not only his smile but also his voice made waves rise in her heart.

'Thanks, but why? I couldn't save the child's life.' She smiled, a little abashed.

'It's not about whether you saved the child or not, but the fact that you came running. I am not surprised that the child died. It was such a massive fall. The child was thrown out of the car window and crashed on a culvert. But have you observed doctor, two- and three-year-olds have the capacity to survive major falls? Nature has given them a special ability for that.'

He said all these with no trace of agitation. Jezebel was a little unnerved. She even wondered if he hadn't gotten to know about the death of his wife and elder child.

'I had some hope in that child's case. That's why I came rushing like that. I was quite sure that the mother and the other child had died on the spot.'

'Then, aren't they your family?' Jezebel asked in disbelief.

He smiled. 'If you put it that way . . . aren't we human beings all one big family? But I don't know this family from earlier. I had accompanied the body of a doctor killed in an airstrike in Saada, Yemen. His family had come to the airport. The ambulance carrying the body went ahead. I was with the family in a car behind. That's when a lorry came and . . .' he sighed. Jezebel stood wordless for some time.

'Are you a social worker?' she asked, swallowing hard.

A smile twinkled in his eyes. 'Sort of. Perhaps you can call my job social work. Can you guess what I am?'

She looked at him again—the way he was lying down, his shoulder bones, the way he crossed his arms on his chest, his fair and sharp fingers . . .

'A neurosurgeon?' She asked.

His smile vanished and his face grew serious. 'Yes! A neurosurgeon.'

The surprise of how she had found out was evident on his face. Her dimples must have unfurled. That is why looking at her, he, too, smiled. Because it was the kind of smile that was infectious. The smile lingered on her face as she walked away without letting him know how she had found out, and even when she entered George Jerome Marakkaran's room. She was happy that she had reclaimed her ability to smile.

The happiness of the heart is one's life, joy and longevity. One lives only as long as one is happy. 'I am alive now,' Jezebel tried to convince herself. 'I will be able to live again, because I am able to smile again.'

George Jerome Marakkaran was still unconscious. Jezebel spoke to Rosamma and her son Richie for a long time. She went on her rounds. She sat in the duty room and spoke to Geethu. She called Sebin and inquired after his health. All the while the thought of that neurosurgeon kept growing within her like the rose of Jericho and the date palms of Ein Gedi. What could be the circumstances that brought him here—sleepless for four nights, accompanying someone's dead body? Where would he go, getting up from the casualty ward of the Medical College teeming with the poor, the helpless and the orphaned, reeking of dirt and blood and pus? What kind of life would his be? How unbelievable the story he had to narrate would be? She was eager to hear that story. She went in search of him. But the attendant was settling another patient in that bed. He had left half an hour ago.

A sense of loss, similar to what she had experienced four days after Ranjith had gone missing in the landslide, gripped her again now. The body froze, its ova forgotten. As she drove back home, she despaired that her smile had vanished like a rainbow. Her heart was about to be uprooted in a storm of sorrow. 'Don't,' she admonished her heart. Sorrow has ruined so many. It was of no use.

The daughter of God was destined to be delivered unto the hands of men. It was also predetermined that she would be put to death by their hands. She, too, had to be resurrected on the third day in her own way.

But except for responding obsessively to nature's prodding, which man would muster the courage to roll away the boulder that covered her grave?

25

Baal, whom Queen Jezebel of Jezreel worshipped, was the god of rain, lightning, wind and resurrection. Baal blessed the earth with fertility. He asked his believers to worship him with dance. The Baal cycle, which lasted seven years, brought either rain or drought to the earth. The belief was that Baal, who was also the god of reproduction, was in battle with Mot, the god of death, for seven long years. If Baal won, there would be heavy rains and a good harvest at the end of the seventh year. If Baal lost, there would be drought and famine. No matter how many times he lost, Baal would return from the netherworld and make it rain on the earth again. And that's how Baal became the god of resurrection as well.

That Queen Jezebel believed in resurrection and in return gave Jezebel hope in her heart. It helped her hope that all was not lost even if she had been buried in a grave. Subjected to nature's obsessive prodding to sustain the bloodline, the body turned restlessly inside the grave just as it had while hanging from the cross.

Jezebel summoned the memory of the neurosurgeon to calm herself. She imagined that they met again, spoke to each other, travelled together, fell in love. In her imagination, he joined the Medical College. In between they would meet in the corridors of the hospital, and when their bodies brushed against each other, sparks would fly. He made her laugh. She made him ecstatic. They walked on waves. They parted the river into two. He listened to all that she had to say. He spoke all that she wanted to hear. In her imagination, she rejoiced that after long years of waiting, she had found the man she desired. He invited her over to his place. In the spacious balcony where the tendrils of vines hung like curls on a forehead, they sat gazing into each other's eyes. A cool breeze tickled the leaves. A drizzle gave the earth gooseflesh. Night fell. Darkness descended. The clouds split open, oyster-like, and a gleaming white pearl of a full moon emerged. In the moonlight they looked like statues of ivory. His eyes smiled at her with love. In the moonlight she caressed his chest and the veins on his neck. Her body rose up into the sky. Just before it could break free of its strings and begin to fly, the memory of Jerome clawed its way out from the dark like long sharp nails. The bubble burst. The broken pieces fell to the ground with a heavy thud. She writhed in agony. Panicking, she tried to forget that stranger.

At first Jezebel did not feel like seeing George Jerome Marakkaran. She would usually go up to the ICU, have a word with the doctors and nurses and return. But one day she happened to talk to Rosamma aunty for a long time, who bared her heart to Jezebel. And that is how she came to know George Jerome Marakkaran's life story.

'Georgekutty cannot stand our family,' said Rosamma. 'First of all, he was an "accident". Jerome is not our Appan's name. It was just a name given by Ammachi. It was the year after she gave birth to him that my Appan married Ammachi. Georgekutty believed that Ammachi was a bad woman. He despised me. My Appan didn't like him either. Every day was full of beatings and swearing. When he was about seventeen, a woman who had lost her husband complained that he had assaulted her. The village folk got together and beat him up. Father Arakkal, the priest in our parish at that time, took him away to work at a care home for elderly priests. The next we saw him was at his wedding. Abraham Chammanatt gave the family a great deal of money to get him to marry Lilly—he renovated the house, gave money to marry me off, got my husband a job in a chit fund company. But Georgekutty cannot stand us. He has forgotten the past and lives like a gentleman now. He has an apartment and a car and all that now. His son is a doctor. But of what use is all the wealth and money? He hasn't got Ammachi even a bit of tobacco, let alone a scarf or a towel. He hasn't once called her "Ammachi" with love. Before she died, Ammachi said she wanted to see him. We informed him. "Let the old hag die, then I'll come," was what he said. In the end, Ammachi's body became bloated. Even her eyelids had swollen up. Still, she would open her eyes and look around searchingly, and then close her eyes. Ammachi was looking out for him. Ammachi's soul must have cursed him. That's why he has ended up like this. And his son too . . .'

As she listened in bewilderment, Jezebel was reminded of the dead bodies that arrived at the post-mortem table. Bodies that looked healthy enough on the outside. Cut them open, and you saw all sorts of damages. Inside George Jerome Marakkaran's body too, there were wounded, festering, worm-eaten sores. She went to meet George Jerome Marakkaran that day with the empathy a doctor would feel for a patient in pain. He was regaining consciousness. He was muttering something. When he recognized her, he shut his eyes tight like one blinded by light. Jezebel felt all the sorrier for him as she realized he was a man who was neither familiar with nor wanted to traverse the path of light, but one who resisted it instead.

Rosamma had followed her into the room. When he saw her, George Jerome Marakkaran's face clouded over. When she sniffled, 'Georgekutty, what has come over you, *da*!', he snapped, 'Who asked you to come here?' When he spoke, his face creased in pain; his words slurred. When Jezebel left the room shortly, Rosamma followed her out, cursing, 'Not for nothing is this wretched fellow in this state!' And then she threatened to go home.

Jezebel could see that the poor thing was in need of money. She had taken a loan to put her daughter through a nursing course. Her calculations that the daughter would go abroad and make money had come to nought. Instead, the girl married a Hindu who stopped her from going abroad. In the meantime, Rosamma tried to send her son to the Gulf after his course in automobile engineering. But the recruitment agency cheated them. Any moment their house could be confiscated. Vareechan's ninety-year-old Appan and Ammachi were staying with them. Where would she go with all of them?

When Jezebel suggested that Rosamma stay back in the hospital to take care of George Marakkaran, Abraham Chammanatt smiled derisively. He told her, 'Georgekutty will not part with even five paisa, *ketto* . . .'

'What if I give the money?'

Abraham Chammanatt looked closely at her.

As if reading his mind, she said, 'It's not so that I will be taken for a good woman.'

Abraham's face changed colour. Jezebel laughed. 'Have I not been disgraced enough in front of the whole world? Why would I need a conduct certificate now? And anyway, which certificate will wipe out all that I have undergone so far? And if at all I need a certificate, isn't it enough if I took care of Jerome? I don't even need to take care of him. I just have to pretend to. No one would suspect a thing. No one would ask questions. I'll be absolved of the bad name of having abandoned my husband in distress, too.'

Jezebel laughed heartily, and continued, 'Shall I tell you what lessons I have learnt from my life so far? People like to see life as if it's a movie. Nothing needs to really happen. Just create the impression that it has. What others want to see in our lives is us acting out roles according to their scripts. Even if they know that it is acting.'

Abraham Chammanatt looked at her miserably. 'Even otherwise, nobody would ask you to look after Georgekutty, *kochey*. Let's arrange for a male nurse. In that case, we only need to pay.'

'What if he cannot put up with Jerome's Daddy's ways? He might leave on the very second day. Or he might do a shoddy job just for the sake of money. If the wound turns septic, it will become a bigger bother for us.' She did not mince her words. 'Rosamma aunty would be better any day. We can pay her what we would pay an outsider.'

Abraham Chammanatt did not disagree.

Days sped by. George Jerome Marakkaran's wounds were taking time to heal. The day the doctor disclosed that the spinal injury would take much longer to heal, Jezebel found Abraham Chammanatt waiting outside Kurien sir's room as she returned from ward duty. 'The doctor said he can be taken home if we want,' he began. 'But I am not sure what to do now . . .' Jezebel grew alert, sensing danger in the way he beat about the bush.

'How will we send him back home in this condition?' He paused and added, 'First of all he needs a lot of rest. Travelling all the way itself is difficult. And who will take care of him there?'

Jezebel heard him out keenly.

'Rosamma said she would take care. We only need to pay her.'

'If it's a question of money, don't worry, uncle. I'll pay, for Mummy's sake,' she said.

Abraham struggled to express what was in his mind. 'Is it a question of money, *kochey*? By God's grace, why would paying ten or fifteen thousand rupees be a problem for me?' He scratched his cheeks with the stem of his spectacles. 'There is no one there to take care of Jerome . . .'

Jezebel's heart beat rapidly. In her mind's eye, she saw a shrunken body, its eyes closed, and a figure sitting attentively next to it. 'Isn't Avinash Gupta there? His real better half?'

Jezebel was merciless. Abraham looked around nervously to make sure no one had heard her. 'Even if that's the case, how can we tell the outside world that?' he said, worried.

Jezebel grew even more hard-hearted. 'The holy book says, "Let your yes be yes, and your no, no, so that you will not fall under judgement." Shouldn't we be speaking about what is actually happening rather than what is good enough to tell the world?'

Abraham Chammanatt was embarrassed. 'What you say is right, *kochey*! But what's the use of announcing it to the world at this point? Can we marry Jerome off to Avinash? Yes, there was something between them. And I have already agreed that there was. And it is to save him from it that I arranged his marriage. He agreed to it too. And he came here as well. I hoped that everything would be all right thereafter. All said and done, you lived happily together for some time, didn't you?'

His words pierced a wound that was still unhealed in her heart. Jezebel was livid. 'On what basis do you say that we lived happily together? What is this happiness you talk about? I haven't felt any such thing. Then again, if whatever you feel could be called happiness, then maybe you could call it that. If that's what you call happiness, Uncle, so be it. I have no quarrel with that. I was very happy. I was jumping up and down with that happiness. Is that enough?'

She looked at Abraham with blazing eyes.

He looked even more embarrassed. 'Whatever you say, you lived together as man and wife for a long time,' he muttered.

'By living together as man and wife, do you mean sex, Uncle?'

Abraham first went pale and then reddened. Jezebel blazed brighter.

'The day I discussed this with my lawyer was the day Jerome's Daddy fell down and broke his bones. Unc*ley*, we can do a test if you want. A "virginity test". You can get any doctor to examine me. Just as in all the other exams, I will clear this one too, with full marks.' She struggled for breath. Fire and water welled up in her eyes. 'True, Jerome and I lived together, playing house for two-and-a-half years. In truth what was I doing? I was washing the clothes of a man I had never met or heard of before. I cooked what he wanted, washed dirty dishes, handed my entire stipend over, surrendered my freedom too. True, what you said is very true, Uncle. I was very happy. There is no lack of happiness even now. Two-and-a-half years later, I am still a virgin, not a scratch on me. How expensive it is these days to reconstruct the hymen. I am in luck. I don't have to spend a single paisa!'

Abraham was stunned. His consternation fanned the flames of Jezebel's rage even more. 'Tell me. What service should I render in gratitude for all those blessings? Should I attend to my father-in-law who is a fount of love? Or should I nurse my husband who is such a paragon of virtue?'

Abraham was completely shattered. Seeing his flushed face, reddening eyes and heaving chest, Jezebel felt a small twinge of relief. But when she saw his distress, the doctor in her reminded her that the man in front of her was a heart patient. She swallowed the rest of her rage and fell silent.

'Pardon me!' Abraham raised his hands in supplication. Jezebel felt like weeping now.

'It's my fault,' he sobbed. Jezebel began to soften.

'Okay, okay, Uncle, tell me what I should do now,' she said hastily.

Abraham looked at her with fear. 'Avinash Gupta's mother died. He is the only son. Their rites are very elaborate. There's no one with Jerome now.'

Jezebel stood there as if she had been hammered on the head. Abraham swallowed hard.

'Either we have to bring Jerome here. Or someone from here has to go and stay with him.' Abraham took out a white handkerchief from his pocket and dabbed at his forehead and neck.

'Who will go from here? My younger brothers are no more. Their wives are staying with their children. Both my children are in America. The wife of the one in California has given birth. Our son has sent us tickets and is waiting for us. Our visa interview is over. Once the papers are processed, we will be ready to leave the week after next.'

Jezebel froze. She felt dizzy. Who is this hefty man in front of me, she wondered. This man with his bald head and dark circles under his eyes and gold tooth, what is he going on about? Who is he talking to?

'What do you want me to do?' Jezebel's throat was dry.

Abraham Chammanatt smiled sheepishly. 'Didn't a priest go to their place to mediate on your behalf, *kochey*? Will he be able to arrange for a home nurse? Or even if he could arrange for some institutional care . . . there seems to be no other option.'

Jezebel called up Father Ilanjikkal right away. She introduced Abraham to him. Father said that he could arrange for someone for the time being. Abraham Chammanatt sighed in relief and thanked Jezebel.

But two days later, as she was preparing to leave for home after hospital duty, Father Ilanjikkal called her. 'There is a problem, *kochey*. We just got news that our home nurse's Appachan is seriously unwell. She insists on leaving immediately. So, until we find someone else, it would be better if someone could come from there.'

Father Ilanjikkal's voice rang in her brain as if from a great tunnel. After a long time, the old fear gripped her—fear of looking around, fear of walking, fear of talking. Fear that the Medical College building was swaying about and that the corridors were lunging at her, ready to strangle her. She was at a loss for words and she felt brain-dead. Father Ilanjikkal continued to talk about this and that. At some point in time, he put the phone down. She left for home sometime. Ammachi served her dinner sometime.

She went to bed sometime, slept for how many ever hours and got up with a start. When she woke up, the past lashed at her like the sea. She swung on the waves and the waves threw her around. Crashing hard against the rocks, her head splitting open and her heart shattering, she woke up. She forced Chachan's door open. Chachan and Ammachi, who were sleeping on the same bed, scrambled awake. Switching on the lights, Chachan asked her what had happened. Her eyes were red, her hair dishevelled. She leaned on to Chachan's shoulder.

'I have decided to go to Jerome,' she whispered. Chachan and Ammachi started. 'What are you blabbering in your sleep, *kochey?*' scolded Ammachi. Chachan smoothed her hair as if to wake her up. Jezebel told them everything that Abraham Chammanatt had told her. All at once, it was as if all three of them had fallen into coma.

'Still, do you have to go?' Ammachi finally asked.

Jezebel looked at Ammachi like one possessed. 'I am going as a doctor, not as a wife,' she said. 'Abraham Chammanatt asked me if we, me and Jerome, hadn't lived together as man and wife for two-and-a-half years. There is some truth and some untruth in it. We weren't husband and wife, but we did live together. When someone with whom you had spent two-and-a-half years is in this state, when you hear that there is no one to take care of him, is it right for me not to go? If this had been either Ahana or Rani, who had stayed with me in hostel, would I not go? Earlier, he had his mother to take care of him, and his father, and his brother, and his brother's wife. Now there is no one. Until his friend returns, another friend is going to take care of him, that's all.'

'Still, you are going alone?' Ammachi worried. 'If something happens to him when you are there, George Marakkaran will throw our whole family in jail' she warned her.

'Then let me and Ammachi come along,' said Chachan.

'No, let me go first. If necessary, I'll call you, Chachaa,' said Jezebel decisively.

Only Valiyammachi, who was still down with a fever, gave her courage, 'You go ahead, *kochey*. Bear that cross all by yourself and then be done with it.'

It was morning soon and Jezebel went about getting ready for the trip. In the morning, she met Kurien sir and applied for two weeks' leave. She booked tickets for the next morning's flight. She called Abraham Chammanatt and Father Ilanjikkal and informed them of her travel plan. The next morning Chachan and Ammachi dropped her at the airport. She checked in. The security check was completed. She sat in the lobby. The boarding was announced. She stood in the queue. As she approached the gate, someone came and put out a hand, 'Hello doctor, what a pleasant surprise!'

She blinked in disbelief. It was him. She looked around. Was it real? Or was she dreaming? Was it really him?

But he did not seem to have noticed her astonishment. He was talking loudly, 'Do you know, doctor, I was looking for you all over the Medical College yesterday. How would I find you? I didn't know your name, or which department you were in, nothing!'

As he took his place next to her in the queue and they moved ahead, her blank expression prompted him to ask, 'You do remember me, don't you?'

She remembered everything—that day, the child's death, his sleep, the empty bed after he left, the house she had seen in her dreams, his chest, his touch . . .

Afraid that he would read her mind, she looked away. She sat impassively as she watched him exchange seats in order to be able to sit next to her. She was reluctant to look him in the eye. She was embarrassed to recall how intensely she had wanted to meet him again. She need not have met him again, she rued. She need not have met him today, she corrected herself. Not today, when she was setting out suicidally to care for a body full of bedsores wasting away in a dark room filled with the asthmatic wheezing of pigeons. She loathed him—did he have to turn up now at this wretched moment? Look at him laughing, smiling, talking—after everything has gone to pieces. She wished she could hate him, but he went on laughing and talking.

'That day I waited for you for a long time, doctor. But the ambulance people were in a hurry. The family waiting to receive the bodies back in their native place were also in a hurry. That's why I left without telling you. Sorry! Actually, I was supposed to return the day before. But somehow, I did not feel like leaving without seeing you once. That's why I came back to the Medical College. Now I know each and every nook and corner of your Medical College. But I could not find you. I have never been as disappointed as I was yesterday.'

He smiled at her with his eyes. She averted her gaze, unable to bear their brightness. As he kept talking about how he travelled with the bodies, how he helped to cremate them, and how he had to shell out more money because he cancelled his tickets, she tried to smile. The flight was about to take off. She leaned back in her seat and closed her eyes. She could feel herself rising up in the air. She imagined soaring higher and higher and then exploding somewhere in space. When she opened her eyes, he was still looking at her. She was mortified. He smiled warmly. She looked intently at him. He was a handsome man—a sunburnt face and dark circles under the eyes. But his eyes smiled. She remembered once again the eyes that had smiled at her in the moonlight that sieved through the tendrils when the moon shone in the sky like a pearl that had emerged from an oyster. She had an urge to link her fingers with his, bury her face in his chest and inhale his scent. A greedy urge, considering that she had set out to care for a body reeking of formalin in an apartment just two hours away, drenched in the dirt of darkness and ringing with the cooing of pigeons that sounded like people gasping for breath on their deathbeds.

Each one of us is put to the test when we are honey-trapped by our own greedy urges. Greed births sin. Sin, when fully grown, begets death.

Jezebel woke up only when someone shook her awake with a 'We are landing.' When she became aware of her surroundings, she looked at the neurosurgeon sheepishly. 'Sorry, what were we talking about? I dozed off . . .' She apologized. He did not reply. 'We were saying something, weren't we?' she repeated. 'That was two hours back,' he said kindly. She looked out of the window, still in disbelief that she had slept for two hours. She saw the earth coming up closer and closer and the sea gleaming in the four o'clock sunlight, as they descended into the outstretched palm of the city. The thought that she would reach the apartment soon and see Jerome's body soon drained her. She said to no one in particular, 'I'm thirsty.' He pulled out a bottle that was nearly empty from the pocket of the seat. She gulped down whatever was left in the bottle. She apologized again for having slept off. 'You've had your revenge for my sleeping off like that the day we met,' he joked.

They looked at each other and laughed. On his face was a simplicity that evoked respect. He seemed the kind of man who would not blow his own trumpet. She liked him even more.

'I slept off that day because I was so exhausted. But what could be the reason for your sleeping like this? Narcolepsy or something? Should we get you tested for it?' There was mischief in his eyes. Her brain shrugged off all traces of sleep. The books she had studied during MBBS came to mind. 'If it were narcolepsy, one would sleep only for a few minutes at a time,' she argued, smiling. He too grew animated. They discussed narcolepsy for a while. Nerves, neurons, hypocretin. 'This neurology is something, I tell you . . .' she conceded. As the door of the aircraft opened, as they moved along in the queue, alighted, and walked towards the baggage reclaim area in the airport, their conversation about diseases continued. He wheeled in trolleys for both of them, talking all the while about the changes in the level of hypocretin caused by the H1N1 virus.

'It was good to see you. I am talking like this to someone after ages.'

She looked away, unable to meet his gaze.

'When I saw you, doctor, I thought you are not the kind of person to be met and forgotten in a hurry. I really like your smile. It's then that I realized that a woman's smile could trigger a smile in my mind too—even as I lay with bruises all over. I felt like seeing you again. That's why I came back. And searched for you for a whole day. If I hadn't met you here, I would have taken leave and come back again at the first opportunity.'

Jezebel's eyes welled up. Her heart beat fast. She was scared of her own self.

'To tell you the truth, I have only one regret now.' His eyes shone. 'After all this, you still haven't asked my name.'

Jezebel trembled. She tried to smile at him, unfurling her dimples. She wished that he would translate her smile into words. She hoped that from that smile he would be able read all that she had imagined about him. She was not sure he could. But his eyes were shining.

'You remind me of Sufi music. Names like Rumi or Amir Khusrau would suit you.'

His eyes shone even brighter. He picked up his bag from the conveyor belt, put it on the trolley and looked at her, tilting his head. 'Would you mind if it were Kabir Mohammed instead?'

She laughed happily. Her bag, too, had made its way down the conveyor belt. He picked it up and set it down on her trolley for her. They moved out.

'When someone tells you their name, it is courtesy to tell them yours as well,' he reminded her as they walked on.

She looked at him mischievously. 'Would you mind if it were Jezebel? Jezebel John?'

He looked at her, astonished. 'Jezebel? The Jezebel mentioned in the Book of Revelations and the Book of Kings?'

'Do you read the Bible?' She was surprised.

'I used to. Once, we had run out of painkillers to give a patient after surgery. He was in excruciating pain. I had no clue what to do. That's when I saw a copy of the Bible around. I picked it up and read the last few pages. That's how I came across the name "Jezebel". And then I began to read out the Bible to that man from the very beginning. That's the only good thing about religions. They teach us to embrace pain as something inevitable.'

'You ran out of painkillers in Yemen?' she asked.

'Well, we have run out of medicines in Yemen too. But this happened elsewhere—in Afghanistan.'

They had reached the exit. At a glance, Jezebel spotted Father Ilanjikkal in his white jubba and mundu, stroking his flowing white beard as he waited for her. Kabir pulled out his phone and waited for her number. She gave him her number and got his too.

'So . . . keep in touch.' He looked at her with anticipation. She was reluctant to look at him.

'Did you know the name Jezebel has many meanings?' He asked as if he wanted to prolong the conversation. She shared the meanings she knew.

'But in the Phoenician language it also means, "Where is the prince".'

'That's news to me,' she whispered, her heart trembling.

'It was also the ritual cry of those who worshipped Baal. In order to summon Baal from the netherworld and bring rain on earth, prophets would dance loudly, chanting "Jezebel, Jezebel!"'

'But that's not there in the Bible.'

'Not in the Bible, but it's there in books about Biblical characters. Queen Jezebel figures in all books about the characters in the Old Testament . . .'

She felt sea waves lashing about within her. Like the waves she saw from the palace in Tyre, they seemed to call out to him with a thousand hands. When he shook her hand to say goodbye, she was on the verge of tears. I haven't touched a hand like this till today, she thought. She hastily withdrew her hand. As she walked away from him and towards Father Ilanjikkal, she thought her body, which had shrivelled up from being hung down from so many nails for so long, was raring to be resurrected.

How would the daughter of God rise from the solitude of the grave which had been sealed with a rock?

However it rose, whenever it did rise, her body was sure to scream out 'Jezebel! Jezebel!'

26

Having passed the nights between the crucifixion and the resurrection, Jezebel wished to declare to the world thus: 'And so my sisters, you may find those nights that each one of us has to cross over as unbearably long and dark. Inside the sealed tomb, your bodies may burn and fester, and your bones and flesh may melt, and only the shroud that covered you may be left in the end. Never again shall the daughter of man return to the world where there is death to reveal whether the body goes in search of the soul or the soul returns to roost in the body.'

In Jerome George Marakkaran's apartment, Jezebel realized that her resurrection would not have been possible without two men in shining garments. Her eyes did not notice anything as she walked past the deafening flapping of the pigeons in the courtyard and stood in the lift that rose, gasping like a soul departing the body. That night in Jerome's apartment, she was like one buried in a grave. Her body lay shivering under the shroud of helplessness. She felt neither anxiety nor fear when Father Ilanjikkal escorted out the home nurse, who was weeping hearing the news of her own father's death, and promised to return the next day. It was only when she received a text message from Kabir Mohammed— 'Jezebel, have you reached your room? Where are you put up? I am staying near the beach. Can we have dinner together?'—that she came to her senses.

That was when she saw that she had returned to square one. The same old apartment, only, more cramped now. Outside, the same old death rattle of pigeons. Inside, the same old sofa. The same old sofa cover. The same old grimy fan. The same old creaking when it was switched on. The same shabby walls. The same old crosses on those walls and Christ's image. A clock whose hands stood still. A television set covered with a yellow cloth on a stand. And below, CDs of religious sermons. George Jerome Marakkaran's bedroom was locked. The cupboards which used to be in Jerome's room had now been moved into John Jerome Marakkaran's room. The dining table lay dark with grime. The kitchen was dark with soot and grease. Everywhere, the shroud of darkness. Everywhere, the smell of death.

Jezebel got up when the sharp odour of formalin pierced her nostrils. She stood at the doorway of Jerome George Marakkaran's room. Later she would recall with shame how her own bodily functions felt strange to her just then—her legs grew weak, a terrible chill gripped her body, her heart stopped beating, and she felt her bladder would burst. She also remembered that the first thing she noticed in that room was an oxygen cylinder and the stand and the tube that hung from it. It was only after that that her eyes fell on the waterbed and the bald form that lay stiff on it. The ribcage that rose and fell feebly under a white apron-like cloth. Hands and feet that protruded under the sheet. The catheter, filled with a little yellow liquid, that hung from under the bed. The overpowering odours of Dettol and phenyl. That face, its muscles wasted and bones jutting out, did not seem to be Jerome's. The bones of the nose were sharper. The jaw bone jutted out. The eyes had sunken so deep into their sockets that only two dark holes could be seen in their place.

She went up to him like a body that had risen from the grave. She touched his wrist. The skin felt like paper. She could not believe that this was the man with whom she lived for two-and-a-half years. The man who had come to see her dressed in an uncreased polyester shirt, his head held high and chest puffed out. Who had stirred her soul with the lie 'We are made for each other.' Who had forced her head down and suffocated her and filled her mouth with bitterness. Who pampered his own body by going to the gym every morning and getting a massage every Sunday.

It was in order to survive the sheer terror of that moment that she called Kabir Mohammed over. The dreadful loneliness of the grave had become excruciating. She needed another soul to come to the door of her grave bearing fragrant oils. Jezebel showered, changed, opened the packet of food Father Ilanjikkal had bought her, washed two plates and two glasses and set them on the dining table. How would the judge and lawyer of the family court have reacted if they had seen a wife who served dinner by candlelight to another man even as her husband lay in perpetual sleep in the next room? Christ on the wall, illumined by a bulb over which a malnourished spider's web gleamed silver, smiled kindly at her. She turned the pages of the Bible kept on the wall shelf and opened 'Ecclesiastes': 'The husband of a good wife is a fortunate man; he will live twice as long because of her. A fine wife is a joy to her husband, and he can live out his years in peace. A good wife is among the precious blessings given to those who fear the Lord.'

Irritated, she shut the book. When Kabir called her again to let her know he had come, she panicked. She imagined that the doors of God's abode were about to open, and that she could glimpse the casket of promise within. She expected lightning, thunder, clamour, earthquakes and a rain of stones. When Kabir walked in, dressed in a loose-fitting khadi kurta and pyjama, his fragrance spread over the stale smells of that apartment. Jezebel welcomed him, acutely conscious of the shabbiness of her surroundings. He asked her whose house it was. 'A friend's,' she said. It was clear that the place, and her presence there, seemed a mystery to him. As for her, she did not have the courage to tell him that she had called him over to clear the air of mystery. 'This is me,' she wanted to confess. 'This is me. Can you accept me the way I am?' Unable to muster either the voice or the energy to ask him that, the body in the grave writhed.

They ate in silence. And then sat face to face on the sofa. Kabir Mohammed cleared his throat and looked around the room once more. 'Are you all alone, Jezebel?' he asked her. 'No,' she said. He waited for her to say more. Before she could anything, the doorbell rang and the door opened. A short, slightly thickset, clean-shaven young man with a tonsured head came in. He stared at Jezebel and screamed at her, 'Get out of this place, you bitch!' He cursed and swore at her in English and Hindi. 'How did you have the nerve to come back to this house? Why did you come? To kill him? I will not let you! Leave this house this instant! Or you will meet your end today! What are you staring at? Get out!'

In a flash, she recognized him. Avinash Gupta! Later she would recall with shame how broken she had been when she did recognize him. Kabir, who had no clue what was going on, stood stunned. Her frozen stance seemed to provoke Avinash even more. He rushed up to her as if to hit her or push her. That was when Kabir intervened, shouting, 'Hey! Stop it! I can't allow this!'

'Who are you to stop me? You *saala kutta*!' Avinash turned on Kabir. Jezebel saw him raising a fist at Kabir, and Kabir blocking and twisting Avinash's arm. She rushed in between them, saying, 'Kabir, please leave. We'll talk tomorrow.' When he asked her, 'Are you all right?', she hastened to reassure him, 'I'm all right, don't worry about me.' Kabir let go of Avinash's hand. 'You both need to leave! This instant!' roared Avinash again. Jezebel turned to him. 'Shut up, Avinash! This is between the two of us. Don't drag Kabir into this. Kabir, I'm sorry, but let's meet tomorrow . . .'

Kabir left without a word, leaving a void in Jezebel's heart. She turned around to Avinash. Their eyes collided. His face turned red. 'Avinash, apologize,' she told him quietly.

'Why should I?' he growled.

'For all the wrongs you have done to me.'

'Wrongs? Me?' Avinash glared at her. His slender lips quivered in anger. He reddened right down to the tips of his fingers. 'What wrong did I do? What wrong did Jerome do? It was you who ruined his life! You are the one who pushed him to his death! Wasn't it for the sake of your lover's daughter that you hired a contract killer to finish him off? If anything happens to Jerome, you whore, I will not spare you! I'll cut you up into pieces and feed you to the dogs!'

Jezebel was silent for a moment. But when she imagined her body being devoured by dogs, she felt like laughing. Her laughter provoked him even more. Jezebel walked up to him. Avinash took a step back. Jezebel grabbed him by the collar.

'What will you do to me? Will you rape me? Can you rape a woman? Isn't it men you want?'

Avinash was shocked. He shrank like a deflated balloon. He looked utterly helpless. His face turned pale.

'What happened? What happened to all that bravado of sometime back?' Jezebel attacked him again. 'You gain confidence only when you admit to being who you are,' she scoffed. 'Aren't you ashamed of pretending to be someone else?'

Avinash stood tongue-tied. Jezebel calmed down, and let go of his collar.

'You don't know what wrong you did, do you? I'll tell you. You knew what the right thing to do was, but you didn't do it. You knew that Jerome is a man who cannot love a woman. You also knew that he needed a man, like you. And yet you didn't try to dissuade him from the marriage. You were not ready to take a risk in front of the world. You could have saved me at least. You called me a whore. I'd rather be a whore than be the virtuous wife of someone like Jerome. Ok, let's just say that my being a whore is your problem. You are a doctor, aren't you? Come, I'll strip in front of you. Examine me and tell me if I'm a whore or not.' She paused, out of breath, and looked at Avinash.

'But if you find out that I haven't slept with any man? Will I cease to be a whore then? Then will you take back the insult you flung at me in front of my friend? Will you make up for Jerome's many acts of deceit? Will you heal the wounds in my heart inflicted by Jerome's family, my relatives, the judge, the lawyer and all those who stood watching?'

He stood blinking. Jezebel grew more ferocious.

'Avinash, my problem is not that you're gay. I don't consider it either a crime or a weakness. My problem with you is that because of your cowardice, and Jerome's, my life got ruined as well. My problem is that you were not only able to ruin another person's life but also felt no remorse about it. How have I wronged you? How had I wronged Jerome? Was denying me the life I wanted to live the answer to society not allowing you to live the life you wanted?'

Avinash stood there as if he had been slapped. He swallowed hard and tried to muster his strength. He looked away, unable to meet her gaze.

'Don't talk rubbish,' he said weakly. 'Who made up these stories? Jerome is a brother to me. How dare you tarnish our relationship like this? I understand your hatred for Jerome. But don't make up such stories about anyone. God will punish you.'

Avinash's lips quivered. Jezebel felt bad for him. She had read that when two men became a couple, one of them assumed a feminine identity. But she was surprised to see that even such a man struggled to hold on to his masculinity when confronted by a woman.

Her silence boosted his confidence. 'How could you bring yourself to talk like this?' he admonished her. 'Who would even believe a lie like this?'

Jezebel felt sorry for him. 'What is there to feel ashamed about, Avinash? The one who told me about this was Jerome's mother,

Lilly George Marakkaran. She has seen you together in bed in Jerome's room whenever you came here to study . . .'

Avinash was stunned.

'Not only Lilly George Marakkaran, but also George Jerome Marakkaran and Lilly's brother Abraham Chammanatt know all about you two. Jerome had promised Abraham that he would end his relationship with you. After all these years, can you not be brave enough to acknowledge this relationship, at least to me?'

Avinash's face drained of all colour. He looked petrified, like a kid who had been caught red-handed. He sank into the sofa, as if he did not have the energy to hear any more. Then he got up and made his way to Jerome's room, head downcast.

Jezebel stood blank, even as she heard sounds emerging from Jerome's room. She was disturbed by the thought that she had hurt him. She regretted having hurt him. Poor thing, he must have felt such rage and jealousy at her for having snatched away his lover. George Jerome Marakkaran must have convinced him that she was the reason behind Jerome's accident. Would Avinash's enmity deepen when he realized that his secrets were out in the open? Jezebel feared that danger lurked around her, like bloodhounds. She could sense their panting. Her heart hardened, as happens when all exits close, at the height of helplessness. What worse could come? What was left to lose?

She went up to the doorway of Jerome's room. Avinash was turning Jerome's body over and powdering him. It was pathetic to see Jerome's naked body. Avinash heated water in the kettle, mixed oats from a tin and filled it into the syringes at the ends of the tubes attached to Jerome's abdomen. He made Jerome lie on his back, fitted the oxygen mask, tucked him in and came out. 'Sorry,' Jezebel told him. 'What for?' muttered Avinash. And then he sat down on the sofa, as if conceding defeat. Jezebel sat down in the chair across him. 'If only you had told me, I could have helped

you, and you could have helped me,' she whispered. Avinash
looked at her indignantly.

'How could we have told you? How would you all have
responded? Would you have accepted us? Blessed us? You would
have stoned us! Killed us! We would have lost all the respect,
regard and love that we had received as doctors. Knowing all this,
how could we risk it? We had no option but to pretend. Even now,
we have no other way. Not because we want to, but because this
world is like this.' His choked back tears.

'My mother just died. But I have wished her dead for such a
long time. I was scared of how she would bear it if ever she got to
know the truth about me. Jerome and I wanted to live somewhere
abroad. You were a stepping stone to that plan. It was because your
brother was in the UK that Jerome agreed to the wedding. Since
no other plan worked out, I, too, was forced to agree to this one.'

Jezebel sat aghast. Avinash pulled out a handkerchief from his
pocket and wiped his eyes and nose.

'America was our dreamland. We have lived in many cities in
India. We tried to rent a house as two doctors and live without
bothering anyone. But it wasn't easy. There was always someone
to gatecrash into a house where two men lived together. Once
a colleague of ours came to stay with us for a week. He caught
us in bed together one day. There was a great furore afterwards.
He went and told everyone. People came to beat us up. We had
to move to another city because we could no longer live there.
One of my mother's relatives came to live with us. With that, we
had to leave that city too. In the meantime, there was tremendous
pressure on Jerome to get married. We had three options: either
become celibate, or live together, cocking a snook at society, or get
married like ordinary men and deceive everybody. The last option
was also the easiest. When you got married, I wept all through
the night. Jerome was a part of my body and soul. No one could
replace him.'

As Avinash wept in front of her, Jezebel recalled her wedding night. Avinash told her that he had often thought of suicide in the days after Jerome's marriage. They had been together since medical college. Avinash became restless after Jerome's marriage. He grew jealous. Every day Jerome promised him that he had not slept with Jezebel. But Avinash was unnerved that Jerome would end up loving Jezebel more.

As she saw the wounds in the heart that had opened out to her, Jezebel was aggrieved. She saw how much more wretched their lives were. Avinash told her how they would meet furtively, after fibbing at home. Jerome had made many trips to meet him without her knowledge. Avinash, too, had visited their city from time to time, and stayed at a hotel next to Jerome's hospital. Jerome would visit him at the hotel under the pretext of going to work. Each time they were together, they were constantly worried about someone informing the police and being arrested and imprisoned for having intercourse against the order of nature.

'Did you have to go to so much trouble?' Jezebel asked, pained.

'There was no other way,' sighed Avinash. 'But I didn't know that Jerome's family knew about all this. He kept that from me.'

It was clear that that was a shock for him. The shock that any man or woman would feel when they realized that their partner had kept secrets from them. Jezebel was not sure if Avinash knew about the assault on Ann Mary. She was worried that it would hurt him deeply. She saw that be it man or woman, in every relationship, one of them was always more masculine. She understood that the more masculine one tended to cheat, take advantage of and control the less masculine one. The tears in Avinash's eyes and the faltering of his words made Jezebel's heart heavier. This, then, was the painful revelation: *no one was happy.*

'I hated you, Jezebel,' said Avinash. 'You were, after all, the one who had snatched my Jerome away from me! When he met with an accident, I was actually happy because it meant your relationship with him was over, at the very least. I was happy even when I got him back in an unconscious state because I had got him back, all to myself. When I believe that he can see me, hear me, and sense my touch, my heart is full. When I first heard you had come here, I got upset. Why did you come back here? What is your pressing need now to take care of someone whom you had not spared a second glance for so long? Is it money? Or is there some other intention behind this visit?' His voice was filled with anxiety.

Jezebel felt sorry for him. 'Just one intention. That Jerome's body should not decay in neglect until you returned from your mother's last rites. That's all. The moment you return, I'll leave this house. Is that enough for you?'

Avinash's face brightened in relief.

'That man hasn't given me any pleasant memories for me to want to take care of him and stay right by his side, Avinash. He never joked or bantered, never made me laugh, never made me feel safe. There are no happy moments to recollect from the time we spent together. A voice from within kept telling me he was hiding something from me. That hurt me terribly. Because he married me, all our happiness—mine, yours, our families'—was ruined.' Her voice choked.

'Jerome's Daddy put so much pressure on him to get married. He was helpless,' Avinash tried to reason.

'I had made my expectations clear to Jerome.'

'I was the one who replied to your email, Jezebel. We were together that day, when he returned after meeting you. I wept a lot back then. Jerome was also upset. He told me to write something by way of a reply to you.'

Cut to the quick, Jezebel glared at him. 'Oh, I was just a stepping stone for you, wasn't I? Neither of you bothered about the injustice meted out to me before making me your stepping stone. In spite of all this education, you hadn't learnt the lesson that you simply do not have the right to ruin another person's life. But I'm much more disturbed by the fact that two doctors were clearly unable to see the value of another individual's life.'

Avinash said, guiltily, 'We even quoted Macbeth in that first email just so you'd get the hint . . .'

'You didn't have to try so hard!' she scoffed.

They sat in silence for some time. He needed to participate in some ritual the next morning. According to his mother's wishes, they had to immerse her ashes in a few holy places. He would return right after. He would take over Jerome's responsibility. 'But for how long?' asked Jezebel.

Avinash's face filled with sorrow. 'I don't know.'

'Aren't you fed up of all this?' asked Jezebel, surprised. 'You're a doctor. How can you look at that body as the person he once was?'

Avinash heaved a long sigh. 'Oh, I got fed up a long time ago,' he muttered. 'I wish Jerome were dead. I pray for it too. I often feel like killing him. How long it has been, Jezebel, since I began to keep vigil over a live corpse. I wish I could love someone like I loved Jerome. But I don't have the courage to go looking for someone like that. I can't, not when he lies here all alone like this. That's how much I loved him. If only he were dead, I could boldly enter into another relationship. But that bastard, that son of a bitch, he isn't dead yet!'

A terrible silence filled the room. 'Are you scared to sleep alone, Jezebel?' asked Avinash. He reminded her of the schedule to change Jerome's tubes. And then he went into Jerome's room again. He kissed Jerome on the forehead and lips, and half-hugged his body. He broke down, sobbing. He averted his face, and wiped his tears. The less hypocritical of the two men, thought Jezebel sadly.

Jezebel would later recall that it was on that night, after Avinash left, as she lay on the sofa staring at the spider that slept in the cobweb that gleamed silver, that she experienced the true meaning of resurrection. At that hour, the apartment felt like a grave. A grave that had gathered cobwebs from disuse. In it, lay her body—shrouded in white and abandoned. It had died a long while ago. Jezebel wanted to forget how she had drifted off to sleep agonizing over who would resurrect the body, and how she woke up with a start, unable to make out whether the strange sound she heard—'*mumhwa*'—was a laugh or a loud sigh or a call.

She was terrified. Because that sound came from Jerome George Marakkaran's room. To her, it seemed that bloodhounds were growling in that room. She rushed to Jerome's room. The sound rose again. '*Mooooohwa*'. Jerome's eyes were open. His irises were staring at her. Jezebel froze. She clutched at the wall so she wouldn't fall. The wall—dry and smooth like Jerome's skin—slipped out of her grasp.

Faith means the certainty that you will get what you wish for and the conviction that what you cannot see does exist. And so, sisters, the resurrection of the daughters of men is also like that. No one has seen it until now. No one has borne witness to it until now. It is only for the daughters of men to experience. Jezebel foresaw that on the first day of the week, when the Mary Magdalenes arrived at her tomb, bearing the fragrant oils they had prepared to anoint the dead body, two men in shining garments would appear to give them the good news. One of them would be more masculine, the other less so. They would have transcended the meaninglessness of masculinity.

27

The point of what we are saying is this: We do have a woman who sits down at the right of the throne of the Majesty in heaven. She ministers in the sanctuary and true tabernacle set up by the Lord, not by man. Since every high priest is appointed to offer both gifts and sacrifices, it was necessary for her too to have something to offer. If she had been on earth, she would not even be a priest since there are already priests who offer gifts according to the law. Now, however, she has received a much more excellent ministry, just as the covenant she mediates is better and is founded on better promises. For if that first covenant had been without fault, no place would have been sought for a second one.

Likewise, if that first 'first night' she had spent with Jerome George Marakkaran had been without fault, there would not have been a second first night two-and-a-half-years later. If someone had asked her to describe the moments before resurrection, Jezebel would have described that night she spent in that apartment with Jerome after two-and-a-half-years. Later, she rejoiced that it had been the first night she had celebrated with him. If her heart had been full of hope the first-time round, she trembled with fear the second time.

Because Jerome George Marakkaran had been as good as dead until then. When he stared at her with eyes she thought would never open again, she was startled. When sounds emerged from the body she thought would never move again, she froze. But any fear is like the human body—open it, and there is only dirt within. Why fear? This is just a body. Just some substance, some energy and some chemicals, she assured herself. That was the gift of having studied science. It had taught her to look at the world and the people and all living beings and her own self, as mere matter. What was the body? A few bones, some flesh, skin, the senses, brain, heart, liver, bowels. A bunch of nerves that controlled all these. And then, water and energy. That was it.

When she looked at Jerome George Marakkaran as just a body, she overcame her fear. A body whose brain cells were almost completely dead. Even in a state of unconsciousness, it may open its eyes, make sounds, move its limbs. But the brain may not be able to analyse what the eye sees. Or distinguish the sounds it hears.

As she stood looking at him, her heart melted. She remembered their first night together. Like she had back then, she went up to him. Her eyes welled up. She gently stroked his left hand, now twisted like a twig. Summoning up the love she could not feel back then, she called out to him, 'Jerome!' She looked at his face to her heart's content. This face, this body, this was what she had thought was hers—the body she had mistook as united with her own by God. She wanted to speak to Jerome. She wanted to pamper him.

'I have never been able to talk to you openly, Jerome, neither before marriage nor after,' Jezebel began, as if she were talking to herself. Slowly, her voice grew louder. That was the benefit of a conversation. When we speak, we can hear our own words. We understand our own selves.

'Jerome, why did I not tell you everything?' she asked herself. 'It wasn't because there was nothing to talk about, or because I didn't want to talk. I was not brave enough. I was scared. Not that you may not accept what I'm saying, but that you wouldn't understand it. And you, you never once spoke to me. Or tried to find out if I had anything to say. Such cruelty! I know there's no point complaining to you about it now, but I can't help telling you either. Right from my childhood, I had many dreams about life. I studied, scored high marks, got a rank, all of it so I would find a special place in the heart of my man. I had dreams about a man who was waiting only for me. I was foolish enough to think that he would accept only me as his life partner. And that I would accept only him as mine. That's why I fell for your line "We are made for each other." Jerome, how eager I was to find my man! If only I had known that you came all the way, travelling for a day and a night, in search of a stepping stone! Have you ever known the pain of a stepping stone? Have you ever tried to find out? Have you thought, at least once, about how you used me like a mere tool on our first night together? And how my heart shattered to pieces even as I waited for your loving touch? I expected love. I expected sex. I expected friendship. I wanted to become part of you. For you, though, I was not part of you. I was just live multipurpose furniture—one that could be used at the same time as a cook, a manager, a sex toy . . .'

Jezebel was close to tears. She could feel pieces of her heart fume and burn, flames flaring up in every breath she exhaled, and her flesh smouldering in pain like wet firewood. His eyes remained open above the oxygen mask. There was a sort of bewilderment in his eyes. It reminded Jezebel of deep-sea divers she had seen in Hollywood movies. He looked like a man who had dived deep into the sea of death and was now resting under a shipwreck at the bottom. Perhaps he did not see her. Or hear her. Perhaps it was only the silence of the endless sea of time that surrounded him. Perhaps all he could see was the cold darkness of the depths of that sea. Jezebel was terrified. She feared that she, too, would drown in that sea.

It seemed inexcusable that he should stay silent like that, without replying, without giving her an explanation, without asking for forgiveness even once. As a human being, he ought to have apologized to another human being for all that he had done to her. As a doctor, he had the responsibility of healing her wounds. He was obliged to restore her shattered life. He was obliged to accept punishment for having wronged Ann Mary. But none of this happened. Instead, he had fled all his troubles and entered this state of silence, oblivion and slumber. Perhaps he could see her. But he would not know who it was. Perhaps he could hear her. But he would not be able to understand what she was saying. Perhaps he could utter sounds. But they would not be lit by his thoughts. His body could not complain of hunger. Or remind him of thirst. This was not the Jerome George Marakkaran she knew, Jezebel reminded herself. Jerome George Marakkaran was a cluster of cells. Most of those cells were dead. If each brick and tile and doorframe and window frame of a church were to come apart, what remained could not be called a church, only a sorry shell of the original. A mere body. A clock that moved to nature's rhythm, bereft of memories, regrets, remorse, joy, sorrow, disappointment, love. It made his eyes open from time to time, then shut them. It made sounds emerge from his throat, then fell silent.

Terror gripped Jezebel. A fire blazed in the pit of her stomach. Perhaps a person gained tremendous energy at the height of helplessness. He was so weak, he would die at the touch of a finger. So, she feared him. His body lay so lifeless, no one could ever hurt him any more. So, she was scared to hurt him. The one who had married her was another man. This man would not know that one's thoughts. This man would not remember that one's desires. How could she take revenge on him? What could she ask him? The next moment, she felt mercy for this man. She thought of that body as a child's. Perhaps Jerome sensed time like a baby in his mother's womb. Like a foetus swimming in amniotic fluid, eyes closed, lost in thought, he was an ark making his way very slowly through the endless waters of time. Her heart ached. Such helplessness. How terrifying this helplessness was!

She understood now why she hadn't been able to talk to him openly in the early days of their marriage. Then, too, he hadn't seen her. He hadn't appreciated her face or her body or her personality. He hadn't heard her voice. He hadn't felt the wetness of her tears. He had done only what his body demanded of him. Whatever he felt was good, suitable and necessary for him, he had taken for himself. Jezebel felt like an ark on fire sinking into the sea.

She grasped Jerome's left hand tight. 'Who are you?' she asked him. 'Who are you to me? Who are you in your own memory?' The papery softness of his skin was unbearable. A palm without the pulsating warmth of life. She bent down, put that palm to her forehead, and wept.

After a while, Jerome George Marakkaran's hand moved a little. She woke up with a start. His eyes had closed. He had moved from wakefulness in an unconscious state to sleep in unconsciousness.

When dawn broke, she woke up, cleaned out his catheter and turned him to one side. She showered and dressed. She grew restless, wondering what she would do with the rest of her time in that apartment. She was hungry and thirsty. She wanted a cup of tea. She craved Ammachi's paalappams and stew. She called Chachan.

'Is there any problem . . .?' panicked Chachan.

'Did you eat anything?' worried Ammachi.

She assured them that all was well. Soon after, Abraham Chammanatt called. She sensed trouble in his voice.

'Georgekutty is kicking up a big row out here. He is bent on coming there right away.'

Her mouth fell open.

'He's screaming saying you'll do something to Jerome. Come to think of it, I'm also a little scared. If something happens to

Jerome, I mean, he's in such a state, after all, Georgekutty will crucify you in all sorts of ways! I'm clueless about what to do.'

'Right, so let him come here and take care of Jerome,' fumed Jezebel. 'I haven't made any offering to sit next to this man who is lying here like a vegetable. I don't want any credit or virtue for leaving my job behind to sit in this rotten flat full of dust and cobwebs. Let him come and save his son. I'll return on the first flight back home! I wasted money on a ticket to come all the way here. That man won't change. Didn't I tell you, Unc*ley*?'

'Forgive him for my sake, *kochey*. I think it's better for him to come over . . .'

'And you want me to stay here and take care of father and son?'

Abraham Chammanatt fell silent. Jezebel grew angrier.

'Uncle, I haven't come here to gain brownie points for taking care of my husband. There is a patient here, left all alone. There's no one to take care of him. I happen to know him. We stayed together in a house for two-and-a-half years. So I thought I'd stay with him, purely on humanitarian grounds, until someone else took over. I have no plan of taking care of him for the rest of my life. I will not make such a promise either.'

'Father Ilanjikkal has promised to bring a home nurse over today itself. Rosamma will also come along for now. I have already credited some money to Father Ilanjikkal's account. And if there's any further need, my manager will take care,' Abraham said in a conciliatory tone.

'I'm so glad! Let Jerome's Daddy come! Just let me know when you're putting him on the plane here. I'll clear out a minute before he reaches. I'd like to know why you had to trouble me like this, though. You haven't had enough of ruining my life, clearly.'

She flung the phone on to the sofa, clutched at her hair and broke down, sobbing loudly. It was as if she had vowed to weep her eyes out and shed all the tears she had stored up ever since she had

first come to that apartment as a bride. She scolded herself, cursed
herself. She was still weeping when Father Ilanjikkal arrived with
another home nurse at ten o'clock that morning. Father Ilanjikkal
said, stroking her hair, 'Why do you lose heart so easily?'

'It's not because I've lost heart that I'm crying,' she wept. 'It's
about Jerome's daddy. When I think about that man's death, I'm
so worried. He won't find peace even if he dies. Father, he will
always burn with hatred for me.'

Father Ilanjikkal smiled sadly. 'That's the right way to think
about it. When someone constantly torments us, rather than seek
revenge, it's better to think about them and weep for them.'

After some time, Jezebel calmed down. She instructed Anila,
the home nurse Father Ilanjikkal had brought, on how to attend
to Jerome. Father Ilanjikkal sent his driver to get food for all of
them. As they were having food, Abraham Chammanatt called
to let them know that George Jerome Marakkaran and Rosamma
were arriving by the three o'clock flight. Jezebel got ready to leave.
She requested Father Ilanjikkal to stay on in the apartment until
George Jerome Marakkaran reached. 'What about you?' asked
Father, worried. She told him she would leave that day itself if she
got a ticket or stay in a hotel otherwise. Father said he would make
arrangements in the convent.

'I wept a lot today. Now I want to laugh. I want to walk about,
see places . . .' she said.

'Have a drink then! I'll give you the money!' joked Father.

'It's because you Fathers preach like this that there are such
long queues in front of liquor shops,' she quipped.

'Oh, we preach about so many things. The lambs take what
they want from it,' said Father.

Before she left, Jezebel went to Jerome's room once again. Her
heart ached at the thought of parting. She felt a bond with him
that she had not felt in the years she had lived with him. Perhaps
that was because this was another Jerome or because now she knew

clearly who he was. She caressed him on the cheeks. Jerome's eyes opened. She wanted to believe that those eyes were looking at her. She stroked his hairless head and kissed him on the forehead. She caressed his arms. The compassion that one human being feels for another made her weep.

When she got into the taxi, she dialled Kabir Mohammed's number. He picked it up on the first ring. 'Jezebel, I've been wanting to call you since morning. And then I thought it's not okay to call without knowing what the situation out there is like.'

'I need a place to stay. Can you accommodate me in your room?'

Her own voice sounded dry to her ears. When Kabir paused a moment before responding, she panicked.

'No problem. I'll inform the reception right away. I need to leave by eleven tonight. But you can stay till tomorrow, *alle?*'

He was staying at a plush seaside hotel. He was waiting for her at the reception. From his room you could see the swimming pool and, in the distance, the sea. Kabir switched on the kettle. She stood by the window and gazed down at the lawn with its fountains, weeping willows and lantana vines. Kabir came up behind her with two cups of coffee. She took a cup and set it to her lips. 'Nice coffee,' she said. He had a sip, and claimed, 'I usually make better coffee than this.' 'I believe that,' she admitted. They looked at each other and laughed. Kabir looked intently at her. She felt conscious.

'Can I ask you something?'

'Is it about why I've been crying?' Jezebel asked.

Kabir's face lit up with a fond smile. It made her happy.

'No . . . I've been observing since last night. There's a sort of stubbornness in your face and voice. Now it has doubled. As if you're challenging someone. It's not me, is it?'

Jezebel's dimples blossomed in spite of herself.

'I feel this sense of stubbornness with the world. You're part of the world too, aren't you? So I feel that with you too.'

'If you're stubborn about wanting something, I'm only too happy to help you get it,' Kabir said.

'Then let's go for a walk, shall we?'

His eyes lit up. They stepped out on to the red-carpeted corridor, chatting like old friends, and walked up to the lift. He made her laugh, telling her about all that had happened since he had arrived at the hotel. He told her about the time he was stuck in an elevator when he was a student in London.

'Were you scared?' she asked.

'There was only a girl with me,' he smiled sadly.

'How romantic! And how did you get out?'

'It took three hours for the lift to be repaired. We got out after that.'

They walked past the door held open by a turbaned doorman, and stepped out into the sunlight.

'And so, did you become friends?' she asked.

He looked away. In the sunlight, the stubble on his face glittered.

'We didn't become friends. We became husband and wife.' His voice sounded parched. 'That too, for three years.'

He walked silently for a while. Her heart lurched a little, but she scolded herself: what's your problem if he's married?

They had reached the main road. He hailed a taxi. They went to a shopping mall nearby. They wandered around for a bit, had juice at a restaurant. When the daylight faded, they went to the beach. They found a space for themselves amidst the huddle of couples twined like lovebirds.

'The one who came last night wasn't your husband, was he?' asked Kabir in the course of conversation.

'Not my husband, my husband's lover, Dr Avinash Gupta.'

Kabir's face turned red.

'Then where's your husband?'

'He was in a room inside. He has been in a coma for the last two-and-a-half-years.'

Kabir sat speechless. Trying to change the topic, she said, 'Whenever I see the blue of the sea, I think of my Valiyammachi.' She disclosed that she had inherited her dimples from Valiyammachi. She made Kabir laugh, telling him about Valiyammachi who always prayed to the Lord to lead her astray.

'My Valiyumma knew four languages—Malayalam, English, Hindi, Arabic. Ask me how she learnt them. By watching TV! We always said it was Valiyumma who gained the most from globalization. She passed away ten years ago, just as she was learning the fifth language, Oriya.'

She replied to his stories about his unlettered Valiyumma with her own stories about Valiyammachi. He asked her about her parents. She told him about Chachan and Ammachi. He told her about his parents, his Umma and Vaappa. He told her about how Vaappa had married again while in Muscat, how Umma had gotten a divorce, sent her four children home to Kerala and then remarried. 'It wasn't easy. Back home, everyone would sympathize with us, saying "Oh! How could your Umma and Vaappa leave you children to yourselves like this," and so on. The four of us went in different directions. All of us studied a lot. There was no dearth of money. Vaappa and Umma vied with one another to send us money.'

He sat watching the eagles soaring in the sky, resting his hands on the sand.

'Was your wife a doctor too?' Jezebel asked after some time.

'Hm . . .'

When it grew dark, they returned to their room.

'I asked for another day's leave, but didn't get it . . .,' he complained to no one in particular when they reached the room. She realized with a pang that he would leave in a matter of hours.

'Don't you have annual leave in your workplace?' she asked him.

'We do, but I don't take it. My job isn't in a hospital, after all.'

His words surprised her.

'Haven't you heard of Doctors Without Borders? Médecins Sans Frontières.'

She looked at him with new respect.

'After the divorce, I joined the MSF—went to the war zone, understood that real war was far better than the war inside the home.'

He tried to smile. He had come along with the body of a Malayali who had died in the war zone. She heard him out, unblinking. That was when Father Ilanjikkal called. He asked her if she needed any help and also told her that George Jerome Marakkaran had reached. Jezebel's blood boiled. She stood by the window. Outside, tiny specks of light floated on the dark sea. Kabir came up to her. 'It is nine o'clock,' he despaired. 'How quickly time has gone by,' she whispered. She thanked him for an evening well spent.

'Meeting you was the high point of this trip. Now I have a reason to come home. We have leave. When it's my turn, I'll come again.'

Jezebel stood there with a heavy heart. She couldn't understand her own self. What was happening between her and that man? Her heart was stubbornly melting into his.

'Do you need any help, Jezebel? To stay here or find a job? I have a few good friends here.' Kabir's voice faltered.

Jezebel turned to him. He looked even more handsome in the lamplight. His eyes glittered like diamonds. She felt dizzy. The air conditioner in that hotel room purred like a lapdog that wanted to be pampered more.

'Any help?' he asked again.

She could see his suitcase, all packed and ready, in one corner of the bed. The bed, done up without a single crease. The table lamp that shed a mellow yellow light.

'Yes. I need a favour,' she said.

'Tell me. Anything.'

She moved closer to him. They stood, face to face. He must have read something in her eyes then, she would later recall. His eyes filled with surprise. His face turned red. She extended her trembling hands towards him. He took them in his, hesitantly.

'Before you leave . . .' Mustering all her courage, she laid herself against his chest. 'A favour . . . a small favour . . .'

Tears streamed down her eyes. Seeing those tears, he seemed perplexed and unsure at first. Then, as if conceding defeat, he gave in and touched her on the shoulder. Like a rubber ball that someone had kicked hard, her heart leapt up, fell down and bounced back again. A man. A man she hadn't tired of. A man she hadn't despised. Her body burst into blossom under his touch. She melted into him without inhibition. He stood holding her lovingly for some time. And then, very slowly, his fingers stirred to life. She found herself slipping into a coma. She experienced resurrection in her subconscious.

Later, whenever she recalled those moments, Jezebel could still see the stars that had burst forth from her brain. She had experienced a whole new body rising from her old self. Another body. Another woman. Another Jezebel. She could not make out the thoughts of the new body. When she tried to go back to the old body, her thoughts and brain feigned fatigue. The old body died. The new body resurrected. It quickly wrapped itself around Kabir Mohammed. There's not much time, it urged. Kabir Mohammed was whispering something in her ear. 'What if something happens . . .?' he demurred. 'I'm the one who should be asking that question,' she shot back like a fearless warrior. Such courage, marvelled the old body from somewhere. At some point, Kabir let go of his misgivings. He gathered her in his arms and took her to the bed. The new body yearned to conquer. The old body wandered about in disbelief. 'Kabir, I lived with my husband for two-and-a-half years. But this is my first night,' blabbered the new body. 'Meaning?' asked Kabir. 'You are the first man to touch my body,' she confessed. That very moment, Kabir's hands froze. He sprang apart. The new body shivered on the bed and wondered, 'What happened? What happened?'

'Sorry, I can't afford to be cheated once again!' Kabir blurted, as he picked up her clothes from the floor and flung them at her before rushing to the bathroom. In the blink of an eye, he had dressed and gotten ready, shut his suitcase, slung his laptop bag on his shoulder and reached the door. While opening the door, he announced to no one in particular, 'This room is available till noon tomorrow. If you want, I can extend it for another day.'

Jezebel sat stupefied on the bed, hugging her clothes to her chest. He had left without saying goodbye. She took a long to time to recover. The new body evaporated. The old body resurrected, nail wounds and all. She did not understand what had happened. In the mirror, she could see the image of a naked woman clutching on to the clothes she had shed. She despised herself. The number of insults she had received over the years made her ashamed. If only she could throw her naked body out of the window as if it were an old dress. In that room full of large mirrors, she saw her own nakedness everywhere she turned. She looked at her body with distaste. It may not have been the fair, rosy complexion of the heroines of stories, but wasn't there anything at all in it that would arouse the desire of a man? She was livid. She felt like running to the heart of the city and asking the masses, 'How many marks would you give my body? My breasts? My behind? My belly? My legs? How many marks? When you compare and contrast with the bodies you've seen and touched, how many marks out of ten?' At once, the body in the mirror turned old. It hung its head in shame.

Jezebel wept, howling, like a child who had rushed home from school only to find, to her horror, that her home had vanished. She wept as she had never wept before. It was a howl that emanated from the pit of her stomach. It shook her body and threw her to the ground. She curled up on the floor and wept her eyes out. Her heart shattered, crumbled and poured out of her eyes as tears. She felt sorry for herself. She felt indignant. And then she remembered that she had died and been buried in a grave. She spent a long time bathing, then looked at herself in the mirror again. She looked at the eyes and face puffed up with weeping, and felt repentant. She booked a ticket in a flight next morning. She sat on a chair by the window. Outside, the city night scoffed at her. The heart was empty. She didn't know what she had to do thereon. Her eyes burned and smouldered. She could not sleep. The bedspread seemed to laugh at her. She curled up inside the chair as if it were a womb. She drifted into a light sleep, then woke up with a start. And decided not to think about Kabir. She thought only about herself. About her little life, and the people who had come and gone.

She tried to recall the face of Ranjith, whom she had been fond of in her MBBS years. She could only remember his ever-smiling eyes. His face crumbled into nothingness like a sand sculpture. If only he had been around, they might have married. They might have lived happily together, in a house filled with children and laughter.

She recalled the day Ranjith had gone missing. It was Rani Kurian who told her, 'Did you hear, Ranjith is missing!' Jezebel laughed. 'Jez, it's not a joke. He was washed away.' Jezebel went numb. For some time, she could not feel a thing. And then her body began to shiver uncontrollably. She felt suffocated. She sat for a long time on the bed, her knees drawn up to her chest, her head on her knees. She looked for her textbook to forget the pain. She tried to read and understand how the body would react when it was buried under mud. She learnt that it was like sinking underwater. She learnt that one remained conscious until the breath stopped, and that those last moments of consciousness were excruciating. She shut the book, lacking the courage to imagine those moments between suffocation and unconsciousness. She struggled for breath till his body was recovered. She thanked God that he had died.

She felt that struggle again now. She wondered if she was buried under the mud. And then reminded herself that she was, in fact, in a luxurious room with all possible comforts. And decided to be grateful and not complain. Praise the Lord that I'm not under the mud. Praise the Lord that when I got ready to sleep with a man, he left the room rather than rape me. Praise the Lord that he didn't trade my flesh, shoot it with a hidden camera and post it on YouTube. Perhaps he did not like her body. He had every right to feel that way, didn't he? Praise the Lord that his rights were not violated.

Jezebel stood once again in front of the mirror. A shrouded body with swollen eyelids smiled at her, mortified. She was convinced that the body and soul were both experiencing resurrection. No one has witnessed resurrection till date. Because it was a divine experience meant to be known only by the self—like a butterfly emerging from chrysalis, like nectar oozing in a flower, like lightning awakening in the clouds. If that first covenant had been without fault, no place would have been sought for a second. Now that a new covenant is being spoken of, the first one has become outdated. The outdated and the old are vanishing.

O object of my affection, the daughter of man shed her body so that we enter the new world made for us and not the holy place which is man-made and only an image of the true one. Sacrificing herself in the fullness of time, she has appeared now in order to do away with sin once and for all. Just as man is appointed to die once, and after that to face judgement, so too the daughter of man will be offered once to bear the sins of many.

And she will appear a second time, not to bear sin, but to bring salvation to those who eagerly await her.

28

Two angels in white asked Jezebel-who-was-Mary-Magdalene, 'Woman, why are you crying?' She said, 'They have taken my soul away, and I don't know where they have put her.' Saying this, she turned around and saw Jezebel-the-rabbi standing there, but she did not realize that it was her own self.

Jezebel-the-rabbi asked her, 'Woman, why are you crying? Who is it you are looking for?'

Mistaking her for someone else, she said, 'If you have carried her away, tell me where you have put her.'

Jezebel-the-rabbi said to her, 'Mariam, do not stop me.'

Jezebel had a long way to understand the revelation that only one could stop oneself. Until then, the body that had lost the soul and the soul that had lost the body floundered about, unable to be one, distressing her. To escape that, the night she returned home, she told Valiyammachi, 'I feel greatly relieved now, Valiyammachi. I'm not angry with Jerome any more. The world was cruel to him; he was cruel to me.'

'When one grows old, we may find it difficult to read letters of the alphabet, but we learn to read peoples' minds better. Is there something you haven't told me?' Valiyammachi questioned her. And so, she bared her heart. 'Valiyammachi, I went to a man in his room.'

Valiyammachi's hand, which was caressing Jezebel's hand that lay across her stomach, went still. The room filled with silence for a moment. And then, Valiyammachi laughed. 'So did something happen?'

Jezebel rolled her eyes at Valiyammachi with mock anger. 'Like that lawyer said in court, you're some grandmother indeed, Valiyammachi! When you hear that your granddaughter spent time with a man in his room, this is just what you should ask her all right!'

'Oh! I have no great hopes pinned on you, *kochey*,' Valiyammachi sighed. 'You would have talked big-big things in that room till daybreak. And in the morning, that man would have run out of the room dragging his suitcase and taken the first flight out. *Ente kochey*, these men are not very clever, *dee*. And they don't know that either. In their eagerness to prove they are very smart, they declare that whatever we say is nonsense. Then they feel very smug about it.' Valiyammachi laughed, her dimples crinkling.

'You don't have to belittle me so much, Valiyammachi. To tell you the truth, a lot of things happened.'

'Except the one thing that ought to have,' Valiyammachi teased her again. Smoothing Jezebel's hair, she threw down the gauntlet. 'Now tell me. What on earth did you cook up there?'

Jezebel lay curled up next to Valiyammachi. 'The name's Kabir Mohammed . . .,' she began. Valiyammachi cut in, 'Ah, religion and caste are not important. Is he humane, is he honest, does he have self-esteem—these are what matter.'

She told Valiyammachi what had happened. 'Oh! Some woman must have stabbed him in the back. Ask him to get lost, *dee*,' laughed Valiyammachi.

Then, seeing that Jezebel's pride was hurt, she reassured her, 'What was it that you told me about Jerome a little while ago, *kochey*? That what he gave you was what the world had given him, *alleyo*? This man too did just that. If you started crying over all this, then you'll have time only for that.'

Along with the power to read others' minds, perhaps some people in their old age also gained the power to turn their grandchildren's tears into laughter. Jezebel buried her face in Valiyammachi's shoulder. When she woke up the next morning, Valiyammachi lay awake. '*Kochey*, he must be a good man . . .' Rubbing her eyes, she wondered who Valiyammachi was talking about. 'That Kabir. He must have panicked when you told him he was your first man.' She didn't understand. Valiyammachi explained, 'A woman no one has touched. That too, one like you who is educated and has seen the world. When such a woman goes to a man on her own, men see it as a great responsibility and burden! He may not have been able to handle it. That's all. Otherwise, these men are generally harmless.'

'But I did not ask to him take on any responsibility, Valiyammachi . . .'

'Try and look at it from his point of view. Won't he be afraid that tomorrow you'll cling on to him using this as an excuse? *Ente kochey*, I'm telling you this from experience. Men are most afraid to love their partners. They will try their best not to love. At the same time, they will insist that their partners love them with all their life.'

'That's not why I'm upset, Valiyammachi. Why do I lust after men like this?'

Valiyammachi's face turned red. 'Let it be, *kochey*. If you're human, you ought to feel love and lust and sadness and hunger.'

'It wasn't like this before, Valiyammachi.'

'If you don't feel it now, then at which age? When you have one foot in the grave?'

Valiyammachi took off her glasses and wiped her eyes. 'Probably because you feel you have been denied it. Love and lust and happiness, isn't it all in one's own mind, *kochey*?'

She agreed that that's what the modern medicine she had studied said too. Each person thought up his or her love and happiness and anxiety. Torture and crucifixion and resurrection— they were all in the mind. How can one who has been resurrected seek herself among the dead, she repented. Her eyes had been blindfolded in such a way that she could not recognize her own self. She asked herself: What are you talking about? How slow your heart is to believe all that the prophet has spoken! Was it not necessary for the daughter of man to suffer all these and then enter her glory? The first ordeal is past. There are two more to come, *alle*? Was she not destined to experience fire and brimstone all over again?

The second ordeal was quick to come. Father Ilanjikkal's call came while she was preparing her documents for a fellowship abroad. 'Georgekutty and his son are in dire straits. The home nurse left after a quarrel with Rosamma. Rosamma isn't listening to Georgekutty.'

Although Jezebel retorted, 'He deserves it!', when she put the phone down, her heart sank. She saw George Jerome Marakkaran and Jerome George Marakkaran in her mind's eye. What would the state of mind of a bedridden father watching his comatose son be like? What would the heaven and hell of his own making be like?

The next day she called Father Ilanjikkal. He told her, 'Georgekutty's foot is infected. Jerome's situation is also pathetic. It would be good if you could come, *kochey* . . .'

'Even my dog won't go back to that place again!' fumed Jezebel. 'This must be another of his plots, Father. He must have found out I'm planning to go abroad. He probably has spies here even now. Earlier his ploy to stop me from passing my MD exam did not work out. Now he's hatching a plan to stop me from going abroad.' She shed angry tears.

'Will I ever ask you to come here after giving up your studies, *moley*? The situation here is bad. I just informed you about it, that's all. Go ahead with your studies. I'll figure out something.' Although Father Ilanjikkal consoled her, Jezebel had lost her peace of mind.

The next morning, Abraham Chammanatt came home. 'Jerome's case . . .' he began.

'Please talk to Jezebel about all that,' Chachan passed the buck on.

'What's left to say?' fumed Ammachi. 'Couldn't that man have stayed on here until he was well enough to walk?'

'He's dragged himself back there just to trouble everyone else,' rebuked Valiyammachi.

'In that case, I'll have to postpone my US trip. Just got the tickets and visa and everything. Only four more days to go,' despaired Abraham Chammanatt.

Jezebel felt sorry seeing the misery on Abraham's face, already creased with age. She asked herself if he would have come to her like this in his youth. She made up her mind that it was not right to inflict more pain on someone who was so miserable.

'Okay let's just say I decide to go. What if he kicks up a racket again?' Jezebel asked after a while.

'Georgekutty is desperate and wailing aloud that anyone will do. Rosamma is returning home today. Father Ilanjikkal arranged for a helper, but her husband won't let her stay in a house that doesn't have other women.'

Jezebel grew restless. 'Why should you go?' she kept asking herself. 'Jezebel, don't stop me'—a woman who had resurrected within her braced for battle. 'I overcame the tests he put me through and passed my MD I will overcome this one too and get my next degree as well,' she prophesied. That evening, Jezebel flew to Jerome's city.

She reached at eight in the night. Father Ilanjikkal was waiting for her at Jerome George Marakkaran's apartment. Fifty-year-old Marykutty, whom Father Ilanjikkal had brought to help out in the kitchen, unpacked her bundle of woes as she helped Jezebel with her luggage, 'Lord, what wrong did I do that I had to cook and serve a man with such a heart of stone?'

George Jerome Marakkaran lay in a bed with caster wheels right next to Jerome's bed. A stretcher lay next to him. George Jerome Marakkaran had reduced beyond recognition. He coughed weakly from time to time. Pus had spread, dark and yellow, over that part of the leg that could be seen outside the plaster. The room reeked of urine and faeces.

'I don't need favours from any daughter of a whore!' he growled when he saw her, and broke into a fit of coughing. Jezebel could visualize his infected lungs. Father Ilanjikkal admonished him, 'Georgekutty, I had to practically fall at the feet of that woman in the kitchen in order to bring her over. She will leave this place this instant if there are no other women around. If you and your son want to stay alive, you had better behave yourself.'

'My Lord will save me! He will make my son walk again!' George Jerome Marakkaran raised his voice. 'My Lord is a living God! He made the lame walk, he raised the dead! How difficult would it be for him to make my son walk?'

Not paying him any heed, Jezebel went over and examined his leg. He tried to pull his leg away. Pain distorted his face.

'It is badly infected. He needs to be admitted to a hospital as soon as possible,' Jezebel told Father Ilanjikkal.

'Let Avinash come, then I'll think about it,' retorted George Jerome Marakkaran.

'Sure, keep thinking about it till Avinash returns after immersing his mother's ashes, keep thinking until worms crawl out of those wounds,' scoffed Jezebel. 'It's stinking already. This room stinks of decaying flesh. You don't understand. At this rate, the whole body will get infected. Have you heard of the phrase "rot and die"? That will happen, literally. The Lord will come in the form of a worm too, *alle*, Father?'

Father Ilanjikkal stood at a loss for words. The veins on George Jerome Marakkaran's forehead and cheek grew taut with fury. 'Get out, you whore!' He tried to swear but failed, as he coughed and doubled up in pain.

When a sound like a burp rose from Jerome's body, Jezebel went over to him. His pulse was weak. She cleaned out the catheter and fixed it again. She detached the feeding tubes, cleaned them out and fixed them back again. She changed Jerome's clothes, wiped his body, powdered him and turned him over. She folded and straightened his limbs to maintain blood circulation. When she turned around after settling Jerome, her eyes met George Jerome Marakkaran's. She looked closely at that darkened, stubbled face. Even his eyebrows had begun to grey. There were great dark pits under his eyes. His cheek muscles had grown taut, indicating high blood pressure.

When she came out and sat on the sofa, tired, Father Ilanjikkal came up and sat down next to her, stifling a yawn. 'Some running around you're doing in your nineties!' she quipped. He laughed as well. 'That's right. To think that I ran away to the seminary fearing family responsibility! And now how many families I'm responsible for,' he sighed. And then he asked her if she had leave and how long she planned to stay there. 'One week,' she said. 'I'll make some arrangement in the meantime,' he promised her. 'Make sure your studies don't get affected, *moley*.' And then he got up to take her leave and asked her with some anxiety, 'Are you scared to stay here?'

'I'm back here only because I realized that I get more scared when I run away from things,' Jezebel reassured him. Father Ilanjikkal repeated that a nun had promised to send him a home nurse the next day itself. 'I was relieved to hear you were coming. But now I'm not so sure. How will you stay here? How will you put up with Georgekutty's cussing and swearing? Maybe you should not have come, *moley*.'

'Swear words are just words, *alle*, Acho,' smiled Jezebel. 'It's the venom in the speaker's heart that turns words into swear words. But the venom spews out either when the person is hurt or when he thinks he is defeated. His swearing is a sort of defence against getting more hurt or defeated.'

'May he not defend himself against you too much then,' sighed Father. It made Jezebel smile.

After Father had left, Marykutty *chechi* served her kanji and curry. Since Rosamma and the home nurse had stayed there for a while, the room John Jerome Marakkaran used to stay in looked tidier than before. The moment she lay down, Jezebel went off to sleep.

She woke up with a start to the shouts of '*Edee*, daughter of a slut, come here, *dee*!' Marykutty rushed in and sat down on the other bed, muttering, 'That man has shat in the bed and wants me to clean him up. I can't do all that.'

Jezebel sat up in the bed as if someone had whacked her on the head. 'I can't either,' she told herself. By then, a foul stench was spreading all over the apartment. She felt nauseated. She sat in the bed, a hand clapped over her nose and mouth. She thought her intestine would rise and spill out of her mouth. She did not know what to do. How will I clean his waste with my own hands, she asked herself. She cursed him. She wondered if he had done it deliberately just to spite her. Let him lie there, let him rot and stink. I won't even look in his direction. This is how the Lord he spoke of is exacting revenge on my behalf.

Panting, she opened the windows and tried to breathe in a little fresh air. A thousand pigeons flapped their wings and rose in flight. She wished she could soar up with them and escape.

George Jerome Marakkaran's yell rose again. '*Edee* daughter of a slut, come here *dee*! Clean me up *dee*! You are being paid to do this, *alle*? The Lord will show you *dee*. The Lord will pay you back for behaving like this with a sick old man! You, too, will lie like this in your own shit and rot and stink to death one day! And I'll die only after seeing that! This is nothing! The game has only just begun!'

Jezebel's head went numb. 'An old man', Jezebel-the-doctor reminded the angry Jezebel. A man who was born without the protection of family or the acceptance of society, and who grew up hearing cuss words and abuse. His limbs and spine are now broken. His leg is infected with pus. His body throbs in pain. He has no one. She took out a towel from the suitcase and tied it around her nose. She wore the gloves she saw on the table. Perhaps they had been left by the home nurse who had been there earlier. She went into the room where George Jerome Marakkaran and Jerome George Marakkaran lay.

When he saw Jezebel, George Jerome Marakkaran struggled to get up. 'No, not you! Don't come near me!' he panicked. 'Oh, but this is the Lord,' scoffed Jezebel, as she went up to him. 'This is how the Lord comes to you!' He raised his other, unbroken arm and tried to hit her. She gripped that arm firmly, and glared at him. 'You have seen only one face of mine so far. If necessary, I can behave more brutally than you. Keep quiet. One more sound from you, and I'll stuff cloth into your mouth,' she threatened him.

She shifted his body carefully, took out the bedpan and cleaned it. When George Jerome Marakkaran tried to say something, she glared at him again and shut him up. Marykutty helped her move him from the bed to the stretcher. They sponged his body with Dettol-infused water, powdered him. He had high fever. His body was full of festering wounds. It was clear he was in great pain. Marykutty found some clean bedsheets and spread them over George Jerome's bed. Together, they dressed him and laid him back on the bed again. Whether out of pain or shame, he groaned pitifully. The groaning slowly stopped. After some time, he went quiet altogether. Jezebel realized with some satisfaction that he had begun to fear her. What would a snake do when its venom had dried up? It would curl up in a corner. In the morning, when she brought him tea, she found him curled up on the bed.

'Daddy,' she called out to him as kindly as she could. George Jerome Marakkaran woke up with a start. He stared at her as if he couldn't believe his ears. His eyes were red, as if he had been crying all that while.

'I have no great wish to call you Daddy. Nor have you ever given me any love for me to call you that. I can't call you anything else, that's why.' She offered him the cup of tea.

'You would have mixed poison into this,' he muttered.

'That's your style,' she shot back. 'That must be how you finished off Mummy.'

'Don't talk nonsense!' he said angrily. 'You can ridicule me all you want now when I'm unwell. Once I get up, then you'll see!'

'Tea will give you a little energy. Then you can swear some more,' she mocked.

'Let that other woman give it to me,' he frowned.

'She hates you even more!' Jezebel was merciless.

He tried to snatch the cup with his unbroken arm, but his hand was shivering. Jezebel snatched the cup back and looked at him angrily. 'There's no one out here to wash clothes every other minute,' she scolded. 'And no place for those clothes to dry either.'

George Jerome Marakkaran gave in. He drank the tea from the cup she held for him. Marykutty brought a bowl for him to rinse his mouth and spit into. Jezebel wiped his mouth and face. She gave him his medicines.

After she had arranged for George Jerome Marakkaran to be shifted to a hospital, called home and discussed things with Abraham Chammanatt, Jezebel increasingly felt the lightness of a soul without a body. After a bath and breakfast, she went to the balcony with a book in hand, and gazed at the city to her heart's content. For the first time in her life, she felt a great surge of energy. She was certain she had resurrected. She could see the many shrouds that had smothered her head and body coming undone. When she saw her own resurrected self, Jezebel-the-disciple trembled in fear. She thought she was seeing a ghost. Jezebel-the-rabbi reminded her: 'Touch me and see—for a spirit does not have flesh and bones, as you see I have.' She raised her own hands and blessed her own self. And thus, she was taken up into heaven. The resurrected Jezebel soared up into the sky with tremendous energy. The sun was rising in the sky. Beautiful red rays swathed her and melted into her. She became the woman adorned with the sun.

29

This is the revelation that Jezebel gave herself to show those who had faith in her what must soon come to pass: *Blessed are the ones who read aloud the words of this prophecy, and blessed are those who hear and obey what is written in it because the time is near. Behold, she is coming with the clouds, and every eye will see her—even those who pierced her. And all the tribes of the earth will mourn because of her. So shall it be! Amen.*

It was the day Christina also descended from the clouds, like another powerful angel. Jezebel was preparing to shift George Jerome Marakkaran to the hospital. He tried not to look at her as she cleaned his body and dressed him in fresh clothes. His old confidence had disappeared. The change that comes over the facial muscles when a person feels defeated was apparent on his face.

There was a bustle at the door even as Father Ilanjikkal was complaining about the delay in the arrival of the ambulance. Before the conversation could get over, the door opened and Christina entered. Behind her was John Jerome Marakkaran, holding the baby and a middle-aged woman with the luggage. 'Why didn't you tell me you were coming?' she welcomed them, surprised and happy. But Christina's face was clouded. 'Did you tell us you were coming here? This is our house!' said Christina loudly, as if throwing down a challenge. 'This house is in Mummy's name. All Mummy's properties are meant for Johnchayan. This is Johnchayan's house. And this is where we will stay from now on.'

She pushed the door of George Jerome Marakkaran's room open and asked the woman accompanying her to set the luggage down there. When George Jerome Marakkaran's voice rose from Jerome's room demanding, 'What's that sound? Who's there?', Christina walked in and announced, 'It's us. We are staying here from now on.' George Jerome Marakkaran must have been taken aback to see the visitor. 'Is this your father's house or what?' he bellowed. When Jezebel went to the doorway of the room, she saw Christina tying her hair up in a knot and bracing for battle. 'This is my child's father's house. We are here to take care of things here from now on,' she thundered.

'*Chee*, get out, *dee*!' George Jerome Marakkaran growled back weakly. 'This is my house. All this is meant for my son when he gets up and recovers.'

Just then, John Jerome Marakkaran rushed in with the baby who was gnawing at her rattle. He looked like he wouldn't think twice before throwing George Jerome Marakkaran down to the ground and tearing him apart. 'Don't shout at Christina!' he screamed in rage. 'If you say anything to her, I'll kill you! I'll chop this leg of yours, mind it!'

Jezebel watched with interest as George Jerome Marakkaran recoiled, unable to believe his eyes and ears. Christina took the baby from John, set her on her hip and repeated, 'This house, and the rest of the assets, are all Johnchayan's.'

Jezebel watched with disbelief as George Jerome Marakkaran's face filled with fear and he fell silent. His face became like that of a corpse's. He shrank back into the bed. Jezebel went up to him, lifted his body and checked the bedpan. Perhaps because of the fear, he had urinated. When she got ready to clean the bedpan, John stopped her: 'I'll do it.' His voice was firm. Before Jezebel could say anything, he had taken the bedpan to the bathroom, cleaned it out and brought it back.

George Jerome Marakkaran simply lay there, his eyes wide with fear. Jezebel was humbled that she was witness to time's sleight of hand, which had now conjured fear in George Jerome Marakkaran and courage in John. John reminded her of a child who wore his father's shirt to look grown up—a man struggling hard to reclaim his rights as firstborn. What an unbelievable moment it had been, she would later muse. When he touched George Jerome Marakkaran, the expression on John's face betrayed the grouse of a child who had not received affection. That face reminded her of Ann Mary's. It seemed that Jezebel was destined to witness how a man and woman, who undergo the same kind of suffering in similar circumstances, experience it so differently.

Jezebel showed John how to wipe George Jerome Marakkaran's body. Christina and John already knew how to clean Jerome and fix his feeding tubes. Without Jezebel telling him, John cleaned up Jerome and fixed his feeding tubes. Jezebel came out of that room and went and sat on the bed in the room which used to be John's. She felt the lightness of having nothing to do in particular. Christina came in with the baby and demanded that a decision be taken with regard to property. 'I don't want any property,' Jezebel told Christina. 'I have lived like a widow even when my husband is alive. It's not property I want, but peace of mind and happiness. If those are there in any account, please give me my share. I'll take it happily.'

Christina began to weep. 'Don't take it otherwise. You know my situation, *alle*? We've got to raise this child, manage expenses. That's why we need to grab hold of every paisa due to us.'

Jezebel wiped Christina's eyes and patted her on the shoulder. 'This house has seen too many tears. Please don't add yours to it too.'

Jezebel watched with interest as Christina and John opened George Jerome Marakkaran's almirah, found his passbook and

other documents, and took stock of the assets. When she helped
them, Jezebel felt the joy of revenge. There was another apartment
in that city in Jerome's name. George Jerome Marakkaran's property
in Kerala was in Jerome's name. John was the heir to Lilly George
Marakkaran's property in Kerala. There were about two-and-a-half
crore rupees in George Jerome Marakkaran's fixed deposits. Jezebel
felt sorry for them when she thought of how worried and frightened
they must have been of her all along their journey back here.

The ambulance, and Father Ilanjikkal's car with the new home
nurse, arrived almost at the same time. It was John who moved
George Jerome Marakkaran from the bed onto the stretcher,
and then carried him down the lift and into the ambulance.
'Jezebel*ey*! How the stone discarded by workers has turned into
the cornerstone!' whispered Father Ilanjikkal. George Jerome
Marakkaran lay terrified, with his eyes shut tight.

The home nurse and attendant got into the ambulance.
Jezebel and Father Ilanjikkal followed the ambulance in his car. It
was a hospital run by Father Ilanjikkal's church. The formalities
and paperwork were cleared quickly. Scolding him for letting
the infection grow worse, the doctors admitted George Jerome
Marakkaran in the ICU.

As she sat on a chair in front of the ICU, Jezebel saw that life
had come full circle since Jerome George Marakkaran's accident.
Back then, she had been anxious about her MD exam. She had
passed that exam, challenging the world, her family and her own
self. Now she was thrown back in front of the ICU at that time of
the year when a fellowship was in the offing. She sounded glum
when Abraham Chammanatt called to inquire, and she told him
all about Christina's and John's arrival. 'Why are they making such
a fuss about the property? It's all meant to be theirs anyway, *alleyo*?'
Abraham wondered.

'Until the verdict is announced, I, too, can stake claim, *alle*,
Uncl*ey*?' she taunted. When Abraham Chammanatt fell silent, she

added, 'That account has my money too. I don't want it, but let people not forget that it is mine too.'

After the phone conversation with Abraham Chammanatt, she opened her book and immersed herself in reading. When she finished a portion and looked up, she found Father Ilanjikkal looking at her, stroking his beard.

'I've been living in this world for so many years. The world itself has changed so much. But I haven't seen someone like you until now,' he remarked.

'There's no one like Jezebel in the Bible either, Acho!' she reminded him.

'That's right,' agreed Father Ilanjikkal. 'King Ahab told his wife Queen Jezebel about how Prophet Elijah created fire and rain through prayer and how he put the prophets of Baal to the sword. Do you know what message Queen Jezebel sent Elijah? "May the gods deal with me, and ever so severely, if by this time tomorrow I do not make your life like the lives of those you killed!" Who was this Queen Jezebel? When she was married off, she must have been a small girl—barely twelve or thirteen. Who was Prophet Elijah? He had Ahab and Israel at his beck and call. And then what happened? The Bible says Prophet Elijah fled for his life, fearing Jezebel. What power did Queen Jezebel command that she could threaten even Prophet Elijah? Imagine!

'Queen Jezebel grew up in a kingdom with many gods. Those gods were very kind. They had forms, and they had kith and kin. Whereas in Israel, there was only one God. That God was alone. He had only worshippers, no friends or family. When the queen married and left for another country, she took her gods along with her. She believed that a world that included them would be better. Her husband's God was an adamant one. And that God's prophet saw her, even more than her gods, as the enemy.

'Why could those who wrote Bible not think from Jezebel's point of view?' wondered a disappointed Father Ilanjikkal.

'When has the world ever thought of things from a woman's point of view, Acho?' laughed Jezebel.

'But she fought back for a long time,' Father reminded her.

'Even though she fought, she fell in the end,' Jezebel reminded him. 'Queen Jezebel of Jezreel was killed treacherously. All the women who have ever dared to question men have met their ends owing to acts of treachery.'

The room for the patient's attendant was ready. Jezebel accompanied Sathya, the home nurse Father Ilanjikkal had brought, to the room and helped her settle in. When she was coming out of the room, Valiyammachi called. '*Edee kochey*, heard the news? Our Sosa's daughter Tresa is now a man! She's put out an ad in *The Hindu*! See if it's there in the city edition there. She is staying there now, by the way. Go and meet her sometime!'

Jezebel was baffled. Tresa, Sosa Aunty's daughter—the one who ran away when she heard Jerome George Marakkaran was coming to see her. Jezebel frantically searched for *The Hindu*'s e-edition on her phone. The data signal was weak, but she managed to find it in the end.

PUBLIC NOTICE

It is for general information that I was previously known as Tresa Maria NavaNazareth D/o Monichan Thomas NavaNazareth and Sosa Samuel Monichan R/o NavaNazareth House, . . . and after undergoing gender transition therapy under the supervision of Dr Kaushik Pandey, have changed my gender to male. I shall henceforth be known as Advait NavaNazareth S/o Monichan Thomas NavaNazareth and Sosa Samuel Monichan R/o Punarjani Apartments, Amartya Builders . . . certified that I have complied with other legal requirements in this connection.

Tresa Maria NavaNazareth

Jezebel read the notice again. When Father Ilanjikkal asked her, 'What is it *moley?*', she shared the news with him. Father Ilanjikkal smiled. 'People have begun to change bodies like they change religions. Good, good. If only some minds could also be changed, how many people would live happily!'

Jezebel could not bring herself to smile. She felt her heart was walking on water. Her feet touched water but she could not feel its wetness. She panicked that she was sinking into a sea of spiritual experience at the height of disbelief. She saw the open doors of heaven in the depths of the sea. She saw a throne of coral reef and a woman sitting on it, making waves. The woman on the throne looked at once like a woman and a man.

Jezebel tried to imagine Tresa in the depths of the sea, amidst blazing torches. But she could not remember her face. Tresa was a couple of years younger than Jezebel. She was of bigger build than Jezebel, yet she was always hiding herself away. On the occasional visit to Sosa Aunty's house, she would slip away like a frightened fish. There was a constant expression of guilt on her face. Jezebel guessed that it must have been guilt about her own body, and that's why she ran away from home the day before the bride-seeing. Jezebel felt a surge of fondness for her. When she realized that Tresa had run away because she did not want to pretend to be someone else, Jezebel felt a new respect for her as well.

George Jerome Marakkaran, Jerome George Marakkaran, their apartment in the city, the tedium of the hospital, the humiliation inflicted by Kabir Mohammed, the crucifixion in the family court, the overseas fellowship—all flew away from Jezebel's mind like dry leaves in the wind. Only Tresa filled her mind now. She told herself that Tresa had been the greatest messenger in her life. It was from her that it had all begun. It was for her that Jerome George Marakkaran's marriage proposal had come in the first place. Sosa Aunty and Monichan Uncle had arranged for another 'girl-seeing' just so the news of Tresa's running away would not become the talk of the town. That is how Jerome happened to come and see her. That is how she happened to marry him. After her marriage, Jezebel had not seen Sosa aunty or Monichan Uncle again. They had played their parts and exited the stage. Jezebel repented that she had never bothered to find out about Tresa either. She looked at the people milling around her. She wondered how many of them lived as their own selves. She was eager to learn the story of a transsexual who lived in a village as a woman. How did she understand the truth of her body? How did she accept her life's goal? How did she bear her life's cross? How did she face her crucifixion?

That day, thoughts of Tresa churned in Jezebel's mind like a whirlwind. She resolved to meet her. Each moment afterwards, with a child's enthusiasm, Jezebel kept thinking about Tresa alias Advait. She worried about him. The day the doctor assured her that George Jerome Marakkaran's infection was under control, she went over to Advait's apartment.

It was not difficult to find Punarjani Apartments with the help of Google Maps. Located in the Amartya Builders complex, which was under renovation, it was the only block of apartments where work had been completed. She got down from the cab and walked past a cloud of dust and the churning of cement mixers. An old security guard noted down her name and address and allowed her in. She took the lift to the tenth floor. She pressed the doorbell of 10C. She waited with a pounding heart.

A handsome young man with a beard and moustache opened the door. She searched for Tresa in his face. It was clear that he had not expected Jezebel at all. He stared open-mouthed in disbelief. His face went pale as if he were a child caught red-handed.

'Advait, *alle*? Do you remember me?' asked Jezebel.

He smiled, like a warrior putting up a brave face when captured by the enemy. 'Jezebel, you gave me a shock!'

Jezebel thought the old Tresa's face appeared in his just then. He welcomed her warmly into an apartment that looked new because it had been renovated and painted. It looked like a garden with a roof and walls—there were green vines everywhere. Little water springs gurgled in terracotta pots. Jezebel wondered if she were on the banks of a stream in a forest.

'All thanks to the women's magazines Mummy used to subscribe to back in the day,' said Advait.

They sat face to face on a wooden settee in that drawing room where the tendrils of the vines that grew in the balcony welcomed her, waving their hands. Their eyes met. His eyes were kind and his gaze was calm. She hadn't seen this much calm in the eyes of Jerome, Avinash, Nandagopan or Kabir Mohammed. His eyes glistened at her. She felt a little uneasy.

'I had often thought of meeting you, Jezebel. But this is a big surprise!' His voice was hoarser than a woman's, softer than a man's.

'Hasn't it been a long while since you've come home?'

'No one wants to meet me back home, Jezebel,' he smiled with no trace of rancour. 'My family prefers to think I'm dead rather than tell people their daughter was not a daughter but a son. Jezebel, can you imagine how difficult it is to live as a transsexual in this world?'

'I can only imagine . . .,' said Jezebel.

He went in and returned with some photographs. The first photo, taken with an autofocus camera, was that of a newborn's genitals. You could not tell if they were male or female.

'This was my body, soon after I was born.'

He showed her more photos—of him at fifteen, at twenty-two—Jezebel's face paled seeing those photos of genitalia, both vagina and penis in the same body.

Advait laughed. 'Jezebel, you're uncomfortable seeing all this despite being a doctor?' he asked her.

Tresa was born when Monichan Uncle was running a business in a neighbouring state. She was born in a hospital there. The doctor said that the baby was a girl and advised that the private part that looked like a penis could be surgically removed later. And so, Sosa Aunty and Monichan Uncle raised her as a girl, keeping her under wraps, literally and otherwise. Monichan Uncle's parents advised him to conduct the baby's baptism in the church there, without informing anyone back home. Tresa herself thought she was a girl until her brother and sister were born. Whenever she was naughty, they began to humiliate her, 'Aanum pennum kettathu, neither boy nor girl!' They brought her up, feeding her an inferiority complex about her own body. Her Ammamma had told her that if the world came to know the truth about her body, the whole family would be shunned. Tresa sprouted breasts and body hair at the same time. But she did not menstruate. Friends ridiculed her, calling her a man. When she had not had her periods even by the age of twenty, her roommate at the hostel in engineering college insisted she meet her mother, who was a gynaecologist. Tresa did not have a uterus, but she had ovaries and testes. When she learnt that her body was that of both man and woman, she was devastated. Doctors advised her it was easier to surgically remove the penis and continue to pretend to be a woman. Her exams were at hand. The friend and her mother suggested she wait until she had a job, to get the surgery done. After she was selected in the campus recruitment for a job in this city, she began to consider the possibilities of surgery. She had a well-paying job in a multinational company. Because money was not an impediment, she explored options of surgery in the best hospitals. She read up and learnt more about her condition. The psychologist whom she met for counselling ahead of the surgery introduced her to a geneticist. The geneticist asked her in jest, 'Do you want to continue to be a woman, or do you want to be a man?' Tresa took it seriously. Should I continue to be a woman and deceive the world when my body is that of a man, she asked herself. The doctor warned her that the world would mock her. 'I've been mocked so much already, doctor,' argued Tresa. 'Take your time, think about it,' the doctor advised. She thought long and hard about it for a month. One night, she called home and informed her family, 'I'm a man.'

'It caused a huge earthquake. All sorts of questions raised their heads—We've brought you up as a woman all along, now what will we tell the world? How will the other two children from such a family ever find a good marriage alliance? They hastily found a marriage proposal for me—a doctor. They decided to hold the wedding at his place. Mummy and Daddy hoped that he would find a way out somehow since he was a doctor. I did not want to deceive anyone, Jezebel. So the day before they were to arrive, I ran away.'

Tresa went to her friend from engineering college. She wept all night, hugging her friend, despairing that she had no one else. 'I'm there for you,' consoled her friend. But when she told her that she had decided to become a man, the friend pulled away in shock. 'If I become a man, won't you live with me?' asked Tresa. The friend slapped her hard. '*Chee* eunuch, how did you even have the nerve to ask me this?'

'That was a huge blow, Jezebel. But with that, I became a man. And then the surgery became just a matter of procedure.'

Even though Advait laughed out loud, his eyes were streaming. Jezebel realized her eyes were welling up, too. 'Men are not allowed to cry, Advait,' she tried to joke. Advait buried his face in his hands, the way women would. Then he wiped his face on his white T-shirt, looked up and smiled.

'To tell you the truth, Jezebel, it's only when I became a man did I understand that there are far more don'ts for men than for women—don't cry, don't laugh, don't fear, don't speak sweet nothings, don't pamper, don't forget yourself in love.'

Jezebel smiled, wiping her eyes. But her heart stung and smarted like a wound on which salt water had been sprinkled. Pain suffocated her.

Trying to change the subject, Advait asked her, 'What would you like? Coffee or tea or juice?'

'Anything,' replied Jezebel. And then wondered, 'Don't you need to rest after the surgery?'

Advait said it had been about a year since the last surgery. 'In the middle of the treatment, I had to quit my job. If I had to apply elsewhere, I had to make the sex change legal. I dragged my feet for the longest time. Finally, it was last week that I put out an ad in the papers.'

Jezebel followed Advait into the kitchen. He put the water to boil in the kettle and turned around.

'This is a huge process. Society will never accept you unless you make it clear that you're a man or a woman. I was a man. It was not my fault that I was brought up as a woman, but that's immaterial. To prove that a man is a man and a woman is a woman, you need a certificate.'

Jezebel looked at him kindly. He was silent as he spooned tea dust into the boiling water. Then he continued, 'First, the notary's affidavit. Then, the advertisement in the papers. After that, the notification in the gazette.'

'I got to know after seeing the newspaper ad,' Jezebel said.

'I'm glad! It was worth the money then.' He smiled.

They returned to the living room with a tray of two cups of tea and a plate of chips. They sat across each other like before.

'Two lives in one life. Isn't it interesting?' asked Jezebel as she sipped her tea.

Advait looked at her kindly. 'Only the body has changed. Inside, I'm the same person. To tell you the truth, now I feel the security that comes with wearing a uniform just like everyone else, after taking off a strange dress that nobody else would wear.'

Jezebel looked at him with interest.

'When I was growing up, I longed to be out and about, Jezebel. But Mummy wouldn't let me go out even during the day. Back then, I thought nights belonged only to men. All that has changed now. One night, I slept on a park bench, another night at the beach, and yet another time, outside a shop.' He paused. 'But then, I realized one thing, nights actually belong to cockroaches, rats and mosquitoes, and men bigger than us.'

Jezebel didn't understand the last bit. He explained, 'There is a more savage and more ruthless kind of masculinity, Jezebel. There is a society that sustains it. So man's predicament is not all that comfortable. The notion that if you're a man, you're safe is true only in virtual reality. We have programmed ourselves to believe that that's the actual reality.'

'How does one reprogramme it then?' asked Jezebel.

'The system must be reformatted,' smiled Advait. Traces of the old Tresa flashed in that smile.

'The Tresa I remember was an introvert,' said Jezebel.

'And the Jezebel I remember was brilliant,' replied Advait. 'Your intelligence always shone in your eyes. But you were also always glum.'

Advait smiled at her. When she realized that it was his eyes that smiled, Jezebel's heart fluttered. Trying to change the topic, she asked him, 'Was the sex reassignment surgery smooth?'

'Not at all,' sighed Advait. 'There were several months of counselling and then, hormone therapy. The top surgery was done quickly. The genital surgery, too, was easier compared to what many other patients have to undergo. In my case, I did not need phalloplasty. So we got to the third stage pretty quickly.'

'Who was there with you at the time of surgery?' she asked.

'Only me,' he sighed. 'I understood that this wasn't going to be easy right when we started on the hormone treatment. I called home and told them about the surgery plan. Mummy said, "Can't you just die instead?" Daddy said my sister's wedding had been fixed and that I shouldn't ruin her future. With that, I erased them from my mind. For the genital surgery, I needed to stay in the hospital only for two days. Because he knew I had no one with me, Dr Kaushik gave me extra care. But the problem came later. I developed bladder infection. How painful that was! Like Mummy said, it might have been better to die instead.'

When he smiled, Jezebel wiped her streaming eyes, embarrassed.

'Oh, I forgot to ask about you, Jezebel. How come you're here? Have you found a job here or something?' asked Advait.

'Yes, a job that Tresa would have had to do if she had been around,' she tried to joke.

Advait didn't understand. Jezebel told her about Jerome George Marakkaran and the wedding. When he heard about the accident and his present condition, Advait was speechless.

'I hadn't meant to hurt anyone by running away,' Advait said repentantly. 'Especially you, Jezebel. You know, I've always adored you. You were my immediate senior, and always the class topper. They moved to me a convent in Chennai by the time I was in high school. Whenever I came home for the vacation, I would ask about you.'

Jezebel smiled, unfurling her dimples. He sighed. They spoke about matters back home.

'Let's have dinner together. I'll drop you back to the hospital,' he insisted.

They drove to a restaurant in his red car. They recalled old memories and exchanged jokes during that drive. She thought he was hungry to hear all about people. She understood that he was like a pup that had always been locked up; now that he was free of the chains around him, he was raring to run around and see the world. It was dark by the time they finished dinner. The city was still in a hectic rush. They exchanged phone numbers and email ids. They took a selfie together. 'Please call me if you need anything,' he reminded her.

They did not bid each other goodbye when he dropped her at the hospital. But she thought his eyes smiled at her. Dimples blossomed on her cheeks. As she walked towards the ICU, she felt both happy and blank. As she sat down in a chair and wondered what a day it had been, his text message arrived, 'When shall we meet again?' 'Any time,' she replied. He sent her a heart emoji. She sent him a heart emoji in return. She felt happy.

Just then, Sister Ashalata came out of the ICU. 'Doctor*ey*, Appachan is asking for the mobile phone. He says his phone and charger are in the side pocket of the handbag.'

Jezebel went to the room, took out the phone and charger and walked to the ICU. George Jerome Marakkaran was waiting anxiously. Forgetting for a moment that his infection had worsened and that his body was close to death, George Jerome Marakkaran's eyes shone at the sight of some faraway object. Although his face clouded when he saw her, he stretched his hand for the phone with a smile full of scorn. The next moment, he switched on the phone and quickly dialled some number. As she walked back to the room, she could hear his weak voice, which hadn't recovered fully from chest infection, inquiring, 'What's up, lawyer *saarey*? Any good news? That's good. I'm bedridden now, *alleyo*? Isn't that why you haven't been able to get through? So, I'll call again on Friday then. By God's grace, you must give me good news that day, *saar*. Otherwise, what's the point of saying I'm a man?'

A bolt of lightning blazed through Jezebel's brain. She remembered it was the day of the verdict of her divorce case. She went out and called her lawyer. 'I was going to call you. They have submitted all their documents. Most likely the verdict will be out on Friday,' her lawyer said coldly.

Verdict? What verdict? Whose verdict? Verdict against whom? In an instant, Jezebel was flung from heaven to the netherworld.

She despaired about the she-who-was, and the she-who-had-been. She felt emboldened thinking about the she-who-would-be, though. Just then, she saw four creatures in the centre of and around the throne under the sea. They had many eyes in the front and the back. The first creature looked like Ranjith, the second had Jerome's face, the third resembled Nandagopan, the fourth had Kabir's looks. The four creatures had six wings each, many eyes all around and within. They proclaimed, day and night. In their midst, she saw a lamb that looked like it had been slain.

The lamb had both male and female faces. Both faces were equally wounded and dripping with blood.

30

Jezebel saw that the day of the wrath of the lamb had come. Who could endure it? The day the sun became black like sackcloth, the moon turned blood red, the stars of the sky fell to the earth like unripe figs dropping from a tree shaken by a great storm and the sky receded like a scroll being rolled up. The day every mountain and island was moved from its place. The day the kings of the earth, the nobles, the commanders, the rich, the mighty, and every slave and free man, hid in the caves and among the rocks of the mountains. The day they said to the mountains and the rocks, 'Fall on us and hide us from the wrath of the lamb!'

One week. Days passed like smoke. Bones burnt like firewood. For, in her second coming, the resurrected one does not need bones, nor flesh and blood. She is meant to wear light, like a robe, and build temples on water. The question of what next, if the divorce came through, troubled her. Would her trip abroad be cancelled? What if George Jerome Marakkaran died? What if Abraham Chammanatt did not return from the US? Would John Jerome Marakkaran and Christina be able to take responsibility for Jerome? If they couldn't, would Avinash take over? Or would they all hand him over to some institution? Would he get proper care there?

The question of what if she were not granted a divorce troubled her even more. Would the court rule that, as a wife, she ought to care for Jerome? Would the court prohibit her from going abroad?

And if she did try to go, would they throw her in jail? If Abraham Chammanatt did not return from the US, who would take care of the finances?

In the midst of these maddening questions, even as she was struggling to focus on her studies, the second coming of Kabir happened, as if to show her that her actions would follow her.

That day, there was another 'sign' in her life. As she sat drinking tea in the canteen that morning bitter with the uncertainty of what next, Advait called. His phone call soothed her. Instead of a hello, he hummed a song.

'Have you heard this song?' he asked her.

'I heard it now,' said Jezebel.

He said the lyrics were by Wayne Shanklin. 'All of yesterday, I was studying about Jezebel. I even finished reading two books!' he said proudly.

'About the old Jezebel or the new Jezebel?' she asked.

'First, one needs to study the old Jezebel, then the new one,' joked Advait. 'Those lines will suit the new Jezebel as well.' So saying, he sang earnestly.

Jezebel felt the fears that had suffocated her until then ease away. She felt a cool pleasantness instead. 'Now that you've become a man, you've learnt to flirt well!' she teased.

'Does one have to become a man for that?' shot back Advait. His voice grew tender. 'And how was the flirting? Sweet enough?'

'A cool sweetness,' Jezebel said truthfully.

'*Sho!* It was worth becoming a man then!' he preened.

They both laughed. Even after the call, Jezebel was smiling to herself. At about ten, just when she was settling down with a book after sending Sathya to pay George Jerome Marakkaran's pharmacy bill, Geethu called from the Medical College, 'A Kabir Mohammed is here to meet you.' And Geethu handed him the phone. 'I came to see you when I got a few days of leave, Jezebel,' said Kabir. 'Lost your phone number, so I couldn't call you. I came straight to the Medical College. That's when I got to know you're there. How long are you there? Shall I come there? I wanted to talk to you. I came to India this time just to meet you. After this, I will be going to Syria—don't know if I'll come back. Please spare me an hour,' he requested. She decided to meet him since she had to pay him the balance amount anyway.

The next day Kabir arrived. He let her know that he had checked in at the same hotel he had stayed at the last time. Jezebel agreed to meet him there in the afternoon. Telling the home nurse she would be back soon, she left to meet Kabir.

It was three o'clock by the time she reached the seaside hotel. As she was waiting in the lobby, Kabir came up to her with a bright smile. 'Shall we talk in the room?' he invited.

'No, I'm a sexually aggressive woman. What if you lose your chastity?' she retorted.

His face draining of colour, Kabir whispered, 'I'm sorry, Jez.'

The memory of the old humiliation stirred again within her.

They sat in the restaurant, by a window facing the sea. She ordered sandwiches and coffee. When Kabir began, 'I was worried you wouldn't come, Jez . . .,' she opened her bag and handed him an envelope with money in it. 'The balance of last time's hotel bill.'

Kabir looked at her, injured. 'Jez, you haven't forgiven me, *alle*?'

'Aren't you the one that needs to forgive? Am I not the one who tried to honey-trap you?' she smiled.

Kabir was silent for a couple of minutes, elbows on the table, face buried in his palms. Then as if mustering his strength, he sat up straight.

'I was stuck with a woman in a lift once. We were alone together for a long time. We talked, got to know each other. And then that woman began to call me frequently, and told me all about the problems in her life . . .'

His voice was parched. He spoke without any emotion, as if he were talking about someone else. At that time, he had been in love with another girl. The daughter of Vaappa's close friend. They had decided to get married after her studies got over. That was when the woman he had met in the lift entered his life. She told him her parents had died early. She told him her marriage had ended in a divorce, and that she had spent only a few days with her husband. She invited him home on her father's death anniversary. She shared a great deal of private details with him. The man she married had had sexual problems. That's why she had sought a divorce. She was still a virgin. Although he was in love with his girlfriend, he felt sorry for this woman. They slept together. Kabir said he felt proud a woman had chosen him as her first man. But later, she would hold him accountable for the virginity that she had gifted him. In the end, he agreed to marry her. He confessed everything to his girlfriend of many years and married this woman instead. But when they began to live together, there were only incompatibilities between them. She was a woman full of all the selfishness and unkindness and greed in the world. Her demands for more money grew by the day. Once day, he chanced upon an old bill in the cupboard—a bill for surgery to restore virginity. Kabir's eyes welled up. 'Can you imagine how a man's world would have come crumbling around him?'

Jezebel sat stunned at this story she had never heard before. Kabir struggled to contain his emotions. 'That day I was furious at having been deceived. I was in a murderous rage. But then when I cooled down, I wondered: why should I be angry with her? Shouldn't I be angry with the world that encouraged her instead? She knew what the world wanted. And she gave it. There was nothing to quarrel or complain about. When you know a woman pretended to love you and made a fool of you, all for the sake of money, what's left of a man's ego, Jezebel? She staked a claim for my father's property. She filed false cases in my name. I lost face at home and outside. I spent a lot of money to settle the cases. I lost everyone dear to me until then.'

Kabir looked at Jezebel, tears in his eyes. 'I don't need any virgin, Jezebel. I need a woman who has been with many men. I can't endure the burden of women's chastity any more. I'm clear that if another woman comes into my life, it shouldn't be for money.'

Jezebel sighed. She remembered Valiyammachi. How the world has put the burden of a woman's body on the man's head as well, she thought, bemused. She felt a terrible hunger and thirst. She wolfed down her sandwiches. Kabir pushed his plate of sandwiches towards her. She had those as well. 'Thanks,' she said. 'For the good food, and for trusting me enough to tell me all this.' Kabir reached for her left hand and clasped it with both his hands. 'I do not lie, Jez. You can trust me. When we parted ways that day, I missed you as much as I did the first-time round.' Kabir looked at her expectantly. 'There was an emptiness in my heart. When we were together in the hotel that day, when we went for a walk, it disappeared. When I left you, that emptiness returned. I wanted you with me.'

Jezebel smiled, unfurling her dimples.

'I'm not joking. If religion is not an issue, I would like to marry you.'

'Marriage?' Jezebel burst out laughing. 'I'm not for anything that involves signing on a piece of paper, Kabir. I've been climbing up and down the steps of the courts for so long, and have swallowed so many insults, all to erase a signature I once put on a piece of paper.'

Kabir's face dimmed. She looked at him kindly. 'All this while, I thought my marriage was the biggest joke but yours is a greater comedy than mine. We don't know, maybe all marriages are comedies.'

'You're still mad at me, *alle*, Jez?' Kabir sounded disappointed. 'I'll wait. Complete your fellowship first. I'm not in any tearing hurry. Marriage can wait, until after we understand each other, after you're sure that you can live with me.'

Jezebel felt sorry for him. 'I'm not angry with you, Kabir. I like you even now. But I've learnt a life lesson. I've taken a decision. I will have one man for keeps only after living with many men first. Like you, what if I too lose my peace of mind over this wretched chastity?'

Kabir turned red. She felt he was racked by the hurt that men feel when they are rejected. He looked into her eyes and said, 'I kept remembering it. That moment we parted. You were aroused . . . I, too, was.'

He looked like a warrior desperate to save face. Jezebel felt sorry for him when she realized he, too, was trying to stake his claim by reminding her they had briefly shared a bed.

'Don't be silly, Kabir,' she said. 'You're a neurosurgeon. You know about bodies. A woman and a man met. The woman was sexually aroused. She asked you for a favour. At first, you gave in, then you decided against. You went off. Isn't this all that happened?' She laughed out loud.

'Jezebel, I'm really sorry,' he said. 'I was not able to think straight at that time. I didn't know it would hurt you this much . . .'

'But you didn't hurt me at all, Kabir!' Jezebel said sincerely. 'I kept remembering that moment too. I remembered how my body was. Before that, I was completely smitten by you. I thought you were the man I had been waiting for. When we walked and talked together, my heart fell for you and my body yearned for you. I also had a complex about not having had sex before. And so, I wanted to avail myself of the first opportunity to experience it. That's natural, *alle*? I have to thank you—it was you who saved me from sex without protection, without understanding you better.'

Kabir was at a loss for words. His face went beet red.

'When I think about it now, I'm so mad at myself. How did I ever dare to have unprotected sex? You work in the battlefield. What if you had hepatitis B or something?'

'Go on, laugh at me, Jezebel. Mock me all you want.'

Jezebel continued without rancour, 'Is this mocking? Aren't we using the science we studied to understand ourselves? What happened that day? My body and your body produced some nitric oxide. Our bodies grew taut. Our heart rates rose. Blood circulation increased. The pleasure centres in the amygdala and hippocampus opened up. For a few moments, anxiety and other worries became unimportant. Some dopamine and some adrenalin were produced. And what was all this for? Nature's little trick to ensure that the species survives. Isn't that what it's all about—this sex that everyone celebrates so much?'

'I have hurt you a great deal, *alle*? I have caused you a great deal of pain, *alle*?'

Jezebel began to feel irritated. 'Is it pain that determines hurt? Is it not the brain that decides whether or not to feel pain?' she laughed. She thought she was becoming ruthless. She thought of that hotel room. She thought of how much her body had yearned to be one with his. She thought of how much she had suffered in the moments afterwards. She regretted having forgotten the science she had studied in those moments. All pain was only the brain's various interpretations of it, she reminded herself. She wanted to ask: when a needle pricks you on the arm, isn't it when the nociceptors inform the brain that something bad has happened that the brain decides whether it should feel pain or not, Kabir? The A delta fibres in the nociceptors pass on the message quickly. You feel the pain instantly. The C fibres are slower to inform the brain but since they connect the brain with so many nerve centres in the body, the pain you feel is gradual and intense. The pain I felt then had been a misinterpretation. There was no wound on my body, and yet I experienced pain for no reason when you left, simply because I thought something bad had happened. She wanted to laugh out loud, but the pained expression on his face stopped her. Nociceptors seemed to have informed his brain that something bad had happened. His stupid brain had believed it too and begun to ache.

As she took her leave, he asked, 'When will we meet again?' She did not reply. She did not wish to meet Kabir again. Her interest in him had turned into vapour. Another wounded one, she thought. He had to heal his own wounds first. The unhealed would not be able to experience joy in love. They would have nothing but pain to give others. No man becomes virtuous until he reinterprets pain.

As she left for the hospital in a taxi, she put everything that had happened behind her, pulled out a book from her bag and began to read. As she opened the book, Jerome's voice rang in her ears, 'You don't need to study beyond MD' And then she heard her own voice insisting, 'I *want* to study further.' Now she told herself stubbornly—I *want* to study more. I want knowledge. I want to take pride in myself. Knowledge is my happiness. Pride is my strength. And I will not let any beast from the sea stop me. Even if it has ten horns, seven heads and ten precious stones on its horns, I will conquer it with my blood and the word of my testimony.

As the taxi sped past the crowds at the beach and got on to a flyover, Advait's audio clip popped up on WhatsApp. It was that song by Wayne Shanklin. Jezebel heard it with interest and laughed to herself. She WhatsApped him another heart.

Friday dawned. At ten o'clock, she called Chachan. Chachan was waiting at the court. She tried to read, but it was the courtroom she saw inside the book. The page number looked like the judge and the margins like the lawyers.

As she sat in front of the ICU, Dr Mahesh Aggarwal came up, quipping, 'Why don't you join us here, doctor? You can take care of your father-in-law, and we'll get a good paediatrician!' He asked her to come in. Inside, George Jerome Marakkaran lay chanting something, a pocket Bible clasped to his heart. 'How lucky you are, *ji*! Does any daughter-in-law in the whole wide world love her father-in-law as much?' Dr Aggarwal complimented George Jerome Marakkaran. Jezebel felt sorry for herself as she guessed what the father-in-law, the object of her love, could have been praying for.

'When can I go home, doctor?' asked George Jerome Marakkaran weakly.

'After you recover completely,' Dr Aggarwal told him.

Jezebel was relieved to see that George Jerome Marakkaran was better. The infection was under control. He could be shifted to a room once the course of antibiotics was completed. Within a week, he could be taken home.

'The living God will make me walk!' he clenched his teeth, looking at her.

'I'm also praying for you, Daddy,' she whispered.

When she got out, she saw Advait at the other end of the veranda. He walked up to her through the corridor, looking like a Christ in maroon kurta and black pyjama. It was a stride that had neither a man's arrogance nor a woman's inferiority complex. Like a tree that knew for sure its place in the universe, he waited for her near the balcony. She walked up to him and extended her hand. He took her hand, hugged her gently and brushed his lips against her cheek. Jezebel was conscious of gooseflesh spreading through her body. She wondered if his eyes shone with love for her.

'I dreamt of you last night, Jezebel.' His face turned a shade of pink.

'What dream did you see?' She played along.

'You were weeping in my dream. I felt like weeping too, seeing that,' he said. He smiled apologetically. 'I cried, even though men are not allowed to cry.'

Jezebel's eyes grew wet.

'Any problem, Jezebel?' asked Advait tenderly.

'I'm not able to study,' sighed Jezebel.

'That's just your imagination,' he assured her.

'I'm not able to concentrate,' despaired Jezebel.

'Whatever it is, tell me. I'll try my best to help,' offered Advait.

'But what can you do about the verdict in my divorce case, Advait?'

Advait looked at her compassionately. Jezebel went and sat down in an empty chair and opened her book. Her tears dropped on the open pages of the book. After a while, she felt the warmth of a palm on her shoulder and looked up. Advait put his hands on her shoulder and hugged her close. 'This is all I can do for now,' he said. Jezebel thought his voice had a touch of manly pride now. She smiled at him through her tears.

'I'll never advise anyone not to get stressed, because I've overcome tremendous stress in order to get to where I am now,' said Advait. 'Is there a greater stress for any human than the question of whether to become a man or a woman? The world would have cast me aside if I were a man. I don't know if you have noticed, but it's a man's world out there. So it's impossible for a man to survive without society. More than a woman, it's a man who needs recognition from society. So it is man who fears society more than women. I first saw that from the way my family reacted to the truth about my body. Society is a great playwright, Jezebel. Our job is to act out our clichéd roles again and again in the ancient play that it has scripted. Every role has its prescribed dress code, make-up, hairstyle, and dialogue. Every movement of each character on the stage has been predetermined. Our job is to play those roles, no matter how ill-fitting the costume, without changing the course of the script. If I decide to change my costume midway through the play, then what will happen to the play? If the heroine on stage suddenly decides to become a man, what will the hero do? What will the director do? What will the audience, eager to hear a story that they like, do?' he sighed.

'I had no clue about the life that lay in wait for me. Have you seen people who have undergone sex reassignment surgery? I hadn't. I did not know this condition of being neither man nor woman. We do not see them. They do not have any place in society. Either they live in hiding or the society neglects them. Until I joined my engineering course, I had not seen transgenders. Their problems were different from mine. I was brought up as a girl. My body had gotten used to limiting the freedom of my legs within the borders of my skirt and containing the freedom of my shoulders with the straps of my bra. I had to learn to walk like a man, to swing my arms like a man, to walk with broad strides like a man, to stroke my moustache . . .'

Advait wiped his face and tried to smile. 'For the past four years, I've been rehearsing day and night to play the role of man as society has determined it, Jezebel. Now I wonder what was all this effort for. It was enough if I had lived just as myself.'

Jezebel clasped his hand tight. She felt as secure as she would have felt holding Rani's or Ahana's hand.

'Jezebel, your problem is not whether you will get the divorce or not, is it? Whether you get it or not, what difference will it make to your present circumstances?'

'I want to go abroad for the fellowship, Advait,' Jezebel confessed.

'Relax. Nothing will affect your studies.'

'Only one more week to get my papers ready.' Jezebel's voice faltered. She wanted to immerse herself in studies, forgetting everything else. Advait thought deeply for a while.

'There are two possibilities, Jezebel. I have no health problems at the moment. Only after the gazette notification can I apply for a job anywhere. I am free until then. If you want, you can go back home. I will take care of things here. Otherwise, you can study at my place. I will stay here in the hospital. Whatever you feel comfortable with.'

'The moment he is shifted to the room, I will go back home,' Jezebel said.

Right after Advait left, Chachan called. 'The verdict has come, *moley*. We lost. The lawyer said we lost.'

Jezebel sensed a pillar of fire descending from the sky into her body and transporting her heavenwards. She immediately called her lawyer. 'Didn't I tell you that day itself?' said the lawyer, disappointed.

'What didn't you say?' laughed Jezebel. 'That the court did not trust women dressed in jeans? That women who cut their hair short are murderers? On what basis has the court decided that I am not entitled to a divorce from a comatose man? That's what I want to know.'

'Doctor*ey*, only when we get the copy of the verdict will we know the details.'

'Once we get a copy of the verdict, we need to file an appeal. Isn't that all? Then another five years like this. The court will not allow me to marry anyone else. Isn't that all there is to it? That's all right.' Jezebel said with no trace of rancour.

'It's not that doctor*ey*. My worry is something else.' The lawyer's voice was weary. 'The court also said something adverse— that the fact that you abandoned your husband in such a situation could constitute a criminal offence.'

Jezebel could not believe what she had just heard. 'Meaning what?'

'Nothing to fear. Whatever it is, we will face it. Anyway, let me get a copy of the verdict first.'

Jezebel wanted to laugh. She did not want to cry. She wanted to stay strong.

Outside, the sky had begun to gleam in the twilight. It looked like a yellow sea. Jezebel saw a beast rising up from beneath the waves of clouds. It had ten horns and seven heads, with ten crowns on its horns, and on each head a blasphemous

name. The beast she saw was like a leopard, with the feet of a
bear and the mouth of a lion. One of its heads appeared to be
mortally wounded. Who would be able to fight this beast? Who
is this beast?

—It was you, Jezebel, it was you!

31

When she was awake, Jezebel had this revelation: *Behold, a great fiery serpent. With seven heads and ten horns. Seven royal crowns on the heads. Its tail swept a third of the stars from the sky and flung them down to the earth. The serpent stood before the woman robed with the sun who was about to give birth, ready to devour her child. She gave birth to a child that was both male and female. When the serpent saw that it had been thrown to the earth, it pursued the woman robed with the sun. But the woman was given two wings of a great eagle to fly away from the serpent to her place in the desert, where she was nourished for a time, and times, and half a time.*

On the day of the verdict in her divorce case, Jezebel understood that the serpent that spewed water like a river from its mouth, to sweep the woman away in its torrent, was within her as well. She sat still in the same place till it grew dark. It was the hour visitors came to see patients in the ICU. Their perfume and the tinkle of their bangles and anklets made Jezebel want to proclaim, 'Therefore rejoice, O heavens, and you who dwell in them! But woe to the earth and the sea!' Time is short, she whispered to herself.

Just then Father Ilanjikkal walked up to her, wielding his walking stick, stroking his silver beard. She followed him. When he heard the news, Father was speechless. He consoled her saying, 'It's all right. We will look for another way out.' He asked her if she had seen Georgekutty. 'No, let's meet him together,' Jezebel told him.

'No, he may say something to you,' Father grew anxious.

George Jerome Marakkaran lay sedated by his afternoon dose of medicines. 'So Georgekutty, you won the case,' said Father Ilanjikkal. George Jerome Marakkaran's eyes lit up. He sprang awake. He tried to get up in vain and sank back into the bed. 'God is great!' he declared. A smile spread on his ashen face. He continued with a slur, 'My Lord made me win. Do not challenge the Lord. The homes of those who do so will be destroyed. Doesn't it say in the Bible, Acho, that Jehovah avenged Jezebel for the blood of his prophets and followers. How did Jezebel meet her end? She was thrown down from the top. That's the punishment for defying God. Man cannot separate what God has united.'

George Jerome Marakkaran laughed out loud, forgetting all his pain. He looked scornfully at Jezebel. Jezebel felt sorry for him.

'Jerome's Daddy is right,' she said. 'But God united Jerome with Avinash, *alle*? And it was you who separated them, *alle*, Daddy?'

She enjoyed watching George Jerome Marakkaran's face dim and his face muscles grow taut. Such suffocation on his face—the suffocation of those who cannot stomach the natural happiness of others.

'The Lord is with me too, Acho' she smiled. 'How will this verdict stop me in any way? It seems the court recommended filing a criminal case against me. Let them file a case. I will appeal in a higher court. Let the case happen. I'll hang around in this city, each day with a different person. What will you do? What can Jerome do?'

George Jerome Marakkaran's face filled with fury and hatred. She thought he would spit on her face. She kept smiling at her own little joke. Once they were outside, Father Ilanjikkal asked her, 'What's the use of telling him all this? The Holy Spirit doesn't reside in his heart. Where there's no mercy in the heart, there's no Christ. Where there's no Christ in the heart, there's no mercy either.'

George Jerome Marakkaran recovered quickly. On the second day after the verdict, he was shifted to a room. She booked her ticket home. When Father Ilanjikkal came that day, George Jerome Marakkaran requested him, 'Let's pray, Acho.'

'If I pray with you, the Lord will despise me, Georgekutty,' Father replied. Without asking for permission Jezebel picked up the Bible kept at the head of the bed and read Kings XVI aloud:

> In the thirty-eighth year of Asa's reign over Judah, Ahab son of Omri became king of Israel, and he reigned in Samaria for twenty-two years. However, Ahab son of Omri did evil in the sight of the Lord, more than all who were before him. And as if it were not enough for him to walk in the sins of Jeroboam, son of Nebat, he even married Jezebel, the daughter of Ethbaal king of the Sidonians, and he then proceeded to serve and worship Baal. First, Ahab set up an altar for Baal in the temple of Baal that he had built in Samaria. Then he set up an Asherah pole. Thus Ahab did more to provoke the Lord, the God of Israel, to anger than all the kings of Israel before him.

She stopped reading and looked at Father Ilanjikkal. And said: 'Poor King Ahab! He ruled for twenty-two years. He was a good king. His only mistake was to marry the Sidonian princess Jezebel. And that too, to improve relations between the two kingdoms and to trade with them. When they got married, Queen Jezebel brought her gods along with her to Samaria. Ahab was a loving husband. Ahab's fault was that he did not behave the way Daddy behaved with Mummy.'

Father Ilanjikkal smiled. George Jerome Marakkaran's face clouded.

'Those who deny God say things like that. Ahab challenged the true God. Jezebel killed his prophets!' he raged.

Jezebel laughed aloud. 'This Daddy is a fool, Acho. He doesn't know a thing. Other than bits and pieces, he hasn't even read the Bible properly. In the Book of Kings, even small mistakes made by Jezebel have been exaggerated. And that bit about killing the prophets . . . Bible studies say that it is not true because it is mentioned in a single line. Why was it not described in detail? Did she kill them all in one row or did she finish them off one by one? Either way, why was it not mentioned in the book?'

George Jerome Marakkaran was shaken. It was an unexpected attack.

'What about Ahab's killing of Naboth then? That has been described clearly. Jezebel wrote letters in Ahab's name, sealed them with his seal, and sent them to the elders and nobles who lived with Naboth in his city.' George Jerome Marakkaran looked to Father Ilanjikkal for support.

'I've been to this place, Georgekutty. Forget vineyard, there's not even a blade of grass there now. So you can imagine those days when wars were waged for water.' Father Ilanjikkal laughed aloud.

George Jerome Marakkaran's face wilted. 'What do you mean, Acho?' he frowned.

'The vineyard is just a metaphor used in the Bible. Maybe Ahab wanted Naboth's land, and maybe Naboth refused.'

George Jerome Marakkaran looked drained.

'Not only that, they recently recovered Jezebel's seal. Those days, the king and queen had their own seals. There was no need for the queen to use the king's seal. Scholars think these were all efforts to demonize Jezebel,' laughed Jezebel.

George Jerome Marakkaran looked even more drained.

'Isn't that why when she decked herself up and looked out of the palace window and called out "Jehu, please take me," Jehu ordered that she be thrown down?' George Jerome Marakkaran's voice grew more obstinate.

Jezebel smiled. 'That was not to seduce him, Daddy. Even otherwise, would a headstrong woman like Jezebel be ready to seduce the enemy? Jezebel calls Jehu "Zimri, you murderer of your master." Those days, to deck up also meant to brace for battle. Those days, even when you went to war, you went all decked up.'

George Jerome Marakkaran looked utterly defeated. 'I know you're a great scholar in many things. No wonder the court ruled against you,' he muttered.

Jezebel felt even more emboldened. 'I couldn't ask you in the court, tell me at least now. What wrong did I do to Jerome to be punished like this? What wrong did I do to you, Daddy?'

'You killed my son.' George Jerome Marakkaran tried to growl, but his voice broke.

Jezebel looked at him with kindness. 'It wasn't me who killed him, it was you.' She looked at him in the eye. 'You are the one who killed him. First, you married a woman for the sake of her money. You made her weep all her life. You tormented her son mercilessly. You brought up your son in a house where his father did not love or respect his mother, and stunted his mind. You destroyed his happiness. You controlled his life. You taught him to deceive everyone. Haven't you heard the proverb: bread gained by deceit is sweet to a man, but afterwards his mouth will be filled with gravel?'

George Jerome Marakkaran writhed as if a burning log had been thrust at him. Jezebel felt sorry for him. How much hate can a man carry in his heart? How much evil can he bear the burden of?

'I'm going back home today,' Jezebel told George Jerome Marakkaran. 'You can call me if you need any help. I'm not coming back here unless I'm requested to.'

George Jerome Marakkaran turned red. 'Get lost! Go wherever you want to, *dee*!' he blurted. 'Who cares?'

Father Ilanjikkal left. Jezebel followed him out. Advait came by in his car and dropped her to the airport. He tried to cheer her up. He kept reminding her to call him if she needed anything. When bidding goodbye, he clasped her hand tight and looked deeply into her eyes. He kept gazing unblinkingly at her until she went inside.

It was late in the night by the time she reached home. When Chachan began to say something about the court case, she cut in, 'I have only five more days, Chacha. I have so much to do. Let's discuss the case after that.'

For the next five days, she kept her phone switched off. She immersed herself completely in the application for the fellowship. On the fifth day, she mailed her documents. Two days later, she received their offer letter. Her eyes blurred with tears, unable to read it. There were exactly thirty-two days for class to begin. When she switched on the phone, the first call was Balagopal's.

'What news?' she asked him cordially.

'One small news.' His voice softened. 'Sandhya left us. This afternoon at three.'

Jezebel attended Sandhya's last rites the next morning. Sandhya lay dead in the small living room of that house. A heavy silence filled every corner. Balagopal held his child's hand and guided him through the rites. After the cremation, he bathed, changed and came up to her. Towelling the child's head, he asked her, 'His health has improved, *alle*?' The child's face looked brighter. 'I've been giving him a lot of leafy greens, as you had suggested, doctor,' said Balagopal. Jezebel petted the child. He had grown a little.

As they walked down to where she had parked her car, Balagopal asked, 'What happened to the divorce case?'

'Rejected. Not only that, but the judge also said I'm a criminal.' She tried to smile. He seemed taken aback.

'These lawyers and judges do not know what it is like to have someone at home lying unconscious for months on end. If they did, they wouldn't pass a verdict like this.'

He looked at her kindly. 'It's ok, everything will get better,' he reassured her.

'What can get better?' she smiled.

'Your divorce will come through. You'll get a good man for a husband.'

'I don't want anyone to rule over me,' she folded her palms. Balagopal clarified that he meant a good partner.

'These days, good people are not to be found,' she countered.

He agreed. 'That's true. Where are the good people of yore? Or is it that when we grow older, our idea of goodness changes?'

'Perhaps it is because we understand our own selves better now,' she said.

'I've got a transfer back home,' he said. 'Please let me know if you need any help. If you need to give any news in the newspaper, threaten someone, get any information . . .'

Jezebel, who was opening the car door, turned around. 'A family of four consumed poison. Three died. Only the youngest child, Angel, survived. Will you be able to find out where she is now?'

Balagopal asked for the date of the incident. Jezebel told him the year, month and the last time she met her.

'Why do you want to find out about that child now?' he asked her.

'There's a need to.'

She did want to admit to herself that even she did not know what that need was.

She met her lawyer the same day. The lawyer agreed to email her a copy of the verdict as soon as he received it. She signed on the *vakalat* form authorizing the lawyer to file an appeal. She told him she had got the fellowship. When he heard that there had been only one seat available for the fellowship, his face filled first with embarrassment and then with respect.

That day, Jezebel met Sebin too, in his house with its yard full of hibiscus blooms. He sat up in the small bedroom, bearing scars of big wounds. She examined the baby Princy had prematurely delivered. She reassured them that the child was healthy and growing well. As they sat having the murukku and the tea Princy served, Sebin fondly stroked the elder child Rupesh's hair and joked, 'I've become like your husband now, Jezebel. You might as well have married me instead!'

'But you must count up to ten without fumbling,' Jezebel reminded him in a low voice.

They burst out laughing like the old days.

For the next two days, Jezebel was busy at the Medical College, preparing her documents ahead of the travel. Her colleagues organized a farewell for her. She gave her friends a special treat. Whenever she called Father Ilanjikkal, he was unreachable. When she could not get through to Father Ilanjikkal the next day as well, Jezebel became restless. In the meantime, Advait called and told her that he was considering applying for a job abroad. After all, Jezebel, too, would be there. 'Such romance in your voice,' she teased. 'I don't know about voice, but definitely there is romance in my heart,' he conceded.

Jezebel smiled to herself.

The next day too she was unable to get through to Father Ilanjikkal. She called Christina. Christina told her that it had been a few days since Father Ilanjikkal had come by. Jezebel inquired about George Jerome Marakkaran.

'We don't know all that. Who knows even which hospital he is in,' Christina shrugged. Jezebel was baffled. When she was wondering whether to make a trip there, a call came from George Jerome Marakkaran's number, 'Doctor*ey*, I have to pay my bill. My cheque book is at home. Can you arrange for it to be brought here?'

It was the moment Jezebel felt herself transported heavenwards again. An unforgettable evening. There, a white cloud in a golden sky. Seated on the cloud was one like the daughter of man, with a golden crown on her head and a sharp sickle in her hand. Then someone cried out in a loud voice to the one seated on the cloud, 'Swing your sickle and reap, because the time has come to harvest, for the crop of the earth is ripe.' So the one seated on the cloud swung her sickle over the earth, and the earth was harvested.

Not heeding Chachan's and Ammachi's and Valiyammachi's objections, Jezebel booked a ticket to Jerome's city and prepared to leave. As she was packing for the trip, Sandeep Mohan called to say he was coming over. When she told him she was leaving for Jerome's place, he asked for all the details. She told him about George Jerome Marakkaran's condition. He inquired about the hospital.

Advait received Jezebel at the airport. He told her the story of how Father Ilanjikkal had gone to visit a fellow priest from the seminary after hearing the news of his heart attack, come down with food poisoning and lost his phone in the midst of all this. Advait was told by the convent that Father would be back in a couple of days.

By the time they made their way past the traffic jams and reached the hospital where George Jerome Marakkaran lay, it was past 2.30 p.m. 'Madam, where were you? Appachan has been so worried,' admonished Sister Ashalata. Jezebel went to the old room. George Jerome Marakkaran had been shifted from there to a small non-AC room. He was in a pathetic state. The moment he saw Jezebel, his tears burst their floodgates. Five days back Father Ilanjikkal had handed him the money to settle the hospital bills. That was kept under his pillow. When he woke up the money was gone. George Jerome Marakkaran cussed and swore at the home nurse. She left in a huff, never to return. The people at the hospital began to pester him to pay the bill. He tried to get the hospital staff to call Father Ilanjikkal from his phone. But the number was switched off. He called Avinash. The phone kept ringing, but he did not call back. He called Abraham Chammanatt, but did not get through. He did not know Christina's number. In the meantime, the hospital management shifted him to a smaller room. He sweated so much he developed chest infection. Followed by urinary infection. His body writhed in great pain. Finally, he had no option but to call Jezebel. 'The Lord made me do it,' he whimpered. Jezebel went to meet the doctor and requested that he be shifted to the ICU immediately. After he was admitted to the ICU, she went up to him. They looked at each other. He expected that she would say something. But she was unable to speak. Finally, he conceded defeat.

'Seen Jerome?' he asked soundlessly. Jezebel shook her head in a no. George Jerome Marakkaran grew distraught. 'Did he die? Did they kill him?' he sobbed.

'I will not go see him unless you tell me to. What if something happens to him after I go there and you say that I killed him?' she asked gently.

George Jerome Marakkaran grew more distraught.

'Don't worry, Avinash keeps visiting him,' said Jezebel. 'When Avinash is there, why should I go? Isn't Avinash Jerome's real wife? If you had let them, they would have lived happily together. I too would have gotten a better husband. There would have been no need for me to lament that I am still a virgin after two years of marriage. I would not have spent sleepless nights thinking about desirable men.'

George Jerome Marakkaran squirmed. She still had the old gripe left in her. And anger. And vengeance. But all of a sudden, everything became meaningless. What was the point of vengeance against a man who was bedridden, his abdomen swollen because he was unable to pass urine? She saw with her own eyes how illness thrashed the soul as if it were laundry against a washing stone, wrung it and hung it out to dry. Pain purifies man. From time to time, pain emerges from the body as grunts, moans and groans. It laments, 'Save me. Kill me, please. Forgive me if I have done you any wrong. Help me. If tomorrow, you, too, fall ill like this, then you will know how much it hurts.'

'If my son had been around, he would have saved me. It's because you made him like this that I've been reduced to this state. Bad times began from the moment you set foot in my house,' said George Jerome Marakkaran. He had said this earlier too. Then his voice was full of scorn and arrogance. Now it had become a lamentation.

Jezebel touched his forehead. 'Daddy, have you ever loved anyone?' she asked.

'The Lord,' he proudly proclaimed.

'Can a man love the Lord without first loving himself? If you had loved, would you be able to hurt others? How much you hurt poor Mummy! If you could not love her, then why did you marry her? Why did you torment her all her life? Why did you torture the child she gave birth to? Have you not experienced the same pain that he did? Did you not know what good you had to do? Where will you go and hide the day your soul would interrogate you?'

George Jerome Marakkaran looked sharply at her. 'How do you know all this?' was the question writ large on his face. 'I know everything,' Jezebel's eyes welled up. 'I know that your cruelty to me was what the world meted out to you. And yet, sometimes, I could not bear it,' she whimpered. Then George Jerome Marakkaran came crashing, deflated. Tears streamed down the corners of his eyes. That whole day, George Jerome Marakkaran lay limp and lifeless. He refused even a sip of water. After a long while, he wiped his eyes, looked at her, and whispered, 'A little water.' She gave him water. He drank it with difficulty. She fed him oats. He ate it without protest. Then he lay silent. When they met again in the evening, he asked, 'Don't you have to go work, Jezebel? How long can you hang around like this? Do you have enough leave?'

That was out of the blue. Jezebel struggled to believe that it was indeed George Jerome Marakkaran who had spoken.

The next evening, during visiting hours, Jezebel had another experience out of the blue—the visit of Sandeep Mohan and Ann Mary. Ann Mary came running up to her and hugged her, showering her with kisses. Jezebel took them to the ICU with the nurse's permission. George Jerome Marakkaran frowned at them despite being in deep pain. 'Do you recognize them, Daddy? This is my secret lover Dr Sandeep Mohan.' Jezebel taunted. 'This is Ann Mary, whom Jerome tried to molest. That's why I walked out on him,' she rubbed it in. George Jerome Marakkaran's face went pale. 'All lies,' he scoffed. Then Ann Mary indignantly put out her right hand for him to see. 'Lies? Uncle, see this. Jerome Uncle's ring tore the skin off my wrist that day. Every time I see this scar, I remember that day.'

'Then why didn't you file a complaint?' he muttered.

'She was in shock. And then Jerome too met with the accident by then,' said Sandeep. 'If this had happened today, you would all be behind bars under POCSO.'

George Jerome Marakkaran squirmed in shame.

Sandeep Mohan had come to say goodbye. He was leaving for the US; Ann Mary was going with him. All the documents were ready.

'You came all the way to say goodbye?' Jezebel asked in disbelief.

'Actually, we came to see someone else,' disclosed Ann Mary.

'Savitha,' admitted Sandeep, sheepishly. 'Savitha is in this city. We have been in touch for the past few months. Savitha has agreed to stay with us and accept Ann Mary as her daughter.'

As she watched Ann Mary leave along with Sandeep, clinging on to him, Jezebel recalled the trial in the divorce case. Was it to leave like this that they had come into her life, she wondered, and felt like laughing. It all seemed surreal—meeting Sandeep Mohan and Anitha, getting to know Ann Mary, going to meet Ann Mary at her house, her running away and coming to stay with them, and Jerome assaulting her. Life had led her through these zigzag paths in order to bring her to this point, she thought, pained. The faces of members of that family that committed mass suicide appeared in front of her. She saw Angel's little face again. She hoped Balagopal would find her.

Father Ilanjikkal arrived the next day. The sight that greeted him was Jezebel softly reading out the Bible to George Jerome Marakkaran. 'So father-in-law and daughter-in-law are friends now!' he remarked as he walked in. 'Aren't we all human, Acho,' quipped Jezebel. 'Yes, never forget,' Father said.

George Jerome Marakkaran grew emotional when he saw Father. 'Did you see Jerome? How is he? Who is with him?' he asked, choking.

'Everyone's there with him,' Father reassured him. 'Seeing John take care of him brought tears to my eyes, Georgekutty. That house looks tidy now. I tell you, Georgekutty, John is a good man. Christina, too, is smart and efficient. John said Jerome was running a slight fever. Mild temperature. Not to worry. Avinash has given him medicine.'

'*Kunjey*, can you go check on him?' George Jerome Marakkaran asked Jezebel. His voice sounded like the squeak of a mouse. Father Ilanjikkal looked at both of them in disbelief.

Jezebel smiled, unfurling her dimples. 'If I go now, I'll end up spending three or four hours in the traffic. I'll go tomorrow,' she assured him.

But George Jerome Marakkaran was unable to sleep even late into the night. He insisted on seeing Jezebel. Jezebel went to the ICU. '*Kunjey*, I'm not well. I feel like my life is being torn away from me,' he cried feebly. 'If something happens to me, please take care of Jerome.'

Jezebel panicked. She feared that the impurities that the kidney could not separate from the bloodstream may have affected his brain. As she massaged his chest, her hands trembled.

Racked by pain, unable to move this way or that, George Jerome Marakkaran gripped her hands tight. 'Go ahead and file an appeal in the divorce case,' he said. 'Marry again. But do check on Jerome once in a while. Consider that I behaved badly with you because of my ignorance and forgive me. That Nandagopan came and met me. He spoke very ill of you. And I believed him then.'

Mice squeaked ceaselessly in George Jerome Marakkaran's throat. 'I can't breathe,' he cried. 'It's like someone's smothering me with a pillow. Jerome is crying. He is calling out to me.'

At about twelve-thirty in the night, Christina called. '*Chechi*, Jerome*chayan* has fits. He's thrashing about violently. What should we do?'

Jezebel called Advait and Father Ilanjikkal. They somehow managed to get Jerome to the hospital. As the ambulance reached, Jezebel rushed over. Even as they moved him on to a stretcher, Jerome was shaking with convulsions. The real Jerome was struggling to break free of that body. The hands that protruded like sticks, the bald head which had lost all hair and the eyes open wide in that shrunken face—it was a horrifying sight. She looked at him, pained. For a moment, the picture of newly-weds posing for the camera in the churchyard came to mind—a bride looking through her veil at the groom, and the groom tilting his face and trying to smile at her.

Her body trembled as she ran alongside the gurney, holding on to Jerome's papery hand. His body had turned an ashen blue. Nobody stopped her even after they had reached the treatment room. Jerome's body arched like a bow with seizures. He was foaming at the mouth. His fingers tightened around her hand, then slackened and slipped away. Slowly, slowly, the seizures stopped. Slowly, very slowly, Jerome George Marakkaran passed away. His heartbeat, blood circulation and breathing stopped. Four minutes. It was all over. A very simple death. Life had pulled its hand free from the grip of that body. Fingers, that had been holding tight, let go. Like a frightened bird fleeing the hunter's grasp, his life had escaped in a trice. His deeds and misdeeds, wishes and wrongdoings, all dissolved into the air like smoke.

Jezebel got out. She stood leaning against the wall for some time. Her body kept trembling. Advait came up to her and placed a hand on her shoulder. She leaned on his shoulder. It was smooth, like a woman's. She gripped his palm tight. It was rough, like a man's. He took her to George Jerome Marakkaran's bedside. The nurses on duty had already heard the news. They made way for her. She held George Marakkaran's palm softly. After a couple of moments, George Jerome Marakkaran whispered, 'It's like touching his hand. He's gone, *alle?*'

Jezebel did not reply. George Jerome Marakkaran tried to move. Tears streamed down his cheeks, vying with each other. 'He's gone,' George Jerome Marakkaran struggled to tell himself. A sort of battered, torn voice. 'He's gone,' he repeated. A simple lament.

Chachan, Ammachi, Valiyammachi, Koshy Uncle and Varghese Uncle came to attend Jerome's funeral. After three fistfuls of mud were poured on him, Jerome disappeared under the mud for ever. Avinash ran away from there, weeping inconsolably.

After the funeral, as people jostled to queue up at the food counter, Jezebel sat a little away, on the steps of the church, next to Valiyammachi. Jerome George Marakkaran seemed to be walking among the scattered crowd. She could see clearly the sheen of his well-ironed polyester shirt. She could see his thick moist lips, and the wounds he had hidden in his heart. She saw his deepest fears, and his feelings of inferiority. She saw his guilt and his feelings of loss. She saw his eternal helplessness.

With a sigh, she switched on her phone. It beeped. 'Who is it?' asked Valiyammachi. It was an email from the lawyer with a copy of the full verdict on the divorce petition she had submitted to the family court.

The petitioner argues that the defence cannot recover his health completely. So PW1 argues that it is not possible to continue conjugal relations with the husband and that married life is no longer possible. PW1 is very young. Her lawyer argues that she does not wish to waste her life. But according to the defence lawyer's argument, after the day of the accident, PW1 abandoned, neglected and avoided her husband. Citing the reason that she had to study for her exams, PW1 neglected her husband. There are enough circumstances to suspect the presence of many other men in PW1's life. Her relationship with her colleague Sandeep Mohan is suspect. Although her husband was taken back home in a critical condition, PW1 did not go there or meet him even once. PW1 has not inquired or tried to understand her husband's present condition. She has filed this divorce petition on the basis of hearsay. But according to the statement given by the defence's father RW1, the defence's health condition has improved considerably. According to the doctors treating the defence, he will recover his health completely within a year. The defence lawyer argues that PW1 is not willing to go and stay with her husband's parents because the husband's father had suspicions about the accident that happened to the defence. PW1's behaviour after the accident was not what one would expect of a loving, caring wife. A virtuous wife would never behave in this manner. A virtuous wife is one who needs to stay by the side of her husband in sickness and bad times. Here PW1 has behaved contrary to this. There is nothing wrong if one argues that her character and behaviour give rise to suspicion that she was the one behind the accident. Both the Supreme Court rulings that the petitioner cited in this connection are not applicable in this case. Because the defence was not mentally ill. The defence in this case fell unconscious after an accident. But this Court is convinced that his health has since improved significantly. A wife ought to attend to, love and care for the husband, however wayward he may be. Instead, what PW1 did was abandon him. This is cruelty. Although I personally feel that this is tantamount to a criminal offence, considering her age and vocation and status, additional references shall be avoided. Having examined the statements of witnesses and other documents, it is clear that the defence does not suffer from untreatable insanity or other physical ailments. I am convinced that the defence will resume normal life within a matter of months. Therefore, I conclude that the petitioner has no claim to divorce.

Valiyammachi burst out laughing. Jezebel silently leaned on Valiyammachi's shoulder and looked up at the sky. Above the trees in the church compound, in the blue lawn of the sky, the clouds had built a great palace. One Jezebel looked down from the palace window above. Another Jezebel who arrived on a horse with a fine white mane, ordered, 'Throw her down!' The new Jezebel flung the old Jezebel down. The horses trampled her. Dogs devoured her. Her body lay unrecognizable like dung in the field of the past. The old Jezebel was no more. The new Jezebel is one who has received the revelation. Behold, she is coming soon.

Sunlight descended on the steps of the church like a pillar of fire. Jezebel turned her face up to the sun. Because the time is near: Let the unrighteous continue to be unrighteous, and the vile continue to be vile. Let the righteous continue to practice righteousness. Let those who love and practice falsehood stay outside forever.

And so, the woman adorned with the sun will weep and wail no more.

Author's Acknowledgements

Jezebel would not have been possible without the inspiration and motivation from my loved ones Dr Dhanya Lakshmi N, Associate Professor, Kasturba Medical College, Manipal, and Dr Piush Antony, Social Policy Specialist, UNICEF, Lucknow. I am indebted to Dr Dhanya Lakshmi for letting me shadow her professional life and for verifying the medical facts and interpretations in this novel.

It was Advocate Joshy Jacob who accompanied me to Kottayam's family courts, where I observed the court proceedings. Advocate G Mohan Raj read and shared his feedback on the first draft of the book, verifying the accuracy of the legal arguments and court scenes.

I do not have enough words to thank my dear Ministhy. S, Ambar Sahil Chatterjee, Navami Sudheesh, Nisha Susan, Madhu Chandran, Sandhya K P, Mathew Antony, Advocate Rashmi K M, A V Sreekumar, V Jayakumar and J Devika for being with me in this journey. I am also grateful to Dr Resmi Bhaskaran for introducing me to the amazing Abhirami and Biju. It was a pleasant surprise to learn that Biju and I share the same alma mater—The Gandhigram Rural Institute (Deemed to be University)—as well as the affectionate mentorship of Dr S Lakshmi.

Affectionate regards are due to the Olympian couple Shiny Wilson and Wilson Cherian who foster cared me in their Chennai home, named Love-Track, where I wrote the first chapters of this book. Most special thanks are recorded to the renowned scholars Dr Devesh Kapur and Dr Juliana Di Giustini and the entire team of the Center for the Advanced Study of India in the University of Pennsylvania for providing me with an elegant office and a wonderful apartment, where the final editing of this book was completed.

For the facts about the Biblical Jezebel, I have relied on *Jezebel: The Untold Story of the Bible's Harlot Queen* by Lesley Hazleton.

My association with Penguin Random House India has completed a decade now. Special thanks to Manasi Subramaniam and Shaoni Mukherjee for bringing out *Jezebel* as truly a woman adorned with the sun.

Finally, I record my eternal gratitude to my ever-inspiring readers.